To Slay the Dreamer

ALEXANDER CORDELL

To Slay the Dreamer

HODDER AND STOUGHTON

LONDON   SYDNEY   AUCKLAND   TORONTO

Again, I owe thanks to librarians, to whom I have turned for help in research, especially to my friend, Mr. John R. Bowring.

British Library Cataloguing in Publication Data

Cordell, Alexander
  To slay the dreamer.
  I. Title
823'.9'1F   PR6053.067s/

ISBN 0 340 22599 8

For Ifor Williams

Here lies half of Spain: killed by the other half.

LARRA *(El dia de difuntos de 1836)*

Historical Note

THE SPANISH CIVIL WAR, the training ground for Hitler's and Mussolini's later attack upon Europe, was conducted with a fanaticism and ferocity worthy of its foreign tutors.

In July 1936 the collectivist revolution dictated by the socialist Azaña overthrew established order and paved the way for General Franco's rebellious coup at Pamplona. Coordinated military risings took place throughout Spanish territory under the banners of patriotism and religious nationalism. The new republic was challenged and overthrown by rebel generals like Francisco Franco and Mola.

At the end of four days the rebels controlled a third of Spain.

Immediately, the country was plunged into a blood-bath in which private vendettas flourished and old scores were paid off, on both sides, with impartial brutality. But Madrid, the glittering prize for which the rebels longed, did not fall. Besieged until republican capitulation some three years later, it stood as an oasis, doggedly defended against the attacks of Franco's Moors, his shock troops, Hitler's Condor Regiment and Mussolini's élite battalions. And beside the Spanish republican soldiers in defence were the men of the famous International Brigades – British, American – men of almost every nationality and creed, who saw in Azaña's failing republic the last bastion of Europe against the onslaught of Hitler's fascism.

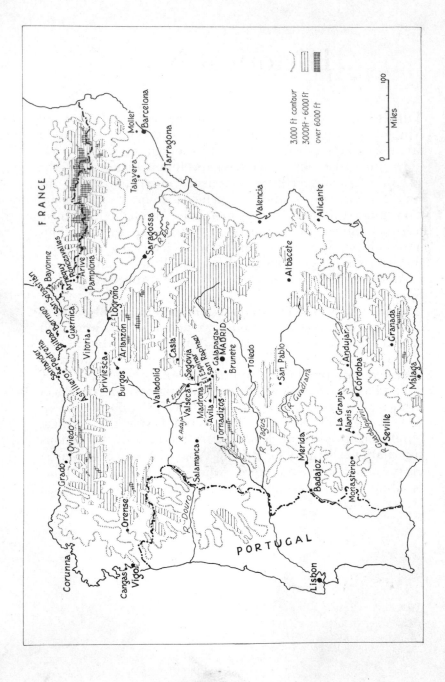

AFTER THE DEATH of General Franco, the Spanish dictator, a secret people emerged from hiding; after forty years of self-imposed imprisonment, they came from cellars and attics, caves in the mountains.

These were the enemies of Franco's fascism; men and women who had fought for the Second Republic during the three year Spanish Civil War.

Mostly, they were unimportant people; minor politicians, the leaders of small republican groups, wounded soldiers unable to escape abroad, partisans who had challenged the authority of Franco's Civil Guard: they belonged to every strata of Spanish society, they came from every part of Spain.

From the province of Old Castile one person emerged whose name had become a legend.

She was Juana de Córdoba, the daughter of the Count and Countess of Avila.

Avila's role during the war was mainly passive. Like Segovia, it was won by Franco practically without bloodshed. But, soon after the end of hostilities in 1939, a series of political assassinations drew Avila's name to the forefront of world news. The murders, beginning that autumn, continued until 1970.

The method of killing was identical – two shots in the head from a small-calibre pistol; one of foreign make; probably a Vostok, according to ballistic experts.

When, by 1960 eleven prominent Spaniards had been executed (all men who had been responsible for war-time repressions) the police were still without clues. But, in the summer of 1961, upon the body of Señor Ignacio Llobet, a member of the German controlled Spanish Secret Police, was found a small medallion: this, clutched in Llobet's hand, commemorated Pelayo, a legendary hero of the Asturians.

Inscribed on the medallion was a small, black arrow.

The assassinations continued, drawing closer and closer to the person of General Franco himself. Each corpse held the Pelayo medallion, which then became known as the Arrow of Death.

In the year 1970 the killings ceased.

Juana de Córdoba came from her hiding-place on the night of the coronation of Juan Carlos, the young king whom Franco had designated as his successor. A cellar door opened in Pío's House, as the people of Avila then called it; Juana climbed the spiral stone staircase to the upper rooms.

By then the old house was almost a ruin on the eastern outskirts of the town. Originally the family seat of the Count of Avila, it had the reputation of being haunted because, when its great lake was drained to make a local authority park, the skeleton of a man was found in the silt; this was popularly believed to be the body of Pío de Córdoba, the husband of Juana, who was last seen walking near the lake on the night his young countess disappeared. Certainly, this was the evidence given by Fonseca, the last retainer of a noble line, who, nearly four decades later, in 1977, was apparently the sole occupant of the house.

Fonseca, beloved by the House of Avila, was rarely to be seen outside its walls. Once a week he would drive a donkey and cart into Avila's market to buy provisions for which he paid in cash; presenting each coin to his thick-lensed spectacles before parting with it. Long-haired, trembling on a stick, Fonseca hobbled among the market stalls with an agility that belied his eighty-five years. He answered no questions, ignored greeting, disdained assistance. His sole aim was to purchase his requirements and return to Pío's House, there to slam the door of the servants' entrance and lock himself in.

In the early days following Franco's victory the Civil Guard entered the house and searched it for what they called republican moles. Finding nothing, they left Fonseca, the recluse, in peace.

As the years passed so interest in the house diminished.

Its windows were curtained, its doors bolted. Sometimes

watching children playing in the park would gather at the public railings that now hemmed the walls, and watch Fonseca, through carelessly pulled curtains, stumbling from room to room preceded by an uplifted lamp; then they would call shrilly and ape his movements.

Electricity served all rooms except the cellars, but he never used the lights.

With the coronation of the young king, a change came over Pío's House.

On the morning of the ceremony, November 22nd 1975, Fonseca rose early and shaved off his straggling white beard; in a looking-glass he cut his long white hair to reasonable length.

But Juana de Córdoba, his mistress, awakened late.

Lying in her cot, Juana's half-closed eyes drifted around the tiny cellar; the only light was provided by an oil lamp; the only ventilation came from a grating in the ceiling.

Within the hybrid of neither sleep nor wakefulness, Juana de Córdoba remembered her past through forty years of waiting for freedom, imprisoned in this room; she heard again the sounds and voices of her youth; a dark siesta that conjured through four decades the sleepless visions of her past. And through it all came the one repetitive dream, the sound of Richard's voice.

Richard said, "When the war is over I think I'll write a book about it."

"And will you include me in that book?" Juana asked.

"Of course. You are one with me now in everything I do."

"And if I have a child as a result of this, will you tell of it, too?"

"If you have a child I will cherish it, because it comes from you. If it is a boy we will call him Jerónimo, or Juanita if it is a girl. If it is a girl she will be dark and beautiful like you; God knows what a boy would look like."

"Were he to be like you I'd be content."

Later, Juana said, "Have you ever stopped to think that we

11

might not get out of this . . .? We are fighting for a new democracy, but will Spain ever be truly democratic? All right, we get rid of Franco, but another dictator could rise. Victory itself could mean the end of us."

And Richard answered. "We love, you and me, in the measure of lovers . . . nothing in the world can alter this and nothing can destroy it."

"How many lovers, I wonder, have said that before?"

"Come on, come on!" and he knelt above her. "If you don't believe that this union will last for ever, how will the world?"

"Then I," said Juana, "will be confident, too. We will live in San Sebastián, I think . . . in a cottage overlooking the harbour . . ."

"We will eat nothing but hot, crusted bread and drink cheap vino tinto . . ."

Juana reached up and brought her mouth to his. "Where is Nicolas . . .?"

"Up there on the crag."

"How long will it take him to cross the gulley?"

"Twenty minutes, perhaps longer."

"Remember, I once said that I would ask you. Please . . ."

Richard replied, "Remember, will you, that you are supposed to be a countess . . .?"

"Please?"

The rain began again in a drumming roar on the barn roof, the moon faded over the Pyrenean night.

These were the things Juana remembered when she opened her eyes from sleep and saw about her not the barn roof and the steepling mountains beyond its door but the stained walls of the sub-cellar of Pío's House; the whitewashed ceiling with its loose plaster; she saw the flag-stone floor that had bounded her feet for nearly forty years; one of republican Spain's *topos*, the forgotten moles of defeat.

Juana de Córdoba closed her eyes again as she heard Fonseca's footsteps thumping overhead.

Dressing in a black, satin suit, Fonseca went about his duties on the morning of the coronation with a new vigour; un-draping furniture, sweeping, dusting, polishing the long refectory table of the dining-room.

At midday, with a flower in his button-hole, he took the trap into Avila and there bought a bottle of San Sadurni de Noya, which was the wine his mistress preferred. The rest of that day he spent in the kitchen, cooking a meal fit for the Countess of Avila.

The wine he laid carefully to cool to correct temperature.

When dusk came that evening every door in Pío's House was open, every curtain drawn back. Fonseca, ever the royalist and with confidence in the integrity of the new king, turned on every electric light bulb in the place. Lamps and chandeliers blazed, the rooms shone brilliantly. People, in wonder, began to throng the railings of the park.

They watched Fonseca light an oil lamp in the hall. Holding it aloft, he descended the spiral stone staircase leading to the cellars and returned with Juana upon his arm.

She was old, the watching people said, but she was still beautiful.

Did she not possess the regal dignity of her mother, the old countess? the older ones agreed.

Of good height, she held herself erect despite her years. Her black dress was trimmed with white lace at the wrists and throat; upon her head was an ivory comb and this held her white hair in a bun at her neck. In her face was a pale, sad beauty, and some of the women wept. But there was a quickness in her step as Fonseca, with a flourish, positioned her chair at the head of the refectory table. He poured her the wine and she savoured it; the people watched in silence.

Pinned to her dress, unseen by them from a distance, was a small metal medallion; a portrait of the legendary hero Pelayo, he who saw the Cross of Victory fall from the sky after his defeat of the Moors at Cangas six hundred years before.

Beneath Pelayo's portrait was inscribed a small, black arrow . . .

One

1937

THE MIDDAY SUN burned down on to the sierra and the saw-toothed ranges were pillars of light. Old mists of morning, rainbow-coloured, barged and shouldered through the narrow gorges and canyons; little waterfalls cascaded down to the purple plain beneath, filling the dried watercourses. Petrified by sun, the lizards clawed at the heat. There was no sound but the droning of the cicadas and the echoing hoof-beats of a mule.

Richard Hanson sat awkwardly in the saddle. Hunched in his big poncho, with his sombrero pulled down to shield his eyes, he moved with the graceless effort of a man unused to riding. And the mule delicately picked a path through the cluttered boulders of the mountain track, raising its head in agony for a scent of water, but there was nothing of water save the distant waterfalls. This came to its nostrils, unsettling it, and Richard had constantly to spur it onward. At times he would rein the animal close; mule and rider motionless on the pass while Richard searched the towering rock outcrops about him for a sign of movement. Eyes narrowed to the fierce light he examined every ledge, crag and gulley for ambush, then settled again to the onward plod, chin on his chest.

The mule stumbled often, sometimes nearly unseating him, and he cursed it silently, for the drop over the pass to the plain was several hundred feet. But not only did he curse the mule. He cursed the heat, the Spanish Civil War and the International Brigade for sending him into the sierra.

He was exposed in the sierra and he didn't like exposure. Fighting in the rubble of Madrid's University was a different kind of war, one he understood. For a start, one fought with comrades. You either attacked or defended; took cover or disdained it, as the situation demanded.

From the moment he had left the Lincoln Battalion, Richard had sensed the isolation of the man who fights alone. If it was necessary for Franco to die, it would have been better, he thought, to achieve it by other means; a mass assault on his Salamanca headquarters? A pattern bombing of his advance base at Burgos? There were a dozen ways of eradicating political opponents without organising far-fetched individual efforts such as this.

This, he considered, as the mule plodded onwards, was where republican intelligence fell down. The Gestapo, which controlled the nationalist secret service, would never adopt such amateurish methods – a single agent backed by partisans in the field. An isolated attack on Franco was dependent upon many links in a chain of organisation, and the more people were involved, Richard contended, the greater the chance of failure. Also, working with strangers, especially gitanos – Estremadura gipsies especially – was not a privilege.

For the past ten months he had fought with Spanish comrades in the defence of Madrid. There was an end-product in war – life or death. The din of the battle with the Colts and sloshers going full blast was an acceptable, if terrifying, certainty. True, one never got used to the sight of broken bodies, but there was within the carnage a comradeship that compensated for the horror. This was why he had joined the International Brigade; not to wander in the mountains in search of doubtful allies.

He was weary, hot and insecure, and his trepidation, Richard knew, was transmitting itself to the mule. The animal slowed its steps. Richard dismounted, took its bridle and led it under the cover of an overhanging bluff. There, in shade, he sat with his back to the rock face, his long legs thrust out, his rope-soled shoes with their canvas uppers cocked up. The mule watched Richard as he unfolded a torn map and spread it on his knees. Automatically, he unscrewed the stopper of his water-bottle, threw back his head and sucked at the hot, sweet water. The water spilled, making white rivulets in the red ochre stain of his face, and laced his stubbled beard with glistening drops. The mule moved, coming closer. Richard lowered the water-bottle. The mule's eyes were unwaveringly upon his.

"You poor old bastard," Richard said.

After resting, Richard tightened the straps of the morse transmitter on the mule's haunches. Mounting, he rode again, watching every gorge and defile for movement, for he did not trust gitanos. Spanish gipsies in the sierra possessed a code of their own: often they fired first and asked questions afterwards – the sight of a new poncho or a Winchester repeater determining their attitude to life. True, Richard reflected, the case might be different when dealing with gitanos of whom the International Brigades approved. The three gipsies with whom he had a rendezvous that afternoon, were, he had been assured, proved patriots. Hans Deimler, the Intelligence chief of the Lincoln Battalion had spoken highly of Old Pep, Nicolas and Manolo. According to their files (and Deimler himself had been specific upon the point) these were gitanos of courage and tenacity; fighters for the republican cause since Franco's rebel coup ten months ago.

Richard, nevertheless, approached the place of rendezvous with care; an area where the mountain track narrowed; where a trained eye could shoot a feather off a man's hat.

It was then that he saw a flash of light; a splintering diamond that pierced the wavering heat, and instantly died.

Field glasses.

Field glasses watching him.

Richard reined in the mule, staring upwards; two hundred yards to his right, below the ridge of the sierra, the light splintered again. He grinned and wiped his mouth with the back of his hand.

From his smock he took a leather pouch and rolled a cigarette, licked the paper and blew on the tinder spark of his trench lighter. Watching the ridge, he inhaled the smoke deeply, his eyes narrowed to sun-glare.

High on the crest something had moved. They were careless gitanos, he reflected, if it was gitanos, for these were men who could tread an enemy encampment at night and return at dawn with the gold teeth of Moors. They were to the Gredos what the Basques were to the Pyrenees; men who knew a trail by an upturned leaf; who could smell the smoke of long dead fires.

Reaching out, Richard gently thumped the mule with a big fist.

"Get on," he said.

Vaguely, he wondered if the flash of light from the crest was a signal. Drawing the big Winchester from its saddle holster he snapped a round into the breach; under his shoulder straps he touched the comforting coldness of his Colt revolver. It could be the gitanos waiting at the rendezvous, as Hans Deimler had planned it; but it could also be a patrol of the Civil Guard who were mopping up in the Gredos.

Richard smoked steadily, staring up at the crest.

The gitano boy, Nicolas Alvarez, lowered his field glasses and watched the pass below.

Earlier, a mile away, he had seen a man riding a mule, but now he could not see him; instead, he heard the mule's hoof-beats and the spit became dry in his mouth. Always, when he heard the sound of oncoming riders he knew this strangling of the senses: he associated it with the hoarse shouts of men, the screams of women.

Raising the glasses he looked again, but the pass below was empty.

The boy's palms grew wet and in his belly was a shivering. When younger, he actually vomited to the sound of hoof-beats. He associated it with the coming of the Civil Guard, they who burned the acorn bags and set fire to the vines. And the vines flared in crackling fire and smoke rose over Alanis, his village, and always, always there was the screaming of the women. But that was a year ago, when he was aged fourteen.

Now he did not vomit. He lifted the butt of the little Kerak rifle and pressed it against his cheek and aligned the foresight with the backsight, aiming down at the pass, and awaited the oncoming rider.

It was then that Richard, now leading the mule, came into his view.

At this point there was an overhanging rock, and Nicolas lowered the rifle and slung it across his back. Retreating from the ridge, he swung his legs into space and momentarily hung there, his rope-soled sandals scrabbling for a hold. The sun ate at his back, spying through rents in his shirt where a whip had cut. Hand over hand, he descended twenty feet, dropping the last six feet to the ground where Old Pep, his grandfather, and Manolo were resting.

Nicolas said, gasping:

"Grandfather, he comes! I did see him. It is a man on a mule – the *Yanqui*!"

Old Pep grunted. "Bide yourself. We saw a man also," and he turned his walnut face upward. "Also, we were just considering the stupidity of it, sitting up here in the Gredos awaiting an accursed Americano on a mule. Eh, Manolo?"

Manolo Quinto, polishing a bullet, spat out of his bearded face; with his short, thick legs thrust out, he tipped up the brim of his sombrero. "Under a sun that would raise blisters on my dead grandmother? I am a madman in a lunatic's war for listening to Felipe Astrada!"

"We are all three mad to be here, instead of taking siesta safe in Alanis," answered the old man. "You saw with the field glasses, my son. Are you certain it is the Americano?"

"I am sure. He is a sore-arse rider. He is also large. His legs hang down below the mule's belly and his feet stick out."

"That sounds like an Americano," said Old Pep. "Did you see the box he is supposed to be bringing?"

"I did not see a box."

Manolo, rising, beat the dust from his smock. "Does it exist, this box without wires, or is it in the imagination of Hans Deimler and Felipe Astrada?"

"Astrada tells us, therefore it must be so," said the boy.

Manolo replied: "Yes? Well, in this war I do not believe the things I see, let alone those I hear," and he raised his big Mauser rifle and smoothed the butt, and his hand, where it touched, left bright sweat on the grain of the wood. "This alone I trust, eh, old man?" and he winked at Old Pep.

It was a good rifle. Earlier in the month, during an ambush in the forest of Chapineria, he had taken it from the body of an Italian officer; also a little crucifix, which, if he returned in one piece to Alanis, he would give to Ana Martínez, who was inclined to the religious, and this he mentioned now.

"Arrive back on earth," muttered Old Pep from the ground, and he scratched under his smock. "Crucifixes! May fleas infest your arm-pits," and he clambered to his feet in wheezes.

"Take me up the slope, Grandson, and we will all look through the field glasses at this Americano."

And Manolo added, "You two look and I will sight him. Perhaps he is not the Americano but one of the Guardia. If he is, he will obtain a hole between the eyes."

Helping Old Pep, the two climbed the slope to the crest; all three lay behind a ledge. The old man sighted with the glasses; Manolo squinted down the barrel of the Mauser.

Richard, still leading the mule, danced on the tip of the Mauser's foresight like a man on fire in the sun. The boy said, "It is he, Grandfather?"

"Put it down," commanded Old Pep, and struck the barrel low. "Nicolas is right. It is for sure the *Yanqui* whom they call the Americano."

Now the hooves of the mule were clattering, and above animal and rider, disturbed from their nest, two vultures were screaming high in the splintering light like the hinges of a rusted gate.

The three watching gitanos could see Richard clearly now against the bright mood of the mountain, and his fingers, bunched on the reins, were white slices of the sun. He looked a man of strength. His broad grey smock reached to his knees, his poncho was folded on his back: his long legs were clad in brown trousers of frayed leather: there seemed no weariness in him, though the mule was spent.

Behind him, on the mule's haunches, was the box without wires.

Manolo said, "He does not know us. Gitanos appear suddenly? He may fight?"

"He will know of us," replied Old Pep. "Felipe Astrada has arranged it with the International Brigade in Madrid."

Mule and rider disappeared in a fold of the pass. The vultures ceased their screaming.

The sierra was empty, save for sunlight.

"He has vanished," muttered Manolo, peering over the ledge.

Richard led the mule into the cover of an outcrop, removed the transmitter and slung it across his back. Facing the mule along the pass he brought down his fist upon its flank. The animal staggered, then reared up, galloping short. Wearying, it slowed to a trot, then stopped and nosed the berm of the pass for water. The three gitanos peered down at the mule below them.

"*Caramba!* He has fallen off," said Manolo, and lowered his rifle. "The mule has arrived, but not the Americano."

Old Pep said, "Americanos are all the same, they do not know the sierras. They come from the big cities and do not know the tracks; the mule stumbles; they fall. And he has taken the box with him. *Dios mío!* Did you hear him go? Felipe will be angered if we report back with a mule and no Americano."

Nicolas said, "Shall I go down and see where he has fallen?"

"Do not worry about him," said Manolo. "Try to find the box." He elbowed Old Pep. "I will go with him – you stay here, old one. Are we agreed?"

"We are not," said Richard, and slid back the hammer of his Colt revolver.

All three swung to him: feet astride on the rocks behind him, Richard covered them, and their hands slowly rose.

Richard said, "We meet, do we? Old Pep, Nicolas, the grandson – Manolo Quinto – Felipe Astrada's gitanos?"

Slowly they lowered their hands.

Nicolas, the boy, was grinning wide.

"*Madre mía!*" said Manolo, and cursed. "We shall never get over it."

Two

RICHARD OPENED HIS eyes and pulled aside his blanket, and there was a redness in the sierra comparable to the beginning of the earth.

Manolo, lying near, awoke also and sat up, scratching under his khaki shirt like a bear after fleas, squinting up at the sky. Old Pep slept on, the sleep of the gitanos.

Having a Spanish mother, Richard knew gipsies, and was not impressed.

At such times when they were asleep, they were wakeful: one could not expect to sleep under the moon as one did under a ceiling; his early days with the International Brigade had taught Richard this. This old gitano, for instance . . . Old Pep.

Rolling a cigarette, Richard considered him.

Here was a reprobate with the face of a saint: nor was he sleeping now, but watching, one eye slitted above his poncho. The boy also, this was the grandson of the reprobate, with a white smile of innocence and a left hand for lifting a sober sailor's wallet. Only in Manolo, the ugly, bearded one with the manners of a pig, was artlessness: Manolo was what he looked – a cut-throat. One could sleep with Old Pep and the boy Nicolas and expect to awake in the morning; to expect it with Manolo was expecting much.

Therefore Richard had slept with his face to Manolo and his back to Old Pep and his grandson, with the cold comfort of the big Colt revolver against his chest. But the hand that had come into his blanket before dawn was not Manolo's, but that of Nicolas. Fascinated, Richard had watched the small, supple fingers, scarcely feeling the feathering touch. But his big Ingersoll watch had flown off his wrist and over the top of his poncho, which was not unreasonable, he thought; his life could have moved just as quickly.

Even in the International Brigade one allowed for peculiarities in comrades.

*   *   *

22

Now crows were protesting at the threat of the sun and the forest clearing was shafted with patterning gold. Old Pep sat up, yawning and thumped his skinny chest.

"You slept good, Americano?" and Richard answered:

"The sierra is a good bed; better than the trenches of Jarama."

"But you will sleep better still when you kill Franco, eh?"

Richard grinned at the old man, and Manolo interjected. "Nobody will sleep better than a Spanish gitano when Franco is six feet down – never mind Americanos."

Nicolas was kneeling, rolling up his poncho. "You fought at Jarama, *hombre?*" His smile was bright.

"Against the Germans in Spanish Legion uniforms?" added Old Pep, and Manolo turned away, and spat.

"It was a February cold," replied Richard. "That is all I remember about Jarama."

"You were with the British on Suicide Hill, against the Moors?" There was expectancy in the boy's face. "There was talk of them even in Alanis, the brave British."

Richard did not answer, he was pulling on his sandals. They were good sandals; he had taken them from the feet of a dead six foot Moor during the battle of Corunna Road, when the rebels had broken through into Madrid's University City. Nicolas said:

"You do not answer me?"

Richard rose and shook out his poncho.

"You talk too much," growled Manolo. "A grandson with a woman's tongue. Make a fire and talk with the belly; one battle is like another and men do not discuss them."

Old Pep was thinking that the Americano was either without imagination or else a sleeping fool.

Like most big men, his movements were slow, his hands were large, like his feet; yet they were feet that moved without sound. Strange, then that the watch had come to Nicolas so easily? Soon the Americano would miss it, and there would be much consternation and searching and where did you see it last, comrade? And where could you have dropped it?

The old man grinned. His yellow teeth rolled drunkenly in his mouth. Nicolas caught his eye and winked.

* * *

23

Richard washed in a stream, blowing and gasping to trickles of freeze soaking down to his belt, and the floor of the valley below glinted with quartz where little waterfalls cascaded white between the pines.

He said, as Old Pep joined him: "Did you see last night the fires of Talavera?"

Old Pep replied, "I saw, and I piss in the milk of the fascist pigs. I knew Talavera from the breasts of my mother. In Malpica we were horse dealers. The soil tastes sweet, the donkeys and the women walk like queens."

"Yet you come from the north?" Richard straightened his naked body to the sun.

"You hear my tongue, eh?" Old Pep's wizened face creased up and he shrugged. "Yes, a man is responsible for the sounds he makes! I am of Basque blood, you understand. Spawned in Roncesvalles and fashioned in New Castile."

"It is a good enough beginning." Richard looked at the sky. "When do we move?"

"After we have eaten."

Richard pulled on his shirt and tucked the flaps into his belt and he smelled the smoke of the fire Nicolas was making and when he returned to the clearing Manolo was squatting on his haunches, stirring coffee in a tin hanging from sticks, and the smell filled the forest. Then Old Pep brought from a bag four wheaten cakes, also a *botijo* of wine.

They ate and drank amid the harsh cawing of crows, and Manolo said, sullenly: "You come from the Internationals, Astrada says."

Richard nodded. Unseen, Nicolas was listening to the ticking of the stolen Ingersoll.

"From Hans Deimler, the secret Intelligence? This is what we were told."

"That is right."

"And you bring the box without wires, the morse transmitter?"

Nicolas whispered in awe, kneeling closer. "The box that speaks over mountains, *compañero*?"

Richard nodded.

"That is wonderful indeed!"

"What is so wonderful?" Manolo moved testily. "In Alanis

24

there is a telephone. In one end you speak and words come out at the other. It can be bad; it is the way the bishops call the Guardia."

"That is why you also need communications," said Richard. "Felipe Astrada has requested it – your leader?"

"Felipe Astrada, he is our leader," said Nicolas, his face going up.

"Where is he?"

"At Salinero, east of Avila," answered Old Pep.

"And we march to him now?"

"We do not. We ride."

"I ride, for I have a mule. You?"

"Soon we will have horses, as Felipe commands."

Nicolas grinned and drew his finger across his throat. "*Ah-ee!* And what horses, Grandfather! Fine, Guardia horses!"

Manolo rose and stamped out the fire. He was squat, broad and surly, with the smell of a man unwashed. Old Pep rose, too, looking at the sky. "The sun says two hours after dawn. If we had a watch we would know the time. You have a watch, Americano?" He winked at Manolo.

"When I left Avila, but yesterday I lost it," replied Richard.

"That is most unfortunate," said Old Pep.

"It is worse. It's a bloody tragedy."

"The strap broke, you think?"

"Possibly, if it happened to be a wrist watch. But is time so important?"

"It is," replied Manolo, turning away. "The Guardia patrol will come before the sun is low."

"And from it you will steal the horses?"

Old Pep spread his hands. "God will provide them. And the Guardia, being dead, will not require them. Besides, I have an important meeting with the Guardia sergeant."

"Of this particular patrol?" asked Richard, strapping his poncho on to the mule.

"Sergeant Tomás Fernández." Old Pep explained. "We are old friends, you understand? For fifteen years I have been coming to the Gredos to find Sergeant Fernández; for longer than that he has been visiting Roncesvalles, to find me. But we do not meet, save once – many years ago."

25

"And when you find him, you will give him more, eh, Grandfather?" cried Nicolas. He was cleaning the coffee tin of soot, and suddenly sprang up, arms outspread, gliding about the clearing and making the noises of an aeroplane, grinning up wickedly at Richard while Manolo cursed him, flapping him into silence.

Old Pep cried: *"Vaya hombre!* – do not act like a child!" He appealed to Richard, hands outstretched. "Not sixteen years under his bottom and he yearns for blood. It is the cruelty of the war."

Richard said, mounting the mule "You owe a debt to this Sergeant Fernández, old man?"

Manolo, hauling his belongings on to his back, replied, "When we meet Sergeant Fernández, *hombre*, you will learn the size of the debt, eh?" and he slapped his thigh and bellowed laughter, and Old Pep shouted hoarsely, his head back and his hands on his hips, but it was not laughter.

Nicolas watched silently, staring at Richard.

"This is a private joke?" Richard now mounted, reined in the mule.

Manolo stopped his laughter. "It is the old man's private business, *hombre*. See to yours."

"As long as it does not delay us," answered Richard. "I am not chasing Guardia sergeants. Felipe Astrada commands you to get horses. All right, we will get horses, but I am not here to help pay debts."

There was a silence. The three, standing together, were unmoving.

Richard said "Private business? Let it be done in private time."

"Por Dios, hombre!" Old Pep showed his yellow teeth, and his face, with the lips drawn back, was the face of a hawk.

"I am sent to Felipe Astrada, not to you. So meet your sergeant, if you like. I have a mule. It is you who need the horses. If necessary, I will go to Salinero alone."

Only the mule moved, gently scraping at the leaves with a hoof.

There were no other sounds but those of the forest.

Old Pep said, "It is required of us that we get horses. Six, our leader says, and we get them from the Guardia."

26

"Then come!" Richard swung the mule about. "Get them!"

Manolo's face was aggressive, his thick red mouth hanging open. Old Pep nodded, his lined cheeks creasing into a smile. "You give instructions, eh? But a few hours here, and you are the leader?"

"It will be different," muttered Manolo, "when we get back home to Felipe Astrada. There we have only one leader; it is he. *Ah-ee*, we go!"

Nicolas was grinning, his fine teeth gleaming in his dirt-stained face. Richard took the mule forward and bent low in the saddle, his hand out to him.

"But first – my watch."

Nicolas's smile died. Uncertain, he looked from Old Pep to Manolo.

"The watch," repeated Richard.

"The watch? What watch?" Old Pep flung up his hands, fury upon his face. "You accuse my noble grandson of stealing your watch? Your mother was born under a dung-heap for you to make such an accusation! *Dios mío!*"

"The watch," repeated Richard, and leaned down and grasped Nicolas by the collar.

"Son of a thousand devils!" shouted Old Pep. "Release him!"

"When I get the watch," said Richard, and the mule went round and round and Nicolas with it, until, shame-faced, the boy pulled the watch out of his shirt and dropped it into Richard's outstretched hand.

"*Caramba, hombre!*" ejaculated Old Pep with incredulity. "You *stole* it, boy? That was unforgivable," and then he grinned wide, growing expansive. "Ah yes, but what a thief!" His face was alight with pleasure. "Can you not admire such honesty? You ask, *hombre* – he produces it! Now you understand my pride in my grandson; he has the belly of a man and the heart of a stallion!"

"Perhaps," said Richard. "Meanwhile, I'll have the skin off his backside if he steals from me again – understand?" and he showed his fist to Nicolas then spurred the mule and rode away, shouting over his shoulder. "Come, now – for the Guardia and their horses. We've wasted time enough."

"Great milking tits!" whispered Old Pep, "this is impos-

27

sible!" and he clouted Nicolas around the head. "Come!"

Manolo said, emptying his hands dolefully, "He orders. We go. Perhaps, if he lives long enough, I may grow to like the Americano."

With Richard leading on the mule, they went in single file through the forest amid the clattering panic of birds.

Three

ALL THAT DAY they travelled in the Gredos mountains, sometimes along the pass that led northward to Avila, sometimes across the eastward tracks to Perameras, the bastion of the town, and the heat did not pity them. Later, when the sun fell down the sky, mist rose, making water, and this ran in rivulets, beading their face and clothes like rain. The sweat steamed upon them, vapouring from the flanks of the mule on which Old Pep rode now, at Richard's insistence. And when they reached Las Navas, where the Guardia patrol was expected, they rested behind a bluff overlooking the pass.

Below this bluff the Guardia patrol would come, said Old Pep.

The sun was low and Nicolas imagined that he saw the guns of Madrid winking diamonds from the east; the others said it was not so.

The sun sank lower. The earth was painted in redness. Even the little waterfalls were as cascades of blood.

Nicolas stripped off his shirt to kneel and wash in a pool, and made small cries of hurt, for the rocks were hot to touch, and Richard, watering the mule, saw the stripes on his back where a whip had cut, and asked:

"How did he get that?"

Manolo had gone to the crest and was watching for the patrol, and Old Pep answered, "He steals from you, yet you are interested in his pain?"

"He is a child in a man's war. What is he doing here, anyway?"

"You are wrong, *hombre*. He is a man in a child's war." The old gitano rolled a cigarette and put it into his beard. "He became a man when his father died."

"And the whip?"

Squatting, Old Pep began to clean his Enfield rifle, one of ancient make, and cackled from a bearded mouth, "You see the patrol, Manolo?"

Manolo, nearby, waved him away, and the old man said, "In Alanis, where Nicolas and Manolo live, there exists the worst landlord in Estremadura. You are interested?"

Richard nodded, scooped up more water in a canvas bucket and carried it to the mule; the animal drank greedily, sucking up the water in gasps.

"My son," continued Old Pep, "his wife and three children – and of these Nicolas was the eldest – were happy to eat acorns, the food of pigs. Such was their poverty that they had to hire the bags in which to gather the acorns from the agent of Villesín – this was the name of the landlord. You understand?"

"I do."

"You do not. One has to starve to understand starvation." The old gitano put his thumb in the rifle breech and peered through the bore. "Then, one day Villesín himself came riding by and saw my family gathering acorns from the forest floor, and asked to whom the bags belonged, and my son answered him saying. 'These are bags we hire from your agent, at one *peseta* a day.' This angered Villesín and he called the Guardia and instructed them to burn the bags, since the profit was not his, and my son said, while the fire was roaring, 'We are landless peasants and the harvest is thin. If you burn the bags, how can we repay your agent?' And Villesín did not answer, but he rode away . . ."

Old Pep lowered the gun, calling, "Son of Perdition, Manolo – are you sleeping? Watch for Sergeant Fernández – he is not a fool!" and he bent again, cleaning the Enfield.

"And then?" asked Richard, squatting beside him.

"Then my son cried out and seized a burning bag out of the fire and ran after Villesín and pulled him from his horse and beat him with the bag, and the landlord screamed, but still my son beat him, there being only Nicolas there to stay his anger. And the Guardia – who had ridden off – heard Villesín's cries, and returned and seized my son. After tormenting him with fire, they took him to the prison in Mérida, but he escaped to fight for the Popular Front."

"And Nicolas, what of him?"

"They tied him to a tree and gave him fifty lashes – his mother also, but not the other children, for they were young."

30

"How long ago?"

Old Pep looked at the sun. "Eight months? – not long after Franco's rebellion last July."

"And your son – the father of Nicolas?"

"Killed in the massacre at Badajoz, by Franco's Moors."

Nicolas, pulling on his shirt, was returning. He exclaimed, "Manolo is waving."

Old Pep rose to his feet and straightened the bandolier across his chest. Briefly, he waved back, then ran in a halting, limping gait to where Manolo was lying. Richard, following Nicolas, crawled to the edge of the crest and looked down into the plain below: westward, the spires of Avila shimmered in the dying sun.

"Look," said Manolo, and pointed, "the patrol."

"It is Sergeant Fernández?"

Old Pep seized the binoculars Nicolas offered, and peered down. He said: "The same time, the same place. You fool! Yes, it is he. Being a creature of habit will be the death of you, Fernández!"

The patrol came on.

Led by Sergeant Fernández of the Civil Guard, it came on warily – the Spanish sergeant followed by seven Moroccans, all mounted.

"The horses look good," muttered Manolo.

Richard and the others took up positions on the crest and spoke in whispers, for the sierra was settling towards the hour of dusk, when all things in the sierra rest.

Sweating under his tunic, Sergeant Fernández was cursing the civil war: Franco for starting it, his rebel comrades for their stupid patriotism, the republican Popular Front for its empty ideals. Nor did he like the Moors who were attached to his command in Avila. He had fought with them at Seville and Badajoz where they murdered republican prisoners with long knives and sent their gold-filled teeth back to their pagan wives in Morocco, a trick they had caught from the Spanish gitanos, and these the sergeant hated, too. And one dead crow of a gitano, he whom they called Old Pep, who said he was a Basque, he hated most of all.

Now, with a six hundred feet bluff rearing up before him,

Fernández turned in the saddle. He saw behind him his drab retinue of Moors; the turbaned heads, the blunted faces. Their blanket ponchos hung limply in the windless air, covering the flanks of their lacerated horses.

"Close up!" The sergeant pulled them on with his arm, yelling hoarsely from a twisted mouth, and the scars of his facial wounds were vivid purple in the dying sunlight.

Manolo waved a hand, and elbowed Old Pep, whispering: "He do not look as handsome as before he took your bullet – eh?" and he passed the old man the binoculars.

"He will look worse after the next one," murmured the old gitano.

"This is your man?" asked Richard.

"It is he."

"Then shoot him and get it over with."

"When the time comes, *amigo*," replied Old Pep. "You just keep arriving, my pretty Fernández."

Leading the patrol up the climb to Las Navas, the sergeant was thinking that he was sick to death of the Gredos, anyway. With luck his application for a transfer to the Basque country might soon come through. With even better luck he might get the Pyrenees – somewhere like the frontier post at Roncesvalles where the accursed gitano lived, he who shot at the Guardia with explosive bullets.

Fernández spurred his mare. Knowing the route, she was picking her way delicately over the boulder-strewn pass. She was a good mare, and he respected her, even if he didn't love her. Fernández loved only the Guardia. One knew where one stood in the force, especially in the mounted section. It combined the expertise of the soldier with the professionalism of the police force. As a soldier you could execute a woman on the spot without official enquiries; as a policeman you could throw a man into a sweat box to cool him off. Vaguely, he wished one could do that to a wife. He had a young bride back home as perky as a filly; she had black hair that reached to her waist and handsome breasts, and in his village it was productive of good conversation to claim that you had slept with María Luisa, the wife of the big, brave Sergeant Fernández of the Guardia.

32

Reining in the mare, he thought of her now.

Things had been reasonable between them until a Pyrenean gitano had caught his face with an explosive bullet. He mopped his sweating brow, wondering how María would settle in the Pyrenees if his posting came through.

Now Old Pep grinned and squinted down the barrel of his Lee Enfield, and Sergeant Fernández, unsuspecting, sat like a marionette on the foresight.

Unaccountably, the patrol stopped.

Richard lifted his head imperceptibly and peered over the rock face.

Faintly the bass voice of Fernández came to him on the heated air.

"Close up, close up!" The Moors moved with the lethargy of men already dead. Fernández cursed them, his big fist raised.

They came on again, closing into the ambush.

Old Pep whispered, "Hold fire until we are sure of them. Nicolas . . .?"

"Yes, Grandfather."

"Watch the recoil on that thing. The first thing the Guardia look for is a bruised shoulder. And aim for the men, remember. Answer to me if you scratch a horse."

Richard, with Old Pep and Manolo on his right and the boy on his left, tightened his finger on the trigger of his Winchester repeater, taking the farthermost Moor. He estimated the range at two hundred yards. Lights up, sights up.

"Fire when I say, and not before," he commanded, and Manolo stared up at the sky like one bemused.

"Here they come," breathed Nicolas.

Sergeant Fernández squinted up at the bluff as he led the approach.

Once past the bluff he could skirt the base of the peak and reach the summit, the limit of his patrol. From there he could dominate the sierra, by binoculars, from Salinero to El Espinar.

It would mean a night's camp on the top of course, and he didn't relish the company of his Moors. But now he began to wonder if there was much sense in continuing the upward plod; with dusk would come restrictions; even now he could see lights appearing on the outskirts of distant Avila. Deciding to stop, he thrust up a hand, reining in his mare. The Moors gathered about him in mute inquiry. Their harsh argument drifted up the face of the bluff. The rifles of the three gitanos shifted to the downward aim. Richard pressed the butt of the Winchester against his cheek.

"They are turning," he said, "Take them now," and Fernández, as if hearing his voice, reined the mare in a circle, staring up. Motionless, the Moors stared also, their faces expressionless.

"Fire," commanded Richard.

The rifles spurted flame in deafening concussions. Nicolas watched a pygmy Moor slip off the tip of his foresight and drop out of the saddle. Horses reared, shrieking. Manolo and Old Pep were shouting, expertly twisting the bolts of their rifles: from Richard's repeating Winchester came the steady *crack, crack, crack* to each touch of the trigger. Moors were floundering about in white robes and ricochets: the horses stampeded; the sun exploded in Sergeant Fernández' face, and his horse pawed the air, unseating him. He slid, slowly at first, down the slope leading to the ravine; then faster, head over heels in a little avalanche of rocks and stones; gathering speed to the precipitous drop to the plains.

When the smoke cleared the sergeant had gone.

Six bundles of dirty clothing, the bodies of the Moors, littered the rock-strewn pass. The horses, methodically accepting the peace that follows war, were grazing at intervals along the berm.

Old Pep rose. Opening the breech of his rifle, he blew smoke out of the barrel. "And that is the end of Sergeant Fernández," said he. "May his soul rot in hell, eh, Manolo? Nicolas!"

The boy scrambled to his feet.

"Good shooting! Go and collect the horses. You and me, Manolo, we will pull the Moors' gold teeth, *ah-ee!*" He clapped Richard on the shoulder. "You agree – good shooting, *compañero?*"

"Good enough – for men who shoot from cover."

"We move again, eh? This time on horses. It is good?"

"It will be," said Richard, "after we have buried the Moors."

"But we do not bury Moors, *compañero*." Old Pep emptied his hands at the sky.

"This time you do," said Richard.

With Richard leading the three gitanos, they went in single file down to the bodies of the Moors, and Sergeant Fernández watched them coming.

With blood dripping from a gashed face, he raised his head and saw them coming over the crest, and the man leading them had a revolver stuck out before him, and this man, Fernández could see, big and loose-limbed was not a gitano, so the sergeant had no eyes for him.

Fernández was waiting for Old Pep, the gitano who called himself a Basque; he who was from Estremadura but lied that he hailed from Roncesvalles, where now he made his home. And Fernández remembered the years of waiting for such a shot as this; one shot for one dead crow of a gitano and may his carcass rot in this forgotten place.

Afterwards? Fernández pondered this. After he had shot the old gitano, the others would probably kill him; they would kill him, and the vendetta would be at an end; his own death a brief entry, with the six dead Moors, in the guard book back at Avila Headquarters. But since many men die for little, he considered, and with less purpose than the way they live their lives, here, at least, was a chance to die for something.

The sergeant squinted down the barrel of his carbine and blood from his face dripped methodically upon his right hand as he gripped the butt, and the sleeve of his left arm was torn, the cuff hanging loose, exposing the muscle of his forearm sliced up to the elbow. The obliterating sun blinded him to everything but pain. His body, after the rolling, sliding downward plunge, was like the body of a man at the stake enduring the first onset of fire. Eyes rolling, the sergeant groaned. His enemies, descending the rock slope to the pass, were talking now; their voices floated down to him on the heated air. Now they had reached the dead Moors whose bodies strew the pass. The sergeant took a sight on the smallest, which was Nicolas; then shifted the carbine foresight

35

to the big one, which was Richard; then depressed it on to the bent figure of Old Pep, and this was his target. Fernández watched the big man kneel at the old man's feet; he was energetically searching the robes of the Moors.

A fresh surge of pain enveloped Sergeant Fernández, bringing him to panic. Soon, he knew, from pain and loss of blood, he would faint, and he must not faint; not until this final task was done, the killing of this rotting crow of a gitano. Old Pep was now shimmering on the tip of the carbine's foresight, which was wavering in the sergeant's weakening hands. Now, gritting his teeth, he fired.

Light flashed. The sun was dimmed in recoil and smoke. And, as Fernández fired, Richard rose from the ground into the carbine's line of sight. The bullet intended for Old Pep struck his head, ricocheted away, and whined into space.

Richard fell flat, face down among the bodies of the Moors.

Dusk came, then night. The sierra howled its silence at the moon. Surrounded in camp by the horses of the patrol, Old Pep and his grandson, Nicolas, sat in silence; between them, his head heavily bandaged, Richard lay.

"He sleeps or dies?" Nicolas stared at his grandfather, and the old man shrugged his thin shoulders.

"How do we know? He is a *Yanqui*; they possess thick skulls," and Manolo called from a look-out crag above them. "Perhaps that is good. Perhaps a *Yanqui* with a broken head is more intelligent than one with a sound one. Astrada will know."

Old Pep hawked and spat. "Did it have to be him? *Cristo!* A little tap like that would stir your brains, if you possessed any. Son of dirt! What will Astrada say? Also, it is not good hospitality to wound a guest. Now he is upon our hands and we are miles from Salinero."

Manolo wiped his bearded face, calling down, "I say put a rosary in his hands and leave him, then he will be here and we will be back at camp."

"That is because you were born of a donkey's womb," cried the old gitano. "Do not pollute the mind of Nicolas," and he reached out and gripped the lad's arm with a bony fist. "This

Americano is a comrade. This morning, he was a stranger, but now he has shed blood with us – see, it is upon my fingers. One does not leave a comrade. Remember this. If the comrade is a mule or a fool, you do not leave him. Understand?"

"What do we do then?" asked Manolo.

The old man rose, looking down at Richard. "First we put around his neck the Pelayo medal," and Old Pep untied a cord from around his own neck and dangling on this cord was a small silver medallion. Kneeling, he tied it around Richard's throat.

"If that is found on him, it will get him hung," announced Manolo, blandly.

"We take the chance. It is Astrada's instructions. If one is wounded, go to Pío's House near Avila, and show the Pelayo medallion."

"Avila is about ten miles, stupid old goat," cried Manolo.

Old Pep said, "It is settled. Ten miles or a hundred, we will take this one to Avila; his box without wires we will take to Felipe Astrada at Salinero. Later, when the Americano is healed, we will collect him from the old countess."

"The moon is giving you vapours," said Manolo. "Who is this old countess?"

"The Countess of Avila."

"*Ah-ee!* Astrada has a fine imagination!" Manolo rose, his body squat against the moon.

"It is so!" interjected Nicolas, hotly. "I heard tell of how she heals wounded republicans, even gitanos."

Richard stirred and opened his eyes and Old Pep knelt to him and moved his hand before the big man's face and the expression in Richard's eyes was unchanged.

"He is blind?" whispered Nicolas.

"I say he sees all," muttered Manolo. "Do not trust a *Yanqui*. Even with shut eyes, they see everything, and their women are worse."

Old Pep said, gruffly, still moving his hand before Richard's face, "You see this hand, Americano?"

Richard muttered and groaned and turned away his face and tried to rise but the old man pushed him back, saying, "Rest, *amigo*. You are with the gitanos, remember? Rest until

37

first light, and then we will take you to Avila." Richard asked faintly:

"What the hell happened?"

"You put your head in front of a bullet, that is what happened," said Manolo. "Can you see?"

Richard shook his head.

"Then rest, I say," said Old Pep, and rose, pushing Manolo before him adding: "You think we can move in darkness?"

"He still has legs, and darkness is nothing to him." Manolo chewed on the butt of a cheroot and his face was lined with ugliness and stained with the dust of the road, and the sky behind him was a scarf of stars and the moon an opal of fire.

"The bullet has taken his eyes on loan," muttered Old Pep.

"At least he will do as he is told. Until now, he has been ordering us. Get rid of him, old one." Manolo smiled. "It is simple, is it not? We have the box without wires and this will please Astrada. If they hang the *Yanqui* in Avila, how bad is that? It is the box that matters."

"It is criminal but it is sense," said Old Pep. "Blind partisans are useless to Astrada. Come, gather the horses."

Four

Pío de Córdoba, Juana's husband, accompanied her mother, the Countess of Avila, to the door of the house. Beyond the columned entrance of marble and Corinthian decoration, the mansion's sixteen acres with its lake and terraced gardens gleamed in the sun. Flowering azalea and calendula, all planted with loving care by Pío, waved along the paths; nun-orchids and wild jasmine, in their seasons, edged the borders of giant rhododendron; convolvulus of many colours lined the road to the little Chinese love-pavilion with its silver dome and door of kruen, gilt and gold.

The Chinese pavilion where Pío de Córdoba, the peasant millionaire, received his lovers, was a legacy from the ancient House of Avila, the home that Juana had known in childhood. The great house, known to the townspeople now as Pío's House, had once been the family seat of Juana's parents, the Count and Countess of Avila. Two years ago it was the dowry that accompanied her parents' settlement on Juana's marriage to Pío de Córdoba, a man nearly twice her age. Now, renovated and refurnished with Pío's money, it was the envy of high society as far as Madrid. And the Chinese love-pavilion, Pío's speciality, was now a hall of treasure; its walls were lined with fine brocades, its floor covered by the weavers of Tientsin; in the air hung a heavy scent of joss. One was seduced, with luck, said Juana, before one reached the bed.

Aged twenty-five, Juana had expected the milder approaches of an older husband: she could even have accepted his apparent inability to consummate their marriage had Pío not been so sexually able with Rosa, her maid, and he pinched Rosa's bottom out of habit, it seemed, while engaging guests in spectacular conversation. Once Juana caught him kissing her; when taxed with it Pío was affronted and sulked for days; explaining to Juana in hurt tones that erotic adventure in the male must never be confused with love; that, as a good

Spaniard, he could do nothing about it since it came from his balls: a standard peasant excuse, Juana was discovering, for adultery to kleptomania, and from this complaint Pío also suffered.

The countess, Juana's mother, understood, she claimed. It was, she said, a perfectly natural phenomenon. Pío, she said, was a peasant, and while a peasant might make love to a servant girl with reasonable success, he could scarcely be expected to repeat it with the daughter of a countess.

Kissing Juana's hands, Pío said now, "Take her out, my love, it will do the old girl good. Tea with Aunt Paquitín always manages to calm her."

"I shall not break bread with that despicable man," called the countess from the drive below. "He is a fascist, and his woman is a harlot."

"Yes, yes, my lady, I do understand," said Pío. Five feet tall, white-suited and monocled, he escorted Juana down the steps of the house with his usual fussy charm.

Juana said: "I am terribly sorry, Pío. Will you put Colonel Carrasco off?"

Pío began to roll a cigarette one-handed. "I beg you, don't distress yourself. Not only is your mother a lady, she is an Asturian, like you, and Asturians and fascists do not mix. I was foolish to have asked the colonel and Lucía in the first place."

"Dios mío! My mother doesn't consider you. Snubbing Carrasco, the party treasurer, is akin to snubbing the Falange."

Pío put the cigarette into his mouth and lit it, hands cupped to the match. "No, it is not, and that's the whole point. Carrasco might have missed a good dinner, but Franco would be delighted; he doesn't entirely approve of poor León, I understand. Lucía García's reputation, you know – though personally, I find her delightful."

The countess called up, "Juana, are we taking tea with Aunt Paquitín, or are we not?"

Pío said, dreamily, "Carrasco, you know, is like the starlings back home in Catalonia; feed him, and he will not take offence. Did I ever tell you about my tame starlings?"

"Only that it was a rumour."

"My rise to riches?" With his arm about Juana he went down the edge of the drive; the countess, impatient, went on ahead. "When a lad I used to lie in the field of my mother's *posada* and watch the starlings stealing olives. After flying from our landlord's estate, with an olive in each claw, the weight tired them, and they would perch on our fence to rest. But to do this they had to drop the olives and I would dart in and pick them up. So the stupid things went back for more. At the end of a month I'd got so many olives that I bought my first donkey and cart . . ."

"And later, I understand, you tired of employing starlings and turned your attention to people."

Pío spread his small hands. "And with what success! But Carrasco, you see, is a starling. With a few thousand *pesetas* – my contribution to the Falange – in each claw, he will not take offence."

"My ████," shouted the countess. "Juana, are you never coming?"

"I love you," said Pío.

"With Rosa watching us from the library window . . .?" Juana lowered her hands. "Pío, this is a quite impossible marriage. In many ways my mother is right."

"But, my love, you take offence so easily. *Madre mía!* You could even be English! I tell you, I tell you all the time. Because I make love to Rosa, it does not mean that I am out of love with you, can't you see?"

Juana called, "Coming, Mother," and added to Pío, "'One day for the winning of their hearts, another day for bedding them. One day for leaving them, two days for replacing them and an hour for forgetting them . . .'"

Pío cried, grandly, "But that is wonderful, wonderful!"

"It is Zorrilla, but I'm not prepared to accept it, Pío. After my mother leaves for Santander, things are going to change in the house, and the first to go will be Rosa. Either that, or I find the captain in the Thirty-third Carlists – the one you are always talking about."

"Now that, my darling, would be extremely sensible. You are so young; it is such a terrible pity . . ."

"Heaven help us," replied Juana, and ran after her mother.

* * *

41

The dying sun was setting over Avila; as she walked, Juana could hear the guns rumbling from distant Madrid.

Like Juana, her mother was dressed in white, her wide-brimmed summer hat enhancing her regal appearance. She said now, quickening her pace. "And it isn't only Rosa, that cheeky little maid. This morning I caught him kissing the cook."

Juana sighed. "He loves Matilde, and she is over seventy."

"I despise your husband – it was a terrible mistake. Not only is he immoral, but at table he has the manners of a pig. By contributing to Franco's rebellion he is betraying us all. Further, that damned man Carrasco is one of Franco's lackeys and his woman is a whore. I refuse to dine with them."

"You've made that clear. Meanwhile, remember that Carrasco could turn us out of the house on a whim – that it's Pío's house and you're here by his grace."

"And you're nearly as bad – nursing in a rebel hospital."

"Rebel or republican, they all suffer the same," answered Juana.

They walked on, passing squads of marching soldiers; the town was embalmed in a strange roseate light.

It was the kind of summer, arriving early, that reminded Juana of the baby-marriage festival of Estremadura, when the corn was golden in the fields and tobacco-faced peasants would lie with their feet on the sun during siesta. Pío had distant relatives down there in Mérida, and during their honeymoon they wandered the lanes together listening to the flamenco guitars.

The countess invaded Juana's thoughts: "I am particularly worried about Pío's contributions to the Falange funds." Red-headed, inches taller than Juana, she strode along. "All right, we are overrun by Franco's rebels and we pay to Franco a sort of diplomatic rent – a blackmail in return for immunity. But a hundred thousand *pesetas* a year is lunacy."

"It's Pío's money, Mother. Leave it to Pío."

"And how would we stand if the republicans win?"

Juana slowed her pace. "Pío says that they will not win."

"That's what the Moors told we Asturians, but we won, did we not?"

"At Cangas, perhaps. You didn't win the Miners' Rebellion."

'*Dio mío!*'' her mother exclaimed. "At least you know your history. If you had any sense, girl, you'd come with me to Santander. Can't you see what is happening under your nose? It isn't as if the man shows you any love. You're aware, I suppose, that he's carrying on with his maid."

"I know."

"And you do nothing about it?"

"I'll try to find a Carlist adjutant. Would that make you happy?"

"Don't be indecent. It doesn't become you!" said the countess.

Many soldiers were on the streets now, and some of these were Moors; squatting against walls, cleaning their weapons: Franco's butchers, said the countess, busy at their meat stalls; perhaps the same butchers, she added, who savaged the Asturians up in Oviedo, and under the same Franco, the Bloodstained Dwarf.

"For God's sake keep your voice down," whispered Juana.

All down the Ronda Vieja army lorries were parked nose to tail, the infantrymen clustered about them being mainly Carlists; they who, less than a year ago, had swept General Mola to power in the coup of Pamplona. A few officers saluted as Juana and her mother went by, their awe proclaiming that, at least, the tall woman must be one of King Alfonso's mistresses, such was her regality: these received a sniff of disdain from the countess.

Juana had seen such obeisance before, of course: a woman of six feet always commands attention. Her mother could descend a staircase at the opera and turn every head, and, half-way down, await the approbation. Now, although her youth was gone, she was still bright-headed and her lips were red; her complexion untouched by the years, her limbs straight and beautifully proportioned. She had worn her gowns in the King's time, Juana reflected, with a symmetry so startling that it had kept her out of court.

"This is an appalling walk among these gaping soldiers."

"Come," replied Juana, "you're loving every minute."

"Do not be insolent. I didn't expect the Moors."

Juana smiled faintly, saying, "Be reasonable, Mother.

43

They have their tasks in life. They kill republicans, but you are killing rebels, are you not?"

"You refer to my gardeners, I presume?"

"I refer to the escape route that is currently running in Pío's House."

"Dear me, little enough escapes you, does it?"

"And right under Pío's nose? Pío might have nationalist tendencies, but is it fair? If a single republican gardener is found, Pío will answer for it, you know, not you."

Clearly the countess was shocked into silence.

Near the church of San Pedro two men were escorting a prisoner; the man was carrying a broom. The prisoner was no longer young; bare-headed, he walked with difficulty, as if after beatings. The left arm of his jacket was torn away, proof that he was a political prisoner. He looked like an elder who had been lifted off his knees in church.

The sun burned down in light-shot rays.

With a guard either side of him the man began to sweep the street.

"What is happening here?" asked the countess, arriving on the scene.

One could appeal, thought Juana; one could pass by with lowered eyes, in shame: her mother did neither.

There arrived from the Calle de Granizo at that moment a train of penitents. In their long Castilian gowns, with their eyes shifting brightly behind the slits of the black cagoules, they wandered past, rocking on their heels, telling their beads in moaning incantations.

A few aged women lined the route, crossing themselves expectantly: to one of these the countess said: "Who is that man? What has he done?"

A woman answered: "He is Profesor Ramírez of the University, lady."

"I asked you what he had done – what is his crime?"

Juana said, "Mother, please come . . ." and pulled at her.

"He sang a verse of '*Hijos del Pueblo*' in the square of Teresa, outside the transept."

"Did he, indeed?" said the countess.

"Mother . . .!" whispered Juana.

" 'Sons of the People, your chains oppress you?' – that song, the one of the Popular Front?"

"That is the song," whispered a second woman. "You are a stranger, lady?"

"I am an Asturian." The countess lifted her face.

"This song is against the law. The Falange is holding Avila? You understand, foreigner?"

"Against the law? Is it, indeed? And this is his punishment – sweeping the street?"

"That we should ridicule him – a professor with a broom."

"We will see about this," said the countess and shook herself free of Juana. Going to the guards she confronted one, saying "Do you realise the identity of this prisoner? He is Professor Ramírez . . ." and she peered into the man's bruised face, adding softly, "Is this the right name, sir? I am the Countess of Avila," and then to the guards: " '*Hijos del Pueblo*' – is this what you do not like to hear?" She seized the broom from the prisoner's hands and tossed it away, crying, " '*Hijos del Pueblo!*' or do you wish me to sing it outside the cathedral transept?"

There came a silence of shocked expressions; not only the prisoner but the two guards were silent and also the women standing near, even the penitents.

The countess said amiably to the guards, "There now, the broom has gone. Go about your business, and you shall come with me," and she took the professor's hand and led him away.

She had got a yard when a guard leaped: the butt of his rifle came down. Struck from behind, the countess fell, but the blow, glancing, only loosened her hair, bringing it down to her waist, red in the sun.

Shrieking, she leaped and clawed at the guard, bringing him down.

There was now much noise.

The guards were shouting for help, the countess was shrieking abuse as she pulled at the professor, who also made noise, being in the middle.

Juana sprang in to help.

The watching woman, too.

The penitents, stripping up their Castilian gowns, waved

45

their arms free, and ran at the guards, crying as they did so, "*Hijos del Pueblo, Hijos del Pueblo!*" and this cry echoed over the square of San Pedro so that others came; many people came running.

With Juana and her mother pulling at the professor and the penitents clubbing down the guards, doors came open along the streets and women peered out, wiping their hands upon their aprons; younger people came, the students lining the walls of the town, in study or sketching, and these were dressed in bright colours so that others noticed the activity.

Then a shot slashed the confusion, as a whip.

The guards crouched, slowly pulling back the prisoner.

Mesmerised by silence, the people watched.

A guard pushed the broom at the professor. "Sweep," he commanded.

Back to back, moving in a slow circle, with their rifles levelled at the crowd, the two guards threatened the people and these bore in upon them, muttering.

The sun burned down on the square of San Pedro.

Again, the professor began to sweep the street: Professor Andrés Ramírez, lecturer in political economics at Madrid University; this was his name and title.

The countess pushed back her hair from her face, and watched, weighing the chances, and beside her was Juana, white-faced and furious. Then her mother smiled, looking about her.

"There is another way out of this," she said, and pulled men and women aside.

With lifted skirts, she ran down the Calle de Granizo to a door.

In moments, she returned carrying a broom.

A cry went up from the crowd surrounding the guards. Running freely, the people were now knocking on house doors, demanding brooms; many offered brooms, thinking help was needed in some respect; others came running with brooms because it was the custom to join queues and follow one's neighbour. It was of no importance politically. One might be a Carlist or of the Falange; a monarchist, anarchist; of the Catholic Party or a Revolutionary Communist; it did

46

not matter. The immediate requirement was to obtain a broom and conform, like others.

Arriving back at the scene, the countess had two brooms now, and one she gave to Juana, saying, "Come. If these fascist pigs want the street swept, we will all sweep it, since we are comrades."

The bells of the cathedral were tolling discordantly, clashing with the bells of San Pedro. And the people chanted and the bells tolled, and all Avila heard this tolling and chanting, so that many stopped in their work to listen: women at housework listened; above the whining of the factory machinery, men frowned up; many in the fields above Avila mistook the time, thinking it was the Angelus. And the bells tolled on in strength and discord and the chanting grew to a roar of sound, and soldiers, cleaning their weapons, paused their hands and rose, listening: the monks of Santo Tomé came from their penance; lovers stopped loving in the middle of love. Telephones were ringing, commands being shouted. And all this time, which was of many minutes, down Granizo, with the Countess of Avila leading them, the brooms came sweeping; scores of brooms of all sizes and description.

A machine-gun spoke.

It spoke in a small anger from the sand-bagged corner of Vacas, in the place where the blind man of San Pedro begged; but few heard it because of the chanting and the bells. Some fell among the crowd, but none appeared to notice. Then the gun spoke again. The countess heard it this time and swung to face it while others fell to the ground about her. Screams began. Again the gun fired in chattering light. Juana, hearing the shots ricocheting from the cobbles at her feet, instinctively dropped flat. And, in the moments before the panic the countess straightened, staring at the machine-gun, and raised her broom.

Crying aloud, she ran at the gun.

It fired again.

Lying on the cobbles, the countess wiped the blood into her hair and smiled at Juana, saying, in the tolling of the bells: "For one who is not involved, you did passably well. One day, with luck, you may be mistaken for an Asturian."

47

Five

ROSA, THE MAID in Pío's House, her afternoon off, was sitting in her attic bedroom a fortnight later, examining the cost of her trousseau – marriage to Señor Luis Avante, who kept a garage in Avila, being imminent. She had arrived at a total when the telephone rang.

Juana, in her early days of marriage to Pío de Córdoba, had often wondered why Rosa was granted the luxury of a bedside telephone.

"Yes?" said the maid.

Whispered Pío, "It is I."

"Where?" asked Rosa.

"Oh come, you stupid girl – the love-pavilion."

Rosa sighed and replaced the receiver, staring through her lattice window to the grounds of the mansion below. She saw Agustín, the old gardener, cranked over his hoe in the dusk. Beyond him the many gardeners (who proliferated in Pío's House) worked industriously; strapping young soldiers – the lightly wounded of the fascist's hospital within the town . . . seeking rehabilitation, according to Matilde, the cook, on excellent rations and light industry.

Rosa, who would have preferred any of these to Pío, bent again to her accounts, making an entry in a large, round hand: 'May 1st, 1937. 200 *pesetas*.'

Preparing to go to the love-pavilion again (once a week, on a Thursday) Rosa remembered the dull seasons of her village outside Mollet, where the land was arid in a stink of urine; a place where the dung-flies danced in summer; of brittle coldness in winter. She remembered the Garbi that blew for three hundred days a year; the hungers of her childhood before she had come to Pío de Córdoba's employ.

Now Rosa saw a wedding in white, the bright-faced relatives, the wedding feast: the little flat above the garage in Avila cascaded over her mind. Rosa pouted, vaguely wondering if Luis Avante, her husband-to-be, would agree with such methods of obtaining a dowry. A man of Navarre, born and bred, Luis wore the Sacred Heart upon his chest, and often, over his head, the black cagoule of the penitent.

There were certain consolations, however, according to Pío.

Naked bodies, he suggested, were possessed of a greater innocence than naked souls.

In his room in the west wing of Pío's House, Calvo Fonseca, butler and old retainer to the Countess of Avila, moved his hands with Spanish restlessness.

A Madrileño born and bred, Fonseca found it difficult to be at ease with Madrid under siege and his beloved countess dead. Earlier, he had seen Juana, his young mistress, in the library, reading. Fonseca was wondering if it might be better to have the encounter with Juana now rather than leave it until later.

From the window of his room he watched her leave the library by the french doors and wander over the garden towards the lake.

Later, near the lake he chanced to meet her.

"You cannot sleep, child?"

Juana smiled. "I've been reading García Lorca; his intensity keeps one out of bed."

She moved away and he thought she looked beautiful; there being about her that indefinable grace of movement that was possessed by her mother, the old countess. Of what madness was Pío de Córdoba, Fonseca wondered, that he should prefer the doll-like Rosa?

"You visited your mother's grave today, Agustín tells me."

"Yes, and the flowers he gave me were exquisite."

"The countess was particularly fond of Agustín's roses." Fonseca brought out a handkerchief and momentarily pressed it to his eyes. His personal grief, like Juana's, was rarely apparent; each minimising the loss to assist the other. He said, brightening. "But she would not have this – can you imagine her intolerance?"

"She'd give us a bad time, Fonseca."

Fonseca's eyes were bright in his heavily jowled face; grief, thought Juana, was not sparing Fonseca; in the fortnight since her mother's death, he had aged.

"Lorca's art brings grief more sharply into relief, don't you think?" His eyes moved over Juana's. "And how could he have existed within this war? Spain is now a charnel house."

The grass was white under the moon; faint shadows of overhanging elms touched their faces. "One day," continued Fonseca, "I will make a pilgrimage to Granada, to pay my own homage to García Lorca. Meanwhile, during the war, I intend to let him rest."

"He's bad for me, you suggest?"

"Practicality is peace, poetry is conflict." He smiled at her.

"And you, Calvo?" The use of his Christian name momentarily surprised him.

"Me?" Fonseca looked at the moon. The sky was painted with faint red flashes. "All my values have gone. For the death of men like Lorca I despise myself. A better Spaniard than I would be at the front."

Bulrushes spiked the silver sheen of the lake; the gutteral music of frogs muttered accompaniment to the distant rumbling of the guns. Madrid, thought Fonseca, was under attack again, and he inwardly cursed the Moors. He said, "Continuity in life, that is all I ask, but I should be doing more. As a soldier I could serve General Miaja and his Popular Front."

"You surprise me, Calvo. I thought you shared Pío's politics."

"The Señor is entitled to his beliefs."

"And what are yours?"

The wind moved and the night was perfumed with the scent of musk. By the wish of the old countess it had been planted, a special order brought in from Ceuta, and Juana remembered the planting.

Fonseca said, "Time was when I sat you upon my knee, remember? Between us then existed the ultimate trust. But, in these sad times when children betray their parents, who is one's child?"

Juana smiled. "You're trying to say that you don't trust me?"

"Frankly, I'm wondering where your sympathies lie – with

the republicans? Or with the fascists, like your husband?"

"With a mother like mine, should there be any doubt?"

"That isn't an answer."

"And the answer is important to you?"

Fonseca did not reply, but watched her from the sagging folds of his face. Juana said, "You distrust me because I nurse rebels at the Hospital of the Sacred Heart?"

"It makes me unsure."

"You should not be unsure, Calvo. My sympathies lie with the republic. If I nurse rebels, it's to counter my mother's activities. Should trouble arise, it's an excellent antidote? Doesn't that make sense?"

"So you know of the escape route?" Fonseca visibly relaxed.

"I know that the number of gardeners we have here wouldn't stand examination. That wounded republicans come and go in the place and that Pío knows nothing of it . . ." Juana smiled at him. "You are also involved?"

The butler drew himself up. "Not only here, but in Oviedo, when we lived there, and I'm proud of it. It is my sole contribution to the war."

"And who else contributes, as you put it?"

"Agustín and Matilde." The butler stared about him as if he'd said nothing in particular.

"The cook? Oh, I don't believe it!"

"I assure you she does, lady. Matilde is a fervent republican and, like Agustín and me, was devoted to your mother. She sews on shoulder flashes, she mends uniforms. Matilde can turn a republican into a rebel at the blink of an eye."

"Rosa?"

Fonseca looked aghast. "Give your mother credit for greater sense, lady."

"And you think I can help now my mother has gone?"

"It is imperative that you do," replied the butler. "The soldiers arrive wearing the Pelayo medallion – this is their passport to freedom. Naturally, they will continue to ask for the old countess, but she no longer exists, more is the pity."

Juana nodded and walked on slowly, then turned for the house entrance. "See me tomorrow, Calvo, and we'll talk more about it."

5I

"On the contrary, we will talk about it now." Fonseca grasped Juana's arm. "Come, please."

Richard was sitting in straw, propped up against the stable wall. A hurricane lamp hanging from a beam above him cast shadows in his ashen face, but his hand was steady on the big revolver he held. Agustín, the tiny head-gardener, was cowering before him.

Juana said, entering: "You're asking for me, I understand?"

Richard nodded. "I am to report to the Countess of Avila."

"I am the Countess of Avila."

Fonseca asked, swiftly, "You have the Pelayo medallion, soldier?"

"Here." Richard took it off and tossed it into his hands.

"It would be more sociable if you would lower the gun," said Juana. "Nobody will harm you here. What is your name?" She was kneeling beside him now, turning his head to the light.

"Richard Hanson."

"From the Internationals?" Juana turned. "Water, Agustín."

"Lincoln Battalion," Richard replied, and took the brandy flask Agustín offered him and tipped it to his mouth. He drank, gasping.

"And you've come through the rebel lines from Madrid?"

"No, from the sierra – Las Navas."

"The Malagar group?" Fonseca was intent now, realisation dawning. His face was bent forward in the yellow light, and Juana watched him; it was a different Fonseca.

"No, I've heard of the Malagar people, but I'm from the Astrada group."

"But Astrada is in Salinero. At Las Navas you were miles off the track."

"I was on my way to him, and was met by his gitanos. They ambushed a Guardia patrol for horses, and I was hit."

Fonseca asked, "Old Pep and Manolo brought you here, then?"

"Also the boy Nicolas, but he stayed in the mountains to watch the horses."

Agustín returned to the stable, slopping a bowl of water, and edged his tiny body around the door.

The butler asked: "Is the house quiet?"

"Like the grave." The old man knelt and placed the bowl with grunts and wheezes.

Juana was untying the bandage around Richard's head and the blood spread in a widening patch in the folds. She said, "This is still bleeding. How long has it been like this?"

"Since yesterday. Until an hour ago I was blind."

She peered at the wound, turning his head this way and that. "Yes, it will have to be stitched, it is a very bad wound."

Fonseca said: "Lady, we dare not risk a doctor."

"Of course not, I will stitch it," said Juana.

Juana saw such men as this a dozen times a day at the rebel Hospital of the Sacred Heart; weary, unshaven bundles of humanity, their clothes starched with blood and in the first stages of consciousness. The man before her was big, and, although clearly in pain, there was about his eyes an intensity that commanded the place; bright blue in his grimed face, they moved steadily from her to Fonseca, who said: "Initially, you came from Hans Deimler, did you not?"

"Yes, republican headquarters in Madrid."

"But you take your orders from Emilio?"

"Emilio is my call-sign."

"Ah, of course!" Fonseca snapped his fingers. "You are the new signaller Astrada asked for. Now I remember!"

Juana knelt back on her heels. "Let me bathe this. It's bad, and stitching is going to hurt." She looked at Richard's blood-soaked shirt. "God, you've lost a lot of blood . . ."

Agustín said in a high, croaking voice, "We will all lose blood if they begin a search, Countess. If he bleeds, could he not do it in the cellar, in comfort?"

"Agustín is right," said Juana. "Take him to the cellar."

With his arms around the shoulders of Fonseca and Agustín, Richard followed Juana out of the stable and over the shippon to the house. She swung the hall door wide, exposing a wide mosaic floor with its spiralling oak staircase winding to the landing above. Next she opened a door in a heavily panelled ante-room leading off the library.

With the lamp held high, she momentarily listened.

Richard watched. He saw Juana's face etched sharply in the light of the lamp, her dark eyes narrowed, the pupils shining. Relaxing, she turned and flashed them a smile, her lips full and red against the straight white lines of her teeth.

Richard had expected an older woman; when the gitanos had talked of the Countess of Avila, they had painted her as an aristocratic scold. But tiredness was now sweeping over him in waves of increasing intensity; his head throbbed; all he wanted was sleep, yet the vision of Juana's beauty persisted in his mind.

They descended stone steps that spiralled down into one cellar, then went through a narrow, bolt-studded door that led even lower, down to another. A thin door creaked open; the lamp made shape, defining a small, low-ceilinged, stone-flagged room with no ventilation save for a grating. In one corner was a wash-stand and water-bowl and jug; in the other a narrow bed.

Through half-closed eyes, in the hybrid between consciousness and sleep, Richard watched the room slowly fade.

Earlier, Pío de Córdoba, standing at a bedroom window that overlooked the stables, had watched Juana and Fonseca cross the terraced lawn. With expressionless eyes he had rolled a cigarette one-handed, peasant style; putting it between his teeth he lit it, hands cupped to the flare of the match.

The lake beyond the house was a mirror of light set against the dark skirts of surrounding poplars; the white portico of the Chinese love-pavilion glimmered in the moonlight. Rosa, the young fool, had left a light on there and he cursed her soundlessly, both for her carelessness at times of ardour and her carefree attitude to waste – she who had been short of a crust when on her mother's farm in Mollet. The young, he reflected, were morons in other respects; no political responsibility, little sense of timing.

For a long time, Pío stood there, watching the shadows dance on the cobbled yard, listening to the sounds of the stables; then, shrugging non-committally, he crossed to the telephone as it tinkled faintly beside his bedside table.

He lifted the receiver.

"Pío de Córdoba . . ."

Six

Next day, Juana said, busying herself around the tiny cellar, "So, you were wounded in an ambush in the Gredos?"

Richard, lying on the bed, nodded. "Trying to get Guardia horses for the Astrada group. You know of Felipe Astrada?"

Rolling bandages, Juana smiled. "I know none of the partisans for this was my mother's province. She organised this escape route, she nursed wounded republicans – a good Asturian in every sense."

"And now she's dead?"

"You knew?"

"Fonseca told me." Richard lit a cigarette and smoked steadily.

He judged Juana's age at twenty-five. Her features, small and well defined, possessed the Iberian darkness of the true-blooded Spaniard, and there was a nobility about her movements that enchanted him. Last night she had stitched the wound on his head, and her hands were small and strong. Now she was bending above him, inspecting the drying suppuration of the bandages for the wound was slightly infected, and this was clearly worrying her. He smoked steadily, smiling up at her, then closed his eyes as Juana turned away. It was hot in the confined space of the cellar and he was sweating badly.

Richard was lying with closed eyes now, and Juana glanced at his face.

It was a good face, she thought, one independent and strong. She had the impression that he didn't care if she attended him or not, and that suited her: he could please himself, she thought, if he didn't approve of her: his very independence demeaned her, but she did not mind. His attitude was a relief from the commoner fawning she got from the nationalist wounded.

55

Richard, for his part, could hear distant guns. It was midday; the usual five minute bombardment of Madrid began dolefully far away to the north. He listened, head inclined, ignoring Juana. Guns called him – a legacy from the Corunna Road, and Jarama.

He glanced at Juana.

So much for the romantic countess, he thought. He'd got the wrong one apparently. This Asturian looked too removed to talk with and too prim to sleep with, though one could never tell. That was the trouble with the true-blood Spanish aristocracy – they were difficult to weigh up, he thought: they did things in the name of God that would not be countenanced by other nationalities: never, he thought, had he met a nation more composed of saints and sinners.

"Your mother was Spanish, they tell me," said Juana, breaking the silence.

"A Basque. My father was a Texan. They were executed after the Miners' Rebellion. It was unfortunate. Soon after I was born they moved to Britain. I stayed there, but they returned to Spain – just in time for Franco's massacres."

"Up in the Asturias?"

He nodded, distant and self-contained. "Oviedo."

Juana tucked in the end of the bandage and tidied the bed. "And now you fight because of them?"

"Not at all. Against fascism."

Juana went to the cellar door, listening.

Her white gown increased her height from a distance; her boy-slimness enhanced it further, Richard thought. He was considering it as astonishing that one day he'd be roughing it with partisans in the Gredos, next day lying within the security of a noble house. Now he began to wonder how the situation could serve the end, by the death of Franco.

"It was a bloody bodge," he said, lying back on the pillows.

Surprised Juana turned from the window. He didn't know the art of subtlety, this one. "The Gredos ambush?" Juana asked abstractedly.

"Ill-timed, badly executed. When they go for Franco they'll have to do better than that."

"And your specific job in life is to kill General Franco?"

"That's right."

"Wouldn't another Franco arise? Assassinate him – we could get one worse?"

Her directness attracted him. He was still tired and wanted sleep, yet she had a peculiar ability to entertain by her presence. She rarely spoke, except to say something: most of the women he had known chattered without direction or effect.

He replied, his eyes still closed: "We must assassinate. It's in the order of things. One after the other, if needs be: it will save lives in the end."

"That sounds more like a directive from the Kremlin."

He didn't appear to be listening. "What do you plan to do with me?"

"Keep you here until your wound heals."

"Yes, but how long will that take?"

"Ten days."

"Ten days is too long. I've got a meeting with Felipe Astrada on the seventh, and that is next week."

"Then Astrada will have to wait," answered Juana. "You won't be well enough to travel."

Richard grinned at her. There was a slight abruptness about her that he admired; perhaps it was part of her outdated aristocracy, he thought; this small sense of domination that pervaded her speech and actions.

He said, "Fit enough, or not, I'm meeting Astrada. The war won't wait."

"There are certain things to be done?"

"There are important things to be done." For the first time she noticed his faint American accent.

"If you went you'd be of little use to him." She was persistent.

"Let me make my mind up about that." He frowned up at her. "Meanwhile, every moment I stay here is a greater danger to you, you know."

"Of course."

"They'll shoot the lot of you if they find me here."

"Possibly."

He said, lighting a cigarette. "You trust these two – Fonseca and Agustín?"

Juana was busy at the sink, her back turned to him. "I've

57

known them all my life. Loyalty is the golden gift of old retainers."

"And your husband? What if he finds out?"

Juana laughed softly. "He'd probably think it lent some spice to life. Pío's one of life's charming idiots, he takes little seriously." Juana dried her hands at the basin. "Everything he takes in his stride – it will all sort itself out, that is Pío's philosophy. The common house-fly, he says, killed more men than the Hundred Years War – what is tomorrow compared with such statistics? – this is Pío."

"His fine philosophies don't prevent him from being a fascist."

"Oh yes, don't get him wrong. A comfortable life, this is all Pío wants."

"And you?"

Juana approached the bed. "Just to continue my mother's work, that's all I ask now."

"The escape route here, you mean?"

"That's right. It's pretty passive, I know, but better than doing nothing."

"You'd prefer something more active?"

"I'd never carry a gun, if that's what you mean."

He smiled faintly. "Somebody has to."

"Not me. I couldn't kill or injure anything." She looked away, aware of his smiling interest; it induced in her a self-consciousness she had never known before.

She had always lacked the self-assertiveness of her mother, who appeared indoctrinated with her own code of behaviour. Before the eyes of this man Juana felt impassive, almost unprotected; his light blue eyes seemed to possess the ability to look into her soul, and she faintly resented it; yet there was about him a courtesy that forbade anger.

"And somebody has to fight, too, you know," he said softly.

"Perhaps, but not me, you understand?" Juana lifted her eyes to his, he was now very much awake suddenly, intent upon her answers. "I hate the war, I hate the cruelty and the killings . . ." She turned away in a sudden despair. "God, how I hate it – the hypocrisy of it all. Rebel or republican – they're both as bad as each other."

58

"But your mother didn't take that line." Richard was watching her above the curling smoke of his cigarette.

Hastily, Juana glanced at her watch, whispering, as if to herself, *"Caramba*, I must go . . ."

"When's the earliest I can leave here, you say?"

"A week, perhaps, if you're lucky."

"Perhaps, by this time tomorrow, it'll be a couple of days?" He gave her his widest smile.

"Leave here in under a week and you'll probably never reach Salinero." She returned his gaiety, but left the room with professional disinterest.

Richard lay back and grinned at the ceiling.

Seven

A WEEK LATER, Fonseca, who strapped his life to time, awoke to a clear sunny morning, remembering with a shock that the war was still on despite the squawking gaiety of the birds. Dressing, he listened to a scratched recording of 'Nights in the Gardens of Spain'.

Later, Agustín, the head-gardener, cranked over his hoe at the western gate of the house, raised high his mole-skin hat as Juana drove her pony and trap out of the grounds towards Avila and the morning market. Agustín's scarred face twisted into a happy smile; there was, he thought, a new gaiety in the young countess these days.

"Good morning, Agustín!" Dressed in white, with a broad-rimmed, summer hat, Juana waved gaily. Agustín winked at the sun; the change in his mistress was in accord with the romantic tenor of his nature.

The coming of summer had brought to besieged Madrid the vital stalemate the Popular Front had sought. The resistance of the International Brigades at Brunete and Jarama had defied Franco's attempts to encircle the capital.

Two months earlier, in March, an army of fifty thousand Spaniards, Italians and Moors had been beaten back from the University City. With over twenty thousand dead and wounded, the nationalists, led by the Italian Garibaldis, had retreated to Avila in disorder.

Juana saw them now, despondent, Italians trudging the pavements about her, the refuse of another's war. Last winter, she reflected they had been up to their waists in snow, starving in the frozen trenches before Madrid.

While buying at a meat stall, a young German officer momentarily paused, saluting. Juana quickly moved on. It might be a Spanish war, she reflected, but it was now being run on foreign lines. The interrogation centres of the *Somaten*, the Spanish Secret Police, were now based on those of the German Gestapo.

Fonseca's window commanded a good view of the western gate of the house.

Earlier, he had seen Agustín hobbling out of his lodge cottage: Fonseca groaned, fearing a visit; made a wry face when a knock came on his door. "*Caramba!* Come!"

"My friend," announced Agustín, entering. "It is tremendous news!"

"Oh God," whispered Fonseca, sighing.

The old man adjusted his mole-skin cap and croaked falsetto. "She has fallen in love, has she not? Our young countess! *Madre Mía!* That will give Pío something to get on with!"

Fonseca said, testily, "Allow her some privacy, you damned old pry."

But Agustín flung out bony hands.

"That American is up and walking the cellar. They are lovers – undoubtedly. Can't you read the language of eyes? I lay you ten to one that last night she was in his bed."

"Last night she was in her own bed, for I visited her room," said Fonseca blandly. "You are evil."

"But my span of evil's run, alas!" The gardener cringed his small shoulders. "The body decays though the heart is young. When I was her age I was the most evil one in Grado, you know."

"Quiet, man. Let me think. If she is in love with the American, it could be important."

"So evil was I that women sought me out to teach them love."

"For Heaven's sake!" Fonseca was now pacing about.

"I became famous. In my spare time I fashioned boxwood pipes with stems of elm. There was a widow who kept a trinket shop outside the cathedral. All men sought her, none achieved her, but she had a weakness for boxwood pipes. In her shop she sold them for thirty-two *pesetas*; she paid me, wholesale, thirty-five."

"When did you see her?"

"Juana? Just now, I say – going to Avila market."

"And Pío was not with her?"

"No."

Fonseca turned away. "It could be dangerous. He always accompanies her to market, it is a weekly ritual. If things are to proceed successfully in this place, nothing should be changed, especially habit."

The old man waved disdainfully. "*Hombre!* Be human! What use is a countess in a convent? Do a few watching fascists frighten you? When empires have been lost within a woman's thighs? Heavens, man, the old countess would have taken on the Washington Battalion."

"Away," commanded Fonseca, "and take your lechery with you."

Pío appeared to be awaiting Juana when she drove the trap back from Avila market that midday. Diminutive in a white, silk suit, with his monocle in place and a straw hat covering his baldness, he waited on the lawn as Juana brought the pony to a halt.

"My love," said Pío petulently, "are you aware that you went to market without me?"

Juana kissed him lightly on the cheek. "Come, you were asleep."

"Where in heaven do you get to these days? I never seem to see you?" Pío waved a small finger. "If I didn't know you better, I'd say you'd taken a lover."

"Your conscience is yours, darling, leave me to mine."

Pío took Juana's arm and steered her across the lawn, crying, "After all, what's a little adventure at such a drab time? As I said to Fonseca – a war is on, let her have a fling. She has a lover in Avila? Excellent! He's probably a smart young captain in the Thirty-third Carlists – or even an adjutant in Miaja's republicans, her taste, like her mother's, being a trifle left of centre." He walked faster, dragging Juana after him.

The lake was lined with waving iris and Juana bent to pick them. "Now come, a name, a name! Who is your chocolate soldier?"

"My God, Pío, it would serve you right, wouldn't it!"

"Is there now coquetry in my sweet Juana!"

Juana began to wonder how much Pío knew.

It was inconceivable that he had learned anything from Fonseca or Agustín. Rosa's face made an image in her mind, but Rosa was supposed to know nothing of what happened in Pío's house. Behind Pío's mock *bonhomie* there was a request for a name, thought Juana.

Pío wasn't a fool. He had not reached the peak in his world of finance without cunning and intelligence. A friend to the likes of Juan March and Juan Ventosa, the richest men in Spain, he was at his most threatening when exuding innocence.

Now he said, clearly exploring another avenue, "I could think of better places to meet a lover than in Avila. No moons exist above Avila, did you know? Cervantes chops them up into stars and puts them over Segovia."

They strolled towards the Chinese love-pavilion in an affinity of sudden quiet: its columned entrance flashed brightness in the sun.

One of the young gardeners – Fonseca's republicans – stood politely aside as they passed, and Pío said, "It quite astonishes me where Agustín gets all these assistants from. Are they paid, do you know?"

Juana replied: "Yes, but apparently on the cheap, and when peace breaks out it'll certainly have to stop. The Falange will then have little use for us."

"And peace is just around the corner, is it not? Any time now Azaña will ask to negotiate." Pío turned his wizened face to the sun.

Juana replied, "If Azaña did that he wouldn't last an hour. The republicans are not losing this war, my love, although you'd like to think it."

"To believe that idiocy one has to be a republican," Pío snapped. "The moment Madrid falls . . ."

"But Madrid will not fall! Not all the time there are men and women prepared to die for the freedom we take for granted!"

He opened his small hands, stopping her to impress his point. "Listen! The Germans and Italians dominate the air – two-thirds of Spain is now in Franco's hands . . ."

Juana interjected; "What do you people want, a ravaged

Spain? Hitler and Mussolini are dictating this war, not Franco. And now we've got to win it or accept national fascism!"

"Oh come, Juana! You accuse a Spanish peasant of wanting fascism?"

She replied earnestly, "I do. And fascism isn't around the corner, Pío, it's here. Toledo, Badajoz – the killings are sickening. What are the Moors doing here, anyway?"

Pío replied calmly. "Excess is the logical outcome of war, dearest one. But, when the killing is over, we'll enjoy a new and revitalised Spain, one free of these damned socialists and communists – don't tell me you agree with their precepts!"

"Yes. If the alternative is your fascism."

They stared at each other. Doves were sobbing from the poplars of the lake; birds of many colours were chattering from the curved roof of the Chinese love-pavilion, its dome shining in the heated air.

"*Por* ⬛⬛⬛, we *are* getting hot, aren't we?" Pío mopped his sweating face. "True, we nationalists are a little energetic in the conduct of the war – men like Mola and de Llano – indeed, Franco's the only one I admire out of the lot of them, but . . ."

"You speak of Franco as a friend!"

Pío nodded assertively. "I find him gracious. His prayer is to build a Spain that is economically and spiritually fulfilled. He's a great family man, you know?"

"Basically concerned about the families of others, I take it."

Pío ignored the sarcasm. "He's devout; hard-headed, true, but then, he has to be. Come! In all great schemes, Juana, there are hideous mistakes."

"My mother's murder, for one?"

Pío shook his head regretfully.

They walked on, turning towards the house.

The sun burned down. Mist was rolling in little billows across the unrippled lake, like herded sheep. Pío said:

"Tonight, I shall be out. You will see your captain in the Thirty-third again? Especially after this unhappy encounter? It is a golden opportunity."

Juana did not reply.

Eight

Fonseca said, "Lady, the American has left the cellar."

"I know," replied Juana, "I have just been down there."

It was the morning after Pío had left for his monthly tour of his business establishments. Juana and the butler hurried round to the back of the house, and Agustín, coming from the stable yard, cried: "He is going, do you know? He is more mad than most, this *Yanqui*. His head is sore and the sun is giving him the vapours." He opened his hands. "I've reasoned with him, but there is nothing to choose between him and his mule."

"He's in the stables?"

"Better than that, lady, he is saddling the thing."

Richard was leading the mule out into the yard when Juana and Fonseca arrived there. She said, "Now come, this is stupidity, man, you can scarcely stand."

Richard said, "It is necessary, I tell you. I've got to get to Astrada."

"Look, we can get a message to him, Fonseca . . .!"

"No, I have got to go myself."

Fonseca said, "Ten miles or more?"

"It is more like five."

"Ten miles using the pass," replied Juana. "We know the country."

The mule was standing in dejection. Agustín appeared, waving his stick, crying, "Let him go. He is a stupid *Yanqui*. The mule possesses more sense."

Juana said, "Food and water?"

Richard patted his water-bottle. "Water in plenty, and I haven't the stomach for food." He faced Juana, smiling and gripped Fonseca's hand.

Strangely, there arose in Juana an empty sense of loss as the mule crossed the shippon; Richard waved once, then took the road eastward, towards the Sierra de Gredos.

* * *

65

The red brick turrets of Pío's House were swallowed into the falling darkness as Richard took the mule into the foothills, traversing the steep hillsides of the bleak mountain district where white water foamed down to the plains.

Here, in the steady clip-clopping of the mules hooves, there came upon him an isolating loneliness. All about him, as he took the narrow track to the east, great forests of pine and ilex stood in stately stillness under the moon. Richard paused at times, listening for hooves, sensing the possibility of ambush.

For this was Guardia country; the embossing olive-groves and vineyards, long deserted and overgrown, excellent headquarters for marauding gipsies. His head-wound throbbed in the absolute quiet. Over his shoulder Richard saw the flat-topped ridge of Avila to the west, and the spires of the town stabbed out of the enveloping ground mist. The moon flash of the Adaja River glimmered dull silver in the treeless plain. To the south and west the lofty mountains of the Sierra de Malagón rolled in dark thunder across the star-lit sky.

And to this barren loneliness there was added a regret – the loss of Juana. It was a nagging emptiness difficult to define. In some abstract way she reminded him of Carla, his wife. Richard smiled at his thoughts and his hand bunched harder on the mule's reins. An Iberian darkness was common to them both, of course; Carla, like Juana de Córdoba, had been a full-blooded Spaniard; such women were not scarce. But there was more to it than looks. There was between them an affinity that he couldn't readily identify, a pleasing phenomenon. Now he swayed in the saddle and the white track before him wavered against the jogging neck of the mule.

Shaking his head to clear it, Richard looked at his watch. He had been riding for three hours, for it was nearly ten o'clock. A little wind blew from the south, fanning the sweat of his face. Reining in, he took the mule into the track-side pines. The sombre gloom of the forest was lightened by great moon-shafts; the chattering of night-birds ceased abruptly to the advent of danger. Dismounting, he was about to tether the mule, when he heard hoof-beats coming along the track behind him.

Instantly, drawing his Colt, he crouched in the bracken. The moon played tricks with light and shade; the boulders

66

about him withered and shrank, a disturbing impression of focal instability. Richard rubbed sweat out of his eyes. The hoof-beats approached without respite, the sound throbbing in his ears; he cocked the revolver, drawing it back into the shelter of his poncho.

The rider came on, now the hoof-beats stammered into silence. Within their indecision, Richard craned forward, looking down the track. He saw, in a sudden scud of the moon, a horse and rider outlined against the stars, and heard a voice call: "Richard Hanson, are you there?" and he recognised Juana's voice.

Rising from the bracken, Richard walked out on to the track; the moon blazed, bringing to shape the forest verge, the white track, boulder-strewn and hostile.

Seeing him, Juana spurred her horse and trotted towards him.

"*Por* Woman, in s name!"

Momentarily, Juana sat unspeaking, then dismounted.

Her face grew in outline before him; he saw the dark smudges of her eyes in her firm, white cheeks; pushing back her riding cap, she said: "We talked of it, Fonseca and I. And decided. 'So what' said he. 'If the American worries you, accompany him to Salinero. Isn't it the least a good nurse could do – see the patient to a place of safety?'"

"You were lucky not to be shot," said Richard. "This is no place for a woman."

"And foolish of you to leave Avila before your are fit to go." Juana led the horse, a young bay, into the cover of the trees. The moon, now clear of cloud, rose bright and clear over the purple rim of the mountains, etching the forest into sharp relief, bringing light and shade to the rolling hills of the sierra. Juana said, tethering the bay, "Let me stay. There is little for me to do back in the house, and I know all the short tracks to Salinero."

"Astrada will not like it."

"Astrada will probably be delighted. He and my mother were friends, according to Fonseca."

Richard sat in the leaves, stretching out his legs. Juana sat opposite him on a boulder.

She looked somehow smaller in her riding jacket and skirt;

the leggings, he thought, did not become her. He preferred her in the white smock she used when nursing: it induced a femininity that now deserted her.

There was in him a small sense of relief that she was near; it atoned for the strange emptiness he had known when he left her standing with Fonseca in the shippon of the house. He rejected the pleasure of her, yet it persisted. He said: "You're foolhardy enough to get yourself into trouble. We aren't going on a picnic, you know, we are going to partisans. There's work to be done, and it will be dangerous."

"The Galapagar convoy?"

The moon faded; tree-darkness enveloped them; Richard could not see her face.

"What do you know of the Galapagar convoy?"

"Little enough, but you talk in your sleep. Is this why you're in such a rush to get to Salinero?"

"It's unfair to listen when people talk in their sleep," he said.

"Oh come, don't be stuffy!" Juana laughed softly, her head back, examining him through half-closed eyes. "Let me put you on the quick tracks to Salinero and then I promise to leave you."

For answer Richard untethered the mule. "That would be wise. They tell me Astrada's tough, and doesn't like strangers. Meanwhile, forget all you've heard about the Galapagar convoy."

"*Madre Mía!* And I thought you'd be delighted to see me!"

Richard heaved himself up into the saddle of the mule. His head was light; shapes of the night gyrated in mist; the roadside boulders floated past him like contorted ghosts in flashes of the moon. Momentarily, as the mule stumbled on the uneven track he lurched in the saddle and was nearly unseated and Juana spurred the young bay up beside him, peering in concern.

In this manner, sometimes riding abreast, sometimes in file, with Juana leading, they entered deep into the Campo Azálvaro, the mountain link between the Gredos and Sierra Guadarrama, and here the track steepened into a pass, narrow and tortuous, winding backwards upon itself in loops

68

and circles and the mountain crags stood out stark against the moonlit sky and the sierra took on a blueness, which was not of itself but the strangely coloured figuration of the clouds. From this high point in the campo they descended into a plateau of greenness, and here, behind a barrier of boulders stretched a smaller river leaping and foaming out of the forest and the river was unnamed, said Juana, because of its smallness; in times of cold it widened its banks and was deep and treacherous; at times of heat, she explained, one could ford it and only get wet to the thigh. But this was before the great heats of the sierra; now both mule and bay would have to swim.

"You've done this before?"

"No, I haven't," replied Richard.

She admired his surly strength; when confronted, as now, with an imponderable, he retreated into silence. She cajoled him, saying as she dismounted, "It's very easy. Look," and she stood beside the bay. "With your right hand you take the reins; with your left hand you grip the horn of the saddle. The horse takes confidence when you wade in beside it. The moment it begins to swim, you straighten your left hand to keep your distance."

"This," said Richard, "is a mule. Has he the brains of a horse?"

"You'll not drown, I assure you."

"I am no horseman," he said abjectly. "Also, I cannot swim."

"The mule will do the swimming, I tell you. Come, follow me," and she led the bay down to the river's edge and the moon was fine and big, hanging like a broken onyx in the sky and all about them was the forest and the roaring of the river cascading over stones. A fish jumped, a silver crescent of terror in the moonlight. Richard followed tentatively, leading the mule.

Juana entered the river with the bay, calling over her shoulder, "When once he begins to swim, lift the reins high – keep them away from his forelegs. Walk until you float. Leave everything to the mule!"

Richard stood in the shallows watching her.

Unaccountably, and he recalled this later, the war was

forgotten. The coming attack on the military convoy at Galapagar was forgotten; nothing was more important than being there with the mule, watching Juana as she waded into deep water. It was an emboldening thought, one exempt from apprehension. Was it possible, Richard wondered, always to stay in this wild, lovely place, and with this good companionship? In this there was no pain, no disquiet; it laid bare the artificial courage, it healed all conflicts. He no longer remembered the bright explosions of Jarama, the rafale shrieking of the ricochets. All was sanctified by simplicity – a woman and a horse crossing a river in moonlight.

Now Juana and the bay reached firm ground on the opposite bank.

Cupping her hands, she called to Richard above the shouting of the river.

"Come on, come on!"

The water swirled about his knees and rose in icy waves to his thighs; deeper now: the mule, uncertain, was rolling its eyes. Richard whispered, digging it with his elbow. "Get up, *get up!*"

Holding the saddle horn stiffly at arm's length, he plunged in.

Juana called above the surge of the river, "Reins high, *reins high!*"

The mule was gasping; Richard could feel its fine body writhing beside him; its forelegs danced, ploughing the swim of the river. Now came a deep silence and he was drawn along by an unseen power, until the mule's hooves struck ground, then it rose, dragging him out of the cold. The river thundered. The mule shook itself, spraying him. Richard wiped water from his eyes and saw Juana standing before him. Her face was shining with wetness; her lips parted in a smile.

"Now then! We've saved two miles!"

"Is this professional nursing? At this rate I'll be dead before I reach Salinero!"

The bay and the mule stood grazing. Momentarily Richard and Juana stared at each other. The spell, instantly woven, was instantly broken.

"We'd best get on," she said.

Nine

RICHARD SAID, "LOOK, Salinero!" and pointed, and dim lights grew out of the mist, burning fitfully.

Juana stood up in the saddle. "You know the site of the camp?"

"Only that it is by a lake to the north of the village, near Miguel."

She replied, "That should be easy to find. One road only goes to Miguel." She reined in the horse. "I shall leave you here."

"And return alone? You will not."

"Astrada doesn't like strangers, you said."

"He'll have to put up with them for once. If you return now you'll be breaking curfew in Avila. A bed in camp for the night is little to ask."

Juana smiled to herself. In retrospect her journey, she thought, had been needless; after a brief rest this man was becoming stronger with every mile. He sat the mule now with a new confidence, his big body jogging easily in the saddle. His face was a dim shape beneath his sombrero where the bandage showed white. She had heard say that some of these republicans were tough enough for ten lives, and this, she thought, was surely such a man – with thirty-two stitches in his head.

She said: "All right, then. Tomorrow, if they're ready, I'll take out the stitches."

They jogged on, now abreast, descending the winding track of the mountain down to the Salinero road.

"You know," said Richard, "you're an enigma."

"What makes you say that?"

"You are singular. One moment you're nursing nationalist rebels, then you're riding to the camp of republican partisans."

"I am one of many," replied Juana. "People who find war barbarous and uncouth – I told you."

71

"A pacifist?"

"Passive enough to keep me neutral. This is a class war; its hatreds fanned by incredible ambitions – Church and State. I could put my tongue to a dozen different factions – from the F.A.I.s to the J.O.N.s – all their ideals based on a futile patriotism."

She rode on, her face upturned to a darkened sky.

"But we republicans stand for the people – come, you are the people."

"You say you stand for the people, but put you in power and things would change, would it not?" Juana flashed him a smile. "It's a political rigmarole and Spain will be the last to benefit."

"You disagree with what I'm doing?" he asked.

There grew in the mist about them a strange diffused light as the moon came out.

Juana replied. "Yes, because you are trying to kill. I've told you – I disagree with killing. What right have you to take a life? As I said – you kill Franco, but another Franco comes; so you kill him, too, then another and another. Killing solves nothing. The only ones who suffer as a result are the defenceless."

Richard said, tolerantly, "Perhaps, if you even were more deeply affected by this war, you'd think differently. A mother with a couple of kids in an occupied village?"

"Probably. Meanwhile, I can only think from my standpoint and only react to what happens to me."

"It's a philosophy that doesn't win wars," said Richard.

They did not speak more because the shapes of three men loomed out of the mist across the Salinero road, and a voice cried: *"Rojillo, dame un cigarrillo!"*

Richard reined in his mule, putting out his arm to stay Juana, and called back: *"Si, camarada! Un cigarrillo!"*

Hooves clattered on the metalled road and there came from the mist a single rider on a fine horse, and he thrust his face into Richard's and the muzzle of a Winchester swung from him to Juana and back again, and Old Pep croaked: "He comes! He lives! It is as I thought – the mule Americano!"

"It is he?" Nicolas spurred his horse and came abreast, and they wheeled about on the narrow road, shouting greetings,

72

until the gitanos reined in hard and turned, and led the way to the camp beyond Salinero, and this was off the road in a forest clearing near a place called Miguel.

Within the clearing squatted a woman, and she was stirring a tin over a fire. The fire was before a cave mouth, so positioned that it could not be seen from the road below; nor from the distant railway along which the rebels were moving the munitions of war towards besieged Madrid. Above the shuffle of the animals' feet in the leaf refuse of autumns, Richard and Juana heard the clanking of distant wagons.

The woman expectantly leaped to her feet when Richard and Juana arrived, then sank down again and pulled the rags of her dress closer about her breast, and her hair, which was black and plaited either side of her head, she swept back. Richard saw her face in the light of the fire. Her eyes were old, her breast was young. The woman stared up at Juana with surly discontent.

Dismounting, Richard approached, while the gitanos called in banter into the cave mouth, and a man came into the dusk, and this was Felipe Astrada.

"*Salud*," cried he. "You bring company?"

Dressed in a khaki jerkin and riding breeches, he stood with his fists upon his hips, addressing Richard but looking at Juana. Richard said, dismounting: "I am Hanson of the Lincoln Battalion, sent by Deimler," and he weighed Astrada.

The man was squat, with a great breadth of shoulders, his movements drunk with strength; his skin possessed the texture of the ape, but his eyes, bright in his bearded face, were good. He said, his hand out, "And the woman?"

"One of whom you've heard," said Richard. "The Countess of Avila."

"The daughter of the old countess, you mean?" Astrada ejaculated, "

Richard nodded. "She nursed me," and pointed at his head. "It is more dangerous round here with your bloody gitanos than in front of Madrid."

Astrada wandered closer to Juana. He said, "Only yesterday I heard of your mother's death. She was a great lady –

my condolences," and he swung to Richard. "But what is she doing here?"

Richard explained and Astrada watched Juana, grunting assent. He said, bassly, "You know the dangers?"

"She'll not be here long," said Richard. "A meal, a rest, and she's back to Avila at first light tomorrow."

"Elisa!" Astrada turned, bawling in command, "Here, take care of our guest."

The woman at the fire rose, walking slowly towards them, looking Juana up and down with obvious distaste.

Near the fire sat Ramón, his pale, aesthetic face turned down, and Elisa spoke to him and joy was in her voice, but he rose, as if not hearing her and walked away to a quiet place and there sat again.

Richard saw this, and wondered, and Astrada, joining him, said: "They are a strange pair, you think?" and he nodded towards Ramón, who, seeing this, averted his face the more. "Of all here, that one has the most potential. Have you heard of the Orphean Choir? This is the torture of the Moors, and this Ramón will collect if ever they find him." Astrada grinned and cocked a cheroot up in his face and lit it. "The body of a woman and the face of a boy. Oh yes, he is queer, though Elisa loves him."

"That is plain," said Richard.

"What is plain?" asked Juana, joining them.

"That Elisa loves him – we are speaking of Ramón."

Astrada drew on the cheroot, nodding towards Ramón. "The gitano whistle after him and make their fancy faces, but Ramón Barro is the best man here."

"Once," said Juana wistfully, "his girl was beautiful . . ." and Elisa put more sticks on the fire and it blazed suddenly, lighting her face.

"She brought Ramón here," explained Astrada. "After escaping from the Women's Prison in Barcelona, she found him and brought him. Before that, it seems, they were lovers. Two months they had her in San Pablo – her looks are gone, you see her face?"

Ramón, as if aware that they were being discussed, rose from the ground and brushed himself down with slow, fastidious grace. Astrada said, "If it comes to trust, Hanson, trust Ramón Barro. Forget Old Pep and the boy, forget Manolo Quinto, for they are gitanos at heart, and may betray you. But, when all else fails – trust him. Who else would act the counter-spy? He marches into the Carlist camps and gets us information, and the nationalists believe he is working for them. Remember?"

"I'll remember," answered Richard.

Later, in the cave mouth, Richard and Juana rose as Astrada came near. He said: "At dawn tomorrow the Franco convoy is leaving Avila. Ramón brings news of it. It is coming on the Galapagar road. And it will be heavily guarded – ambush will not be easy . . ." He smiled at Juana. "Is it asking too much . . .? We could do with a nurse . . ."

Astrada drew his poncho closer to him.

Behind him the others moved like wraiths and coffee-smell killed the perfume of the forest. He added, "This is Elisa's country. We need a tree struck by lightning, and she knows of one near to Pinares, where the railway crosses the road. The exploding tree is gitanos' business, not mine, but I have seen them use it before. They find a tree, cut it down, hollow out the hole to a ten foot length and bind it with halter rope to strengthen it like the barrel of a gun. This they fill with gunpowder and stones. Set in an ambush, it can strip a hundred men down to their skeletons." He smiled into Juana's face.

"I will drink to that," said Manolo, overhearing. "Tonight I will drink to skeletons."

Old Pep cried, bringing a can of water, "To the skeleton of Franco I will drink especially – and in best *manzanilla*."

"You will help us, lady?" asked Astrada, kindly.

"As a nurse," replied Juana.

Ten

WINDLESS AND DARK, an hour before dawn, the moon hung on the pines.

With the animals' hooves muffled with cloth, Elisa led them, single file, across the open valley that led to the bridge of Pinares. Reaching the Avila road without incident, they travelled parallel to the berm until they came to the bend in the road; here they were to position a tree-gun.

Richard glanced at Nicolas, who looked racked with loss of sleep. This was the trouble with the young, he thought, as the boy dozed in the saddle.

Boys of this age, and younger, fought with men at Jarama, and bravely, when they were awake. But most of the time, through hunger and cold, they were asleep. In the University City, when the Moors broke through, they died in dreams.

Old Pep and Manolo were dragging the tree-gun; the Don Quixote and Sancho Panza of Spain – the lean, tall and sad; the short and fat, like the heroes of Cervantes. Astrada, as usual, rode alone. Elisa and Ramón rode together, and occasionally, Richard noticed, her hand went out to him.

Ramón, his eyes constantly searching the dark emptiness of the road to Galapagar appeared alert to everything but her.

Along this road the convoy would come.

In a clump of undergrowth they tethered the animals.

The preparation to position the tree-gun and flank it in defence, was easily and swiftly done. Clearly, the gitanos had used this weapon before. Richard watched as they worked; gathering wayside stones, they packed them down the empty tree-trunk as shrapnel.

Richard said to Astrada, who was bending near the work: "How is it fired, by fuse?"

"In the Carlist wars, by fuse. But this required a road block to bunch a convoy. Now they are fired electrically; it gives surprise."

76

"An electrical detonator. Where is the battery?"

"We have no battery, but we can use the dynamo of your transmitter for power."

"Who will fire it?"

"Ramón has volunteered."

Richard said, "Who better than I? It is my transmitter. But keep Juana in the rear."

"As you wish. He who fires it will be the last away. Ramón will not mind." Astrada crawled down the bank of the road, calling the gitanos to him when the weapon was positioned.

Richard examined the tree-gun, thinking of the carnage it would create among the convoy. Its snout was cocked up so that a line of vehicles, breasting the slope, would take its full discharge; and so laid that it would rake them as they slowed for the bend. He unwound the drum of electric cable and laid it over the ground, seeking cover behind a boulder; running to the mule, he unstrapped the transmitter, passing Astrada, who said softly: "Fire when I call, and not before. Listen. The art of the ambush is to kill everything that moves. But withdraw on my command." He pointed out the positions of the others. "If we become scattered, rendezvous at the site of the tree the gitanos cut, understand?"

"I understand."

"And tell Juana that if she cannot get away, to keep a bullet for herself. Franco's bodyguard is mainly Moors. Everybody talks, for they are experts. If one talks they'll have the lot of us by nightfall."

Richard nodded, and Astrada said, "One last thing. If anything happens to me and you become leader, disperse the group after this attack – successful or unsuccessful – disperse it. Send the three gitanos back to their village – Ramón and Elisa can take care of themselves. For a week or so, until things cool down, you understand?"

Astrada crawled away: Richard knelt, with the transmitter between his knees.

In the light of the moon, a trail of peasants had passed them on the tree-fringe of the road fifty metres away on their way to Avila, despondently ignoring them as they went by; the men sitting on the haunches of their animals, hunched under their wide sombreros. Behind the daintily-stepping donkeys their women stumbled bare-footed, carrying their babies in their shawls or in their stomachs; dishevelled women in coloured gitano dresses, their thin faces gleaming with night mist, their black hair hanging in thick, wet strands on their shoulders. Out of the mist they had come, and just as quickly gone; down the road to Avila along which Franco's convoy would come. Astrada, as surprised as they, gave them no greeting, nor they to him; the little retinue of misery passed, and for Juana it established the eternal suffering of Spain; women's inferiority, male dominance.

"That was bad luck," said Astrada, turning in the saddle. "Where did they spring from?"

"They are gitanos," remarked Manolo, "they will not talk."

"Let us hope not," replied Astrada.

But such as these, Richard thought, would be herded into the barbed wire compounds of the rebels after the attack on the convoy and tortured for information; for this was so clearly a gitano ambush and these wandering people of flamenco singing and dancing would pay for it.

Richard sighed and raised his head, staring about him. Juana, in a nearby clump of trees, was preparing her medical bag.

The pines, spearing the stars, stood in regal stillness, the sierra, craggy and barren, raised cathedrals of monolithic immensity; nothing moved. On such a night, Richard thought, one might hear the winging of a sierra buzzard or the scuttling of a vole. Now there came a rustling of branches and he drew his Colt revolver. A face rose from the heather before him; an ashen corpse of a face with smudged shadows for eyes, and it was Elisa.

She said: *"Yanqui?"*

"I am here."

"The convoy is coming."

"I cannot hear it."

"The gitanos can. Old Pep has ears to hear a donkey dreaming. He puts his face to the ground."

Richard said, "Best you go, Elisa." He stared through the blackness, but could only faintly see the road.

Elisa replied: "*Vaya hombre!* You do not know the sierra! – for half an hour at least it will whisper, then rumble. But it is coming and that is all that matters. Why do you not trust Ramón?"

"Did I say I did not trust him?"

"Of all here, he is the best – you understand? And this you will find, *hombre*, if you live long enough. No, you did not speak distrust with your mouth, but with your eyes. Your woman also. I see it."

Now she was kneeling before him and there was in her scarred face a strange beauty; in her voice an urgency. "Ramón Barro is a brave man. Are they as brave, I wonder, in the International, where all fight together?"

"The convoy is coming. It is all that matters."

Turning her head, Elisa spat. "But trust does not require proof, it is based on comradeship, and I hate you as I hate the dirty gitanos, who whistle and giggle when my Ramón goes past. To them he is a clown, to me he is a god." She thumped herself. "But you will see! All in good time. He is worth ten of you rogue elephants of strength and hair."

"Best you go, before Astrada comes for you," said Richard. "He is hairy, too."

Elisa spat again. "*Mala sombra! Tozudo!* Pig Americano! Even magic could not protect you from your criminal stupidity, and your woman is a whore."

Earlier, after making many checks of his connections on the transmitter dynamo and cleaning his Colt revolver, Richard waited for Juana to come to him.

Earlier, despite Elisa's hostility, Juana had gone to her and helped in the preparation of the meal, which was cold sausage and bread washed down with a circling porrón. And so Richard waited in a quiet place away from the others; within sight of the transmitter which controlled the tree-gun, yet in isolation, and knew that when she had finished helping Elisa, Juana would come.

Every so often he would rise from the bracken of the forest floor and look out into the sierra. The moon-struck road to Galapagar, along which, earlier, the gipsies had travelled, was shining wet among the rolling hills of darkness.

Until this time, which was close to dawn, Juana had shared the ground with Nicolas; it was his habit now to come within reach of her and curl up in his poncho and lie there staring above his log pillow at her face, and every time Juana opened her eyes she would find the eyes of the gitano boy upon her.

On the first night of travel Juana had made her bed with Elisa, but then Elisa had gathered up her blanket and wooden pillow and taken it to the side of Ramón, who slept apart from the others, and Old Pep saw this and grunted, as old men do at lovers.

Then Juana no longer slept with Elisa, so Nicolas came.

"*Salud*, Señorita," he said. "May I sleep with you, as with my mother?"

But later – still before the dawn – Juana awoke and saw that the boy slept, and rose quietly and went to the place of bushes where Richard lay beyond the sight of the others, and he, knowing that she was coming, moved his body so that she could lie on the warm earth where he had lain. This Juana did and his hand went out to her, touching her hand, and they lay together, and none knew of this, except Old Pep, who slept awake. And he smiled again, as he had done with the lying together of Ramón and Elisa, and grunted.

So Richard lay and watched the dawn come up and Juana slept, and he traced with his eyes each line of her features and watched how the moon played tricks with her hair, which was black against the pallor of her face, and he would have touched her but dared not, for fear of waking her.

Lying thus with Juana took him back to his days with Carla, his wife, when they would run together on the beaches of Santander in the sun, and the sun was burning then as the moon burned now, and there was only the two of them and nothingness; no earth, no sea, no sky; only they, Richard and Carla. And Carla, his young wife, had been like this, also; fair of face and dark-haired.

Hand in hand they had run on the sands, which was hot to their feet, and the nakedness of their bodies was like the gold shining of the sand, and sand was on her arms and hands and the salt spray of the sea upon her lips when he kissed her, as he wished now to kiss the lips of Juana, who was lying near.

And the hand that he held against him now was, for Richard, the hand of Carla; the body stretched beside his was Carla's; also her eyes when she opened them and saw him; these were not the eyes of Juana. Even her voice, when Juana spoke, was not her own voice.

"Richard," she said.

"I knew you would come," he answered.

Now there was no more loneliness in him.

It was as if Juana's coming had brought him a companionable love, a strength beyond himself that he had known but once before. The touching of this one, who was not Carla, the smoothness under his hands, the warmth, all was a rebirth of what had gone before; a knowing of something long forgotten that had come to life with a touch.

"Lying here with you like this is lovely."

"Do not speak," Richard replied, and put her fingers against his lips.

The convoy was coming.

The sky was faintly lightening over the pine-tops, etching the summits of the Guadarrama into a deeper blackness.

Nicolas, now positioned on a high point, raised his field glasses and trained them on to the Avila road; and saw, like a fairy chain in the darkness, pin-points of light moving against the black mass of the sierra. Three times he made the sound of a screech owl, and Old Pep heard and raised his hand to Felipe Astrada. Manolo heard it, too, and settled behind the butt of his Mauser, training it on to the road. Ramón heard it, and pushed Elisa aside, snicking back the bolt of his stub-nosed tommy-gun. She pressed her cheek against the cold muzzle of her little Slossack rifle. Old Pep curled back his thin lips in anticipation, and spat.

The convoy came at speed.

Richard, crouched behind cover fifty yards from the road, could now hear it grinding up the hills and whining down the slopes of the road from Avila.

In the eye of his mind he saw it coming, the escort motor-cyclists leading; an armoured car, the prime target, with its squat grey body lurching in its wake. Behind this would be the lorry-packed Falangist infantry sitting shoulder to shoulder, their Galician helmets of German design crammed down on to their faces. Always they sat like this, for he had seen them coming in the battle of the Corunna Road: dull automatons of war, the poor bloody infantry, their faces swaying and expressionless; humans who pinned their future on the next command on how and where to die. Their impotence was never more revealed, he thought, than when packed together in lorries; going nowhere, or returning from it.

Suddenly it began to rain, lightly at first, then harder, and Richard cursed the sky. The road to his left began to shine more wetly in the coming dawn. He stared through the rain, trying to identify the positions of the others, and failed. The rain fell harder, lashing down on to the dull, forbidding country; thunder rolled and reverberated in the mountains, faintly detonating among distant summits; lightning faintly flowed, dimly lighting the scene before him – the rock outcrops wetly shining on either side of the glimmering road. He saw a flash vision of Elisa's arm upraised. Nicolas suddenly appeared, running across the muzzle of his Winchester. Richard cursed obscenely.

"Americano!" The lad pointed excitedly, his face streaming with rain. "They come, *they come!"*

"I know – get back – look, go back to Juana," Richard waved him away.

"No, *amigo*. I stay with you."

"Go, sod you!"

"I stay! We fight together, you and me! *Listen!"* The boy put up a finger, listening to the approaching convoy. "They come, Holy Mary! Now I kill this devil Franco! You and me, *compañero!"*

Richard fixed the second wire to the dynamo and waited, his fingers gripping the handle.

The muzzle of the tree-gun, fifty yards to his left, gleamed in the pouring rain. He could hear the convoy clearly now, the high shriek of its tyres – the metallic whining of a half-track – probably Franco's armoured car, he thought, if Ramón was right. Subconsciously, he heard Nicolas rotate the bolt of his rifle and slam a round into the breech. It was an appalling noise that split the growing clatter of the approaching convoy. Richard estimated it was a hundred yards now; heard the half-track driver change gear as it struck the slope. Timing was important, he thought. He would fire the tree-gun as the armoured car breasted the slope, exposing its soft under-belly to attack.

"*Look!*" shouted Nicolas, and straightened, pointing over the boulder, and Richard, with a curse, hauled him down. But in that instant, through the rain, he saw the black-out pin-head lights of the leading motor-cyclists on a distant bend; two of them – combinations, with sidecar passengers sitting behind the black muzzles of their machine-guns. He saw a fluttering pennant as the armoured car emerged out of a blanket of spray; saw the swaying canvas of the infantry lorries before they disappeared into the road dip. Tense, he waited, his whole being tuned to the coming of Franco's armoured car. The clattering half-track consumed the dawn. Nearer. Tyres began to whine on the flooded road; louder.

Richard rose, disdaining cover, and peered through the rain, the transmitter on the boulder before him.

The noises of the oncoming convoy abruptly ceased.

Brakes shrieked beyond the hill.

Silence.

Richard heard no sound but pattering of rain.

"*Que va!*" Nicolas stared up at him from a puddle of a face. "The convoy has stopped!"

A faint report echoed from afar, then another; a low whining began of growing intensity, that ended in a shriek. Richard pushed Nicolas down and crouched above him. The earth before him detonated in spuming fire, shooting up stones and smoke. Another whining, another explosion. Another, another. The mortaring grew in pace and pattern, the bombs combing the position around the tree-gun. And in an interval of the explosions, Richard saw small white figures flitting in the trees beyond the wet road.

Nicolas saw them, too, and cried: "*Moors!*" and threw the muzzle of his rifle across the boulder beside Richard's Winchester.

83

Light began winking from the pines beyond the road. The ambush was being attacked. Bullets began their impact thudding. Slowly, the dawn filled with howling ricochets, the dull thumping of rifle-grenades and mortars. And, as Richard's repeater stabbed fire from the boulder, he saw scores of figures emerging from the pines, bunching together; wildly gesticulating forms running like white witches with their capes flowing out behind them; others crawling across the road towards the tree-gun. Now they multiplied, streaming from the halted convoy. Nicolas was saying, "Hail Mary, full of grace, hail Mary full of grace . . ." and punctuating each prayer with a bullet from his Slossack. Richard was firing coolly, his repeater jumping to the concussion. Commands were shrieked from over the breast of the hill. And then, amid the explosions, the nationalists came storming over the hill from the convoy, yelling their battle cries. In a solid block they came, their boots thumping in the unison of a massed attack. With their rifles held at the hip, bayonets fixed, the dull blue uniforms of the Falange mingled with the white robes of their comrade Moors.

To his right Richard could see stabs of rifle fire from Astrada and the others as they stemmed the attack. Moors dropped as fusillades raked them; the wounded flailing their limbs in search of cover; the dead lying like heaps of dirty washing, for the Moors were always in the van.

But the Falangists came on, leaping over their writhing comrades.

Orange flashes lit the scene as grenades dropped before them and they momentarily hesitated; a German stick grenade sailed out from Astrada's position, landing among Moors on the other side of the road, but still they came on. A man with his clothes on fire was walking aimlessly among them as Richard wound the handle of the transmitter's dynamo. The dawn erupted in a deafening flash. Light flared. Smoke billowed and darted through the shattered pines. When the smoke cleared the road had been blasted clean, as if swept with a broom. A few bloodstained Moors, hopelessly concussed, were wandering about in the trees on the fringe of the road.

A blanket of silence dropped on the scene. Save for the

diminishing echoes of the tree-gun in the mountains, there was no sound but the rain.

Dazed with the shock of it, Richard bent and gripped Nicolas as realisation returned, hauling him to his feet.

"Quick, the horses!" Richard swung the transmitter box over his shoulder, shouting "Juana! *Juana!*"

"She went back with Elisa!" yelled Nicolas

Leaping from behind the cover of the boulder, they ran.

Richard's mule and two horses were still tethered among the trees.

At their feet Felipe Astrada lay dead, his arms flung wide. Bending, Richard swiftly turned him over.

"Dead?" whispered Nicolas, staring nervously around in the quiet.

Richard nodded. *"Look . . ."* and pointed to bullet holes across Astrada's shoulders.

"Soon they come, *amigo,*" said Nicolas. "The Moors . . .!"

Richard knew no emotion. Swiftly he searched Astrada's pockets for identification, gathering up his small possessions. From Astrada's neck he snatched the little silver medallion of Pelayo, then, with his own handkerchief, covered the dead man's face. He was in the act of rising when Nicolas's rifle exploded flame: Richard was just in time to see a Moor in a nearby thicket fling up his arms. Nicolas crossed himself. "We go. Leave him!"

Two Moors came crashing through the bushes, one with a levelled rifle. Richard drew his Colt and shot him, and the man's rifle exploded harmlessly upwards: the other came leaping in, his curved knife swinging, and Richard missed with the revolver as the Moor bore Nicolas to the ground. The blue uniform of a Falangist made shape amid leaves. He came bravely in a limping stagger, a pistol levelled from behind the tethered horses: swinging about, Richard shot him, and he dropped at the feet of the mule. Turning, Richard clubbed the Moor on top of Nicolas with the butt of the Colt and pulled the man aside. Bleeding from the face, the boy swayed to his feet; Richard tore the little Slossack rifle from his hands and gave him the Falangist's pistol; gripping his collar with his free hand, he dragged Nicolas towards the tethered horses.

85

These, frantic with fear, were wheeling and tugging at their halters. Freeing one horse, Richard bundled Nicolas up into its saddle, crying, "The place where they cut the tree. Go!" He thumped the mare's flank with his fist, turned, as Nicolas galloped away, and came face to face with a Moor. From the ground he fired the Colt; the Moor dropped soundlessly across Astrada's body. Kneeling, Richard turned in a slow circle within the little clearing; then raced towards the mule.

The dying Falangist was crying from the ground. *"Viva Cristo Rey! Viva Cristo Rey!"*

Richard untied the mule's halter and tried to mount the animal, but the horse beside it was impeding him. Wheeling the mule free, Richard spurred it. As he did so, two Moors leaped out of the undergrowth and clawed him off, bearing him to the ground. One he shot with the Colt even as they fell. With the other Moor on top of him, Richard saw the curved knife above the man's squat, passionless face. And even as he fought for the knife other Moors were rustling through the undergrowth. Faintly, in the fight came galloping hooves. Richard had the Moor by the throat now, swinging him away, and the man's knife sliced at the forest leaves. Then Ramón, leaping down beside him, scrambled upright and swung the butt of his tommy-gun, knocking the Moor senseless. Kneeling beside Richard, he levelled the weapon and raked the undergrowth with streams of fire.

The Falangist was shouting as Richard climbed weakly to his knees, *"Viva Cristo Rey . . .!"* His bright fair hair contrasted the dull red of the forest leaves. Swinging to him, Ramón levelled the gun; light chattered. The soldier's body leaped and twisted to the shock of the bullets.

Ramón shouted; "Quick – the horse! The mule is dead. Quick! More are coming!"

"The transmitter . . .?"

"It's on your back, man."

As he galloped out of the small clearing, Richard saw Ramón kneel. Pivoting on his knee, he calmly sprayed the undergrowth, the tracer of his tommy-gun curving streaks of fire into the pines.

Richard clung to the galloping mare. Gunfire lending speed to her terror, she was leaping the brooks and striding over strewn boulders; swaying her fine body expertly through the impeding trees. Richard let her go. With a loose bridle, he clung on. The transmitter was thumping his back obscenely to the rhythm of the gallop, and with one hand he tried to steady it. Bullets were ricocheting off the trees about him as the mare took him blindly on.

And then, to his astonishment, another horse drew level with his, and he saw the face of Ramón ducking to wet, overhanging branches. He cried: "Those bloody Moors!" and reached out and thumped the flank of Richard's mare with his gun. "You're going in the wrong direction – this will lead you back to the convoy," and he spurred his horse, calling in his strangely high-pitched voice, "Follow me, follow me!"

The dusk was poking remnants of sunlight out of the sleeping trees.

"Is it bad?" whispered old Pep, bending above Manolo.

"Bad enough, by the way it is bleeding," replied Juana, and slackened Manolo's belt and pulled up his bloodstained shirt, and the path of the bullet grew across his matted chest in a line of blood from hip to breastbone.

"I am dying," said Manolo.

"Tie it and get him on his feet," said Old Pep in disgust. "Listen to it – a scratch, and he calls for the priest."

"Wine, in the mercy of God," mumbled Manolo, and took the porrón Richard offered and guzzled at it, the red wine running through his beard and down his throat. "*Santo cielo!* These bloody Moors!"

"This accursed Ramón, you mean," cried Old Pep, and he thrust out his scraggy chin at Ramón. "We make the tree-gun, we fire it good. But where did your Franco get to, *compañero?*" He opened his arms in disbelief. "The convoy stops?"

"Perhaps they got wind of us," Elisa said.

"*Sí, sí!* And perhaps somebody told them!" The old man stamped about in fury. "Where is your Bloodstained Dwarf who is sitting on ten thousand dead? – not in the convoy!"

Juana worked on, unheeding of them: from her small medical bag she took a bandage and fed it under Manolo's arched back and bound him, and stretched it taut and bound him again from hip to chest, and he made no sound. Richard asked:

"Are the ribs broken?"

Juana shook her head. "This is the test. Under a bandage this tight he would be screaming."

"Scream low, *amigo*," muttered Old Pep, showing Manolo his fist. "For what you have done today the Falange will hand you two hours of the Orphean Choir." He glared at Ramón, who turned away. "What you say, Falangist? Franco arrives but does not keep the appointment? Astrada is dead, but the Dwarf is alive."

Richard said, bending to Manolo, "Leave it, old man."

"Why?" Manolo shoved his face up belligerently from the ground.

"Ask questions later," said Richard, and the old gitano elbowed him and pulled out his ear like a fan, and said, "*Hombre*, you see this ear? It is the one I keep for listening to Manolo, who is a fool with a tongue. But this time I ask, too. Why did the convoy stop?"

"*Caramba!*" muttered Manolo. "We were ambushed before it got to us!"

Nicolas said, tears upon his face, "Felipe Astrada is dead. He was good to me."

"We will all be dead, *amigo*, if we listen to Ramón Barro," grumbled Old Pep, and Richard said, getting up:

"Astrada is dead and you quarrel before he's cold?" He pointed at Old Pep. "Had your father sense and your mother a husband we'd be miles from here instead of arguing like washerwomen."

"All right, all right!" Old Pep waved him down. "Continue to trust this one, my friend?" and he nodded at Ramón. "But I shall not."

"You son of a goat gitano," whispered Elisa, her face furious.

"Yes, yes, and you a daughter of a bitch! But we find one big mistake fighting with you and him. When Manolo is on his feet — we go, we gitanos!"

Juana said, "Come, help Manolo up, somebody," and stood aside and Manolo rose, knees bent and blood grew in a widening stain upon the white bandage about his chest.

Old Pep elbowed him upright, crying: "Stand properly, ride properly, so that we can leave this accursed place and go back to Alanis. Ana Martínez has softer hands."

"None has softer hands than the lady of Avila," grumbled Manolo, "for I did feel them. Softer even than Ana's."

Nicolas said, "With luck I will one day have a wound, and then she will put her hands on me?"

"*Dios mío!*" exclaimed Old Pep, and boxed the boy's ears.

Nicolas wound the handle of the transmitter dynamo, and all sat around while Richard tapped out the message and there was no sound but the sounds of the forest and the chattering of the morse transmitter key:

Hanson to Emilio. Hanson to Emilio. Come in. Over.

This he repeated several times, and then the key trembled, and Richard wrote the message on his pad:

Emilio to Hanson. Receiving you. Over.

Richard tapped out,

Galapagar attack unsuccessful. Astrada dead. One wounded. Instructions please. Over.

The message came,

Message received. All disperse. Hanson takes leadership. Next action Segovia. Await instructions. Keep daily midday contact. Over.

Richard replied,

Message received and understood. Over and out.

Ramón said, quietly, "All right. You explain; we understand. Elisa and I, we will go to lodgings in Avila. What about the gitanos?"

Old Pep replied: "It is of small consequence to you, my

delicate friend. We take orders from the *Yanqui*, no other. Manolo, Nicolas and me, we will go to Alanis, and there wait until the *Yanqui* calls us," and he spat on the ground.

"And what of the lady of Avila?" asked Nicolas, and went to Juana and stood close to her and touched her, smiling into her face.

"Do not question your betters," said Old Pep, and reached out and pulled him away. His thin face jerked up to Richard. "The box without wires?"

"The box without wires is the leader's business, old goat – see to yours," growled Manolo. "Meanwhile you may not reach Alanis, for I will kill you long before."

"I'd be happier," said Richard, "if there was a little more love between us, for we quarrel like fish-wives. Ramón, Elisa – you two away to Avila, then, and give me a contact address." He nodded at the gitanos. "You three to Estremadura and get there in one piece. Come the moment I call or you will answer to the International Brigades, not to me."

All that day they travelled slowly and the sun showed no pity but hung in his bowl of molten glass, a season of extraordinary heat. But with dusk came cold, a cold that froze the bones and a night mist hugged the forests of the sierra, and in this coldness the three gitanos journeyed to the south and Ramón and Elisa to the west.

Richard and Juana, hunched in their blankets, sat crosslegged before the red embers of the camp fire. For a long time they sat there unspeaking, watching the moon rise ice-cold in a frosty sky and listening to the silence of the sierra; one by one the cicadas shivered into quiet and then there was nothing but the emptiness of the forest.

Eleven

"I MUST GET back to Avila," said Juana, and looked at her watch and the luminous dial glowed in the forest darkness where they walked, she and Richard. Her young bay and Richard's horse grazed nearby.

"I do not want you to go."

Before them, at the end of the path through the forest, the serrated peaks of the sierra rose up in the moonlight. Earlier, they had looked down into the valley where fields of vines and wheat glimmered in a wilderness; squat cottages curled smoke into the rain-laden air. Beyond lay the town of Avila shrouded in night mist.

They walked slowly, removed in time and space, now that the others had gone their different ways, and the death of Astrada was heavy on their minds.

Near midnight, on a cairn above the track, they sat, and the traffic of war rumbled southward to Toledo; this and the wind were the only sounds of the night. The noise and violence of the Galapagar ambush receded within the intimacy of their nearness.

Richard said, "You are not as I imagined you. When first they told me of the Countess of Avila – it was Hans Deimler, I think – I gathered the things one associates with a countess; romance, vitality, aristocratic indifference."

"That was because he was speaking of my mother."

"And you are none of these things?"

"Not if you were to ask Pío."

"Is Pío a good judge?"

"Of women, yes. His experiences include his paramours."

"But not the daughter of a countess?"

Juana smiled. "The fault is probably mine. I could have been a more tolerant wife."

"You don't love him?"

"Of course I do; everybody loves Pío. To me he's a cherished friend."

"You'd not consider me like that, if I were your husband."

Juana lay back on the pine-needles; the forest floor was vibrant beneath her head. "But you are not my husband. Anyway, how can love be perfected under conditions of war?"

Richard said, "I love you, Juana, war or not."

"You must not. It is dangerous. Take Elisa – she loves Ramón, so every moment of her life is filled with fear. You're pledged to kill Franco. Nothing will be accomplished until that is done, and it is a wall between us." She touched Richard's face as he leaned above her. "I could just as easily love you, but I must not, either. The moment I do, I shall be terrified."

"Isn't that a cost lovers have to pay?"

There was about them the night sounds of the forest; the pines shook their branches in the wind.

Richard said, "You speak, but I don't hear you, because I know that what will happen between us is inevitable." He lay back on the leaves beside her. "Soon after Carla died, I was once in Mérida. The day was windy and hot; a gale was blowing yellow dust in the street. Rebel execution squads were rounding people up and shooting them in batches. In a doorway, within the sound of the shooting I saw two youngsters making love. It was beautiful. I watched them with no sense of witnessing. It was like drinking iced water during siesta."

"Sometimes you speak like a poet."

He shifted moodily above her, staring down into the moonlit valley. "You and I know that yesterday is dead and that tomorrow isn't here. Carla's gone, Pío is lost to you. For us there is only today – the war says so. Love-making's a good therapy – on a day to day basis."

"It seems to me you've done this before."

Richard smiled. "Haven't you?"

"Only once."

"Oh come, I don't believe it!"

"Please believe it, it's true. Only once, though I have been married for two years to Pío de Córdoba. And it happened so long ago now that I've nearly forgotten it!"

The wind was quiet. Guns grumbled in the earth beneath them.

"My mother," Juana said, "was a standard Asturian countess of her day. I suppose I could have been sired by any of the attractive men to whom she offered favours. My father, a roué – was either drunk or away. I was home from boarding school at the time, sleeping in a bedroom next to my mother's, and one young lover lost his way."

Richard grinned down at her.

"He was only a few years older than me and a member of the Anarchist Doctrinal Vanguard – he had brown eyes and black hair – my mother liked them young. I was in bed, and opened my eyes as my window slid up and a man's booted leg swung over the window-sill. I was enchanted."

"And then?"

"I thought he looked beautiful taking his boots off. He had all the qualities of an anarchist – assertive, handsome, and he possessed a beautiful moustache. He was wearing a white, silk shirt open to the waist, I remember. 'Where's the old man, then?' he asked, referring to my father. 'In bed next door,' I replied, which was true. 'You, Countess, look a great deal younger in bed than up,' said he, and tried to turn on the light, but I stopped him, saying, 'And you're very ill-mannered for taking me for granted. Would you ravish a woman against her will?' 'Señora,' he answered, 'yes, if needs be,' and got into bed beside me."

Richard turned over, laughing softly. "Did you enjoy it?"

"It was absolutely delightful. For weeks I clapped my hands in joy at the very thought of it. When my mother came down to breakfast next morning she was sour, complaining that she'd been up half the night. So had I."

"And your anarchist, did he return?"

"Never, although I left the window open for a week. Clearly he hadn't enjoyed it half as much as I." She added. "I was only sixteen, of course. I'd be better at it now, given the opportunity."

"You know, you're amazing. You give every impression of being so damned straight-laced!"

"Isn't it right to be natural about it?" She touched his hair and the touch brought them a nearness and intimacy they had not felt before. "What shame is there in such a gift? If you tried to make love to me now, and I resisted you, it would not be because I thought it wrong, but because you needed protection."

"God You didn't do a lot to protect your anarchist!"

"I didn't love my anarchist."

"Do you love me?"

"Yes, but as a comrade. How can I love you in any other way, and at such a time? Consider it. In all my years I have only given once. When I give again, it will be because I am enjoying peace. Then you will not have to make a play for me. I shall ask you if you want me."

"You are strange, and beautiful."

Richard saw in the faint light the sharp curve of her cheek; her eyes, the pupils shining, the lashes patterned on her pale skin. Her hair was black, like the hair of the young Asturians' wives he had seen washing in the Deva River, when he was young.

"And if I were to ask you now?"

"I would allow it, if it gave you ease."

"Because I'm a comrade?"

"Yes, but reluctantly."

"*Caramba!* You're the queerest woman I've ever met," said he, and kissed her lips.

Juana said, "You kiss me, you hold me, but you do not love me. You are still in love with your wife. You kiss me now because I am convenient, like the others who have tried for me."

"You are untrusting?"

"Uncertain. My anarchist didn't come back, remember?"

Richard drew her to her feet and held her against him.

Twelve

THERE MUST BE compensations, Juana thought, in being a courtesan; especially when as beautiful as Lucía García, Colonel Carrasco's mistress. Tall, bright fair, her bosom, like her name, preceded her: in an off the shoulder dress of pleated pink, she sat at table on the night after Juana returned from the sierra . . . and left the talking to Carrasco.

Juana, facing Pío at the end of the refectory table, wondered what Franco's Junta thought of Carrasco's woman. The General's opinion would certainly be interesting because his puritanism was famous; brought about, his enemies said, by the piety of his mother and the indiscretions of his father, who once kept a mistress in the country.

For lesser crimes than sleeping with the likes of Lucía García, better men than Carrasco had faced a firing squad: she who was known privately as the Whore of Madrid.

Fonseca, serving at table, assisted by a black-haired, confident Rosa, was wondering at the ability of Juana to come and go from Pío's House with such ease. She had arrived out of the sierra as if called by the imminence of Carrasco's arrival. Pío would have been hard put to explain her absence, he reflected.

Carrasco asked, raising dark eyes across the table, "They tell me there's been another ambush in the Gredos, have you heard?"

Pío, noisily eating boiled mutton, was snapping at the food like a dog at flies, apparently unhearing. Juana lifted her wine glass and drank steadily, looking at nothing.

"Something will have to be done about the sierra – the Gredos especially," added Carrasco.

Pío replied with a full mouth: "Something is always going to be done about the Gredos, but it never is. These damned bandits rule the place. Another ambush, you say?"

"This time an attempt upon the life of the Caudillo."
Juana lowered her glass. "So near to Avila? Who would
dare it?" She glanced at Fonseca, whose face was expressionless.

The previous evening, with Pío already returned from his
tour, she had come in from the sierra before curfew, leaving
Richard in the foothills of the mountains. And Fonseca, with
his usual ability to learn everything that happened, had been
passing by the west gate as she stabled the bay. She had
managed to gain her room without detection, but on her way
downstairs the butler was standing on the landing.

"It is well timed, lady," he had said. "Colonel Carrasco is
due for dinner tomorrow."

"It's a date I remembered," replied Juana.

"And the American?"

"I left him at Tornadizos."·

Now Fonseca stood near Pío's chair with a nonchalance
that Juana found astonishing; his eyes, like the eyes of a
hooded crow, moved around the room with a lifeless stare.

"Who would dare to attack Franco so close to Avila, you
ask?" Carrasco smiled at Juana. "Many would dare, believe
me, Señora. Outrages occur in Avila itself – don't you read
the papers?"

"Imagine it," interjected Lucía García, apprehensively.
"Supposing the General had been killed?"

"Fortunately, he wasn't with the convoy that was attacked."
Carrasco added, "Happily, the bandit's espionage is not well
informed."

Pío said, breaking bread, "Is it possible, these days, to
consider Spain without Franco?" He munched on, his eyes
vacant.

"Once it wasn't possible to consider Spain without
Sanjurjo," answered Carrasco. "And what happened in Lisbon
could be repeated here in Avila." He glanced at Juana. "The
sierras are a cancer on the back of the war. Every damned
movement in it costs nationalist lives."

Pío put down his knife and fork. "Partisans, you mean?"

"Bandits, I mean."

"I thought the Moors had mopped them up, León." Pío
began to pick his teeth.

96

"Try mopping up the sierras. The Gredos is bad enough, the Guadarrama is one worse. Both are infested with anarchists and spies – most of them controlled by the Madrid Internationals."

"You are sure?" Pío was sipping wine.

"We are certain. Normally, for instance, they bury their dead. This time we found a body – a certain Felipe Astrada. He was leading this particular group, and we know he came from the Internationals."

"And the convoy?" asked Pío.

Carrasco moved uneasily. "It was halted in time, but even so, we had casualties – nineteen killed, fifty-two wounded."

"In return for one dead bandit?" Pío smiled wryly. "That's bad statistics."

"Not if it guarantees the safety of the Head of State."

There was a silence, and Lucía García interjected, "I think it's scandalous! These damned anarchists interfering in Spanish affairs."

"Anarchists?" asked Juana, innocently.

"Well . . . foreigners!"

Fonseca refilled Juana's glass, his eyes on Carrasco, and Juana said, "And the Italians, the Moors, the Germans – they aren't foreigners?"

"Technically, perhaps, they are," snapped Carrasco, "But they're also allies."

"Allies to the nationalists, but foreigners to the republicans! What decent Spaniard approves of the Moors?"

"*Vaya!*" ejaculated Carrasco, his hands high, "We've hooked a radical!"

"A radical, you call me?" Juana smiled. "Not at all, I'm stating a political fact."

"You have borrowed your mother's precepts, you mean." Carrasco returned her smile.

And Pío interjected swiftly: "Oh come, now, you're turning this into a turkey, the pair of you, and it gobbles. Let us change the subject, eh, Lucía?"

But Juana said: "No, that isn't good enough, Pío. Until Hitler and Mussolini came into the war no International Brigades existed – come Colonel, be fair."

"But they were formed to fight Spaniards – you approve of

97

that?" Carrasco opened a case and selected a cigarette with care.

"No. To fight fascism," answered Juana.

And Lucía said weakly, her hand to her chest: "Oh dear, I wish I hadn't started this . . ."

"Spanish fascism?" asked Carrasco, evenly, meeting Juana's eyes.

"Yes, if you like."

"So now you are implying that the Caudillo supports fascism?"

"You twist my words, Colonel. I didn't say that."

"No, no! You did, Countess – you be fair." Carrasco sat back in his chair and fluttered a wink at Pío who looked ill at ease.

Juana replied: "No, I don't believe Franco's a fascist – he's not even political, to my mind. Examine it. He appeals neither to Monarchist, Carlist, nor the Falange. Not even to the Church. Franco's here for what he can get out of it – power."

"He'd be enchanted to hear that!" said Carrasco drily.

Pío said, swiftly, "Juana that's very rude."

"So, you label the General an adventurer?"

Juana answered, "They're all adventurers. How can any junta be otherwise? Lose, and you hang. Win, and you're a Head of State."

"*Por Dios!*" ejaculated Carrasco. "And I thought the free thinkers in this house died with the old countess, rest her soul! Undoubtedly I'm wrong." His voice raised. "You don't like the Moors, either?"

Fonseca momentarily broke the tension of the room by leaving it.

Juana was thinking of the quiet of the sierra, the companionship removed from the artificial friendships of this room and the cut and thrust of its argument. Vaguely, she wondered where Richard was. Now that he was lost to her his presence kept returning to her with increasing force.

"Isn't it true – you despise the Moors?" persisted Carrasco.

"Of course – be reasonable. I'm an Asturian! Have you forgotten their part in the Miners' Rebellion?"

Pío said softly, "Juana, for God's sake . . .!"

"And have you forgotten that the Caudillo is the Commander-in-Chief of the Army of Africa?"

"I have not."

"And that he's sensitive on the subject of his Moors?"

Faintly, from the hall, a telephone bell rang.

Juana sat in silence. She had said too much and was inwardly cursing her foolishness. Carrasco, as financial secretary of the Falange, was a powerful man.

He said, quietly: "I doubt if your views would stand repeating in public, Countess."

And Pío interjected: "León, don't be damned stuffy! This is an argument between guests and in private. You don't really mean all that political claptrap, do you, Juana?"

Carrasco relaxed, smiling tolerantly. Fonseca entered the room, saying softly, "Lady, you are wanted on the telephone."

"At this hour?"

Pío asked swiftly, "Would it, by any chance, be the hospital?"

Fonseca bowed. "The hospital, sir. Casualties are coming in from Madrid, and the countess is required by the authorities."

Pío said, "So there, León, you have your radical free thinker! They call her to nurse in the Hospital of the Sacred Heart, a hospital opened by the Caudillo himself."

Colonel Carrasco didn't reply.

In the hall, Juana said: "They appear to have rung off, Fonseca." She replaced the receiver.

"They didn't ring at all," came the reply. The butler hesitated, his eyes moving shiftlessly. "That conversation needed terminating. I took the liberty of doing that – for the sake of the master, you understand? Such talk could land him in very serious trouble. You understand?"

"I do now."

Fonseca added, "You are such a child in all this, and Carrasco is dangerous, can't you see? Financial secretary to the Falange? Personally, I doubt that. Never, never take issue with him again."

They stared at each other.

Thirteen

Señor Jorge Pelán, Assistant Clerk to the Waterways Committee of the Segovia Council, knew the history of the Roman aqueduct in the town with the assiduity of a dedicated artisan. He had been in water ever since he could remember, as had his father before him and his grandfather before that. Certainly, generations of Peláns had diligently pledged their lives to the maintenance, and rightly looked upon the aqueduct as a Roman wonder of the world.

Jorge Pelán, Mayor-elect of Segovia, could quote the history of this famous aqueduct.

Constructed of Guadarrama granite, the blocks dove-tailed into each other, he would explain, needless of mortar or clamps: composed of one hundred and twenty-eight arches, it began at the Caserón Tower, which collected the waters of the Riofrío, and ended at the Alcázar in the south-west corner of the town.

In his capacity of Assistant Waterways Clerk to the Council, he visited it daily, always being devout before the statue of Our Lady and St. Sebastián, who graced its highest keystone; as he was also devout before Our Lady of Fuencisla, she whom Franco had recently elevated to the rank of field-marshal for her defence of the town against the Reds . . .

This Señor Pelán considered was his official duty as well as a diplomatic necessity, since he was secretly a devout republican . . . He knew the statistics, geometry and wetted perimeters of the aqueduct's pipes and conduits; he knew the points of access and egress to the channels serving the town; he knew the areas where entrance was easy or difficult, safe or dangerous. He knew, did Señor Pelán, that the overflow of the aqueduct discharged into the confluence of the Rivers Eresma and Clamores, that washed the foundations of the ancient Alcázar.

He was further aware, early in the civil war, that visiting dignitaries used the hotel Las Sirenas, which was situated nearby in the Calle de Juan Bravo. Therefore, soon after

Franco's coup at Pamplona, he rented the house next door.
It was such technical expertise and foresight that gained for
Señor Pelán the post of Assistant Clerk to the Waterways
Committee; his genius for advance planning granted him
public confidence as Segovia's Mayor-elect.

Now, on May 20th, in the attic of number eighteen Juan Bravo,
Señor Pelán sat at his morse transmitter and listened to the
clatter of the key in code. Taking down the message on a pad
beside him, he wrote:

> Emilio to Pelán.
> Franco visit to Basque front confirmed. Staying night May
> 20th at hotel Las Sirenas. Send guide to meet Hanson
> partisans midnight Caserón Tower. Provide access Las
> Sirenas roof. Equipment. Explosives. Escape via aqueduct
> conduit. Over.

And the Mayor-elect tapped back:

> Pelán to Emilio. Message received and understood. *Viva
> España*.
> Over and out.

Señor Pelán, wheezing, wiped his sweating face. He had just
removed his head-set and covered the transmitter when his
wife opened the door of the attic. Short, fat, she stood there
weeping in a blueness of tears, and Señor Pelán eased his
gross body out of the chair, saying, "It is all right, I tell you,
Agueda. It is all right."
"The aerial will be seen!"
"The aerial is in the chimney. It cannot be seen."
"The transmission can be traced – you said so yourself!"
Her husband replied, "It cannot be traced over short trans-
missions. Agueda, please . . .?" He held her.
She streamed tears, shivering in his arms. "Jorge, I am
afraid!"
Footsteps sounded on the stairs behind them, and she
swung around.
"We are all afraid," said their daughter, Consuela, stand-

ing in the doorway, "but if you are that bad, you'd better leave, hadn't you?"

There was little beauty in the Peláns, the people of Segovia said. If one wanted beef, then vote for Señor Pelán at the next mayoral elections. And there was no beauty at all in Consuela, though the washerwomen of the little streams above the *cementerio* said that she was sharper than most.

It was a pity, they also said, that one so promising at school, and now working for a university degree, should be possessed of the gross appearance of her parents. The mother, it was agreed, was a sight to behold; and if she ever reached the exalted position of mayoress, she'd be no help to Señor Pelán socially – an egg-head woman of fat; no spunk, no fire.

How, in God's name, the tradesmen said, did she ever produce the charming Consuela?

In Castilla they were particular about mayoral dignity; they who had known good mayors since the departure of the Moors.

"But think of your position!" Señora Pelán cried now, clutching at her husband. "The German Gestapo is in the hotel next door – think of the danger!"

"Danger is proportional," said her husband, still holding her. "Come, Agueda, pull yourself together. Franco is also in town, so the rewards are also greater." He nodded towards his daughter. "Consuela, make her coffee, for God's sake."

"You have heard from Emilio?" asked Consuela, nodding towards the transmitter.

"Later, later," replied Señor Pelán. "Comfort your mother."

"Send her away, she is useless to Spain," said Consuela.

"You will please show her respect!"

"She is a danger to us and to the Hanson partisans." The girl went to the attic window, looking down on to Juan Bravo. The bells of the cathedral were sounding the Angelus. She said, "More townspeople were arrested last night, Father. *Por Dios!* Be practical. If the Guardia search us, she'll come out with the lot!"

"They will not search the house of the Elect!"

"I shouldn't depend on it."

"If they do, it will be the will of God."

"Don't depend on that, either. It will be the will of the German Gestapo."

Señora Pelán wept on, staining her bosom with tears and mascara.

"You've *got* to get her away," said Consuela. "It isn't fair to Hanson," and Señor Pelán said gently into his wife's tear-stained face:

"You will go, Agueda? For me? Yes, yes, it is arranged – you must leave for Valseca. It would be better. Consuela will take you to the bus . . .?"

"Now you're making sense," said Consuela.

The three of them stood in their grossness.

Yes, said the people of Segovia, the advantage of having a fat mayor might denote commercial prosperity, but, if his wife and daughter were also fat, there could be social disadvantages. Could they all sit comfortably behind the banqueting table at social functions, for instance? Would it entail the expense of a larger mayoral car? But there were also advantages in promoting Jorge Pelán to high office – he was a devout before the glory of Our Lady of Fuencisla, and believed to be a loyal Carlist. One cannot have everything, said the people of Segovia.

Now the Mayor-elect said to his daughter, "Consuela, bear with your mother. She has been a loyal wife to me and a good parent to you. All right, she possesses little courage, but can one have every quality in life?" He took his daughter's hand. "Now listen carefully. Yes, it is confirmed. Franco will soon be in the town. More, he will be staying at Las Sirenas."

"I could have told them that. When will the partisans come?" asked Consuela.

"At midnight tonight. All is ready; it is organised down to the last detail. You are sure of the suite Franco will occupy?"

Consuela answered, "I've attended important guests in it often enough. The first floor suite above the main entrance."

"The one whose window faces Juan Bravo?"

"As I say." Consuela appeared impatient. "The window

above the main entrance. All other rooms are occupied by Germans. They are mainly of the Condor Regiment – and, of course, Gestapo. Incidentally, General Mola will be arriving later today."

"So I've heard. Yet Emilio made no mention of the Second-in-Command in his transmission."

Consuela said, "He is coming right enough. It is a local conference – Franco and Mola leave for the Basque front tomorrow."

Señor Pelán lit a cigar and smoked with the grace of one who compromises with evil. He said, "The presence of Mola will be a bonus; greater than riches. Two birds, one stone." His calm eyes flickered with inner amusement. "General Miaja would give much for the head of Mola on the same plate as Franco's. He would raise me to the rank of grandee. You would be canonised as a modern Spanish Salome!"

"Let us concentrate on the head of the Caudillo," replied the girl, without humour. "The explosives are ready?"

Her father pressed himself up from the table in grunts and wheezes. "Forty pounds of gun-cotton; primers; detonators; fuse and percussion caps."

"I do not know the technicalities."

"Also ropes and grapnel hooks – in the cellar. A risky business. The Gestapo are not fools."

"And I rendezvous with the partisans at the Caserón."

"At the Caserón Tower – the conduit serving the aqueduct. At midnight."

"How many in the partisan group?" Consuela asked.

"Three. Hanson, the leader; Ramón Barro, a mountaineer – a man much used to heights. And Elisa."

Consuela's eyes were shining. "Elisa?"

"Emilio guarantees her. She is an escapee from the women's prison of San Pablo, Barcelona; her loyalty is proved."

They stood in silence. Touching the lace curtains of the attic, Pelán looked down on to the activity of the street below.

The Juan Bravo pavements fussed and strutted in the sun; German and Falangist officers mingled with drab-clothed inhabitants of the town; monks and nuns walked in a bowed idolatry of the beads, mumbling incantations amid the timorous yelping of suicidal dogs. Columns of military traffic hooted and honked; the bells of the cathedral bellowed a welcome to the Caudillo, who was there to plan with Mola the butchery of the Basques.

Consuela asked, breaking out of pensive thought: "Three, then – Hanson, Barro, the woman Elisa? Let's hope they're professionals."

"They were appointed by Deimler; Emilio controls them operationally. The rest is up to God."

"God is a peasant," replied Consuela. "He is dressed in the clothes of a *bandido*; his face is brown through rubbing it with walnut juice; also, he is blind. In peace he sells lottery tickets; once he shone shoes; in the midst of blood he just sits and bloody stares."

"*Mala sombra!* Please do not blaspheme!"

A blind man was squatting on the pavement on the other side of Juan Bravo; his opaque eyes seemed to stare up at the window of the attic. Involuntarily, Señor Pelán shivered, and Consuela said with cold practicality: "Right, then. I meet the partisans at the Caserón Tower and bring them in along the aqueduct. What about the aqueduct guards?"

"I have checked. There will be none. All spare soldiers will be on duty in the town."

"And after the explosion, they escape through the underground conduit?"

"Correct – through the overflow. The descent via the cellar is easy . . ."

"Even for me?"

Her father smiled faintly. "Even for Peláns. Through the manhole and into the conduit overflow. Within ten minutes you'll all be out at the river."

"And if the Germans get wind of it?"

"They will flood the conduit."

Consuela scratched her chin and smiled at the ceiling. "There are worse ways of dying?"

"One could always be caught by the Gestapo."

His daughter said with slow charm. "I hope to God you're the only one who knows about that manhole, Father."

"I am. All reference to it on record plans have been erased."

The morse transmitter key clattered. Pelán sat down again

and adjusted his head-set, and wrote, while Consuela watched his hand:

Hanson to Pelán. Emilio orders rendezvous midnight May 20th at Caserón Tower north-west of aqueduct. Confirm intention. Over.

The Mayor-elect replied, tapping:

Pelán to Hanson. Have been contacted by Emilio. Intention confirmed. A guide will be there. Over and out.

He removed the ear-phones, saying, "That was Hanson, as you see. He sounds amazingly close . . ."

"Yes," said Consuela, and bent above him, tracing her finger on a wall map. "They're probably in the Carpetanos, coming down from El Paular – at a height; that's why reception is so clear." She turned to the door. "Well, by this time tomorrow, the Caudillo will be dead. Incidentally, have you heard that he has just approved a death sentence on Major de la Puente, his first cousin?"

"Is his own grandmother safe?" asked her father. "Consuela! Do not concern yourself with trivia. What is one Caudillo more or less? Have you confessed?"

"No," said Consuela.

"May God pardon you. Meanwhile, death to Franco . . ."

"Death to Franco," repeated Consuela. "*Viva España!* And how do you get away?"

"See to yourself, child. My life for Franco's is not unreasonable."

Before leaving, Consuela bowed to him.

That afternoon, Consuela took her mother to catch the four o'clock bus to Valseca.

After her mother's departure the girl walked down Cervantes and through lounging German soldiers to the street of Juan Bravo, where she lived. This took Consuela past the entrance of the hotel Las Sirenas, where once she had worked. The entrance was guarded by giant Moors in ceremonial robes and turbans, Franco's bodyguard from his Army of

Africa. The foyer appeared full of expectant officers; staff cars came and went in hurried consultation. To her surprise Consuela recognised the owl-like bespectacled figure of General Mola standing on the pavement. Clearly, she thought, it was going to be an eventful day, and this she mentioned to a woman standing in the crowd.

"An eventful day, indeed!" replied this woman. "Our beloved Caudillo is coming! I saw him, you know. He has not visited since he freed the town from the Reds. Death to them! *Viva Cristo Rey!*"

"Long live Christ the King," said Consuela.

Given good fortune, she thought, it would also prove an eventful night.

When Consuela approached her house she saw that it was guarded by an armed soldier. A neighbour passing in the street, told her that her father, the Mayor-elect, had just been taken away by the Germans for routine questioning.

"Oh, God," breathed Consuela.

"But do not be afraid," said the neighbour heartily. "It was all very polite. 'Señor Pelán,' they said, 'Would you oblige us by stepping this way? It is purely a security measure, you understand? With the Caudillo staying in the hotel next door, it is natural that we would want to take every possible precaution.' 'You realise, I hope, that I am the Mayor-elect?' asked your father. 'This we understand,' they said. 'We assure you, Mayor-elect, that you will be caused a minimum of inconvenience. Where is your daughter?' 'She has gone with my wife to a relative in the country,' said your father." The neighbour stared at Consuela. "Yet you are here, child?"

"But not for long," said Consuela, and smiled. "God Almighty," she said, under her breath.

Consuela entered the house by using her back door key. She saw the outline of the soldier on the glass of the front door as she went silently through the hall. Fearful of noise, she tiptoed up the stairs to the attic. No entry had been forced, nothing appeared to have been disturbed. Even the seal on the attic door – always positioned when anybody left it – was intact. The morse transmitter, therefore, had not been discovered.

Consuela stood in the middle of the attic and listened to the growing clamour of the streets. She saw a staff car arrive with out-rider motor-cycles; she saw it stop at the hotel next door. A small, pot-bellied man with bald, wet eyes got out of the car and was greeted by General Mola, then disappeared from her sight, into the hotel. Juan Bravo was now a bustle of activity. Consuela, with clasped hands, wandered about the attic. The nervous anticipation of a coming disaster was draining her of hope and strength.

In desperation, she sat at the transmitter and tried to contact Emilio, as her father had instructed should he be taken; any danger to the partisans must be reported at once, he had said.

Failing to make contact after an hour of trying, Consuela looked at her watch. It was five o'clock.

Señor Jorge Pelán, Mayor-elect of Segovia, followed the captain of the Condor Regiment into the Gestapo Head-quarters. There two men were seated at a table.

"Good afternoon, Señor Pelán," said one. "You realise, of course, that this is purely routine questioning – your house being so close to the hotel Las Sirenas, where the Caudillo is staying?"

"There are many people close to the Caudillo's hotel," replied Pelán.

"And the fact that your daughter – Consuela, is it not? – once worked in the hotel . . .?"

The Mayor-elect raised his sweating face.

"Also, your good wife having left for Valseca a little while ago?"

"What has that to do with it?" asked Pelán. "In any case, she has not gone to Valseca, but to Madrona." Offered a chair, he sat down heavily. "The town council will want to know about this, I hope you are aware?"

The man from the Gestapo bowed, saying:

"Be assured, Señor Pelán, of our greatest possible respect."

Fourteen

RAMÓN AND ELISA, led by Richard came down from El Paular from the Carpetanos Mountains and through the outskirts of La Granja. Segovia rose up through the ground mist, the spires and turrets of its antiquity spiking the moonlight as a ship in full sail upon a sea of silver.

On the tree-fringe of the river they waited; here the Clamores leaped and sparkled against the sombre pines. The tower of Caserón stood like a gowned monk in the mist. Richard peered at the luminous dial of his watch.

"Midnight, and the contact does not come?"

"The name of this guide?" asked Elisa.

"Emilio did not give a name," Richard's breath steamed in the windless air.

"But Pelán confirmed it?" asked Ramón.

"As I told you."

They crouched, listening for footsteps on the narrow road and the wind murmured in the pine clothing of the woods, and nobody came as Emilio had promised.

"Listen," whispered Elisa, who had the ears of a cat.

There came to the Caserón Tower in the moon's light a young girl; reaching it, she paused, looking about her, and drew back her hood, and the cloak she wore swept about her in a sudden wind of the river and her dark hair beat about her shoulders. The girl began to walk to the west, and Richard saw this and said, "It is a signal. She is walking towards Segovia . . ."

"A girl?" asked Elisa, "We are meeting Señor Pelán, surely?"

For answer, Richard rose and stepped into the road and called softly, "*Salud*, Señorita . . .!"

Consuela turned. "You are Hanson?"

Richard went to her. "We are the partisans. Where is Pelán?"

"My father is not available. He told me to come."

"Is Franco in Segovia?"

"Better, he is in Las Sirenas." Consuela looked about her. "There are others?"

Richard whistled softly and Elisa and Ramón came to the road.

"Quickly, along the aqueduct," said Consuela. "My father said to waste no time. Tell Hanson, said he, to move faster than light."

"He has the explosives?"

"Yes. Also iron hooks and ropes for climbing, in the cellar of our house."

They hurried on; Consuela opened the door of the Caserón Tower; their footsteps echoed on a spiral staircase that led upward to the aqueduct. Consuela said: "There is a thirty foot gap between the buildings – between the roof of our house and the roof of Las Sirenas, you understand?" Her obesity was exhausting her and she paused for breath on the staircase . . .

"And the tray for the explosives – how do we carry such a thing across?"

"The wooden tray is already on the roof of Las Sirenas – in pieces that have to be fitted together."

Ramón asked, "And Franco has arrived, you say?"

Consuela nodded. "This afternoon."

"You know this for certain?"

"I know it because I have seen him before. A dwarf with large eyes and a big stomach. General Mola is also there. He arrived earlier – it is a conference."

"How can that be?" asked Elisa. "Why is he not up at the Iron Ring at Bilbao."

Consuela swept back her hair. "Because I say he is in Las Sirenas. Do not question; take it for granted."

They reached the top of the tower; this led to a footwalk and through a door; above this was the aqueduct; the waters of the basin placidly shining, a broad road of light that tapered to a needle through moonlit country a hundred feet below.

Richard hesitated. "Aren't there guards on this thing?"

"There are no guards on the aqueduct. My father said they would be withdrawn for point duty in the town."

Richard drew his revolver from underneath his smock.

"Let us hope your father is right."

"You once worked in the hotel Las Sirenas?" Ramón asked. And Consuela answered: "Not since the Germans came. 'Out,' they shouted. 'You are a fat girl with the looks of a Jew. Out!' And I said to them, 'Do you realise who I am? I am Consuela Maria Pelán, and I am Spanish. My father is the Mayor-elect of Segovia. How dare you speak to me like that!'"

"And then?"

"'Out,' they said. But, before I went I took the wooden tray and hid it on the hotel roof; the wooden tray that will blow them all to pieces." Consuela smiled at Richard and he saw that she was young, judging her age at fourteen.

"You are a brave girl," commented Elisa.

They were walking hurriedly, Richard and Consuela leading along the bank of the aqueduct, Ramón and Elisa following, and Consuela said breathlessly over her shoulder: "Not I. My father is the brave one. Today the Germans came and took him away for questioning . . . Also, they have put a guard on our house!"

"Que va!" ejaculated Elisa. "And you didn't bother to mention it before?"

"I didn't mention it because they have no proof against my father." Consuela said to Richard. "Soon after you and he talked with the morse, they came and took him from the house."

"Where there is a transmitter, I understand," added Ramón.

"I have checked. They have not discovered the transmitter; also, my father will die before he talks. Do not be fearful."

"Oh yes?" Elisa raised her face. "To me it sounds as if we are walking into a trap."

"All life is a trap, Señorita," replied Consuela. "Is not one patriot dependent upon the next? My father is Jorge Pelán, the Mayor-elect of Segovia. He will spit in the faces of the Gestapo."

"You have a mother?" asked Richard.

"I have."

"And she, too, will spit in the faces of the Gestapo?"

"No," said Consuela. "She is without courage. She would weep, whine and beg. Therefore we have sent her to my aunt in Valseca."

Elisa said with cold practicality. "A guard is on the house, which holds a transmitter. Her father is in the hands of the Gestapo. Why ask for death?" She added to Richard, "Turn back. This is madness."

Consuela replied: "Death happens once, Señorita; we who work with the partisans are not afraid of it. You are free, we are in chains. Living with the fascists makes it reasonable to be dead." She looked around their inquiring faces. "Go back if you like. I shall kill Franco."

They walked on and soon the town of Segovia with its maze of crooked streets grew about and below them. Consuela led them along the high level aqueduct until they came to the Alcázar. Here they descended to a door in the wall of the aqueduct, and Consuela opened it. Within bare concrete walls they went down steps. Consuela flashed a torch. Lower, lower they went, until they reached a conduit overflow, a five feet diameter underground pipe. In single file they went now, stooping to the curved roof, the overflow of the aqueduct. Rushing water grew about their ankles and reached icy fingers up their calves. The pipe sloped downward; the overflow foamed, growing into a roar.

Richard asked: "Where does this lead?"

"To the river," said Consuela. "Also, to the cellar of our house."

"And the guard?" asked Elisa, and her face in the light of the torch was like the face of a corpse, with grimacing mouth and black hollows for eyes, and her teeth shone like jewels.

"He is at the front door," replied Consuela. "But what is the guard to us? There are men here."

To this Elisa did not reply.

Soon they came to an opening in the roof of the conduit; step-irons were built into the wall of a vertical shaft. They climbed.

Richard climbed first with the torch. Twenty feet up his head struck a manhole cover.

"It is on a hinge," whispered Consuela behind him. "Push it, and it will open."

Soon they were standing in the cellar of number eighteen Juan Bravo.

"Is it safe to go up?" asked Ramón.

"It is safe," replied Consuela. "There is another guard on the roof, but he is dead."

Fifteen

THE SKY ABOVE Segovia was storm-black behind scudding clouds of night and interlaced with stars. Richard and Ramón – with Elisa on guard outside the attic and Consuela guarding the hall below – gripped the guttering of the Pelán roof and looked down on to Juan Bravo. A hundred feet below, the town lay in a ground mist that swirled through the narrow streets and alleys: row after row of flowered balconies and criss-cross roofs sloped crazily around the aqueduct. Around its base the Eresma and Clamores, bright silver, swam in confluence.

"Look," breathed Ramón, and pointed down; double sentries, with rifles slung, were wandering the cobbles outside Las Sirenas. The town slept beneath the obliterated moon.

Richard was curling the grapnel rope for the throw. Ramón took the grapnel and swung it in balance.

"The near chimney?" whispered Richard.

"Thirty feet – if we can reach it."

"Don't miss, man, for God's sake."

Elisa appeared beside them like a wraith; crouching behind the guttering of the roof, she whispered, "Look, the clock. It will strike on the hour . . ." and she pointed: a clock face glimmered in the mist; the hands said two o'clock, and Ramón threw as the clock boomed the hour. The triple-hook grapnel sailed against the clouds, struck the chimney, momentarily gripped, dislodged, clattered over the slates: there it struck the parapet, and held.

All three peered down at Juan Bravo. A sentry paused in his wandering, staring up.

The clock boomed on, reverberating into silence.

Richard peered over the gap. "It's hooked on the parapet wall."

"Is it a grip?" asked Ramón.

"We'll take the chance." Richard strained on the rope, winding it around a chimney upstand. "I'll go first." Bending, he swung a necklace of gun-cotton slabs around his chest. Ramón and Elisa were testing the rope; it sang with horizontal tension from the chimney of the Pelán house to the parapet of Las Sirenas. Gripping it, Richard swung into space, edging himself feet first across the gap between the buildings. Inch by inch he went. The wind rose, swirling the mist in little eddies about him. He looked down. The cobbles of the hotel yard gleamed wetly in a flash of the moon. When he was halfway over the gap, a Guardia van appeared below, crawling down Juan Bravo; it stopped outside the hotel entrance. Richard hung motionless as three civil guards got out. Bunched together in the middle of the road they began a noisy conversation. Plaster broke off from the hotel parapet where the grapnel had its hold, trickling down the side of the building, pattering on the road. Richard watched with fascinated intent.

Ramón said: "Get on, get on, man!"

Swaying on the rope, Richard edged forward again. The guards below began to smoke. A match flared; Elisa saw the cupped hands, the grotesque shadows of a man's face, red and black. The grapnel kicked under the tension, almost dislodged and gripped again. The jerk flung Richard upwards on the rope; his body began a violent swaying. Light glowed on the distant horizon and Ramón saw him suspended as if in a vacuum.

"*Santo cielo,*" breathed Elisa. "Don't go Ramón, please don't go!" She clung to him, but he pushed her away.

"Don't lose your nerve now!"

"There's no need for the two of you. Ramón . . .!"

"Get back on guard. *Por Dios*, it's all you're fit for!"

Ramón rose. Richard had reached the hotel parapet; waving briefly, he climbed out of sight. Gripping the rope Ramón swung himself out over the gap.

"We appear to have mislaid your daughter, Consuela," said the Gestapo questioner, and Señor Pelán raised his haggard eyes.

"I fail to see what my daughter has to do with this questioning."

The man smiled. "You are of Jewish extraction?"

"Is it of consequence?"

"Of no consequence at all, sir. I apologise for the question."

Pelán looked at his fingers. In one corner of the room a secretary was taking notes.

"In your capacity as Assistant Clerk to the Waterways Committee, you have access to the records of the aqueduct, I assume?"

"That is correct."

"Therefore you have knowledge of the access points of the overflow conduit, sluice doors and such other technical paraphernalia?"

"Of course." Señor Pelán lit a cigarette.

"Is there such an access point in the cellar of your house?"

Pelán stared at the cigarette. "If there is I am not aware of it."

"Your wife is, Señor. Where did you say she went today?"

"To Madrona . . ."

"Yet, at this moment she is being questioned in Valseca. How could you possibly make such a mistake, Señor Pelán?"

On the flat roof of Las Sirenas, in the shadows of a stack, Richard found the wooden pieces Consuela had hidden. Ramón joined him and they swiftly assembled a tray about four feet square; on to this, like a slab of chocolate, they packed the slabs of gun-cotton: to this they linked the primers and fuse. To the side of the loaded tray they attached lowering ropes, then carried it to a spot above the main entrance of the hotel. Their target, the hotel suite occupied by visiting dignitaries, was directly above the entrance and below this lowering point. Carefully, they lowered the tray vertically down the face of the building. The sentries below were now engaged in animated conversation, their voices drifting up.

"Watch Elisa!" whispered Richard.

Elisa, positioned to judge the tray's descent, governed this by signals. Each with a rope, Richard and Ramón lowered; the tray with its packed explosives descended inch by inch; occasionally caught by the wind, it bumped the face of the building in frightening delays.

"Wait," commanded Richard, and peered over the parapet at the street below.

The sentries, above whom the tray was descending, grew voluble in argument; one thumping his fist into his palm. As he vehemently emphasised a point a light went on above the hotel entrance.

"*Guard commander!*" A window swung back upon its hinges. Richard and Ramón sank down below the parapet, but Elisa saw the sentry clearly as he sprang to attention. He bawled, "Yes, sir?"

"Your name!"

"Corporal Lobera, sir!"

"Report to me in the morning. Meanwhile, stop your bloody chattering!"

"Yes, sir!"

The window slammed shut.

Richard saw Ramón's face in a sudden blaze. The moon came out from behind thunder clouds and painted up Segovia. Spires and turrets leaped up out of blackness; the town walls with its turrets; the domes and steeples of ancient palaces, the Plaza San Martín, the Gothic arch of Corpus Christi . . . all made shape in silver beauty from the Alcázar's towers and bartisans, eastward to the Correo. And the cathedral surmounted all, perched high in monolithic splendour.

Before this brilliance Ramón cowered, and Richard whispered: "That voice!"

"It was not Franco's."

"Of course not. Probably an aide."

"Are we on the right window?"

"Yes, according to Consuela."

In the silence of the frightened sentries, they lowered the tray again. There was no sound but the singing of the descent ropes and the bumping of the tray.

Ramón whispered, paying out the rope: "What are you doing?"

Richard was bending, blowing on the wick of his trench lighter.

The fuse lit; spluttered, died, then leaped again into life as the black powder caught. Its hissing consumed them both. Acrid smoke drifted upward against the moon. Then clouds rushed again and the moonlight died. Segovia sat in blackness. Elisa was frantically signalling. The tray sank lower,

lower. A man asleep within the hotel suite, opening an eye, would have seen the black drape of its shadow over the window glass; the slow descent, like the lid of a coffin. The wind touched the tray, gently swaying it within the recess of the window. One corner touched the window glass before it sank again, inch by inch until it settled on the window-sill. Ramón secured the ropes high above.

"Right. Out of it," said Richard, and ran to the wall where the grapnel was lodged.

"You first," said Ramón.

Replacing the telephone receiver, the Gestapo interrogator said, "Señor Pelán, you are being very tiresome. Your wife in Valseca has told us everything . . ."

The Mayor-elect raised his bloodstained face. "Then you're wasting your time with me, aren't you, my friend?"

"But some things your wife simply does not know. Who is Emilio? Who is Deimler? Who is Hanson?"

"I've never heard of these people."

"Your wife says that there is a radio transmitter in your house. Is that correct?"

"If there is I am not aware of it."

"We will shortly know – the Guardia is on its way there, you see. Where is your daughter?"

"Please God, a long, long way from here."

"Who is Emilio, Hanson, Deimler? Would they, by any chance, be within the espionage organisation of the International Brigades?"

The Mayor-elect stared doggedly ahead; the Gestapo interrogator smiled, crossed the room, and nodded to his assistant, who primed and lit a blow-lamp.

Richard took one last look at the fuse. It was spluttering sparks on the wall of the parapet; creeping upward in melting bitumen to the edge of the drop. Soon it would descend to the gun-cotton.

Richard imagined the explosive blast as the window blew in; nothing would survive the holocaust of forty pounds of gun-cotton exploding into a hotel room. Soon, he thought, a pall would hang over Segovia, the death-shroud of Franco.

Now, gripping the rope above the gap, Richard edged his body feet first back to the Pelán roof. Elisa gripped his boots as they came within her reach; leaning out, she supported him as he twisted into safety, then stared back across the gap.

Ramón was running. Reaching the rope, he gripped it with the practised hands of a mountaineer, and swung himself skilfully into space.

Richard and Elisa hauled him in.

"Right," said Richard, "down the stairs to Consuela. I hope she remembers the escape route."

"I hope to God she does," added Elisa.

Sixteen

THE GUARDIA RUSHED through the front door of Señor Pelán's house as Richard, Ramón and Elisa raced down to the cellar where Consuela was waiting. She held back the hinged cover of the access manhole. One by one they scrambled down into the conduit.

"A torch? Have you a torch?"

"Here!" cried Consuela, and flashed it around the damp walls of the chamber. Richard closed the cover above his head. The walls of the chamber made shape in dripping dampness; a continuous oval vault of ancient stone that thrust its finger into the blackness. Bending to the low roof, Consuela led the way, the torch held out. With his Colt at the ready, Richard followed with the others, their feet churning the slack water of the pipe into foam.

They arrived at a branch in the pipe; Consuela hesitated.

"Which way?" Faintly, above the sounds of rushing water, Richard heard the drumming feet of men and bawled commands.

"To the left."

He stared up at the dripping roof. "You're sure now?"

"The pipe descends. It leads to the river."

"Where does it come out?" whispered Elisa, and her face in the yellow light was the face of a starved ghost.

"Below the Alcázar – near where the rivers meet."

The drumming of activity in the cellar above them crystallised into a roar. They heard a faint clanging.

Richard seized the torch from Consuela's hand. "Come on!"

He led the way; another branch in the tunnel walls came into view, a cul-de-sac surmounted by iron-studded doors.

"What's that?"

"The sluice gates serving the aqueduct," gasped Consuela, breathless.

"What are they for?"

"An overflow. When the water level's too high after rain, they open them from above."

"And this tunnel takes the storm water?"

Consuela nodded, her hand to her chest, gasping.

"I could think of better places to be at a time like this!" Richard waded forward. Now they ran in stooping haste, crouching low to the vaulted roof, their feet splashing as the descent steepened to the river outfall.

"*Dios mío!*" said Elisa. "If your father talks, girl, this will be our grave."

"My father is Jorge Pelán. He will not talk." Consuela's fingers formed a cage over her mouth to stifle her laboured breathing. "*Listen!*"

Unmoving, they crouched together in the light of the torch.

From the end of the tunnel came faint voices; Richard pointed at dimly flashing lights. "They've found the manhole. Quick, get on!"

"Holy Mary!" whispered Elisa. Ramón whispered, "Look, let me go back. There's cover at the sluice gates. I can delay them!"

Elisa clung to him. "No, please . . .!"

"Later, perhaps." Richard reached out and hauled Ramón after him. "For God's sake, where's our explosion?" he stared at the dripping roof.

"They must have caught the fuse," said Elisa.

"It should have blown by now, for God's sake!"

"If it had we'd have heard it "

"*Ave María!* They'd have heard it in Madrid," said Consuela.

"Let's get on," said Richard, and swung the torch and the yellow beam probed the blackness ahead: the tunnel narrowed, then branched again. They momentarily stopped, indecisive.

"To the left," said Consuela. "Follow the descent – down, always down."

"The water's coming up," said Elisa.

The fact stopped them yet again. Richard lowered the torch. The water at the bottom of the tunnel was rising.

"It has increased its speed," added Ramón.

"Holy Mother, I can't bear this," said Elisa, her hands to her face.

"They've opened the sluice doors," said Consuela.

"What?"

"The sluice gates – the ones we saw back there. They must have opened them."

The water at their feet increased in pace, the surface tension breaking from a gentle swim into little ripples of foam. A low hissing began, growing out of the darkness. A piece of driftwood came down, innocently gyrating, touching their legs in passing as if in greeting; boat-like, it shot away into the darkness before them."

Richard asked "Consuela – how much farther?"

"To the river?"

"To the end of this accursed pipe," demanded Ramón. "We've come a hundred yards already."

"I . . . I can't remember . . ."

For answer, Richard waded on, towing her after him. "Think girl, think. You've been down here before, haven't you?"

"Only as far as the sluice gates."

"But you've seen the records?"

"No."

"Then how far is it, for Heaven's sake? Good God – is it a hundred yards or a mile?" Richard was wading more swiftly now, and the tunnel water, suddenly quickening, beat over his ankles, splashing up his calves. Consuela's breath was coming in gasps, her throat contracting to the effort of wading.

"I do not know, I tell you – I do not know how far."

"It comes out below the Alcázar, you say?" Elisa's eyes were protruding in her white face, frog-like in the light of the torch. Consuela staggered, leaning against her.

"Then how far is that?"

"You're wasting time," said Richard, commandingly.

"Are we going the right way, even?"

"Should we have turned right at the last branch?"

"Left, left, you've got to keep left."

"Are they in the tunnel?"

"Who? The Guardia?"

"Who else, for God's sake?"

"Of course they're in the tunnel. The sluice gates are open, aren't they?"

"But she says they're opened from the top."

"If they're open, it's the end of us!"

"We've still got a chance!"

"One in a hundred. This pipe carries the water in the aqueduct!"

"Somebody's talked!"

"But not my father!"

"Your father, your mother – does it matter now?"

"Oh God, my mother . . ." whispered Consuela, and sank to her knees in the rising water.

It was a flood now, nearly two feet deep; the pace of it terrified them. Racing now, the flood water of the aqueduct head was swilling up the curved walls of the conduit; tumbling in a growing roar of sound. The tunnel reverberated; small, staccato detonations filled their world of the roaring pipe. And from the darkness of stone niches, inches above their heads, small twin lights appeared in the glow of the torch: rats. Rats in little groups at first, whiskering and preening themselves; staring down at the stupidity of humans; rats safe in the knowledge that the pipe never ran full bore; that havens lay in the cavities of stone work where ancient artisans had stood their lanterns. Swimming rats now, altering their positions as rushing water bellowed in the conduit.

Consuela, her hair streaming out before her, her face inches above the foaming water, floundered onward; slipping, falling constantly, clawing at the wet walls of the pipe in her headlong flight. The water surged, pressured by the distant Riforía; it cascaded about Richard's crouching shoulders, swept him along. Consuela was clinging to his belt and he dragged her unceremoniously on; Ramón waded doggedly, giving no heed to Elisa.

The water was within a foot of the roof now; they went in staggering rushes, pausing to gasp at the life-giving air above them. And the air was whining against the tunnel roof, forced into the confining segment bounded by stone and water; ice-cold from the underground caverns.

Richard was going blindly now, driven on by instinct.

Consuela, half-drowned, was being carried against him, her billowing skirt tripping them both. And then, quite suddenly, the pressure lessened; the water slackened, released from its pent forces. The space above them between water and roof widened. Gratefully, they breathed warmer air. And a dim light began to glow at the end of the conduit; a segment of moonlight that grew out of the darkness like a fractured, opal moon. Richard cried, "Look! *Look!*" and pointed onward.

Behind them the clangorous noises thundered still; in scores the rats swam, their brown bodies lithely twisting, articulately steering themselves past the awkward, plodding humans, making for the river. Moonlight grew in strength and beauty at the end of the conduit as if greeting their escape into life.

And the flood water, as if now with restive humour, pushed them one by one, dishevelled bundles of clothing, from darkness into light.

They lay together on the bank of the Clamores and the river swam and the water of the overflow conduit poured in white loveliness, and the moon sat in the sky over the turrets of the Alcázar in sad contrition.

Richard said, "Well, that was one easy way of getting out of Segovia."

"So much for Franco," said Ramón, cleaning his pistol.

"The cat with ten lives."

"Could the explosion have happened while we were in the conduit?" asked Consuela.

Richard nodded upward at the stark, turrets and bartisans of the Alcázar rearing above them. "It did not go off. Either the fuse went out or somebody cut it in time. Segovia's as quiet as a summer night."

"It won't be quiet for long," added Ramón, and stood up and looked over the river to the far confluence where the moon glimmered bright on rippling water, and the stars were big above the town.

"We'll dry as we walk," said Richard. "Ramón is right. We'd best get on."

"And I?" asked Consuela.

For reply, Elisa put her arm around her. "Come."

A bullet cracked out.

It struck the ground at Ramón's feet and whined into space; struck a stone on the river bank and screamed into a ricochet. Falling flat, Richard pulled Elisa and the girl down with him.

"Stay here and we'll be outflanked." He stared about him. "Where did that come from?"

"From the Alcázar," said Consuela, and as she said it, light winked along the black outline of the turrets to their right; a rafale of bullets beat the ground and air about them. Richard moved first, gripping Consuela's hand.

"Down to the river," he said. "It is the Guardia!"

They ran, crouching, merging into the dark shape of the shore.

There, in the cover of the river bank, Consuela, wiping wet hair from her face, pointed. "Keep to the river; this will bring us to the outskirts, south of Socorro; then to La Granja and into the sierra."

"The Guadarrama?" asked Richard.

"To safety, Señor – the Guadarrama."

"And you?"

"I shall go back to Segovia, to my father."

They went east, for Picos and the mountains.

Consuela guided them back to the Caserón Tower, and they reached it as the tip of dawn's tongue touched the sky.

And Consuela said suddenly: "My father called my name then."

Hearing this, Elisa went to her, saying, "Soon everything will be all better, child, and you will be back with him."

But Consuela said to Richard, "He called my name. You understand? He called to me. My father is dead, Señor. Will you take me with the partisans?"

Reaching a place where the track sloped upwards, Consuela, now leading them, breasted the rise, and this was a height that led down to Picos.

Now it was midday; the vertical sun was melting in a sky of gold: here they were to rest.

It was as Consuela turned to face the others coming up the track that the bullet took her.

She fell, gently tumbling down the hill into Richard's arms.

He knelt beside her, and the girl said: "I can stand, Señor. It is nothing, I tell you. Look, it is but a scratch."

Ramón whispered, in anger, "A sniper." He pointed. "Down there on the road."

There was no sound then but the wind, Consuela's hoarse breathing, and the faint whining of a lorry five hundred feet below on the road to San Rafael.

"A wandering patrol," said Elisa. "God, they are murderers! They will fire at nothing."

A Moor in white robes shouldered his gun and walked back to the lorry on the road.

"~~████~~," whispered Ramón. "Give me a rifle . . ."

Richard probed Consuela's wound for the bullet, but failed to find it; when she slept, exhausted, blood was upon her mouth.

In the cool of evening they made a sling of two coats threaded on to saplings; on this carried Consuela and the moon was the colour of meadow-saffron along the mountain track that led west, towards Avila.

Seventeen

Rosa, close to tears, called Juana from the greenhouse.

"The telephone, Señora . . ." said she, and screwed at her hands.

Juana gave her a meaningful look.

"I'll take it in the library."

Richard said on the telephone, "Juana, is that you?"

"Richard!"

"We need you badly, darling. Can you come?"

Juana lowered her voice. "Of course! Where?"

"You remember Tornadizos?"

"Yes."

"And the road to Salinero from there?"

"I do."

"The first crossroads. Bring your medical pack. They hit us approaching Avila. We can't travel by day – a wounded girl . . ."

"Elisa?"

"No, not Elisa. Another. When can you get here?"

"I'll leave in an hour."

"We'll wait until midday."

Rosa was waiting in the hall when Juana came out of the library.

"Señora . . ." she began.

Juana paused before her. "Yes?"

"You're leaving again . . .?" Rosa's dark eyes, ever more evident first thing in the morning, were red with unshed tears.

Juana said curtly, "Yes, what of it?"

"She's coming, you know . . . Señorita García."

"To dinner tonight? Yes, I know that."

"But she's staying, lady. I'm preparing a room for her."

Tears filled Rosa's eyes.

Juana took a breath, saying evenly, "And supposing she is, what's it to you?"

The girl moved her feet in restless agitation; unspoken words trembled on her lips. "I . . . I just thought you ought to know, lady."

"What made you think I didn't know? Prepare a room for Señorita García. It was I who invited her."

It was inadequate. Juana knew it, even as she walked away.

Pío was taking his early morning walk around the lake when Juana found him.

He was watching the ambulances rumbling in from the north; lightly wounded, the overflow from the ambulance trains, were being evacuated from the Ring of Iron where the Basques were stubbornly opposing General Franco's push.

Juana said: "I am going to Santander, Pío, my father is ill."

"Really?" Pío gave her a bland look. "As a result of that telephone call?"

They stared at each other.

Agustín was in a boat on the lake; he moved it across the shining water with dabbing strokes of a paddle, his thin body cranked to the effort. Always, at this time of year Agustín tended the waterlilies; the scene was stridently removed from the rumbling ambulances of war.

"You'll be missed at the hospital," Pío said, watching Agustín.

"The hospital will have to do without me for a bit."

Pío said, turning, "Don't underrate my intelligence, Juana. To get to the coast you'd have to go through Bilbao, so you'd never reach Santander. And you'd be wise to instruct your terrorist friends not to use an open telephone. You're not involving me in your under-cover activities."

"Meanwhile, inviting Lucía García here might involve you with León Carrasco, remember that." She added assertively: "Pío, for heaven's sake! She's his woman!"

Pío's monocle dropped from his eye. "León himself suggested it – to keep Lucía amused while he's away in Burgos." He wandered on and Juana joined him.

The morning was bright with sun and air, the Chinese love-pavilion shimmered in the early heat.

Pío continued adamantly, "All Lucía's friends will be in Burgos – a conference – León, bless him, is actually travelling with the Caudillo."

"He'll enjoy that."

Juana spoke rationally, but her thoughts were racing. Franco was flying to Burgos. Given that all the Caudillo's movements were secret, it was astonishing information. She said, casually, as they approached the house. "Talking of Franco, I doubt if he'd approve."

"Of Lucía? He was charmed with her. I took her to the Subscribers' Meeting at Salamanca, on the 20th."

"The day before yesterday. Wasn't I available?"

Pío smiled, gesturing airily. "You were around, for a change, but I didn't think you'd be interested." He sighed. "It cost me another stiff donation, but then, it always does. Not that it's much appreciated, but it helps to keep the place intact, my love."

"I was here. Did you really have to take Lucía García?"

Pío shrugged. "Now don't tell me you're jealous – not after your own perambulations."

She only vaguely heard his reply. Juana was wondering about Richard's attack at Las Sirenas. Clearly, he'd been instructed that Franco would be there, when in reality he hadn't been within fifty miles of Segovia. Republican intelligence she reflected, having failed at the Galapagar attack, was again under par.

Pío's voice invaded her thoughts: "You appear disturbed. I trust your partisan friends are safe and well."

Juana did not answer. Ring-doves were calling from the woods, their voices sobbing on the sunlit air. Then she said, recovering herself, "Forget about me, Pío – see to yourself. Franco's basically too prim for the likes of Lucía García. You might get away with an affair with your maid, but if you really want to keep this place intact you'd better keep away from the harlots."

Pío replied as if he hadn't heard her. "Be careful, Juana. For God's sake, be careful. If things go wrong, I cannot save you."

Fonseca was in the stable yard as if awaiting Juana when she went there to saddle the bay. The animal, bright-eyed and nervous, whinnied at the sight of her. The butler said lightly, "A morning canter, my lady?"

Juana removed her medical pack and put it on the ground. "Come on, Calvo, you know perfectly well where I'm going."

His plump respectability was searched by the sun, making him suddenly drab. He said, flatly, "Certainly, we try to keep abreast of events in the house, lady. You are going into the Gredos again?"

"Worry about Pío. He's the one who needs it."

"You refer to Señorita García arriving?"

Fonseca, she thought, was a phenomenon. Butlers of abundant personality often ruled households like this one by general consent, but this butler ruled without permission. And he knew everything that was going on. He said, "You don't approve of Lucía García?"

"She'll be all eyes, Calvo – watch your gardeners." She opened the stable door and led out the horse.

Fonseca said, out of context: "It is important, Juana, that no suspicion falls upon the master. Whatever you do, he must be free of it; his position here is delicate, as you know." He helped Juana saddle the horse and held the bridle for her to mount, adding, "Working with the partisans is dangerous – all right, I asked you to help the man Hanson, and you did. I am grateful; it is what your mother would have done. But she would not have gone further. If you are caught the retribution will be terrible."

"I realise the dangers, Calvo."

"I cherish you. Be careful." Fonseca stood watching as Juana rode out of the stable yard, then, turning, walked in the direction of the Chinese love-pavilion. Here Pío was idly strolling.

Juana rode eastward through the sierra to Tornadizos, returning the morning greetings of soldiers and villagers, many of whom were on their way into Avila for the market. The town had settled into the humdrum activity of a secondary headquarters and supply base, neither in the war nor out of it. With the fighting on the Madrid front stagnated, things were quiet. Not for Avila the mass executions that had recently occurred in unfortunate Málaga; there, five thousand republicans were shot by Italians. And, although Avila's curfew was still in force, General Mola, who made a headquarters there for the final assault upon Madrid, had given permission for bull-fights to recommence in the summer for the benefit of hospitals.

Juana rode slowly at first, one of the Spanish élite who, war or no war, would not forsake her morning gallop. Only after she had left Tornadizos did she break the filly into a canter.

The Falangists had been at work here, the road littered with corpses; buzzards were crying hoarsely in the sky, vultures pecked in bald-necked chattering groups, ignoring the German aeroplanes droning overhead. Faintly came the double-thumping of cluster-bombing from Madrid.

The Germans were practising for Guernica.

Such a journey, out to contact partisans, Juana reflected, would have been impossible in the vicinity of Málaga, for instance, where nine battalions of Italian Black Shirts operated under General Roatta.

The sierra grew steeper; the mountain peaks began to spear the sun.

Juana heard the motor-cycle coming above the clatter of the filly's hooves; instantly, she turned off the road, dismounted, smacked the horse's flank to send it deeper into the trees, and flung herself down into the cover of the roadside ditch.

Pressed into the overgrowth, she listened to her heart thumping against her shirt.

Nearer came the motor-cyclist; a growing roar of sound that ended in a shrieking of brakes beyond her.

Raising her head Juana peered.

The motor-cyclist was young. Broad-shouldered and helmeted, he was wearing the blue uniform of the Falange. Now he swung himself out of the saddle, unslung his automatic pistol and approached to where Juana was lying.

Juana saw him coming. Pressing her face into the earth, she listened to his jack-boots thumping the road; nearer, nearer.

The boots stopped a yard away from her head.

The soldier was looking over the ditch at the filly grazing

contentedly. His eyes switched and he turned in a slow circle, his knuckles white on the gun.

The soldier had killed before, but not often. He had killed in Mérida at the beginning of the war, and had enjoyed it because his brother had been executed by peasants with fifty of the Guardia Civil.

Every time he saw a peasant he thought of his brother: every village he passed through he kept an eye open for solitary peasants; every one he shot was one for his brother.

"Bastard!" the soldier said.

God only knew where this one had got to.

The filly raised its face and focused him, chinking its bridle. He suddenly hated it, momentarily raising the automatic in its direction, but swung and fired a short burst of the tracer at nothing. Juana's world exploded into light and concussion: hot cartridge cases sprinkled her back. She thought it was ridiculous that the soldier had not seen her. He was too close, she reasoned; had he been even ten feet away he could not have failed to see her. And then the soldier grunted.

Instinctively, she knew she was discovered, and raised her face.

The soldier's finger moved on the trigger of his gun. Juana was on her feet now, awaiting the thudding impact of the bullets. As the muzzle lifted a voice cried: *"Down, down!"*

Juana went flat as bullets raked the trees beside her.

The soldier slowly turned, sagging at the knees; his weapon chattered aimless fire before it dropped.

Elisa leaped over his body, her little automatic pistol loose in her hands, and cried: "Are you all right?" and knelt. "Hanson sent me. I was waiting for you at the crossroads when I heard the firing."

"*God* that was close!"

"Quick, get the horse – where's your medical bag?"

Juana was clutching it against her. She said, nodding down at the dead Falangist, "What about him?"

Elisa spurned him with her foot. "Leave him. He got what he came for. He's one of the Orgaz trainees – provisional officer, certain corpse – that's their private joke."

*　　*　　*

132

Juana was bending over Consuela.

The bullet traverse was clean, but a splintered bone had severed an artery. Consuela said, smiling, "You'll tell my mother that Franco is dead?"

"I will tell her myself," whispered Elisa.

The girl raised her head. "It is true that the Dwarf is dead – you have proof?" She looked into their faces.

Richard replied, "When midday comes, we'll have Emilio's confirmation – meanwhile Juana has brought the news. Franco is dead – tell her, Juana."

And Juana said: "It is true, Franco is dead. This morning, before I left, I heard it on the wireless. You killed him at Las Sirenas. You did not hear the explosion, you say? Segovia did."

"*Que frío hace,*" said Consuela, and died.

Juana said, "Listen to me. You attacked Franco believing that he was in Las Sirenas? I tell you, he was nowhere near Segovia the day before yesterday."

"Where, then?" asked Richard.

"He was at a Subscribers' Meeting in Salamanca."

Elisa cried, "That is ridiculous." She nodded down at Consuela's body. "She saw him. She saw him going into the hotel – Consuela identified him."

Richard said to Juana, "You're quite sure of this?"

"I am. Pío took and introduced a friend to Franco. Unless Pío's lying, and I've no reason to think he is, it wasn't Franco that Consuela saw in Segovia."

"Who then, for God's sake?" asked Ramón.

There was a silence. Richard said, "A doppelgänger?"

"A double, you mean?"

"Yes, a stand-in."

"That's ridiculous," interjected Elisa.

"Oh no, it's not. It's happening all the time."

"You're saying that the nationalists knew of our attack? Had they known, why didn't they stop it?"

"Because, quite possibly, it suited them to let us carry on – up to the point, but not including, the actual explosion . . ."

"You mean, they've been using us. What for?"

Richard replied, "To kill Mola? He was in Las Sirenas all right, we know this for sure."

"Do we know anything for sure?" asked Ramón.

"Counter-espionage?" asked Juana.

Richard nodded. "An attempt to wipe us out, to eliminate the cell? It scarcely puts republican espionage at the top of the tree, does it?"

"Or raise Emilio in my estimation," added Ramón. "Do you realise that since Emilio's been handling us, things have gone wrong – first the Galapagar ambush, now this." He looked about him in quiet disgust. "What happens now, for God's sake?"

"We give Consuela a decent burial," answered Richard.

"And then?"

"Then I contact Emilio for further instructions."

Ramón said, "Hanson, don't you ever question authority? Doesn't it ever strike you that the people at the top could be blatant idiots?"

Richard knelt beside Consuela and took her hand. "It strikes me all the time, but I know this. Unless we have the discipline to trust them, where do we stand? What did Astrada die for, or this one? Alone, we'd just wander without direction. No, Ramón, we've got to trust someone. Things can be at their cleverest when they appear the most idiotic – this is espionage."

The sun was blazing in the sky as they buried Consuela.

Eighteen

MANOLO, RIDING DOLEFULLY on a donkey, led the way back from Alanis to Las Navas, and the rendezvous with Richard, who had sent word for them to join him for the next attack upon the life of Franco.

Behind Manolo followed Old Pep; his Guardia mare, the property of Sergeant Fernández, was sure-footed on the tracks. Old Pep dozed, eyes shut but wide awake. After him came Nicolas, upright and alert, his bright eyes switching across the giant panorama of peaks and sun; his mind full of thoughts of Juana. Had she not reached out in the night and touched his face? thought Nicolas: would not such a woman, given time, be the pride of his mother's *posada*, back in Alanis?

For the past week, while they had been in Alanis, it had not rained; all was sun, siesta for many, and early morning sowing under the lead-labourers. On the nights of the big moons there were bonfires and even a little *fiesta* dancing among the young ones who did not think in terms of war.

For Manolo, this had been a time of hatred.

As the donkey swayed him in the saddle (he had sold his Guardia mare for marriage money) he thought of Ana Martínez serving in the village shop of Alberto López; he remembered the sleepless siestas when he squatted in the shade of his mother's kitchen amid the strutting hens, and watched Alberto's shop on the other side of the village square. Every time the villagers went into the shop the bell would clang; when they came out it clanged again, and there was no other sound on the heat-laden air.

Ana was dressed as a Mexican rose, with a red, tight-stretched blouse across her shoulders, and her skirt was tight also so that it showed her bottom when she walked, and the other men said, 'Look at Ana Martínez, *hombre*. If I had a waggling bottom like that and a black skirt to cover it, would I be gathering vine?'

And another said, and Manolo listened, 'You think she hates Alberto López? I doubt it. He has become a habit. Anything can become a habit. Even a fat shopkeeper. After all, she could leave if she wanted to.'

'She cannot leave,' replied Manolo, hearing this.

The man who had spoken was eating black bread dipped in olive oil, and spread oily hands at the sun. 'Of course she could leave if she wished to! But perhaps Alberto has a large one – larger, even, than the general's horse which stands near the Retiro in Madrid; undoubtedly this is necessary to the Virgin of Alanis,' and he winked and tore at the bread with big gnarled hands.

'*Mala sombra!*' Manolo had cried, and dived upon him and tipped him up, and white dust rose to the tearing of their cotton jackets as they wrestled in the sun, Manolo uppermost. Dashing away the bread and oil, he held the knife at the labourer's throat.

'All right, all right,' the other labourers said, 'You are in love with Ana? Aren't we all? Is it needful to kill poor Ignacio for love?'

Then there was much jesting and Manolo sat brooding, and in his sweating palm was gripped the bullet he had polished for Alberto López, and when the shop door opened in the dusk, he watched still: Manolo watched, though the others had gone. Ana came out of the shop and went up the steps to the barn across the square, and Alberto López followed. And although the sun went down on Alanis, Manolo was there still, though his mother called him many times from her kitchen.

Dusk came and they did not come out of the barn, Ana Martínez and Alberto López.

Still Manolo watched. He took from his pocket the polished bullet which he had been saving for Alberto López and rubbed the sweat of his hand upon it, and polished it more.

"Of what are you thinking, *hombre*, if you had anything to think with?" asked Old Pep now from the saddle, but he knew what Manolo was thinking, and gave cruelty to ease the cruelty of the sun.

The rocks of the sierra were as diamonds of light. Manolo did not reply, so the old man called, "You are in trouble enough already, now we are going to have another try at Franco. That accursed American is trouble twice, do you realise it? He wags a finger at us from Tornadizos and we arrive – all three of us. We were safe in your village. Now, serving this mad *Yanqui*, many bullets will arrive in our direction."

Again Manolo did not reply, and Nicolas beat himself with his hat for dust, and shouted, from the rear, "Leave him, Grandfather! He grieves for Ana Martínez. Soon, says my mother, she and Alberto will elope to Toledo. What is elope?"

"They will have departed together," said Old Pep. "It is an American politeness for fornication."

"Old Man," said Manolo, not turning in the donkey's saddle, "you have a dirty head and a dirtier tongue. Continue like this and I will step off this donkey and slit it."

Old Pep laughed at the sky. "Poor fool, listen to him! The sun has cooked his head. He is sensitive about Ana and that old fool, Alberto."

In the evening the sky darkened and rain-clouds rolled up from the northern hills. All that night it rained, a drumfire that cascaded off their sombreros and churned up the forest leaves into mud; a deluge that filled the narrow gulches and defiles with foaming water. Dawn came, fine and big with stars. The three of them circled a fire and ate panecillos and drank, and the smoke of their fire drifted upward and there was a smell of leaf dampness in the trees, and coffee.

Before they travelled again, to the place where they were to meet the others, Manolo mended his donkey, who had a loose shoe, and talked much to her in the process.

"There is a great understanding between those two, you notice?" Old Pep said to Nicolas. "Both having kissed the arse of the chief sorcerer."

Nicolas did not answer; all night he had dreamed of Juana and the softness of her hand when she touched him, and there was in him a sickness that he could not define. Getting no response, Old Pep repeated his statement, and Nicolas said, "Poor Manolo. Do not give him cruelty, Grandfather."

Manolo put down the donkey's leg and stretched himself. "Does it sicken you, too, to hear the old fool croak?" And he bent under the donkey to find his hammer and at that moment the donkey made water, soaking him over his head and shoulders and Manolo rose, shrieking and scrambled up and booted the donkey on the rump and hit her with his hat and booted her again, cursing her, while Old Pep was silent, squatting on the ground, holding his stomach with mirth. But Nicolas did not laugh.

"The trouble with you, *amigo*," said Old Pep, laughing still, "is that you do not understand women. Remind me to give you lessons – how to handle women and donkeys."

Later, before they set off again, Nicolas saw Manolo returning from a stream in the valley where he had gone to wash. The water was still on the face of Manolo.

Nicolas was cooking, on a triangle of sticks, a leveret that had come into his snare within the thickets: two he had caught, the first being with young, and her he had released since it was bad sense to eat the source of leverets; the second he had skinned, gutted and set over the fire, and while awaiting its roasting, the porrón had gone from mouth to mouth. "Thinking of Alanis sickens me also," said Nicolas. "By the time I'm home after killing Franco, there'll be a new pair of rope sandals in our *posada*. – Diego Díaz will be there."

"My son, your father is dead, Nicolas," said Old Pep, and he tore at the leveret's leg with his yellow teeth and wiped his bearded mouth with his hand. "But your mother's belly is still ripe for children. She is in need of another man; be reasonable."

"She has me." Nicolas thumbed his chest, chewing. "What need of another?"

Old Pep said at the stars. "Can you make your mother's children?"

"I am her son."

Manolo, now recovered in temper, said, "Of course, but do you not also feel the wind up your shirt when girls walk by?"

Nicolas did not reply to this; he was thinking again of Juana, and hated the *Yanqui* who had taken her attention. How could it be, he thought, that one of his strength and hair could persuade such as her into love? Indeed – how could one as fair as his own mother rub skin with the skin of Diego Díaz, who was wrinkled with age? Women, he thought, were strange, and he angrily said: "My mother is young, as the lady Juana is young. Diego is old. It is indecent."

"Oh, yes?" With heavily-lidded eyes, Old Pep squinted at the moon. "My son, my son! Do not assume that everybody above the age of thirty has one foot in the grave." He gave the leveret's thigh-bone a final suck and tossed it over his shoulder. "When the Bloodstained Dwarf is six feet down, I shall retire and take another woman to my bed, to warm my old bones in winter. You, in your turn, will one day understand."

Nicolas slept, again dreaming of Juana.

As they rode again, taking the sierra tracks to Las Navas and the rendezvous with Richard, Manolo thought again about Ana Martínez.

He had waited outside Alberto's shop for Ana – near enough not to miss her when she finished work for the day; far enough away not to be seen.

It was not in the evenings that Alberto demanded her, but in the afternoons when the wine was in him and the day was hot: in the evenings, sober, he went home to his wife.

Therefore Manolo, who waited until dusk, was surprised to see Ana come out of the shop followed by Alberto; and still more surprised to see her mount the stairs to the grain barn on the other side of the square, as if of her free will.

She, Ana, had not known of Manolo's presence.

In Manolo's pocket were pastries; little cakes of wheaten flour which his mother had made: he had intended that he and Ana would go to a quiet place and eat these, first drinking a little wine. Therefore he had also brought with him a small porrón, and in this was the best wine of Alanis.

He and Ana would drink and eat, and it would be good, thought Manolo.

Seeing Ana climbing up to the barn, Manolo would have called her and followed, for deep in the hay he could have held her and told her what would happen after the war, when Alberto had gone from Alanis, and there would be only them – he and Ana Martínez, for love. Would not Diego Díaz, the lead-labourer speak for him, he being a friend of Nicolas's mother? And perhaps, even, the agent would speak to the landlord and grant him a cottage.

139

All this Manolo planned to tell Ana Martínez; and all this would come to pass after she had freed herself from Alberto López.

Now he called to her, his hand up, but the call stopped upon his mouth.

After Alberto had closed the door of the barn, Manolo came from his hiding place; there was no sound but the cicada's song and the croaking of bull-frogs from the pond; this and the guitar of Gustavo, the blind mute who lived behind the inn.

Crossing the road, Manolo stood at the bottom of the steps leading to the grain loft, listening, but heard no sound other than the sounds of the village.

Manolo mounted the steps to the grain loft, until he reached the platform serving the door, and the timber here was stained white with flour and golden husks; these, disturbed by his sandals, drifted down to the ground in a golden rain.

Again Manolo listened, this time outside the barn door.

Silence.

Carefully, he turned the handle of the door, but the door did not open to him.

Above him was a ball-hook, used for swinging the grain bags.

Manolo measured the chain length, the hook, the crane arm, the radius of the swing. At full stretch, he calculated, the hook would take him opposite the loft window where the grain was loaded.

It meant swinging from the platform into space. But, once in position, dangling over the fifty-feet drop to the ground, he could command a view of the interior.

Leaping up, he caught the hook; reached out with a foot, and pushed.

The jib arm swung with a creak.

Dangling from the hook, Manolo twisted from the waist, thrusting out with his legs, propelling himself in space.

The jib arm began to move to a position opposite the window.

Rigidly, Manolo hung upon the hook, staring through the window into the loft.

Nineteen

THE SHORTEST ROUTE to Burgos would be to strike north along the road to Valladolid, but this, added Richard, would be madness in view of the disposition of the rebel nationalists. The longest way being sometimes the shorter, he led them first east from Tornadizos through the Sierra de Gredos, then struck north-east upwards into the Sierra de Guadarrama, where the occupying rebels were thin on the ground.

"We will keep to the mountains, Old Pep, does this make sense to you?"

The old gitano replied sullenly, "We will stay alive that way; that makes sense to anybody."

At first they travelled by night and rested in the day, and on the second day of travel passed through Galapagar, the area of the convoy ambush. This took them near to the spot where Felipe Astrada had died, but none spoke of it. The crescent moon sat on the bony shoulders of the sierra, and they rode in single file, with Old Pep leading and Richard and Juana behind him. Then came Ramón and Elisa, with Nicolas and Manolo following.

In this manner they went along mule tracks in a wilderness of mountains: sometimes on high ground overlooking the valleys, sometimes over deserted plains of bush and scrub. Buzzards and eagles moved here; the lizard ran in quick swerves, young fawns watched from thickets.

"Look," said Old Pep, "a patrol," and Richard and Juana looked, and saw in the valley a thousand feet below the tiny snake of a Guardia patrol, and Old Pep grinned and drew his finger across his throat, speaking of Sergeant Tomás Fernández, his old enemy, whom, he said, was happily dead.

"You are sure of this, Old Pep?" Richard teased him.

"As sure as my mother who knew it was me," cried the old man, turning in the saddle. "One falls, the sierra buries you. First come the little voles: later, the buzzards pick you cleaner than a jewel."

"Do not be too sure," called Manolo. "I agree with the *Yanqui*. True, he fell, but Sergeant Fernández has the lives of a cat. You boasted that you killed him once before, remember? – it is old crow talk."

"Defile your penis – he is dead!" cried Old Pep.

After this they were quiet; the mood of the sierra had changed. Its moonlit beauty dulled into a sombre darkness; black fingers reached into the forests of pine; the animals placed their hooves more gently on the rich, resisting earth, rolling their eyes at imagined shadows – sierra tigers feasting.

With dawn the temper of the sierra changed again. The sun came raging over the peaks, shedding golden light. The forest danced to a jangling orchestra of birds.

The day warmed them. They made camp above Casla, north of the road that led to Segovia.

This was on the third day of the march.

Casla, said Old Pep, was a place of *pistoleros*, the paid assassins of both sides of the war, who killed for a pair of boots. Nicolas went first on guard, since he had dozed in the saddle. The others, in the shelter of a hollow clear of the pass, lay down and slept.

Sitting on a crag, Nicolas remembered that in such a manner he had sat before; watching as before, but not for *pistoleros*: on that occasion he had waited and watched for an American, and that, he thought, seemed a world and a year ago.

Before that, he was home in Alanis, the country of the fighting bulls.

There was nothing better, he thought, than practising the dexterity and fleetness possessed by the great bull-fighters of the past – Montes, Romero, Candido; side-stepping the young bull's maddened rush, lightly leaping the fence an inch in front of his horns. Nicolas smiled, remembering his urchin friends of the village. But that was before the war; before the starvations of their landlord, Villesín, and the torture of the *bimotor*.

How beautiful his mother had been, he reflected, in the days before the war hungers came. And what ambitions he had known! Not for him the role of a second class *banderillero* or a third class *picador*. No! He would prove a maestro of the quality of the great Manolete – in his opinion the greatest of them all!

Now the sun told him that it was six o'clock; Nicolas, sitting there with his rifle across his knees, forgot the bulls and remembered his mother.

Since Ramón had galloped into Alanis and ordered them to Burgos to kill the Dwarf, Nicolas had thoughts of his mother upon his mind, and the thoughts brooded like the rotting carcass of a chicken.

How could an old woman of thirty years or more, he speculated, bring a new man to the bed of his father? – he who had died in the massacre of Badajoz? She, who was so prim before strangers when washing at the tub . . . this same woman could despoil herself before Diego Díaz, the lead-labourer of Alanis?

It was regretful, he thought, that his father was not alive to put an end to such degradation.

Nicolas remembered his father when the Guardia came and arrested him for beating the landlord Villesín with the burning acorn bags. The Guardia had tied his father's hands behind his back and pulled the rope over a branch. And, as he dangled there, in view of his family, one had opened his jacket and trousers, and with a smouldering acorn bag, burned away first the hair of his arm-pits, then the pubic hair of his legs.

His father was silent.

Then the Guardia sergeant, angered at this silence, seized his father's testicles and swung him to and fro, then round and round in a circle on the rope, while the others made the sound of an aeroplane diving, and this was called the torture of the *bimotor*.

It was as if it was a sack the sergeant was swinging, because still his father made no sound, though his face was the colour of a man dying. And, as his wife wailed, the Guardia cut him down and pegged him out and flogged him. After this, they tied both Nicolas and his mother to the same tree and flogged them also. His mother had screamed, but he had made no sound.

The watching children wept.

143

Nicolas moved his shoulders now, remembering the whip.

With a rope around his neck, they had then led his father away, and the other end of the rope was tied to the horn of the sergeant's saddle. Later he died under the knives of the Moors, in the bull-ring of Badajoz.

Now Nicolas recalled that, not long ago, he had demonstrated the torture of the *bimotor* to the leader, the man Hanson; that he had childishly held his arms outspread and ran, making the sounds of an aeroplane. Remembering this now, he lowered his face in shame. But that, he reflected, was when he was a boy. Now he was a man. Much had happened in between.

Now this, his mother's remarriage.

It was not even as if Diego Díaz was young, he thought – he who possessed wizened hands and a face scarred with a life of labour. Also, his thighs were withered and his stomach wrinkled, for Nicolas had seen him washing at the village pump. Earlier, he had seen his father washing at the same pump, and there was a cleanness about his muscular arms, and the dung and dirt staining them swilled down the drain in brown streams, until the water became white again, and his hands and arms were clean, like the breakers in the sea off Santander.

But the limbs of Diego Díaz would never become clean, he thought, for they were stained with the dirt of age, though his mother's skin was flawless; no gitano, this one; she was black-haired and her lips were red, like the lips of the lady who now lay beside the *Yanqui* and whose sleeping face he had watched in other dawns.

Old Pep had once said, 'Women and donkeys, my son, think of them as one. What do you do with a worn out donkey? You take him up into the mountains and push him over the top. Women, like bottles of wine, should be cast aside when they have fulfilled their function.'

How strange, therefore, thought Nicolas, that the Americano was so attentive to this Asturian lady; never eating until she began to eat; never resting until she was comfortable.

With his almond eyes narrowed to the dawn redness, Nicolas looked to the place where Juana lay, and saw her and realised that, if thirty years difference was acceptable to Diego

Díaz and his mother, what was ten years between him and this Asturian lady?

True, he thought, he did not possess a chest like a doormat, as did the *Yanqui*; true also, he was not greatly interested in the nothingness between the legs that ladies possessed, although Manolo, who was despicable, was always discussing it. Many times he had seen village women in labour; the sweating and tears, the drumming of their heels on the board. If this strange place of nothingness and pain was favoured by Manolo, he himself did not find it of any great attraction. But it would be good, Nicolas thought, to place his head on the softness beneath a throat; to hear a woman breathe, like his mother breathed upon his face when he was young.

Did such privilege cease when one became sixteen?

From his pocket he took a ten *peseta* piece, long worn to a shine. Nicolas held it up to the sun. 'Take this from me,' his father had said. 'Use it not for hunger or lodging, but give it to a woman – not to one or twenty, but to the woman you take into my *posada*.'

And so Nicolas flicked up the coin against the sun and caught it and gripped it in his hand, looking down at the sleeping form of Juana, and his mind traced a finger around the nipple of her breast, and on this spot he placed the coin in his mind, and she did not resist him.

And so he rose when the cocks began to crow from a distant village, and went past the sleeping Elisa to the place where Juana slept. Richard, lying near her, opened one eye to the whisper of a twig bending, and his right hand moved.

And Juana awoke also, because eyes were upon her face, and sat up, smiling, and said: "Nicolas . . .?"

The boy did not reply, but stood and looked upon her, then turned and went.

Juana said, "How strange were his eyes. What on earth did he want?"

And Richard turned over upon his back and tipped his sombrero over his face against the redness of the sun, and chuckled in his hat, and did not answer.

Twenty

WITH THE COMING of next day's dusk they were still in the hair of the sierra, and the moon was like a quarter Dutch cheese on her back in the sky. They moved in single file through the clustered poplars and pines, and Richard ordered them not to speak for fear of rebel patrols.

They could hear the traffic of war rumbling up to the Basque front, but only the daintily stepping hooves of the donkeys made sound in the forest; the creaking of harness, the chinking of bridles. And so they threaded the sierra rocks as a woman threads a needle, north for Burgos.

In this manner, before darkness of the fourth day, they came to a signpost on the sierra track, and here a man was standing. Dressed in a poncho was he, with a captured Moor's turban flat on his head and a carbine over his shoulder.

"Gitano!"

"Greetings, greetings!" As the man moved forward, other figures rose up on either side of the track.

Richard reached for his Colt, but the man whispered beside him: "Do not fear, *compañero*. You seek the Pradales partisans? You find them – this is our camp," and Old Pep spurred his donkey and trotted up to Richard and Juana, saying, "No noise, Señor. The road is close but you are among friends. This one I even know," and he clapped the man on the back. "Not two years back, in Roncesvalles, *eh, eh?* Ah, *compañero*! You fight on the Burgos road?"

The stranger spoke from a bearded face. "In the Pradales sierra; here we fight. Tomorrow dawn we attack a rebel convoy. They have medical packs for our wounded and paymaster's *pesetas* for Mola's northern army!"

The men nearest laughed softly, their hands over their mouths.

In the dim light the faces of the partisans crowded about

146

them; scores, thought Juana, perhaps a hundred dirty, dishevelled men, but armed with the latest Vostok subautomatics, of Russian origin. The animals moved nervously, their hooves scraping the flinted track. The first man said, simply, "We speak for Señor Deimler. He grants you free passage. 'Await the Gredos people,' said Deimler. Look, we have it here by special messenger," and he held up a paper. "'See them north of Revillas and keep them high at a thousand feet.' You come? We know the rebel front."

Old Pep opened his gnarled fingers before Richard. "Señor, welcome him! He is our guide, commanded by Deimler."

"He who talks much but never appears!" The partisan thrust out a ragged arm and Richard grasped it. "They fight with pens – no blood!"

"Salud, *compañero*!" said Old Pep. "Go in God. Make sure that we are not too far behind."

The guide moved off. A man said, "Long live liberty and down with fascism! *Viva la República!*"

Away from the main body of the Pradales partisans, Juana and Richard walked together and the night was fine with a big moon speared by the hunting pines, and over the forest was a silence and this contained them so that they walked unspeaking in a brittle agony of expectancy that each knew but did not declare; it was the foreboding of a loss, an undefended nakedness.

At first they walked as friends do, hand in hand, and sat for a while looking at the moon, as lovers do: then they sat on a crag that overlooked the valley of the Pradales, and Richard took from his pocket the burned cork he used for night hunting and struck a match and burned it again, and with this he painted Juana's face, dubbing out the whiteness. She knelt before him and her face was upturned and she acted pertly, turning her face this way and that, and every so often, in the blackening of her cheeks, her forehead, the pale curve of her throat, Richard bent to kiss her lightly, first on her cheeks, then on her forehead, then upon her lips. He saw before him in the light of the moon the white mask of her face slowly disappear behind the camouflage so that where once there was whiteness, now was blackness.

147

When he had finished this task, Juana painted Richard's face with the burned cork, and when the moon faded and the forest became dark, they saw nothing before them but their eyes rolling white, and the straight white lines of their teeth; their white-palmed hands moving disembodied against the dark foliage of the forest darkness. They kissed, tasting upon their lips the acrid soot of the cork, and they laughed softly. Night-birds heard this laughter, and listened.

Then there was a place of bushes and shadows where the moon did not enter, and here they sat, at first in quiet; then Juana caught her breath as Richard's arms tightened about her, and she lay back on the forest floor in what each knew was kinship. Richard felt Juana's body against his and the pressure of her breasts upon him, and Juana did not resist when he opened the buttons of her shirt and the warmth and softness of her was upon the coldness of his hand, and Juana turned away her face.

So they lay, and there was a new aching in Richard that grew first in his throat, bringing a new strength; and with this strength he gathered Juana against him and their breath was one and their trembling was one to the other. The minutes passed and they knew each other in the heat of it: so come upon them that the present was obliterated in the cherishing, when words were not of themselves; spoken but unheard; the endearments part of the night; the touching, the kisses. One with them were the wind-topped pines also, the moon and the dark, the silence and the warm, impetuous earth. And from the quickness of this loving came sobriety and humour, and Juana opened her eyes as their breath chastened them, and she smiled, seeing above her Richard's face which the moon made into shape; his white teeth, the blackness of his hair she saw, and reaching up, kissed his lips.

"Now?" he asked.

With one finger he traced the smoothness of her breast.

"Oh, ⟨illegible⟩" she said, "is there time?" She stroked his face. "The Pradales . . .?"

"Yes, there is time."

Then there was no night and no leaves, no sky, no sounds: save for wind that rustled the floor of the forest, there was nothing; nothing in nothingness: no time, no happening, no existence, and he bared his body to her and they were one in the oneness of nothing. "I love you, I love you," Juana said.

Nicolas watched.

Presently, within the absolution of love, they rose from the leaves; and unspeaking, went back to the partisans.

From the camp of the Pradales partisans, they followed the guide, first marching parallel to the Burgos road; that night descending into the foothills of the sierra. Before the light of the next dawn, within a few miles of Burgos, they reached the Mencilla Sierra.

"What now?" said Old Pep, his temper frayed by the presence of another gitano, the guide.

"We rest," said Richard.

By a little waterfall they watered the animals, and slept, with Ramón and Elisa on guard, and the horizon was faintly alight with gun-flashes where Mola's army was attacking the Iron Ring of the Basques.

Outlined against this horizon, its towers and steeples pinnacling the explosions, was the town of Burgos.

That night they stayed in the cover of the sierra, and listened to patrolling nationalists and the rumbling of lorries, and at midday, Richard adjusted the morse transmitter and made the call-sign, and the message returned:

Emilio to Hanson. Operation Dwarf. Give position and casualties. Over.

Richard replied:

Position one mile north Hontoria. No casualties. Over.

Emilio answered:

Emilio to Hanson. Guide Don Pita at roadside bridge near Arlanzón. 0600 hrs. Wayside shrine Eulalia. Destination Café Suizo. Bury transmitter. Over.

*　　*　　*

149

Richard waved a hand and the guide came to him, crouching, in quick swerves from the elms.

"You called?"

The man screwed at his hat. His face, above his blanket poncho, floated in darkness. Richard said:

"We have instructions to go north to Arlanzón, to a roadside bridge over the river."

"Señor, there are two bridges! Is it the bridge near the Seminario, in Burgos? Or is it the bridge of Arlanzón, on the road to Logroño?"

Juana whispered, "There is a wayside shrine of Santa Eulalia, man – that bridge."

The gitano said, "That is on the Logroño road. Yes, I know it. I know, also, that it is on the edge of a Carlist camp, an outpost of the Burgos Infantería."

"Dangerous?" asked Richard.

"It is suicide. The last guide to Arlanzón hanged on a tree until midday."

"That is nothing to what could happen to you," said Richard. *"Lead!"*

Until first light they marched, always climbing, and the bastions of the city rose up before them, its high summit crowned with a ruined castle. They were in a thickening mist now, but saw through a gap in the trees the turrets haloed with clouds.

Silently, with care, they moved through the dense tree-mist for Arlanzón village, and the bridge near the shrine of Santa Eulalia.

Near the bridge a man was kneeling in the mist. Richard looked at his watch. It was 0600 hours, the appointed time. As Richard drew closer he saw that the man was small, like monumental stone, and he knelt praying. He didn't even glance up as Richard drew near.

He was a monk.

Before a small wayside shrine he prayed, and Richard knelt beside him.

The little monk was no longer young. The gown he wore was more ill-fitting than most, and he raised his bearded face as Richard joined him, and said, "You pray to Eulalia, too, my son?"

"Also to Pelayo," replied Richard, "he who saw the Cross of Victory fall from the sky after his defeat of the Moors – see, I have his medallion," and he opened the top buttons of his jacket. "See the medallion." The man said unmoving:

"*Salud, compañero.* From whom do you come?"

"From Emilio."

"For *Operation Dwarf*?"

And Richard nodded.

The monk looked over his shoulder. "And your comrades?"

"A whistle, and they will arrive."

"How many?"

"We are seven. We had a guide in the Pradales, but he has left us."

"He is the only sensible one among you," came the reply; the man rose and Richard saw to his astonishment that he was little taller than when kneeling, but his voice was bass and beautiful.

Seeing Richard's astonishment, he said, "Do not be confused, comrade. Franco, not I, is the Dwarf they refer to. *Viva la República!* Do you support the clerics?"

Richard said, "Can we have the humour later, brother?"

"The humour is now, *amigo* – that we should be here at all." He pushed Richard aside with an inborn arrogance, and said. "You seek the Café Suizo?"

"We report to the Café Suizo, yes: this is our brief."

"As clerics you may reach it . . . the place of penances." He tugged at Richard's poncho. "In this rig-out, never. Are you a faithful servant of the Church of Christ?"

"*Hombre*, you can imagine it!"

"May it rot in Hell, its priests and bishops." The monk crossed himself. "Only as penitents will you get into Burgos. Make your confession at the Café Suizo and there seek absolution." Reaching up, the little man took Richard's sleeve, pointing. "In that ditch you will find nine cagoules, which was the number Emilio demanded. At midday the bells of the cathedral toll the Angelus. As a trail of travelling penitents, we'll enter Burgos."

"In daylight?"

"In darkness you will get bullets across your backs, penitent or heretic. Challenge nothing, *hombre*. Listen!" He lifted his small head, near bald, save for a ring of greying hair. His eyes, bright with an inner peace, moved in his lined cheeks. "Who is commander now, then? You or I?"

Richard said, "You, quite clearly."

"Good." The monk clutched at his beads. "Dress in the cagoules and leave me to pray. You are ready to move?"

"We are ready."

"Excellent. We will take the main road into Burgos."

"The main road, Venerable Brother," said Richard.

Later, abandoning the animals, they left the cover of the trees and walked the road to Burgos, mingling among the people entering the city for market. Don Pita led them. With his cagoule back upon his shoulders and his head bared, he held high a crucifix.

Following him was Richard, his gown straining at the seams; the three gitanos, then Ramón supporting Elisa and Juana. In their black penitents' gowns they went in a shuffling gait, their cagoules, slitted for eyes, covering their faces, and Don Pita cried: "Make way, good people, make way for the penitents! A family in disgrace. Make way for the Franciscan and the sinners of Arlanzón!"

In this manner they crossed the river bridge and into the Espalón crowds, then dispersed.

Each made his way, individually, to the Café Suizo.

Twenty-one

NATIONALIST ACTIVITY IN Burgos was increasing hourly as the military tempo increased towards the Basque front farther north. Reports came from the Basque Ring of Iron protecting Bilbao that Guernica had fallen after obliteration by German bombing; that Bermeo had been overrun by Mussolini's Black Arrows. The Basques fearing encirclement, were falling back before General Mola's Army of the North, Richard heard.

"But the biggest crime is Guernica," said Don Pita, "it is the home of the Basque parliament; the town of the church of Santa María . . ."

"And holy in the eyes of Spanish kings," added Ramón.

Elisa, surprised, turned up her eyes at this.

"It is nothing," said Don Pita, "compared with what there is to come."

"And what is there to come in the Café Suizo, Legionnaire?" asked Old Pep slyly. "Emilio promised us many things, but I doubt if we will get them from the Legion," and he inhaled his cigarette and blew a smoke ring at the ceiling, baiting Don Pita; no love being lost between the Legion and gipsies, as Richard knew.

"Weapons, explosives, all as Emilio ordered," Don Pita replied. "Also a Mercedes motor-car for gitanos who wish to show a clean pair of heels."

"Enough," said Richard. "Save your dislike for Franco, whom you've come to kill."

Later, Richard and Juana were sitting at a table in the attic of the Café Suizo.

Below them they saw, through heavily laced curtains, rebel military convoys bunching along the waterfront; the cobbled Espalón facing the river was filled with activity.

Blacksmiths, their forges glowing, hammered, clanked and sweated at their bellows while horse teams of gun-limbers were lined up for shoeing – these same blacksmiths who later struck their horse-shoes on to the naked feet of captured Basques. Canvas-topped lorries rumbled northward in never-ending convoys.

Market women cried their wares. Water-sellers, leading donkeys loaded with mountains of *botijos*, threaded a path through the market crowds, the red containers gleaming between their netted coverings, and their cries rose to the curtained window. The river flashed in brilliance off the whitewashed terraces of the waterfront. War wounded from the battles of the Basque fighting sat in their white bandages, passively accepted as the refuse of war.

An armoured car preceded by motor-cyclists was coming along the Espalón.

With General Dávila (head of the junta administration in Burgos) in front with the driver, the big Hispano came at speed. Sitting at the back was Franco in his usual passive calm; Juana caught a glimpse of a face paunched and white; the large, bald eyes surveying the lines of soldiers with obvious disinterest. Beside Franco sat General Mola, who had met him at the air-strip – the lanky and bespectacled Cuban, his owl-like face incongruous under his peaked cap; looking more like an accountant, thought Richard, with his horn-rimmed spectacles, than Franco's Second-in-Command. And the animosity, the reported intrigues for total leadership appeared evident, Richard thought, in Mola's attitude now: he sat with aloofness, seemingly unaware of Franco's presence, one arm languidly raised in greeting to the crowds.

Before the war was over, Richard reflected, the acrimony that existed between these so-called brothers-in-arms would degenerate into a conflict for power. Indeed, according to the rumours of the streets, such a conflict had already begun.

Facing Franco and Mola in the back seat of the staff car, sat Colonel Carrasco, his dark face beaming; clearly, he was enjoying the company of Spain's new Head of State.

Juana said, "So Pío was right again. There he is – Carrasco!" and she nudged Ramón, who was beside her. "Look!"

Ramón stirred uneasily, watching the cavalcade, then said,

"Yes, and I was just thinking. We plan, we scheme, and people die – good people like Astrada. Yet one machine-gun at this window now and it would all be over."

The Espalón was erupting with cheers. Nationalist flags were waving, the fascist salute being given. The car and its out-riders swept past and disappeared from view.

Richard replied: "True, but you create a martyr."

"Is falling out of a car or falling out of an aeroplane so different?"

"Quite different. One is seen as an accident; the other's an assassination, a patriotic death."

The door opened then and Don Pita, the landlord of the café, entered with a bottle; now a man of sweating wine and wheezes. No longer a Franciscan friar, this one, but a typical Burgos landlord. Richard wondered where they got these actors from, but they were excellent in espionage, and easy to get hold of, according to Deimler. Easing his little shining backside down into the nearest chair, Don Pita sat in unbuttoned meditation: the transition, thought Juana, was remarkable. He said, quietly, "I have been on the roof, Señor. The transmitter is ready." The little man put the bottle on the table. "Meanwhile, let us drink together. Death to Franco."

"I will drink to that," said Richard, and the landlord slopped red wine into four glasses.

"The gitanos are comfortable in the stables?" asked Juana.

"That is where they prefer to be. It reminds me of the Legion to see these fighting gitanos; siesta gitanos, most of them, but when they are fighters there are none better. The old one – him, even!"

They laughed together.

"You were in the Legion you say?" asked Elisa, and her hand, Richard noticed, went out to Ramón, but he pulled his away. Don Pita sipped at his glass. "In the Legion, on the stage, in the bull-ring – mine has been a varied career." Blearily, he examined his wine. "All of Spain is in the slant of a glass of vino tinto," said he.

"Not a matador!" Ramón leaned forward, his eyes shining, his small, aesthetic face suddenly alive.

155

"Yes, yes," said Don Pita. "But though small, I was slow, too slow. ~~Cristo~~! I was no Manolete! I was gored, so I married. It is in the order of things. One is gored, one settles down."

"Your wife is here with you in the café?"

"God forbid! Her name was Paulina. She was a beautiful, but a fevered woman, either praying or making love." He drank and refilled his glass. "And all the time she was loving she was looking at the bull-ring – in her mind, you understand – so that she would birth a matador!" He pushed up his impish face at them. "I used to say to her – *Cristo*, woman! Pay attention to what is happening to you. I am a good Spaniard – give this bull-fighter a little consideration." He peered at them over the table. "Was that unreasonable?"

"She was a fool," exclaimed Elisa, entering into the spirit of it, for the landlord was plainly tipsy. "To have a bull-fighter in one's bed is very reasonable."

"It was a ridiculous marriage," declared Don Pita. "I used to have to dress up as a matador. But, as I told her, bull-fighters are conceived in the soul, not the womb." He grimaced and wiped his mouth. "I've known some actually born in the dens who died of pneumonia when the first bull went past. I left her, of course. Life was too much of a palaver."

"And then?" asked Richard, enjoying it, and flickered a wink at Juana.

"And then I married my Josefina. More wine, my friends! More wine!" The little man went round them, filling their glasses. "But that was after I left the stage."

"Josefina?" asked Juana. "This was your second wife."

Don Pita lifted his glass. "To my Josefina."

They drank, watching him. He said, "And that is why I am here, to kill the Dwarf. In the Legion we killed by instinct, like a cat kills a rat . . ." He stared blearily about him, adding: "She was not as other women, this one. She was plump and plain, but merry of face and excellent of temper. I loved her well. We married a month before the coup, and went on our honeymoon to Pamplona, to the house of her sister."

"Pamplona? Of all places!"

"Yes, and we were there when Franco's rebellion started with Mola's eight thousand Carlists, and no chance of getting out." The landlord wiped his sweating face. "The relatives had little food in the house, and my sister-in-law said, 'Josefina, today is the day for bread. Go to the baker's queue on the square,' and Josefina went and joined a queue of women standing at the back of a lorry. Bread was short in the town . . ." He stared at them.

"Continue," said Elisa, softly.

"Well, the women were gossiping – you know women – interested in Josefina because she was a stranger. And while they were chattering, an officer comes up and orders them into the lorry, and the women protested, making much noise, saying that they were only waiting for bread. Then soldiers came and goaded the women into the lorry with bayonets, and all got into the lorry which was driven to a place east of the town. There they were made to stand by a ditch and were shot."

"Good God!" whispered Juana.

"And . . . and when the Carlists came back to Pamplona they saw, on the other side of the square of Castillo, a lorry with women roped together, standing behind it, awaiting execution – school-teachers, intellectuals."

Elisa said flatly, "They'd got the wrong lorry . . .!"

"They'd got the wrong man in making an enemy of me," said Don Pita, and drank again. "To the death of Franco, the Bloodstained Dwarf. I will kill him for Josefina!"

They drank again, watching him. None spoke until the landlord said; "Now upstairs! I have done my part, now do yours. The transmitter is ready, Señor," and Don Pita rose, bowed, and led Richard up to the roof.

Later still, waiting in the downstairs bar of the Café Suizo, Richard glanced up as Ramón approached. Apart from two men drinking in a corner, the bar was empty; Don Pita was lethargically polishing glasses behind the bar.

"You sent for me?" asked Ramón. Sitting down, he faced Richard over a table.

"The attic gets overcrowded. I wanted to see you alone."

"As a result of your transmission to Emilio?"

Richard nodded. "Yes, and I'll come to the point. Emilio's orders concern you directly."

Ramón lifted his pale thin face, smiling faintly.
"You expected it?"
"It was inevitable, was it not?"
Don Pita brought wine and Richard drank, but Ramón did not; instead, he stared through the door of the café to the river beyond.
Richard said, softly. "You were at school in Santander, I understand. While there, you made friends with one named . . ."
Ramón interjected, "Let me tell you, *amigo*. It will save much time. While at school I made friends with Gil Vega – now Captain Vega of the Spanish Air Force. Attached to the German Condor Regiment and stationed in Burgos."
"You read my mind!"
Ramón nodded. "Now it is required that I renew the friendship?"
Richard nodded. Lighting a cheroot, he watched Ramón. A nerve in the man's temple was beating violently; at the best of times Ramón was psychologically disturbed; never was it more apparent.
Ramón said, his lips trembling: "Could you spare me that? I beg you, Hanson. I'm finished with Vega."
Richard replied, "According to Emilio, it is necessary. This old friend of yours is in direct contact with the pilots who fly important people in and out of Burgos."
"So, it is final. Franco is going to die as Sanjurjo died, is that it – in a plane?"
"An accident in the air is the surest and always the most convenient way." Richard drew on the cheroot, watching Ramón closely.
"I'd rather not do this."
"Dishonour an old friendship?"
"Renew a dead friendship."
"You're talking in riddles. If Vega's friendship means nothing to you now, isn't it easy to take advantage of it?"
Ramón raised his eyes. "It involves old affections. Vega is a homosexual."
Seconds passed. The landlord was cleaning glasses with a new flourish.
Men suddenly flooded through the door; peasants, mostly,

coming in from the stalls of the market day, and the room was filled with their banter. Richard said, quietly, "We all serve, my friend. Sacrifices have to be made. Vega has information we want – Franco's movements by plane. It's vital you obtain them."

"My God," whispered Ramón, "life is a mess of chaos and despair."

"You're prepared to die, aren't you? Is this asking so much?"

"Would you sell your honour like a bawd? You don't know what you're asking, do you?"

Richard glanced about him at the room.

The wine was going down now; men guffawing and pushing with boisterous intent.

Richard said earnestly, "It has got to be done. You are our only chance. Headquarters knows your record, and they're pitiless."

"Need Elisa know of this in detail?"

"Of course not."

"When do I go?"

"Now. Every moment's important, says Emilio. Listen. You tell them that you're stationed at the army camp at Arlanzón – remember it? It was there we met Don Pita. It's a detail unit there – redisposal of lightly wounded – you are just back from the Basque front, understand? A torn muscle – anything will do. And you've just heard that Vega is attached to Mola's headquarters. Contact him. Find out all you can about Franco's movements."

Ramón was already moving away.

Minutes later, in the stables, watched by Old Pep, Manolo and Nicolas, Ramón changed into his uniform of a lieutenant in the Carlists.

"~~Christ~~ Almighty," said Richard aloud, and finished his glass.

Yet, deep within him Richard knew a faint but nagging suspicion. This time Ramón was going right into the rebel Infantería. It only needed a hint . . . and the rest of them were sitting ducks in the Café Suizo, a quarter of a mile down the road.

Richard stared out on to the bright Espalón.

If Emilio was wrong, he thought – and he'd been wrong before – heads would roll, but not Emilio's.

He watched Ramón walking swiftly over the bridge to the other side of the waterfront, going in the direction of the Cuartel de Infantería, General Mola's rebel headquarters.

Twenty-two

ELISA WAS SITTING alone in the attic when Juana entered; it was one of the few occasions, Juana reflected, when they had been alone together; the lack of contact had not served to bridge the hostility that Elisa held for her. Juana said, sitting down, "Do not worry, Ramón will be back."

Elisa said, her eyes empty of hope, "Yes, he will come back. Always he comes, but is he really here . . .?"

"I do not understand."

Elisa stared down on to the Espalón. "Of course not. How can you understand? With you and your man there are no such complications – this is your luck! Everything is right in your world."

"I wish it were."

As if unhearing, Elisa said, wringing her hands, "But, whether he returns or not, I will kill every fascist I can lay hands on in this war."

"Do not hate. It takes two sides to make a war."

"Oh yes? Two sides for a war as comfortable as yours! You've had it easy. You snap your finger, people come running. Even now, being a nurse, you are playing at war. But this war has destroyed Ramón and me. So I will kill every fascist, I say!" She made a fist of a hand and put it against her face. "I have killed many already, you know that?"

Juana lowered here eyes. Elisa continued. "Oh yes, yes! When I was in Barcelona, after escaping from the prison, I killed many!"

"You were in the women's prison of San Pablo?"

"For months, and for what? For being the daughter of a woodcutter who supported the Popular Front."

"Many suffered for that," Juana observed quietly.

"But me . . .?" Elisa turned from the window and thumped herself with a fist. "What did I know of politics? Nothing! I did not know the difference between the fascists, the U.G.T., or the meaning of the Cortes! Shall I tell you what happened

161

in San Pablo?" She began to pace the room in growing restlessness. "They took me to the Guardia Interrogation first, and there beat me until I could not stand. Then they dragged me to San Pablo where the warders were women, and these strapped me to an iron bed – many of them, shouting and jeering, and one said, 'Do not be impatient, lover. Here is a bridal night for Señorita Elisa Santona, one of the Reds . . .!'"

Juana said, "Elisa, it is finished. Why torture yourself?"

"Because I cannot forget."

"Try to forget. Think about Ramón . . .!"

"So now I kill fascists . . ." She swung to Juana. "Do you know Montjuich, in Barcelona?"

Juana nodded wearily.

"Well, after sentencing them we would take off their handcuffs because of ricochets and bind them with rope, pack them into lorries and drive them up to Montjuich. You should have seen their faces! There we would haul them out and line them up to face the city, and we would say to them, 'What fools you are! Because of your stupidity in joining the rebels instead of the Popular Front, you are now looking at Barcelona for the very last time!'" She smiled brilliantly, moving around the room in fevered agitation.

Juana interjected: "Elisa, for God's sake, don't boast of it."

It turned her, and she shouted in Juana's face, "Why not, lady nurse? Certainly I boast of killing fascists! Aren't we here to kill the biggest of them all? I took pleasure in doing it, I can tell you!"

Juana saw the madness of her face; Elisa's eyes were now glittering with an unholy light. "We would sit behind the sand-bagged guns – their backs were to the guns, you understand? – and we'd call to them, 'Look, *amigos*, you can see the dawn come up over the city! Oh, how beautiful is the Plaza de Cataluña in springtime! The flowers! But no more will you hear the Sardana Band, or go with your people to the Toros. How stupid of you to become rebels when you could have been republicans! Now, had you been workers and got up in the morning, you'd have seen the dawn more often! Turn, if you please, and face the guns.'"

"Elisa, *Elisa* . . .!" She was close; Juana reached out to draw her nearer, but Elisa twisted herself away.

"Do not touch me!" She dashed away the tears of her face. Richard, entering the room, shot a brief, inquiring look at them both, and went out again.

Later, when Richard, Juana and Elisa were in the attic, Ramón returned from the rebel Infantería.

Elisa, at the window, saw him first, and cried: "Here he comes!"

Ramón, accompanied by Don Pita, entered the room like a man rejuvenated by events. Elisa ran into his arms, but he firmly and gently rejected her.

"Wine?" whispered the landlord into his face.

"Wine, wine!" exclaimed Ramón, and sat down at the table.

"You're late," observed Richard, while Don Pita slopped wine into a glass. Ramón snapped, "Be reasonable, man, these things take time."

"You met Vega?"

"I met them all – Vega, Chamorro, Fidel Quinto, even Major de Haya . . ."

"Major de Haya? Franco's personal pilot, isn't he?" asked Don Pita.

"He flew Franco here in his Blériot."

Richard said: "If de Haya flew Franco in, he's no doubt flying him out . . ."

"But he isn't," interjected Ramón. "The Caudillo and Vidal Mola are going together by car to Vitoria after the conference here . . ."

"By car? They've both got planes – why travel by road?"

"Because they're inspecting troop units on the way, and visiting the big sub-depot in Miranda. Listen carefully. Mola has his own personal Puss Moth and an allotted pilot – I mentioned him – Captain Chamorro. Chamorro is flying the Puss Moth and Major de Haya's flying the Blériot to Vitoria the day after tomorrow."

"And what happens then?" asked Richard.

"They're to wait on the air-strip at Vitoria to pick up Franco and Mola for another outward journey."

"Where to?"

"Major de Haya flies Franco to Salamanca; Chamorro

163

takes General Mola on to the Basque front – tour of in-
spection."

"But Franco, man, Franco. To Salamanca, you say?"

"Yes. He's due in Salamanca at seven o'clock for a meeting
with the Headquarters staff, and then he goes on to breakfast
with the Portuguese ambassador."

"God," said Don Pita. "He likes his early starts . . ."

Richard said, "But both planes – the Blériot and the Puss
Moth – are flying from the air-strip here the day after
tomorrow – what time?"

"Estimated time of take-off is five a.m. I saw their squadron
orders."

Richard groaned. "The bloody complications! Why the hell
do they want to go by car. Both in the same plane from here
and it would have been easy . . ." He stared into space. The
others sat silently.

Ramón added: "Don't expect him to be convenient, man!
He's Franco."

And Richard said, thoughtfully, "This means that, if he
keeps to his timings, he'll be in the air between Vitoria and
Salamanca between six-thirty and seven a.m.?"

"It would appear so."

Don Pita said, quietly, "If Franco dies as a result of this,
you will know the honour, Señor." He smiled at Ramón. "It
is remarkable espionage."

Ramón said, "It was easy, as I said. I was well received – a
renewal of an old friendship. On this I traded, God forgive
me. Gil is now an important man, and . . ."

"Gil?" interjected Elisa.

"Vega . . . Gil Vega. He's rich and influential. The officers'
mess was full; I became the toast of all. 'How is the war going
for the poor, bloody infantry?' they asked me. 'Are those
Basques still shooting you up? Do not worry, my friend – soon
we fly-boys will be up there in force, then we will give them
Separatism!' I tell you, they are in great form."

All were silent. Ramón stared at their eager faces.

"Tell us more," said Elisa, and bitterness was in her voice.

Ramón warmed to the subject. "Somebody – I think it was
Gil – sent his servant for a gramophone, and on this we
played 'Face to the Sun'. Captain Chamorro's father – an old

Carlist colonel, became very drunk, boasting about his son. 'Look at my fine boy,' he said. 'He is becoming important, is he not? – flying General Mola about. True, Major de Haya here is the Caudillo's personal pilot, but is not my boy equally important? Or does one have to train turkeys to get one's name in the papers . . .'"

"What did that mean?"

Ramón said, "He was referring to the relief of the nationalists at Andújar. Major de Haya trained turkeys to fly in medical supplies. It . . . it was all very embarrassing for Gil, who was throwing the party. Then people started getting drunk. We left the mess, and went to Gil's flat." He smiled apologetically at Elisa. "He has the most beautiful flat, you know, in the Calle de la Merced. His valet called us at dawn and drove us out to the air-strip."

"What for?" demanded Richard.

Ramón said, "Gil was insistent. 'What good is an infantry officer if he doesn't put his head in the air,' he said." Ramón was smiling nostalgically. "He's mad, you know – quite mad, but charming." He turned his eyes to Elisa. "It's marvellous in the Spanish Air Force now since the German Condor Regiment have taken over. 'Take my situation,' Gil said. 'I breakfast late, fly north to pepper the Basques, then back home for a round of golf. A leisurely lunch, another little sortie, then return to the mess in time for a film – last night it was Katherine Hepburn.'" Ramón added, shuddering, "Can I have more wine?"

Don Pita poured him another glass.

"I . . . I was glad Gil took me up. I was able to see the air-strip here properly. There were three planes outside the hangars at the end of the runway – Franco's Blériot, Mola's Puss Moth and another old *bimotor*." He turned to Richard. "The Blériot's in the middle." He raised his hands. "Well, there you have it. Get a bomb into the Blériot."

"If the timings are right," added Juana, thoughtfully.

Ramón raised a pale face. "Could I have done more? I've betrayed a dear friend to get what Emilio wanted."

Don Pita rose in his most elegant manner, saying, with a bow, "It is brilliant, I say. What need of Mata Hari?"

The room was silent after Elisa slammed the door.

* * *

Later, alone in the attic with Richard, Juana said, softly: "She is strange, you know."

"Elisa?" Richard sighed. "Their lives, she and Ramón, are involved with magic, according to Deimler. To quote him – they're an ill-assorted pair. The son of a country gentleman and the daughter of a woodcutter."

"That takes Ramón into a very different society."

"Exactly. One day, apparently, Ramón accompanied his father's agent to Elisa's cottage for the rent. Elisa's father was out and she answered the door. That happens. It's life."

"During the war?"

"Just before the war," answered Richard. His hands moved carefully over the explosives on the table before him. "Ramón's father was a fascist and Ramón followed suit. Then the Guardia shot Elisa's father for supporting the Popular Front; they burned her cottage and sent Elisa to prison. There she was tortured – you've seen her face."

"Yes, I know – she has just told me."

"Ramón was appalled. Overnight, it seems, he changed sides, and became a republican."

"How do you know all this?" asked Juana.

"There's files on everybody in Madrid H.Q."

"Elisa's clearly in love with him. If he loves her, then everything falls into place."

"But he doesn't, does he? That is obvious."

"Does Ramón ever visit his home?"

"At odd intervals. His father lives in the Valles de Ambles. The old man believes he's fighting for the nationalists."

"Do you trust him?"

Richard shrugged. "Deimler gives the orders." Richard put a length of fuse in a detonator and crimped it with his teeth.

"Yes," persisted Juana, "but do you trust him?"

"I'd like to have notice of that question," said Richard.

Richard was making the petrol detonator.

The casing of the detonator was cylindrical, an inch in diameter water-tubing filled with plastic .808 explosive.

Having fashioned the little cylinder, Richard turned his attention to the timing-mechanism: this he constructed from an old wrist watch, removing the minute hand and fixing a

small insulated upstand of wire out of the luminous face.
Another wire fixed to the body of the watch, through a tiny
battery, completed the circuitry.

"I told you to stay out of here, you know."

"Is it so dangerous?" Juana asked.

"Not until I put the explosive in, but it's best done alone."

"Anything that happens to you happens to me," said
Juana "Ever since the Pradales, and it is your fault." She
kissed his face. "I warned you, but you took no heed. Now I
am in love with you, and that is bad."

"On the contrary, it is wonderful."

"No, it is bad. Things will be more difficult because of it."

"That's the penalty of loving, dearest, and we must accept
it. Ramón and Elisa have the same difficulties."

"There is so much danger to come, and I am so afraid."

He kissed her face. "We will do things all the better because
we are lovers. Now there is everything to gain and nothing to
lose. Think of it!"

"I am thinking of that thing on the table," said Juana. "So
small a thing can blow an aeroplane out of the sky?"

He released her from his arms. "It does not have to be
large. A plane is self-destructive through its petrol." Richard
wrapped up his tools.

"This is how you brought Sanjurjo's plane down?"

"No, with a limpet mine. In those days I was closer to the
Internationals. Now I live off the land – improvisation." He
added: "Has Don Pita hired a car?"

"Yes, a big Mercedes. It is in the stable yard."

"Right, fetch the others in for briefing."

Juana called Ramón, Don Pita and Elisa from the bar
below; the gitanos came from the stables. All filed into the
attic.

Richard said: "Listen. This is the outline in brief. I'll give it
to you slowly. Try hard to remember your part in the plan."

Twenty-three

A THREAT OF DUSK was laying a mantle of soft light over Burgos. The snubbed turrets of armoured cars nosed the dying remnants of the sun. Fire-boats, contrasting with their brilliant red, snouted the river mist. The drab crowds of the front-line city were gathering in groups with growing excitement at the prospect of *fiesta*. Mola, the military commander, was allowing a bull-fight on the morrow to boost morale; the proceeds going to assist the Hospital de la Concepción; the matador Manolete being flown in from Córdoba especially for the occasion.

By contrast with the city's spontaneous gaiety, long columns of dejected infantry were coming in from the fighting of the Iron Ring. With their weapons sloped at desultory angles, they tramped along, and the flowers tied to the muzzles of their rifles were withered.

Don Pita standing at the window, said, "Not for you tomorrow's bull-fight, *amigos*. Soon you will be outside Bilbao again. And the Basques will be waiting for you, as before."

Richard jerked his head at him. "Sit, Don Pita. Time's short. We move from here in an hour. You have petrol and oil in the car?"

"The car is ready, Señor," sang the landlord. He crossed himself. "God help him from whom we hired it."

"And rifles – the Winchesters – and Mausers – hand grenades?"

"All packed in the boot, and loaded."

Richard said, "You, Don Pita, and you, Nicolas, will stay here when we leave. But before curfew tonight you will take the car over the river and park it in the grounds of the Convento de la Merced. There you will sleep in it and wait until we come."

"Understood," said Don Pita, and Nicolas scowled. Richard had attached him to the ageing legionnaire, and Nicolas was disgusted.

Richard continued, "The convent is the rendezvous for our escape out of Burgos. Wait there until we join you; defend the car if necessary." To Old Pep and Manolo, he said: "You come with Ramón and me. There will be guards on the air-strip and they'll have to be taken care of . . ."

"Manolo and me, we take care of guards pretty well," said Old Pep, "eh, my son?" and he shoved Manolo. "Leave the guards to us."

Richard asked Don Pita, "You have the uniforms ready, you say?"

"Of the Falangist Militia, Señor. It was the best I could do."

Manolo said with finality, "Old Pep and me, we do not wear the uniform of the fascists, understood?" and he scowled.

"Donkey's arse, do not argue with your betters," cried Old Pep, pushing him. "Me, I would wear the drawers of a woman to kill the Dwarf!"

Richard said, "Juana, you stay here with Elisa and be ready with the medical kit if things go wrong at the air-strip. Elisa, you will serve in the bar."

"Oh, no, I do not! I came to Burgos to fight fascists, not serve them wine!"

And Ramón answered swiftly: "Like Manolo, you will do as you're told. It is dangerous to close the bar on *fiesta* day, is it not?"

"It will look suspicious," confirmed Don Pita. "Manolete fights in Burgos – there will be much drinking. A bar is closed, questions will be asked." He opened his small hands, smiling. "All you do is pour the wine, little lady. And if you do not, the customers will do it for you – remember, please, to take the money."

Juana asked. "When do we join Don Pita at the car?"

"Be there by midday. If we are finished earlier at the airfield, we will contact you here, at the café."

Old Pep said, "Midday is a good time. Many people will be on the streets, going to the bull-fight. Now, what about the weapons?"

"Distribute them."

Ramón lifted a box on to the table and handed out the weapons; a big Colt revolver he gave to Richard; little snub-

nosed Russian pistols he gave to the others, chiefly Vostoks.
Juana refused a weapon; Elisa spun her small-calibre Vostok
round on her fingers, and said, "I come to Burgos to fight
fascists and end up serving them wine." She shoved the pistol into
the hem of her skirt and turned away in disgust.

"And my gun?" asked Nicolas.

"You, my young friend, will share Don Pita's excellent
Kovaks pistol-automatic!"

Richard tossed a Luger pistol across the room and Nicolas
caught it in mid-air, turning it over in his hands with growing
interest. "A present from a German – compensation for
having to stay with Don Pita!"

The first June day had baked Burgos in sun; in contrast, the
nights were cool: low clouds blanketed the moon, the town
stagnated in mist. When Richard, Ramón and the two gitanos
left the Café Suizo before dawn, the wind was cold: before
them, dominating the night, the fortifications of Castillo
reared up like a mailed fist. People were wending homeward.

A few patrolling Guardia Civil were on the streets, especially in the Plaza Mayor; sentries watched from the doors
of the theatre.

They walked briskly, Richard and Ramón in noisy argument. Avoiding the Infantería, they took the Calle de Paloma
eastward from the cathedral: stray dogs peered from the
shadows: the bull-ring turnstiles were barred and shuttered.
Northward, the Santander road was empty. They reached the
outskirts of the air-strip; the clouds paled, the moon came out
in sudden brilliance.

"This is bad," said Richard at the sky. "I preferred the
mist."

The mist hung only in gaseous patches, filling the bomb
craters of the early Burgos fighting; a lunar landscape.

Richard said, "Two sentries, you say?"

Ramón said, "Two. They patrol the wire perimeter, and
are based on the mechanics' hut."

"You're sure of this?"

"I saw them when I flew over the strip with Vega; the same
two were patrolling when we returned from Vitoria."

"Arms?"

"Rifles, I think."

"Would there be a telephone link between the hangar and the Burgos barracks?"

For reply, Old Pep raised his eyes at wires slung in the branches of trees above them.

"I say cut them," grunted Manolo, looking incongruous in his tightly fitting uniform of the Falange.

"No. Later, we may need the telephone."

They went in single file now, seeking cover over the sodden fields where the dew was heavy; it sparkled on the grass in myriad tips of light, a faint penetration of the moon. Richard knelt; they followed his example.

Before them, in the mid-distance, the dim outline of the airfield hangar lumbered into shape.

"The mechanics' hut?"

"To the north of the hangar. We can't see it from here."

Ramón pulled out his Vostok and examined the magazine; seeing this, Old Pep shoved his hawk-like face between him and Richard and drew out his knife. The blade glinted and he drew a gnarled finger across his throat. "This, *amigos*, is the weapon for night; you grip, you hold, you push between the ribs, ah ee!"

"One gurgle, and it is finished," Manolo explained.

"God Almighty," whispered Richard.

"You stay here," commanded Old Pep. "Americanos have big feet and they are noisy. One dies, eh? The knife or the gun makes little difference," and he gripped Richard's shoulder and pulled Manolo after him. Crouching low, they slipped away into the mist.

Crawling after them, following their wet swathes in the grass, Richard and Ramón neared the hangar. Above them was a pole and a wind-sleeve hanging lifelessly. The corrugated mass of the hangar obliterated everything. The mist was wavering in strange shapes about the roof and eaves; wetness gleamed upon the black walls of the massive building.

"Somebody's coming," whispered Ramón, and out of the vapour lumbered Manolo like a bear feasting, and his form was mounded with a burden, and he stooped before them, tumbling from his shoulders the lifeless body of a militia guard. Old Pep slid up behind him. His face was beaded with

dew. His beard hung in wet tendrils on his scraggy chin, and
he said, chuckling, "We present our credentials, comrades –
republican undertakers."

Ramón said, "Only one?"

"Only one guard we could find. Two others are patrolling
in the hangar."

"And the mechanics?"

"In their hut, asleep. But a light is burning in its window."

Richard said, "You do not touch the mechanics, understand?"

"You are wrong about the guards, Señor Ramón,"
whispered Old Pep. "Four we have seen already – one, at
least, is patrolling the outside wire," and Ramón said softly:

"Reinforcements, because Franco is here."

"Get the one who patrols," commanded Richard. "Where
do the telephone wires lead?"

"Into the mechanics' hut, I saw them," answered Manolo.

"Wake the mechanics and they'll telephone the barracks
before we can get to them . . ."

"The knife for gitanos is easy, I tell you," said Old Pep.
"He makes no noise."

"Go, then – get the patrolling guard. Leave the guards in
the hangar to us."

All four crept away; the gitanos to the airfield perimeter
wire, Richard and Ramón to the entrance of the hangar.

Through the mist the mechanics' hut glowed a dim beacon of
welcome. Reaching it, Richard rose noiselessly from his knees
and peered within through a chink in the curtains. On
opposite sides of the small, bare room, two men, the mechanics, lay silently amid the disorder of men who live alone;
strewn papers, the ashes of a dead fire tumbled untidily from
a stove in the middle of the floor.

"Just keep on sleeping," whispered Richard, and lowered
his face from the window. With Ramón leading now, they
crept on all fours to the gaping entrance of the aeroplane
hangar. Outside this, standing on the tarmac, was the old
bimotor Ramón had described.

"Down!" hissed Ramón, and they sank lower into the
soaked grass.

Richard peered. A sentry was lounging against the open door of the hangar. With his rifle slung and tenting his groundsheet, he appeared statuesque, as part of the landscape. Beyond him Richard saw grass move. A head momentarily appeared, then sank back into cover.

"The gitanos!" Ramón whispered. "Leave him to the gitanos!"

The sentry stirred, his first sign of life. The rifle muzzle inadvertently struck the iron door of the hangar; the noise seemed to shatter the night. Then he foraged in his pockets, produced the butt of a cigarette and put it between his lips. His trench lighter glowed as he blew upon it. A faint fragrance drifted over the wet fields. Inhaling deeply, he exhaled the smoke at an obliterated moon. And, at that moment, Manolo came noiselessly out of the grass. He came bare-footed, like a tiger hunting, in crouching swerves, his body wriggling to the obstacles of patchy vetch-grass: Richard saw him sink down. The grasses ceased to wave; the night was still. The sentry smoked on, a man dreaming of life within a yard of death. And then, unaccountably, Manolo rose before him, motionless. The cigarette dropped. The sentry's mouth opened for the cry. Old Pep stepped out of the shadows behind him. The knife flashed in its horizontal glide. With his forearm around the sentry's throat, the old gitano lowered him slowly to the ground and nodded briefly to Manolo, who joined him at the hangar door.

"~~Pablo~~, you said get the patrolling sentry. They don't even obey orders, these two," whispered Ramón.

"They've probably got them all!"

Rising, they ran swiftly to the hangar door and turned to face its blackness. Before them rose the snouted nose of the Blériot, and almost instantly the gitanos came.

"Any more in here?" demanded Richard.

Old Pep grinned, showing his big teeth. "None. We have checked. But three more sentries are patrolling – perhaps two hundred yards away. Three we have killed already."

"Then stand guard," commanded Richard. "I'm going in," and he opened the haversack he carried.

Manolo dragged the dead sentry away.

Kneeling before the Blériot's propeller, Richard drew from

173

the haversack the petrol detonator; the steel cylinder gleamed; it was six inches long, surmounted by the watch, its dial glowing luminously. Richard turned the hour hand of the watch and wound the spring.

Ramón asked, softly: "What time will it explode?"

"Six-thirty."

"And Franco's due to land at Salamanca at seven."

Richard nodded. "This should get him in the air soon after de Haya takes off from Vitoria."

"And if his time-table alters."

"~~Maybe~~, don't mention it!"

"But if it does?"

"Then we fail, don't we – and try again."

Ramón said, his voice strange, "God, you're a queer one, Hanson. This is hit and miss."

"It has to be. We're dependent upon Franco keeping to the time-table."

"But it's all so bare – Emilio sings and you dance to his tune. Who is Emilio, do you even know?"

"I've no wish to," said Richard, his hands working on the fuse. "How do I know what's going on higher up? I take my orders through Deimler."

Ramón glanced about him. The two gitanos were now on guard; Manolo at the hangar door to intercept a patrolling sentry, Old Pep outside the mechanics' hut.

"Aren't you interested in the boys at the top?" asked Ramón.

"Of course not. My role is in the field. I do what I'm told."

Ramón shrugged, disinterested. "I am nosey, that is all. If I am going to die for somebody, I like to know who it is . . ."

"If you're dead, who cares?" Richard climbed up on to the port wing of the Blériot. Ramón stood on guard below.

Richard's immediate world, the moment he unscrewed the plane's petrol intake cap, became filled with the nauseous fumes of gasolene. Taking from his haversack a length of string he attached it to the fuse, positioned himself over the pilot's cockpit above which the intake was located. The control dials glowed like elfin faces from the dark. Behind him another cockpit yawned its emptiness, the one in which Franco would sit.

There came to Richard the calmness that always pervaded such actions, he had found; the ice-cold incomprehension of all about him, save the task in hand. After he had performed this obscenity, he thought, two men would come and sit in the places where he was working now; sit together in the comradeship of soldiers: and in oblivion to danger travel suspended in air, while below them the implement designed for their destruction would tick away their lives. They would talk through the inter-communication; discuss the progress of the war, their families, perhaps, even the state of the weather. And in their conversation give no thought to the man who, with cold design, had planned to blow them to pieces.

The metal fuse clanked dismally down the pipe of the gasolene intake as Richard lowered it, inch by inch.

It was a sheer paranoia, he knew, that such thoughts should come to him; when he had fixed the limpet bomb that killed General Sanjurjo, he had suffered the same emotions; an inability to detach himself from the sufferings of others. It was unprofessional but he could never divorce himself from the relentless pursuit of conscience; the wet faces of wives, the wailing of children rose before him with vivid intensity. But this was war and the job had to be done. A man could die in a million ways and one in war; the manner in which de Haya. the innocent, and Franco, the guilty, would die was a death of relative comfort: one moment sitting with the sun upon their faces, next moment fragmented into oblivion. Did one experience, Richard often wondered, the momentary second of delay, the red blaze of the gelignite . . . before the brain was decimated by skull splinters? The thought haunted him in daytime dreams. Did one feel an instant of limbo as the limbs were blown assunder? Or did one fly from material stability into nothingness with the living's undaunted smile?

If so, then death itself was a fake, he thought. If one had the joy of living, should not one be granted the sadness of dying?

He was sweating badly beneath the tight tunic of his uniform, but not with exertion or fear. It was an emotion he had experienced before, when fitting the limpet mine into Sanjurjo's plane in Lisbon eleven months ago; a combination

175

of exultation and shame. One did these things in the name of patriotism, he had thought afterwards, but paid the eternal penalty of conscience.

It was the action of the dishonourable; a levelling with the extortioner or blackmailer; one who shoots from the dark, aiming for the back.

Trying to obliterate reason, Richard leaned above the tank, inhaling its heady fumes. And saw, in the moment before it disappeared from view, the luminous dial of the watch glowing through the waterproof bag.

Amazingly, the ticking of the watch, despite its immersion in the gasolene, was heavily pronounced: Richard could hear it clearly, funnelling out of the filler-pipe, as out of a megaphone. The detonator was down now, resting on the bottom of the tank; he suspected that it was against one of the baffle-plates of the anti-swill; the tank was only half-full. Swiftly, he worked, knowing that soon the mechanics would arrive to fill it.

Snapping shut the petrol-cap was like snapping off the noises of the earth.

The staff car bringing Major de Haya and Captain Chamorro arrived at five o'clock: now the fields of Fuento were shining gold in weak sunlight.

"They're smack on time," whispered Richard, peering over the ditch.

They came without escort, these two, in a battered old car, and wandered from it towards the aircraft. De Haya was short and stocky, a hero in the eyes of the nationalists; Chamorro was tall and slim. And they walked with a swagger, in flying coat and fur-lined boots, their helmets dangling from their hands. Chamorro, with a glance towards the mechanics' hut, put his fingers to his mouth and whistled shrilly. The hut door opened and the mechanics came out carrying cans of petrol. The two pilots wandered about while the tanks were filled, then de Haya climbed into the cockpit of the Blériot and Chamorro got into the Puss Moth. The mechanics swung the propellers. The two engines burst into sound and smoke. A minute passed while they were warmed, and the airfield was detonating with staccato reports. Then the mechanics pulled away the chocks, and the two planes, led by de Haya's Blériot taxied over the grass and turned into the wind. In wing-sag and smoke, they waddled to the runway, then accelerated, engines thundering.

Richard looked at his watch. It was now five-thirty. There would now be a further long wait, he reflected, before they left to join Don Pita and the women at the car. At that moment Manolo's hairy face peered up from the grass.

"Where's Old Pep?" asked Richard.

Manolo shrugged. "He has answered a call of nature, perhaps? Am I his keeper?"

"And Ramón?"

"Perhaps the same, Señor."

"Then come with me to get these mechanics?"

"We kill them also?"

"We do not kill them."

Ten minutes later, with the two shivering mechanics propelled before them, Richard and Manolo made their way to the hut.

"*Mare del bon Deu!*" exclaimed Manolo, and started forward.

Old Pep was lying across the steps of the mechanics' hut with a knife between his shoulders.

"Pepi, Pepi!" whispered Manolo, and knelt, turning him into his arms. "*Valga'm Deu!*" and he turned a distorted face up to Richard. "Look he is dead. My Pepi is dead . . .!"

The two prisoners stared from one to the other in horrified perplexity. Manolo rose from the ground, his hand going to his knife, and Richard said: "Not them. How could it be?"

Manolo shouted. "Before they left the hut . . .?"

The two mechanics argued in terror, their hands protesting. One knelt, trying to help by drawing out the knife, but Manolo kicked him away, sending him sprawling.

Richard said quietly. "Where's Ramón? Seizing Manolo's shoulders he shook him for sense. "Find Ramón, man. Find Ramón! The same thing might have happened to him."

Before Richard could stop him, Manolo fired twice. The mechanics collapsed together, squirmed feebly, and lay still.

Manolo knelt again and gathered Old Pep against him, saying, "Pepi, *Pepi* . . .?"

Twenty-four

COLONEL LEÓN CARRASCO, attached Gestapo, picked up the telephone in his office at the Infantería, and said, "An urgent call to Avila, please. Pío de Córdoba, I forget the number." Carrasco rose from his desk and looked out over the river. The scene before him appeared like any other day in Burgos, yet this day, he knew, would prove different. From the window, he could see nationalist wounded lying in their cane chairs in the grounds of the Hospital y Presidio. Nuns moved among them in white stateliness; it was a purity that continued with soothing serenity, day by day through the war.

But with General Vidal Mola, Commander of the Army of the North, Second-in-Command to Franco himself, missing on a flight from Vitoria, this day would not be as other days.

The telephone rang. Carrasco returned to his desk.

It rang, too, in a bedroom in distant Avila. Raked from sleep in his Chinese love-pavilion, Pío put a hand out of the sheets and lifted the receiver.

"Pío de Córdoba."

"Ah, Pío! This is León Carrasco."

"God, man!" ejaculated Pío, "the streets aren't aired . . ."

"They are here," replied Carrasco. "Are you still abed?"

Lucía García emerged from under the sheets, saying sleepily, "Who is it, darling?"

Pío waved her away, saying, "It's not yet eight o'clock, Carrasco – don't you ever sleep?"

"*Mala Sombra!*" ejaculated Lucía. "León!" and dived under the bedclothes.

With his hand out to keep her there, Pío said into the telephone: "All right, Rosa, put the tea here."

Carrasco shouted angrily: "Pío, don't fool with me, this is important. Get up, get dressed, and come to my office in Burgos at once – the Infantería."

"Burgos, man? At this time of the morning?"

"Come. It's a matter of life or death."

"It'll have to be." Pío clambered out of the bed and sat on the edge of it. "What's happened, for God's sake?"

"It's Juana."

"What about her?"

"I promised her immunity from arrest, remember? You increased your party subscriptions, I turned a blind eye to her activities, but this time, I fear, she has gone too far."

"What's she been up to?"

"She's right up to her neck with the Hanson partisans. Something big has happened and she's involved. Intelligence are bringing her in and it's out of my hands."

"*Dios mío,*" groaned Pío. "Where is she?"

"Here, in Burgos. Look, I can't say more on an open line." The colonel glanced at his watch. "Can you come straight away?"

Pío smiled at the ceiling. "I've a few things to do, León – but I hope to be with you soon after midday." He glanced at Lucía García who was now pacing the room in panic, a long white negligée flowing out behind her nakedness.

Carrasco said, "Put Lucía on."

"I beg your pardon?"

"Pío, don't trifle with me. I said escort her, not sleep with her. Put her on."

Pío held out the telephone to Lucía who cowered away from it.

"You'd better take it. He knows all about us, my poppet."

Lucía did so, saying tremulously, "Oh, León, my love . . . !"

Carrasco said, "Get out of there, Lucía, do you hear me? Something's about to break. Get out, and don't go back. At this moment especially, I can't afford a scandal."

"Oh ██████," said Lucía, her peasantry showing, and gave the receiver back to Pío. "He knows about us . . . He knows!"

"I must say his tone was a trifle peremptory," said Pío.

Carrasco rang a bell on his desk; as Major Ritter, his aide entered, the colonel asked, "Have you got the time-table?"

"Here, sir."

"Read it to me." Carrasco lolling in his chair, lit a cigarette and blew smoke at the ceiling. The major said, "This is as close as we can get to things, sir, until more information

179

comes in from field intelligence," and he read from a signal form:

0600 Hours   Major de Haya and Captain Chamorro, piloting Blériot and Puss Moth respectively, landed at Vitoria from Burgos. Both planes service-checked and refuelled; normal procedure. Puss Moth had a firing defect; taken to hangar.

0615 Hours   Generalísimo Franco and General Mola arrived by car from Basque front, ready to emplane: the Caudillo to fly to Salamanca, Mola to Burgos. Discussion on air-strip.

0620 Hours   Telephone message from Salamanca; Portuguese ambassador ill, cannot keep appointment with Franco. Franco handed Blériot over to Mola, deciding to wait for repair of Puss Moth. Meanwhile tour military installations in Vitoria arranged.

Major Ritter glanced at Carrasco. "There was now no urgency for the Generalísimo to get to Salamanca, you see. . .?"

"Of course, I realise that," snapped Carrasco. "Read on."

0620 Hours   Urgent telegram from General Dávila, Burgos Infantería, to General Mola, asking him to return without delay – general staff requirement.

0630 Hours   General Mola took off for Burgos in Blériot. Piloted by Captain Chamorro.

Carrasco was smoking steadily. "And no news since – no wireless or morse reports from agents?"

"Nothing at all, Colonel."

"The Blériot was serviced at Vitoria, you say?"

"A service-check, sir, nothing more."

"Somebody's head will roll for this."

"Looks to me like sabotage, sir. Chamorro was an excellent pilot."

"Really? I think that's a particularly stupid observation, Ritter."

Carrasco was pacing about, sending glances of disdain at his aide, who stood clutching the signal. Major Ritter didn't like Carrasco, and was aware that the colonel didn't like him. Further, the major realised with some pride that, as a fighting man, he wasn't much good at administration. He had a young wife down south who was expecting a baby and they feared the birth would be difficult. Also, his wounds ached, but he could not tell such weaknesses to the colonel, whose treasurership of the Falange was only a cover for his role of espionage director. Men like this, Ritter knew, could liquidate another on a whim.

Carrasco barked at him, "Are we certain that Burgos was Mola's destination?"

"According to Movements, yes. The air-strip log at Vitoria . . ."

"Yes, yes, but you know Mola. He's a variable fellow . . ."

"Argumentative, is the word, sir, according to the Caudillo!"

Carrasco narrowed his eyes, mildly surprised. "Don't be a fool, Ritter."

"No, sir."

Distantly, Carrasco heard the Gestapo telephones ringing. Outside in the yard a clutch of apprehensive republicans were awaiting transport after their interrogation, their hands tied with rope; always a bad sign, thought Carrasco, vaguely. Some, bloodstained, were having to be supported.

Carrasco said. "Surely a crash-landing would have been reported by now? *God*, Ritter – Mola left Vitoria at half-past six. He's two hours overdue already."

The aide replied. "Peasants are notorious for curiosity. If they found a wreck they'd have to fetch the mayor before reporting it."

"I'm a very worried man."

The major clicked his heels. "The moment there's news, I will let you know, sir."

After Ritter had gone, Carrasco put his feet up on his desk and looked out on to the bright river. Unhappily, he thought, this would put an end to his hope of attending the bull-fight: though that, he reflected, could be unspectacular unless Manolete was certain to perform. Then his office door opened and Major Ritter returned: his face was pale under its tan. He said, "A telephone call from Briviesca, Colonel. The wreckage of a plane has been found."

"By whom?"

"A Guardia patrol, sir. Two occupants; one not yet identified, but they think it's General Mola."

"Oh, God!" Carrasco rose from his chair. The aide continued: "They believe it's the general, but they are certain it is Captain Chamorro. His log book has been found – name, rank and number. Colonel Chamorro, his father, is stationed at Valladolid, and he has been informed."

"They're that sure!"

"It's the Blériot all right," said Ritter.

Carrasco sat down and covered his face with his hands. Telephones had stopped ringing in the building, as if a pall of grief had descended. Ritter said, softly, "Can . . . can I get you anything, sir?"

"No. Mola was a dear friend, Ritter. Please leave me . . ."

When the aide had gone Carrasco got up and locked the door.

Into the telephone he said: "This is Colonel Carrasco, Gestapo Headquarters. Put me through to General Dávila, please."

The line clicked. Carrasco waited.

A voice said: "Dávila."

"Ah! Carrasco here. Listen carefully, sir. Briviesca – a few minutes ago – both dead."

There was a pause. Carrasco heard the other take a deep breath.

Then: "When . . . when did it happen?"

The colonel glanced at his watch. "I'd say about seven o'clock this morning. They've only just been found."

"This news is accurate?"

"It's Mola all right. The pilot – Captain Chamorro, has been identified."

"And the Hanson people? Don't let Ritter in on that, for God's sake."

"I'll handle it personally, sir."

"Excellent. Thank you. God, what a mess! I'm appalled."

"Of course, sir."

Carrasco replaced the receiver and rang for Major Ritter, who entered.

The Colonel said: "The General of Administration is very upset, which is to be expected. He is a little concerned about the Hanson partisans, too. There's no proof, you know, that they are actually operative in Burgos. Let sleeping dogs lie, he suggests. Contact Captain Echevarría of the Guardia. I want the woman Elisa Santona – she's the escapee from San Pablo, remember? – the only one the Guardia have a case against. Tell Echevarría to get rid of her. Where is she at the moment?"

"The Café Suizo, with the de Córdoba woman."

"And after he has done that to wait for me there. I want a word with the young countess."

Carrasco lit a cigarette and stared out at the bright river. "But the rest can go, as I say. We don't want Hanson and his people cluttering up the interrogation centre. Mola's death was an accident, pure and simple; Captain Chamorro was flying too low in the mist. Large scale arrests at this stage could give an impression of enemy success."

"I understand, Colonel."

Carrasco glared at Ritter. "Yes, but do you? Half the time you don't, Ritter, and that's your bloody trouble. Make a mess of this and you'll account to General Dávila."

"I . . . I'll do it now, sir."

After the aide had gone, the colonel said into the telephone, "Gestapo Liaison, please . . ." He waited. "Señor Tano?"

"Tano, Gestapo Liaison."

"Carrasco here, Tano. Look, I don't want Ritter hanging around here any more. He already knows too much. He's got a couple of things to do today, but I want him out of it by this time tomorrow."

"Yes, sir."

"And Tano . . ."

"Yes."

"Get rid of him – not the Basque front; be original."

"I understand. Is everything all right otherwise?"

"It has gone perfectly."

Carrasco was about to leave the office when the telephone rang again; he picked up the receiver.

A voice said: "Colonel León Carrasco . . .?"

"Speaking."

"Colonel Carrasco, attached Gestapo Administration, Burgos Infantería?"

"The same."

"Generalísimo calling from Salamanca Headquarters. Please hold, Colonel, until required."

Carrasco smiled at the ceiling. "Certainly."

After a full minute of waiting, a soft voice said, "Is that you, León?"

"Speaking, my general!" Automatically Carrasco came to attention.

There was a pause; then: "In a word, thank you."

"Thank you, my general. It is an honour to serve you."

"And . . . and give me a hand-written report on these proceedings, will you? – short and concise. Bring it to Salamanca tomorrow, I would also like to see you personally . . ."

"I will write it now, my general."

The colonel replaced the telephone receiver. With a new and jaunty step he moved around the office. Franco, he thought, always signed death warrants after their execution; it was an irony he reserved for his enemies. For his friends he reserved an unerring gratitude. Success such as this – the death of Vidal Mola – one of the Caudillo's most argumentative and ambitious comrades-in-arms, could be gloriously repaid. It could even extend to a provincial governorship; even a position of influence in the junta itself.

Carrasco decided to write the report at once while it was fresh in his mind. This he did, excluding everyone from his office. It was nearing midday when he walked along the Espalón towards the Café Suizo where he was due to meet the captain of the local Guardia; there to interview Juana de Córdoba in the presence of Pío, her husband.

Twenty-five

OVERNIGHT, DON PITA and Nicolas had slept in the hired Mercedes in the grounds of the Convento de la Merced and listened, before sleeping, to the evening vespers of the nuns in plain-song; their soprano voices drifted down to them into the car.

Te Deum, non nobis Domine, nunc dimittis . . .

Faintly to Don Pita's nostrils came the smell of incense, and Nicolas, asleep beside him in the front seat, remembered . . .

Once, in the fortress cathedral of San Juan, in Badajoz, after a pilgrimage there to pay homage to the soul of his father, he and his mother had knelt in the pews within the great gilt and gold, and listened to such chanting.

Nicolas saw again his mother's face in profile; her black mantilla draping her face as she prayed. Now the face was not the face of his mother, but that of Don Pita, and when the old legionnaire spoke it was not his voice in the pews of the cathedral San Juan:

'Nicolas,' said his mother, 'I have but one ten *peseta* piece in my pocket as alms for the priest when the plate comes round, you hear me?'

'I hear you,' replied Nicolas, and his mother opened her hand and he saw the coin lying in her palm.

'I have nothing to give you to put upon the plate in offering and it is wrong that the plate should pass you by, this would shame us,' said his mother. 'You still possess the ten *pesetas* given you by your father?'

'It is here,' answered Nicolas, and held up the coin and it shone bright silver from long wear in his pocket.

'Give that then, my son,' but when the alms plate came round the pews Nicolas rattled the money therein with the tips of his fingers and put the ten *peseta* piece back into his pocket, maintaining, as he did so, that he owed nothing to Christ.

Nicolas had expected to hear the chanting stop at this perfidy, but it did not. Now, sitting in the car, Nicolas heard it again.

"You doze, Small One?"

"Not now, Don Pita, I am wide awake," said Nicolas, and watched as the landlord tipped a flask of *anís* to his lips.

"Can I have some, too?" asked the boy.

"Later, when you're a man, you can swig *anís* to your heart's content."

Nicolas cried, "I see. I can fight the Moors, but I am too young to drink *anís*, is that it?" He was wrathful, his face red with outrage.

"Señor, I apologise to you," replied Don Pita. "I cannot imagine what came over me," and he gave the flask to Nicolas who tipped it, eyes clenched and then choked, coughing and Don Pita struck his back for breath.

Later, still waiting for Richard and Juana and the others to come, Nicolas said, "For years now I have been fighting with the Guardia, and have killed . . ."

"And now, like me, they leave you behind, eh? It is disgusting."

"When I am older, I will return to Burgos to repay you wine – we will drink a bottle together, old man."

"You repay me with your company."

The old legionnaire thought of the nights of summer and the moon over Burgos, and the attic where he had loved Josefina; unknowingly, Nicolas invaded the kisses of Josefina's mouth.

"That is good *anís*. I doubt if I've tasted better. I drink quite a lot, you know," said he.

"Doubtless, you can hold your liquor."

"The lead-labourer of my village drinks much, but it makes him vomit. He is disgusting."

"Who is this?"

"Diego Díaz, who is to marry my mother. When I return home he will be in my father's bed. His sandals will be in our *pueblo*, his cattle will be in my father's stalls. Yet he is twice my mother's age!"

"Small worry for that. I was twice the age of Josefina."

"Age is not important?"

"Not if this Diego Díaz loves her twice as well."

Nicolas dozed, dreaming, in the fumes of alcohol, of the shining ten *peseta* piece he would one day give to the woman of his choice. "Do you admire the lady Juana?" he asked suddenly.

"Greatly," answered Don Pita, collecting himself. "As you say, she is a lady. You have said it all."

"With only eight years or so between us, I think I will give a ten *peseta* piece to her," said Nicolas. "I was worried about the difference in our ages before, but now I am not."

Don Pita rubbed his chin and smiled at the moon. "Without doubt, my son, this is a truly excellent *anís*. Remind me. I beg you, to order more."

Elisa was behind the bar of the Café Suizo when Captain Echevarría came.

The room was full; outside the crowds, awaking that day to a *fiesta*, went arm in arm along the crowded pavements; their excitement quenching as a Guardia squad threaded through them to the door of the café. Clamorous expectations of the Manolete bull-fight died to a whisper within the bar; glasses lowered, feet moved uneasily. People rose singly and in groups, trooping out into sunlight. Soon the bar was empty, save for Elisa and the policemen.

Captain Echevarría approached heavily, saying, "You are Elisa Santona?"

Two of the men raised their rifles; another secured Elisa's wrists with handcuffs. She whispered, "*Què Veleu . . .?*

"It makes no difference what we want, if you are Elisa Santona," said the captain, and seized the handcuffs and twisted Elisa away from the bar, and she stood, head bowed, unspeaking.

"Search her."

A man did so, running his hands over Elisa's thin body; another cried: "There is a gun here!"

Echevarría jerked his head. "Who else is here?"

"Nobody," said Elisa.

"Where's the de Córdoba woman, then?"

"She's out. She has gone to the bull-fight."

"I think we'll take a look," said Captain Echevarría.

Juana, given new medical equipment by Don Pita, was rolling out bandages in the attic when the door opened and Captain Echevarría, with a pistol held out before him, entered.

"Juana de Córdoba?"

"Yes."

"We'll make ourselves comfortable until Colonel Carrasco arrives."

"Colonel Carrasco?" said Juana, askance.

With an unconcern she did not feel, Juana continued to roll bandages.

The captain sat down heavily, his jack-boots cocked up on the table.

Colonel Carrasco entered the Café Suizo. Captain Echevarría, upstairs with Juana, saw him arrive and hurried down to the bar to meet him.

Carrasco asked immediately; "You've arrested Elisa Santona?"

"Yes, my Colonel."

"And Señora de Córdoba?" Carrasco's eyes drifted slowly around the room with its bright little bar and clustered wicker tables.

"She's upstairs, sir."

Carrasco pushed passed the Guardia, wandered to the bar and helped himself to cognac. He asked quietly, "Your name again?"

"Echevarría, sir."

"Echevarría . . .? That's a Basque name, isn't it?"

"Why, yes, sir."

Carrasco smiled, turning away. "Unhealthy, surely, at a time like this? The Basques, you know, are causing some difficulties . . ."

The captain shifted uneasily.

"Still," continued Carrasco, "who can help his antecedents? You're responsible for the town security, are you not, Captain?"

"Yes, my Colonel."

"And that includes security at the airport?"

The man nodded.

"So, is the airport secure?"

The captain paled. His dark jowls trembled, and Carrasco said, "You are in trouble if it is not, my friend. General Mola has been killed, and the plane that killed him took off from here this morning."

"Mola, dead?" Echevarría crossed himself. *"Por Dios!"* He stared about him in agitation. "But surely, an accident . . .?"

"Probably," replied Carrasco. He watched the captain over his glass. "But the search will be for whipping boys, my Basque friend, if airport security is as lax in Burgos as it appears to be in Vitoria."

Echevarría was sweating. The trembling of his hands grew; sweat beaded his forehead and he wiped it into his hair. Turning his back upon him, Carrasco said, softly, "I have just received a telephone call from one of our agents. Security up at your air-strip is a bloody shambles. Get up there and tidy it up. Are you listening, Echevarría?"

The captain was now rigidly to attention.

A clamour was growing beyond the café door. People were chanting, "Manolete! Manolete! Manolete!" Soon, Carrasco thought vaguely, when they hear of Vidal Mola's death the chanting would change to wailing; the Navarrese troops Mola commanded worshipped him.

Carrasco said now: "A bloody shambles, so clean it up, Echevarría, unless you want an official inquiry. Get up there now. Arrest the mechanics, the guards – anyone on duty. Execute them summarily, you understand? On the spot. I want no questions, no chatter, and I want no witnesses. And neither, unless I'm much mistaken, do you."

"Yes, my colonel."

"Land in front of me under interrogation, and you'll know what to expect. You've fallen down on your job, Echevarría, and I won't spare you. Neither will the Gestapo. When you've finished at the air-strip, report back here."

Carrasco poured himself another glass of cognac, smiling faintly as Captain Echevarría hurried away.

The colonel was about to go upstairs to Juana when the figure of Pío appeared on the glass of the café door.

"Why, Pío!" The colonel was effusive. "You're on time for once!"

Beyond Pío's diminutive figure Carrasco saw the *feria* crowds gaping in admiration at the enormous Hispano standing by the kerb.

Carrasco closed the door behind Pío: he, dapper in a white cotton shirt, monocled and well-groomed, entered with aplomb. "Where's Juana?"

"You're alone?"

"I drove myself. Fonseca's of another generation when it comes to speed. Where is she, León?"

"Upstairs. Compose yourself, my friend." Carrasco went to the bar and poured another glass.

Pío said with fussy charm: "God! What's she done this time, for Heaven's sake?"

Carrasco gave him the cognac. "This time, Pío, I can do little for her. This is why I sent for you. There's been a partisan attack on the airfield here and Vidal Mola is dead."

Pío's eyes widened; "General Mola?"

"Actually his death was an accident – his plane crashed in the mist. But you can see the dangers, can't you? Mere public grieving for an accident, but a Gestapo hunt if assassination is proved."

Pío sat down at a table. "Oh my God!" he said.

Carrasco shrugged. "Normally, you could take Juana back to Avila – get her right out of it. But this time I simply dare not overlook it."

"You're sure Juana's involved? You're absolutely sure?"

"You know damned well she is! For Heaven's sake, Pío – what's she doing up here in Burgos?"

"What happens now, then?" asked Pío.

Carrasco sipped at his glass. "They've got one of her accomplices, an Elisa Santona. The others, as far as I know, have already got away."

"But so far you've managed to keep Juana out of it?"

"Yes, but for how long?"

There was a silence. Pío said flatly. "It'd be a dreadful scandal, you know. As a major subscriber to the Falange, questions concerning the loyalty of a countess would raise the nationalist roof. Would the junta like it?"

"That's why I sent for you, my friend. I'm in a terrible quandary."

"But what can I do to help?" Pío spread his small hands.

"Possibly you can save her Gestapo interrogation. It's only a question of time before the other woman talks and the Gestapo aren't much concerned with Falange party funds. The rank of countess won't mean a lot to them, nor the great name de Córdoba. But I'll tell you a name that will."

Pío frowned up at the colonel.

"Emilio," said Carrasco.

"Emilio. Who the devil's he?"

"Emilio," said the other with tolerant charm, "is the operational director of republican espionage. We know Deimler runs the International circus in Madrid, but we don't know the identity of the man operating the field groups . . ."

"As a financial secretary you're well versed . . ." interjected Pío.

"I . . . I have, shall I say, my espionage contacts?"

"Why is Emilio so important?"

"Because he runs the groups, as I say. People like Hanson take their orders from him; the cell here in Burgos is only one of four, apparently. They exist to one end; the assassination of Franco. The attempt here, for instance, was upon the Caudillo, but they got Mola."

"Good God!"

"Thank God, you mean. Mola can be replaced, Pío. Franco cannot."

"And the attempt is not to be made public knowledge?"

"Of course not. An air accident. Assassination produces martyrs and that's the last thing we want." Carrasco began to wander the room, glass in hand. "Things aren't going well up at the Basque front; what we badly need is a nationalist success. The arrest of Emilio would produce public acclaim."

"Therefore the necessity for Juana to talk."

The colonel nodded.

"Perhaps she doesn't know?"

"She knows all right. She's Hanson's lover, or perhaps you're not aware of it?"

Pío said, examining the end of his cigarette. "Torture?"

"A little persuasion." Carrasco nodded towards the door.

Juana was standing by the attic window when Pío and Carrasco entered, the latter locking the door behind him.

She said, staring, "Pío! What are you doing here?"

Pío kissed her hands. "Oh dear, you're in trouble this time, make no mistake . . ."

"Where's Elisa?" She was looking past him at the colonel.

"The woman serving in the bar?" asked Carrasco. "She's been arrested. At this moment she's under interrogation."

"As you will be," added Pío, "unless I can make you see sense . . ."

Juana was watching them both. Her heart was thumping against her shirt. She didn't trust Carrasco, and Pío little better, and she was inwardly frantic for Richard's safety. She heard a clock in the town strike one and saw Carrasco glance at his watch. With luck, she thought, Richard and the others would be at the convent by now. But Elisa . . .

"Then what do you want of me?"

The thought of pain brought to her a numbing weakness. Elisa had known so much pain . . . the thought suddenly incensed Juana.

Carrasco was speaking and she turned to him. He said, ". . . in minutes the Guardia will return. And the moment they take you I can do nothing to help you, Juana. But help me in my inquiries and you can return with Pío to Avila. Nobody will be the wiser. I will even promise to get the woman Elisa Santona away to safety, but you must do your part . . ."

"What do you want to know?"

"What does the name Emilio mean to you?"

Juana turned to the window.

She was no actress, and she knew it. At school, in childhood, she was always seconded to minor roles in the drama classes, and she was aware now that the immediacy of the question had shocked her into betrayal.

Pío said quietly, behind her. "My darling, it's quite obvious that you recognise the name. For God's sake . . ." He joined her at the window.

Juana said, screwing at her hands: "I don't know. I've never heard it before."

"That's remarkable," said Carrasco. "Morse transmissions were continuous between Hanson and Emilio . . ."

Juana swung to face him. "I tell you, I know nothing. And Elisa knows nothing, either!"

Pío said, still facing the window. "I think you should know something, Juana. You're not talking to the treasurer of the Falange now, my love; León is the director of nationalist espionage, without a doubt – are you not, Colonel? Probably also the founder of the *Somaten*, the S.I.F.N.E., perhaps, even the Mapeba people in France. His proposal is to torture you for this information – no dead cats being allowed to land in the lap of the junta!" He raised a hand, gesturing slightly. "He will torture you, without a doubt. For this you can take my word."

Carrasco frowned at Pío, and said, "Your husband's well informed." He lit a cigarette. "Meanwhile, who is Emilio?"

Juana moved away, but Carrasco caught her wrist and twisted her down on to a chair. There he stood with his feet astride, the cigarette in his hand. "Now listen to me. I want his identity – what is he, a businessman, a military man like Deimler? Where he is based. What do the others care about you? Hanson is gone – Ramón Barro, the gitanos, while the controllers like Deimler and Emilio sit in safe places. Who is left? Two women – you and Elisa Santona. Are men like this worth protecting?"

Pío said, "Tell him, for God's sake, Juana. We'll get no peace until you do."

Carrasco held the lighted end of the cigarette before Juana's face. He said, softly. "Look, look. Into your eyes? And this will be nothing to what the Gestapo will do to you. They have your record – the Galapagar attack on the life of the Caudillo – you even harboured Hanson under your roof . . ." He smiled at Pío. "Did you know that? – in your own house, Pío." Carrasco bent over the chair. "One last chance now – who is Emilio . . . who is Emilio?"

A fist hammered the door. Carrasco turned his head. "Open it, that will be the Guardia." He straightened. "Well, perhaps, in your own time now, you'll tell the Gestapo."

Pío unlocked the door and swung it back.

Fonseca stood on the threshold with a gun in his hand. He said, his pale, fat face expressionless: "Don't move, Colonel . . . Move a finger and I'll shoot."

Carrasco slowly turned.

Fonseca said: "Get his revolver."

Pío did so, moving swiftly across the room, saying: "God, where did you get to? I thought you were never coming. The Guardia are due in minutes." Pío turned to Carrasco. "You, come with us!" Gripping the colonel's arm he pushed him towards the door.

Fonseca grasped Juana's hand. "Quick, lady, *quick*! Down to the car."

Pío, with Carrasco's own revolver held against the colonel's ribs, followed Fonseca and Juana down into the bar. Elisa's little Vostok pistol was lying on a table; Fonseca automatically picked it up, and swung open the bar door. Light and air struck Juana's face. The *feria* beat about them. She saw a small sea of bobbing heads; the war appeared to have been forgotten; it was more like the madness of an *encierro*, she reflected.

Suddenly the crowd parted and Captain Echevarría and four policemen came striding down the pavement, brushing people aside. From the back seat, while Fonseca started the Hispano's engine, Pío prodded with the gun.

"You are returning to your headquarters at Avila," he said. "A word out of place, León, and you are dead."

Fonseca, Juana noticed, averted his face as the captain stooped, saluting.

"Reporting, sir," said Echevarría, "as you ordered."

The engine started with a roar. Pío, beside Juana in the back seat, prodded harder into Carrasco's body.

The colonel said: "Stay on guard here, Captain. I am returning to Avila."

"Avila, sir?" Echevarría looked nonplussed, staring at Juana.

"You . . . you've got the Santona woman all right . . .?"

"Why, of course, sir."

"Then do as you're told. Stay here on guard. I'm returning to Headquarters at Avila." Carrasco barked the words.

Instantly the captain drew up to attention. Juana closed her eyes with relief. Fonseca passed a hand over his pale, sweating face as he let in the clutch. Pío, for his part, grinned amiably at Carrasco's stern profile, saying, "Well done, León. That was really quite professional, you know." His expression changed. "Try to maintain the standard until we're clear of this bloody place."

Juana frowned. Despite the tension, the words engaged her. She had never heard Pío swear before.

Twenty-six

Fonseca nosed the big Hispano through the *feria* crowds. On the bridge of Santa María an unsuspecting sentry gave Carrasco a salute, which he returned with a wave, under threat of Pío's gun. On Juana's directions the car turned into the grounds of the Convento de la Merced. Seeing it coming, Richard and Manolo ran to firing positions; from the front seat Don Pita and Nicolas levelled their weapons.

As the Hispano swept up, Juana slid down her window and cried: "Quick, we're getting out."

Richard straightened, staring at Carrasco while Fonseca turned the Hispano in a circle. Richard shouted, running beside it, "Where's Elisa?"

"I'll tell you later. Follow us!"

Don Pita started the Mercedes' engine; its wheels skidded as he swung it after the Hispano: He reached the convent entrance just in time to see the bigger car speeding eastward along the Calle de Madrid, out of Burgos.

Incoming crowds, the after-work labourers of the farms, were thronging into Burgos, slowing the cars' progress: passing squads of Navarrese troops, unaware of their general's death, came to the salute in harsh commands at the sight of Carrasco's uniform; a few officers, slowing their pace, peered into the back of the Hispano at Juana with faintly questioning glances.

Rain began to fall; the crowds thinned. The butler increased the big car's speed.

Carrasco said, speaking for the first time since his capture: "This is madness, Pío. You won't get away with it, you know."

"Don't lay a bet on it." Pío clapped his small hands together as if with delight; the imp, thought Juana, had apparently returned.

The colonel said: "There are questions Juana can answer and it was a legitimate interrogation."

"Without a doubt," said Pío, suavely. "If I recall you threatened to blind her. God alive, man, I had to do something." He looked aggrieved.

"You'll answer to the Falange, not to me. You are abducting a nationalist officer. The Caudillo himself will be interested."

"No doubt it'll cost me a few hundred thousand *pesetas* for the Caudillo's charities," said Pío.

Juana interjected, "Where are we going, Pío?"

"At this moment, anywhere away from Burgos."

"Back to Avila, you said?"

"Not us, eh, Calvo?" Pío shouted it at the butler in front. "Paris, London – Calvo, León and me. What does it matter, my love? You insist upon getting yourself into these impossible situations, and we have to get you out of them, don't we?" He patted her knee confidentially. "You and your chocolate soldier are going to France?"

"That, I believe, is the intention," added Juana.

"To France, to France! *La Belle France, vive la France!*" Pío waved the gun about. "There you can make love to your heart's content and give the poor French the taste of a dedicated republican. *Vaya, hombre!*" and he pushed Carrasco. "You said once, I believe, that I'd be safer without her, and there's a lot in that. Are the others following?"

Fonseca, leaning to look into the driving mirror, nodded silently.

Juana watched them both, her eyes drifting from Pío to the butler.

The change in them, she had suspected earlier, was being confirmed as the miles flew under the Hispano's wheels. It was a different Pío, Juana reflected: true, the impish drollery was still present, but it was forced; it was like a man acting. Fonseca showed nothing of the warmth and concern he had expressed for her in the past. And in the disarming and capture of Colonel Carrasco in the café – himself a trained soldier – both had moved with the assurance of gangsters and the speed of athletes. Certainly, she knew now that the butler's entrance at the right moment had been planned – no doubt, she considered, by a signal from the window. Meanwhile, Fonseca was handling the big car more like a racing driver than a butler, swinging it, one-handed, around the narrowing bends, and the following Mercedes, with Richard aboard it, was clearly having difficulty in maintaining the pace. The sun had gone now, obliterated by thunderous clouds, a premature dusk; the rain was scything across sodden fields and blustering about the car; the wind, rising to a gale, bending the roadside trees into crippledom.

Big sierra country began to loom about them, and Pío said, breaking the endless silence: "Where are we now?"

"A mile or two from Eneríz," replied Fonseca.

"Stop the car."

The Hispano slowed, pulling towards the verge, then stopped.

"What happens now?" asked Carrasco sardonically, "the official execution?"

"*Por Dios!*" exclaimed Pio. "It would be no less than you deserve." He touched the butler's shoulder. "Calvo, back to the others and tell them to wait. And to stay closed, too. I don't want an audience . . ."

Through the rear window Juana saw the Mercedes stop at Fonseca's signal, and he hurried towards it.

Pío said, turning to Juana: "Right, Juana, here we part. This is what you wanted, I take it, and this is what you've got." He smiled faintly. "We all get what we deserve, don't we? As I just said to the colonel here . . ."

For answer Juana stared at him, and Pío continued, "Get out, go back to Hanson, get in with him and drive away – north, if he's got any sense, over the border. Stay in Spain, Juana, and you'll answer for it – I won't help you again."

"And you, Pío?"

"We – that is, León and I?" He clapped Carrasco on the shoulder, the old Pío momentarily returning. "We are going to Avila – temporarily, shall we say, until we sort things out? My God, León, there's a lot to sort out, isn't there!"

The colonel sat in moody disregard, hunched like a bear at feed.

Juana said, "Back to Rosa, Pío?" and his eyes instantly danced.

"Possibly," he replied. "Or Lucía García, eh, Carrasco? We will take the choice between us, eh? 'How tedious is honour

– I am bored by what is good for me,' remember *Los Vargas*, Colonel? 'All lust is life, all life is then perfection!'" Pío chuckled at the car roof. "What discerning husband sticks to one wife? Women! Only a fool turns the pages of last year's almanac." Reaching out, he swung open the car door. "Just hope and pray he sticks to you, you know these Americans."

"Goodbye, Pío." Juana stood at the door. The rain beat about her.

Fonseca was leaving the Mercedes. She could hear his complaining voice and Richard's deeper replies. Hurrying past Juana he entered the Hispano without a word and started the engine. Reaching out, Pío took and kissed Juana's hands.

"Goodbye, my darling," he said.

She stood watching while the Hispano roared away. Richard, now driving the Mercedes, slid it up beside her.

"What was that all about?" he said.

Strangely, she could not reply.

Despite the presence of Colonel Carrasco in the front seat, they had delays at the road blocks outside Avila; it was therefore near midnight when Fonseca turned the Hispano through the western gate of Pío's House. Only Agustín saw the car slide up to the lakeside and park in the cover of the willows beside the Chinese love-pavilion. Here, from a side window, a small light was burning. Pío knocked. The entrance door of the pavilion opened; Lucía García stood aside as the men entered. Pío brushed past her without a word or glance; Colonel Carrasco followed, projected in front of Fonseca, who held a gun.

"*Caramba!*" The ejaculation was quiet; the shock of seeing Lucía there was in Carrasco's face.

Lucía García said curtly: "You have searched him?"

Reaching a little room, Pío turned to face them. "Of course. And found this." He held up the report that the colonel had written for Franco, adding, "Yesterday's date. It's my guess that he was due to present it at the Salamanca Headquarters tomorrow."

Fonseca said, glancing at his watch: "Señor, it is already tomorrow."

"He has talked?" demanded Lucía.

199

"He is of the *Somaten*, lady," replied the butler. "He will not talk."

"He will talk all right, will you not?" Lucía smiled into Carrasco's face, and he said, smiling faintly, "Well, well, who would have believed it. The Whore of Madrid . . .!"

"A whore for the republic," said Pío, and pointed to a chair. "Sit."

Colonel Carrasco sat; raising a hand he wiped blood from his face.

Lucía said, joining Pío at a desk, "We all have our opera cloaks, León. Yours, if I recall, was that of party treasurer?" She smiled at him, her face in shadow, but her hair was bright fair in the light of the single lamp.

The colonel said, and he was no longer smiling, "The tragedy of this game is that one can become quite fond of people . . ."

"Not a game, León – that was your trouble, your weakness – that was how you played it. A drama, my friend." Lucía nodded down at him. "A Spanish tragedy. For you, I fear, an unhappy dénouement."

Pío asked, rifling papers at the desk, "There can't be time for this – is everything here, Lucía?"

She assented, bending above him. "The boat, the *Marie Tours*, leaves Vigo at midday – that gives us twelve hours from now – ample time . . ."

"Bound for Bordeaux? Why Bordeaux, for God's sake?"

"Because Deimler orders Bordeaux. *Por Dios!*" Her voice rose and her eyes opened wide. "Am I the International? You tell me to ask him . . ."

"All right, all right," snapped Pío. "The Gestapo official stamp, what about that?"

"It is there, man, if you look."

Turning, she ran her fingers through her hair in exasperation. "It is all there. What the hell do you think I have been doing? Matilde's forger has managed military passes through Salamanca and Orense – stamped and signed. The passports, the sailing tickets, the French visas . . ."

Pío interjected: "You could have argued about Bordeaux, woman. What about extradition?"

"All right, what about it? Isn't Deimler supposed to know?

France, he says, Bordeaux, he says. You try arguing, *hombre!*"
Pío sat back, his small hands clasped, his elbows on the
desk. "I prefer Lisbon."

"*Santa María!*" Lucía tossed up her hands. "He prefers
Lisbon." She broke into a tirade of protest.

Carrasco, from his chair in a corner, watched. In anger, he
thought, she was even more beautiful.

Within the containment of approaching death, he was
experiencing a calmness he had never expected. Soon, he
knew, he would be interrogated. They had already found on
his person the report he had written for Franco. It was top
secret and they had found it, so even if they spared him now,
the nationalist junta wouldn't. Franco himself, earlier so
complimentary, would order his death sentence. He had been
a fool – he who so often called Ritter a careless fool – to the
extremity of foolishness.

Strangely, Carrasco was relieved that the play, at last, was
over; Lucía was right, he reflected, it was a Spanish tragedy, a
drama. And yet, within its acts, he thought, he had enjoyed
her. Yes, he had enjoyed Lucía García as few men enjoyed a
woman: there was a deep privilege in the ownership, however
brief, of such astonishing beauty. The Whore of Madrid. How
well she had played her part – even Franco had been charmed
by her at the Subscribers' Meeting, he'd heard it said. No, not
a whore, not at all . . . she who made love like a prim Spanish
wife, then knelt at the bed in prayer. Vaguely, Carrasco
wondered now if he loved her. He lifted his eyes to her face.
Even here her loveliness was enhanced by the ornate room;
she appeared as part of the tapestries, of the kruen, the gilt
and the gold . . . despite her drab travelling clothes of brown
tweed.

Now she was angrier than ever with Pío, growing furious in
protest, and she cried, her hands twisting together: "All right,
all right – you want Lisbon, you go to bloody Lisbon. In a
week they will extradite you. Deimler says Bordeaux and it is
Bordeaux for me!"

Pío thought, watching her; good in bed but a woman of
tantrums. God help me if I have to put up with her in
Bordeaux, Lisbon or any other place, a Jezebel if ever there
was one; God Almighty, what we do for the republic. And he

cried, "All right, all right! Bordeaux it is, then," and he smacked his hand down on the desk, and rose, pushing Lucía aside. "León, you are to sign these."

Going to the corner opposite Carrasco, he sat down at a table and adjusted head-phones; reaching out, he switched on the transmitter before him.

Carrasco inclined his head; Fonseca, too, listened to the morse:

Emilio to Deimler. Emilio to Deimler Madrid International. Come in. Over . . .

Pío tapped out the message on the brass key, then sat back in the chair, waiting.

Silence. They waited, their eyes turned to the transmitter. Suddenly the brass key chattered. Carrasco made the message in his head:

Monitor International replying. Monitor International for Deimler replying. Loud and clear. Come in Emilio. Over.

The colonel licked his dry lips. He had never suspected that Pío de Córdoba was Emilio, the most wanted star in the republican firmament; true, he had suspected that Juana de Córdoba, whose countess mother was a confirmed republican, might have some inkling of the identity of Emilio . . . but not Pío! Never in this world had Carrasco suspected Pío . . . The colonel saw Pío's finger moving expertly on the transmission key. Pío handed him the code card.

Emilio to Deimler. Top security. Code X4. Message begins. Hanson partisan cell infiltrated by Colonel Carrasco. *Somaten* Gestapo Liaison. On Carrasco's orders agent Ramón Barro, repeat Ramón Barro, diverted Hanson attacks from Franco to Mola. General Mola died air crash 0705 hrs June 3rd. Alert all cells. Ramón Barro free but Carrasco in custody. In possession of counter-espionage report signed Carrasco to Caudillo. Instructions please. Over.

*　　*　　*

202

Almost a minute passed before Deimler's reply came. Fonseca, arms folded, but with a gun in his hand, watched Carrasco. Lucía García watched Carrasco; the colonel's eyes were lowered. The message from Deimler seemed to hammer in the little room.

Deimler to Emilio. Message understood. Instructions follow. Agents Emilio and Lucía proceed Vigo and Bordeaux as arranged. Not Lisbon. Repeat not Lisbon. Operation Dwarf continues. Maintain daily contact Bordeaux and Madrid. Interrogate Carrasco and dispose. Repeat dispose. Over and out.

Pío switched off the transmitter and turned in his chair, staring at the colonel. Carrasco raised his head.

"You read morse, I suspect?" asked Pío.

"Yes, Emilio, I read morse," said the colonel.

"Then you will realise that, for me, there is absolutely no alternative, León?"

"I realise it."

"The . . . the further interrogation is not necessary, of course," added Pío. "Fortunately for you, we have your own personal report concerning Ramón Barro." Pío smiled, taking the report from his pocket. "We will see that the Caudillo gets it, of course . . . it being essential to us that all remains exactly as it was before."

"With the exception of your disappearance, of course," added Fonseca, speaking for the first time. He gestured with the gun and the colonel rose.

They stood together, as if indecisive, then the colonel said: "By my own hand, Pío?"

"Of course," Pío answered. "Most willingly. It is a ridiculous business and in many ways I regret it." He took the gun from Fonseca and broke it open, taking out all the bullets except one and laid the weapon on the desk. "Half a minute, León. Do not make it longer."

Then the three of them – Pío, Lucía García and Fonseca left the Chinese love-pavilion and stood by the lakeside, looking at the moon.

Three wild duck, alive despite the war, rose from the lake

surface in a clattering panic of wings as the shot split the night's silence.

After regaining the bank of the lake and mooring the little punt belonging to Agustín (with this he tended the water-lilies) Fonseca stood in the shadows of the Chinese love-pavilion and watched the moon hanging above the turrets of Pío's House. Agustín, the old gardener, approached, his feet soundless on the grass. He joined the butler who was now standing beneath the willows.

Earlier, after he had lowered Carrasco's body into the lake, the butler had watched the rear lights of the big Hispano disappear through the western gate. Now he said, as Agustín approached:

"It was a mistake, you know. They will never get on. He'd have done so much better with my small countess."

"It certainly was a mistake," said Agustín, and waved his stick at the lake. "He will kill the fish."

"Possibly," answered Fonseca, "they do not like rebels, I understand, but perhaps he'll be good for the waterlilies. I still say," he added, staring at the western gate, "that it's a very great mistake."

Pío turned the Hispano along the Paseo des Rogue, which would lead him north-west to Salamanca and thence to Orense and Vigo where the boat was waiting.

"I leave with some regret," said he, and driving with one hand, expertly rolled with the other one of his home-made cigarettes. "I quite liked Carrasco, you know. León had charm; this was inevitable, I suppose, being a gentleman."

"Which is more than you'll ever be," snapped Lucía García, and she put out her hand and touched his face. "But then, like you, I am the essence of the revolution, and am reasonably happy with my peasant."

Had I not loved her so well, thought Pío, as he clasped Lucía's hand, I could have been reasonably happy with my small countess.

Twenty-seven

AFTER PÍO, IN the Hispano, had dropped Juana on the road and driven away without her, Richard took the Mercedes another mile or so and stopped on the deserted road.

Don Pita was the last to leave the car, and said, pulling on his monk's cassock, "Now for a pilgrimage to Pamplona. I, of all of you, know exactly where I am going. First I shall visit the grave of my Josefina, which is a wayside ditch on the road out to San Sebastián; there I will place flowers. Later, I will go to the house of her sister, her husband now being deceased."

"It could not have been better planned," said Richard. "And you, Manolo?"

Manolo replied, "I walk also, but in the opposite direction, and will go to Alanis. There I will burn a candle for the soul of Old Pep, who is in Hell."

"And with a polished bullet send Alberto López after him, eh?" cried Nicolas, and he opened the boot of the Mercedes and brought out all their travelling bundles, also the small Kovaks sub-automatic that had belonged to Don Pita.

Juana said: "Surely you've had enough of killing, Manolo! Isn't Old Pep's dying enough?"

At this Nicolas moved close to Juana with the bundles and laid them on the ground at the feet of those to whom they belonged, then stood beside her and looked into her face, and said, "He is a killer gitano, lady. Do not deal with him, you who are so pure."

Manolo showed his yellow teeth and tipped back his sombrero. "Only one more, lady – only one . . .!" And he put an arm around the shoulder of Nicolas. "Come, little one. We begin together, we finish together, eh? But first we kill for horses."

"I am not coming," replied Nicolas.

"*Caramba!* What do you mean?" Manolo, staring, was outraged. "Of course you are coming! Old Pep is dead. The old goat will haunt me if I do not take charge of his grandson!"

"I shall not return to Alanis," said Nicolas firmly. "Because Diego Díaz will be there. His cattle will be in my father's stalls, his hat will be on the peg where my father hung his sombrero. I shall never return to Alanis!" He spat furiously.

"What nonsense!" Manolo swiped at him with his hat.

"Wait!" Juana intervened. Nicolas was backing away, his rifle at the ready, and Manolo was incensed at the disobedience, shouting, "You will come, I say! The old goat would demand it!"

Juana said gently, "Where then, Nicolas, if you do not go with Manolo?"

"I will come with you, lady."

"That's all right," said Richard. "Why not?"

"You will take me?" asked the boy eagerly.

Manolo waved a disdainful hand. "Take him, then, for I have done with him. Relative of a goat. Fool of perdition! You are worse than your grandfather! Will his soul rest? You travelling with a *Yanqui* instead of a gitano? Bah!"

"Go in God. Do not think ill of me," said Nicolas, now serene.

For answer, Manolo strode away; he went to the south to Alanis: Don Pita to the north, to Pamplona.

Richard, Juana and Nicolas got back into the Mercedes and Richard started the engine, saying: "We'll drive east as far as we can, along the Erati river to Arive; at a convenient place we'll leave the car and go over the border on foot."

"Into France?"

"Into France. Through the Sierra de Abodi, keeping clear of the frontier post, and past Larrau."

The car was racing along now and the night was black, with an obliterated moon. Richard turned to the back seat where Nicolas sat hunched, his hat pulled down over his forehead, his gun across his knees: from under the brim of his hat he watched Juana's profile; Richard could see him reflected in the driving mirror. He asked, "Nicolas, do you understand what exile means?"

"I do not, Señor."

"It means," explained Richard, "that you will live in France until the end of the war. It could mean, too, that never again will you live in Spain."

"I will live anywhere, as long as I live with the lady."

Richard made an expression of whimsical speculation, and Juana said, "Don't bother him with it. When we are walking I'll explain it in detail."

"Which ever way it's done, it's important that he understands. He's a gitano, they live in their clans. I can't see him being happy anywhere out of Estremadura. Also, there's his mother to think of."

"By the way he's hanging on to me, I can't think he'll miss her much," and Nicolas, as if overhearing, cried above the engine:

"In France I will burn a candle to the soul of my grandfather; one for my father also, who is dead, and one for my mother, who is alive. But being married to Diego Díaz – that, I say, is the same as death." He knelt forward and gripped Juana's shoulder. "But we, lady, we are alive."

There was a silence.

"It's clear that you intend to stay with us," said Richard, wryly.

"Not with you, *amigo*," replied Nicolas, "with the lady."

Beyond Arive the roads narrowed and steepened and the peaks of the Abodi began to hunt the sky. Through sleeping villages they passed and then came again into open country. By the side of the river Richard stopped the Mercedes. Here was a tree-filled ravine. The mountains either side of the road stood in a monastic quiet as if the world was holding its breath; from some distant village a clock chimed the hour of ten. Opening the boot of the car Richard took out the bundles again, thrust his Colt revolver into his belt and loaded the big Winchester rifle; this he had brought with him from the battles of Madrid, when first he joined Astrada.

"Do we need guns for exile?" asked Juana, beside him.

He offered her Elisa's little Vostok, saying, "Here, take it. Fonseca brought it from the Café Suizo; he gave it to me, thinking you would like to have it, since it belonged to your friend, he said."

Juana did not take it; instead, she turned away. "We are going into peace, I hope, not war. Keep it, I hate all guns."

Nicolas saw this, and did not speak.

Then Nicolas joined Juana on the road and watched Richard as he started the engine of the Mercedes and ran it, roaring it, as he took the car into the forest, its wheels skidding and sliding on the autumn refuse; turning it, ploughing up the forest floor, edging it deeper into the trees away from the road. And even as they stood there so the noise of the engine died into a whisper and from a whisper into silence, and there was only the two of them, Nicolas and Juana; it was as if there was nobody else in the world. Nicolas slipped his hand into Juana's, saying, "Now he is gone, and there is only you and me."

Richard returned on foot. The night was fine, with a cooling breeze coming from the west. With their bundles on their backs they went, Richard and Nicolas with their weapons slung, Richard with his Winchester and a bandolier of .303 bullets, Nicolas with the lighter Kovaks pistol-automatic. The roads steepened and narrowed into paths. Up, upward they went, mounting hill after hill, crest after crest.

Because the rope-soled shoes Nicolas was wearing broke their straps, they stopped in the shelter of a cairn; and lay there, Richard and Juana, with Nicolas between them. And before dawn Nicolas reached out and touched Juana. Half sleeping, she put her arm about him as a woman does to a child, and he slept.

At dawn Richard awoke and stretched himself, shivering with cold; kneeling, he took the blanket he had left and put it over the two of them, and stood there, smiling down, for Nicolas was lying with his arms around Juana and his head was upon her breast.

"Lucky little bugger," Richard said under his breath. Then he looked to the west and the road sloping down to the Spanish plains was empty; he looked eastward, towards France, and saw the sun rising in a great confusion of fire, red and gold, and the Pyrenees reached up monolithic fingers into the redness like a world in flames.

Awaking, Juana said from the ground, "I dreamed, Richard. I dreamed of Pío."

"It is about time you changed that dream," said he, and gave her a grin. He was rolling a cigarette, his big hands heavy but skilful, and Juana remembered how Pío, the peasant, rolled his cigarettes. "In any case," added Richard, and nodded down at the sleeping Nicolas, "it seems to me that you've already got your hands full."

Juana rose. "As I said before. He pretends that I am his mother."

Richard grunted, cupping his hands to the wind and the air was filled with the perfume of the cigarette, but it was not the brand he preferred, he said, and added, "Not so much of the child. He's knocking sixteen. A year or so from now and he'll have hair on his chest."

"Even now I have hair on my belly," said Nicolas, opening an eye. "Shall I show you? I am a man. I have much hair on my belly, look now . . ." and he began to unbuckle his belt.

"Not now, not now," said Richard swiftly, and bent to him. "Later, we will bathe, and you can give us all a treat."

Nicolas left them then and Juana knelt to tie up the blankets; the sun was full now, each leaf sparkling with dew.

Richard knelt, too, and said: "Take my tip, Juana. He is not a child in arms, you know. Treat him more like a man."

"Would that be so wise?" said she.

They spoke much of Pío and Colonel Carrasco and the death of General Mola; of Consuela they spoke as they trudged into the sun, and the rays of heat began to spy at the sweat of their clothes.

Twenty-eight

ALL THAT DAY they walked, trudging up the steepening tracks of the foothills of the Pyrenees, and below them saw the fertile Valley of Lavenden; here the stubbled trunks of the elm and pine forests stood as sentinels to an age of luxurious country, and high above, enshrined in cloud, floated hawks in ragged isolation. Here spouted waterfalls from the riven sides of the mountains, tumbling in cotton-wool streams to the plains below, and from them rose mist, filling the gorges and canyons with rainbow colours.

Richard went first, Juana following him, with Nicolas, now bare-footed, labouring after. In this manner they climbed upward, first to the topmost bastion of the foothills, then onward along the mountain pass that ribboned the flanks of the peaks.

Reaching a crest, Richard leaned against the rock face and pointed into the valley, and Juana saw in the foreground the scattered farmhouses of the Spanish Basques; then he pointed northward.

"Look!"

Nicolas joined Juana and she put her arm around his shoulders, and they looked to the north where Richard's hand pointed and beyond the foreground was a frontier post with pin-point vehicles scattered loosely about it, many on the Spanish side of the border, but more to the north.

"Is it France?" asked Juana.

Richard did not reply to this, and Juana sensed in him a strangeness, for he had looked at her and she knew in him that which was of herself; an emotion beyond longing. Also, she knew that this pain in her would not be lost to her; that nothing could assuage it save his nearness. Within the moment when her eyes found his there were no mountains, no sky; no presence save Richard's. The proximity of Nicolas beside her was not a part of her. The boy's hand was upon her arm and the warmth of his fingers came, but she did not experience it. She existed in that moment of time for one only, and Richard saw this in her face and smiled and Nicolas saw this smile and drew away.

The wind moved from the Valley of Lavenden and Juana smelled the ice-coldness of the white-decorated peaks, but the live warmth of the man came to her again, and he spoke.

"Soon it will be night," and lifted his face to the wind.

The boy said, "I am tired. Can we rest?"

"It is better to go," Richard answered. "You agree, Juana? It is safer to go; to stay here could mean capture."

"I have no wish for that," said Nicolas. "Not the Guardia, God, not the Guardia!"

"I have a wish only to sleep," said Juana. "To lie in a bed and sleep and forget the war; forget all, save remembering dreams of sleep. Have you not slept in such dreams, when you were young? A double sleep? When to awake was like coming out of death?"

"I sleep to awake to life," said Richard. "Come, a mile or two more before dark? Then we will be safe."

Nicolas cried, "And I will go down into the valley and snare a leveret and cook him on sticks over a fire. We can find a cave?"

"We will easily find a cave," said Richard. "There are ten thousand."

"I will build the fire red, with peat from the little stream beds, and it will glow, for that is the way to cook a leveret. Would you eat the flesh of a leveret if I cook him, lady?"

"I would eat a vulture if you cook him, Nicolas."

And Nicolas went past her, and past Richard also, and breasted a new rise and pointed down and there below was a little pasture on a plateau in the mountains and this was crowned with clumps of swaying elms and pines, a magical visitation out of barrenness. There was greenness to its boundaries and little white brooks and streams intersecting it.

Therefore Nicolas clambered over the edge of the pass, slipping and sliding down the slope of the crags, down into this valley of greenness that beckoned them, and Juana put out her hand to Richard and said: "Come!" And he took her hand and went with her as Nicolas had done, slipping and sliding in laughter down the slope of the crag to the bounty of the plain, and here the wind was soft and the great trees swayed in the valley wind and no longer cried in the crags of the mountains.

Nicolas ran ahead, calling to them.

"Oh, he is such a child," said Juana.

"He is a child with a man's heart," replied Richard. "Where has his youth gone? Look at his face. He is old in suffering."

"Do not speak of suffering."

She knew only the wish for peace; without Richard's hand in hers there was only war and blood and the savagery of the mountains where the steepled peaks wounded the clouds. But as they walked together a solace came to her, bringing her to calm, and she knew only him, and was of him, in a oneness she had not known before. His very treading on the grass was of her, the rustle of his clothes; all was of Richard; it brought to her a richness of companionship.

Until this moment, Juana thought, his body had been but the nearness of a comrade.

One ate and drank and talked with such a comrade; within the fight for survival, within the lonely majesty of the sierra one travelled, as now, with such a comrade; and slept with him, body to body for warmth in the coldness. It could not have been so with Manolo, who possessed fleas and little intelligence, but it was certainly acceptable with one like Don Pita, a man she scarcely knew: certainly it would have been acceptable to sleep with her arms about Nicolas, the boy.

This was the way of partisans, she had discovered. One lived, argued, quarrelled on equal terms: few loves existed, because love is chastened by thought of danger, and danger was ever present. Intimate things were done in each others' presence, like washing naked or dressing without an attempt at covering oneself; modesty had no place in a sierra camp: in small measure some privacy existed, such as in the daily toilet.

Men spoke like men spoke, swore like men; a woman accepted this. Male vulgarity was part of an accepted existence. One shared the last cigarette or crept to a comrade for small gifts; or shared a bottle without the wipe of a mouth: as you shared the dirt, hunger, wounds. There was little of sex in a partisan war, save to indulge in it as a passing relief, knowing that one might be dead tomorrow: to be alive today was usually enough.

"Look!" cried Nicolas, a long way off, and waved his arm.

So they stopped, Richard and Juana, and peered through the gathering dusk and saw there a ruined barn, and outside the barn Nicolas stood waving, and they ran together; slowly at first, then swifter, still hand in hand, and came to him.

"Now you can sleep, Señora!"

Laughing, breathless, Juana put out her arms to him. "Now I can sleep," she said, and the boy led her out of the dusk, into the dark greeting of the barn.

Within the barn was warmth and the smell of humans, and dry straw formed to the bodies of animals, and the roof was torn so that they saw above them the pale stars and the blackness growing over the sierra; there was no sound here save the whispering of the wind in the eaves and the crying of the owls in the valley below Visaurin. Richard was clearing the earth floor of straw and piling it in heaps against the wall that faced the valley.

Juana helped him; for a time they worked unspeaking.

After a little while Nicolas entered and hanging from his wrist was a hare. The hare's eyes were open, large and bald and glazed and matted blood was upon its muzzle where the trap had snared and one hind-leg was grotesquely doubled back in death. Squatting, Nicolas laid the hare down upon the floor of the barn and with his belt knife skinned and gutted it. Richard built a triangle of sticks and Juana collected fuel for a fire. Nicolas had found peat and cut the sods small, and these he packed around the leaping flames and presently the gas caught and the peat glowed and a savoury smell filled the barn.

Nicolas turned the naked carcass of the hare on a spit and Richard and Juana sat watching, their faces red and black in the flickering flames. A warmth slowly filled the barn where the shadows danced.

"This is the way the gitanos cook. See, it is good?"

"It is wonderful!" cried Juana.

"He is better than a French chef," announced Richard, and

took the meat from the spit and quartered it on a stone, giving each a share, and they squatted on their haunches in the glow of the fire, and ate in gasps; Nicolas cried at the scald of it, tearing at the flesh of the leveret with his white teeth and the fat was shining upon his fingers. They laughed together, blowing and gasping within the comforting heat of the fire, so that the sighing of the wind outside and the coldness of the night were as nothing to them.

"First watch? Who is first on watch?" asked Richard.

Juana wiped her hands on straw and saw his face in the redness of the fire; the shadows were deep in his eyes so that his face was without shape or contour; only his eyes she saw in that redness, and the whiteness of his teeth in his bearded cheeks.

Richard rose and stretched himself and went to the barn door and looked out on to the night which was fine and big with stars, and he knew a comfort in him that they had found this protecting place. Bending, he picked up his Winchester and snicked back the bolt and was ready to go, but Nicolas said:

"No, *compañero*. You stay with the lady. I will take first watch."

Richard did not reply, but turned and looked at Juana who was still squatting before the fire, and she smiled, so he said:

"As you wish. But sleep *amigo*, and I will have the tail off you. The Guardia could be near. Understand?"

Immediately Nicolas had left the barn, Richard slept, and Juana lay beside him, listening to his breathing; and her own breathing she made one with his, rhythmic and gentle so as not to disturb his sleeping by her breathing, and there was no other sound but the distant lowing of animals from the valley.

Almost immediately Juana slept also, but awakened soon and was aware of Richard's warmth beside her in the straw and this warmth brought a comfort so that she stretched out her hand and touched him.

The touch of Juana's hand, so softly upon his face brought to Richard the realisation of her presence, and he turned to her in the straw and looked at her, and Richard saw that, despite Juana's steady breathing, she was awake, like him, and knew that her touch had awakened him.

He lay, unspeaking, and Juana was silent within the calling of the wind, and there grew between them an understanding of their need, one for the other, but this they did not betray by word or gesture. And even when the voices of hunting dogs came up from the Valley of Lavenden, they did not speak, but Richard's hand moved and clasped hers, and the barn entrance was darkened as he leaned above her, and she thought: how can I hold back tonight and delay tomorrow, so that this shall continue without end? How good it would be to make a house here, far away from the dirt of the encampment and the stinks of war; never to count the days to an inevitable parting. To stay with this man in this place and to be one with him when ever he needed me.

As the seasons came and went in this lovely place, she thought as he kissed her mouth, so the pale coltsfoot and meadow-sweet would cover the mountain slopes: in summer the marshes would be alive with iris. Hand in hand with this one I could walk in seas of buttercups and columbine. And then she smiled, for these were the thoughts of a girl, not of a woman: for a woman would be practicality; the cooking, the cleaning; not all would be romantic in a village in the Pyrenees.

But now Richard's hands caressed her and there was a richness in the opening of her body and she forgot all that she had thought, remembering nothing but his kisses and his hands touching her.

It did not matter to her that she was in the midst of danger; that the Guardia sought them, that the frontier police, French and Spanish, would be ringing their telephones and soldiers loading their rifles. All that mattered to her now was Richard's immediacy, and she reached up and pulled his face down to hers, cherishing his mouth, his cheeks, his hair, and said: "Oh God, Richard. Oh God . . ."

Within the pain of it Juana knew a sudden terror that soon, indeed, this man would be lost to her, and then there would be no more of this, but the pain would remain, though none of the beauty.

She heard a voice say: "I can hear the beating of my heart."

Richard did not reply, so she said, "Never before have I heard my heart beating . . ."

"It is not your heart," he answered, "it is mine."

She lay like a child whose strength had gone while he enjoyed her.

"What would your anarchist say about that?"

"He didn't come back, remember?"

"God, Juana, you're so intense!"

She turned away her face and saw beyond the barn entrance the vast summit of the range and the stars ringing the peaks were as candle-fire. Richard added, "He must have been a fool of an anarchist; as a lover he was an idiot."

"Nevertheless, I am afraid . . ."

He saw her face in the faint glow of the door; the deep smudges of her eyes, her shadowed cheeks. "What a child you are, and how uncertain."

"That is because you have taught me to love you, and now I have done so, I am fearful. Did I ask for this? Now, what alternative is there but to love you back? The fault is yours."

He smiled down at her. "Yes – a schoolgirl. I knew it. You are not grown up."

"But I am, I am now. And this is the trouble." Richard made to move but her arms held him. "No, don't go. Please don't go. Not yet."

They lay together in the pattering rain and the barn roof leaked and splashed them with an icy coldness. Richard whispered, "But I must, my love. Soon Nicolas will be back."

"Oh God! Of course! I'd forgotten him."

So Richard drew away from her and gently covered her with the blanket and they lay together, and Juana said, her eyes closed; "What are you thinking?"

Raising himself on an elbow, Richard stared through the door into the night, and there was a silence in the forest; he saw above the lofty pines the saw-toothed ridges of the Pyrenees and there was no movement, even the rain had temporarily ceased, as if the earth itself was listening.

216

He said, softly: "When the war is over I think I'll write a book about it."

"And will you include me in that book?"

"Of course. You are one with me now in everything I do."

"And if I have a child as a result of this, will you tell of it, too?"

"If you have a child I will cherish it, because it comes from you. If it is a boy we will call him Jerónimo, or Juanita if it is a girl. If it is a girl she will be dark and beautiful like you; God knows what a boy would look like."

"Were he to be like you I'd be content."

"Have you ever stopped to think that we might not get out of this?" asked Juana. "Tens of thousands of people have already died, some of them so close to me. My mother, for one – Felipe Astrada – and like her, he died for nothing; Consuela, Old Pep . . ."

Richard rose and walked to the barn door. And saw, outlined against the stars the distant form of Nicolas, sitting on a crag. Richard replied, "We are survivors, and we will get through – into France first, and lie low for a time. But we will be back . . ." And Juana interjected: "But in all your marvellous self-confidence, have you stopped to consider that Franco might win? We are fighting for a new democracy, but will Spain ever be truly democratic? All right, we get rid of Franco, but another dictator could rise – Spain stands for extremism, she never takes a middle course. Victory itself could mean the end of us."

He answered, "Forget the war. This love between us now is only the beginning. Can you sweep aside its marvels because of a mere war and Spanish dictators? And the outcome of this stupid fight – that is even less significant." Richard turned at the door. "We love, you and me, in the measure of lovers. You are a part of me now, I of you. Nothing in the world can alter this and nothing can destroy it."

"How many lovers, I wonder, have said that before?"

He smiled and came back to her, kneeling. "They all do. This is the unique confidence of lovers; without it the world stands still. The talk of all lovers is immortal. Come on, come on – if you don't believe that this union will last for ever, how will the world?"

Juana said, touching his face, "Then I will be confident, too. We will live in San Sebastián, I think, for I love the Basques. We will rent a cottage overlooking the harbour, and while you are writing your book I will sit in the sun and dabble my feet in the sea."

Richard said, "We will eat nothing but hot, crusted bread and drink cheap vino tinto – bad wine is good for lovers . . ."

The words died on his lips as Juana reached up and brought her mouth to his. "Where is Nicolas . . .?"

"Up there on the crag."

"How long will it take him to cross the gulley?"

"Twenty minutes, perhaps longer."

"Remember, I said once that I would ask you. Please . . ."

"Remember, will you, that you are supposed to be a countess . . .?"

"Please?"

The rain began again in a drumming roar on the barn roof, the moon faded.

Twenty-nine

MANOLO ARRIVED IN Alanis with the sun going down.

As he walked down the lane that led past the doorway of Nicolas's *posada*, a voice called:

"Manolo, is that you?"

And the mother of Nicolas, whose black hair was newly oiled, drew away from the washing-line where she was pegging out Diego Díaz's trousers in the sun, and cried again, "Manolo Quinto!"

Manolo continued to saunter past. With his cheroot cocked up in his bearded face and his poncho thrown over his shoulder, he went, and his peasant smock was stained with dust and dirt

The mother of Nicolas, now the wife of Diego Díaz, the lead-labourer, ran after Manolo and swung him to face her.

It was as if this marriage had brought new blood to her face, Manolo thought. Her eyes were bright, her lips red. She said, "Manolo Quinto, what of Nicolas?"

Manolo did not answer. She asked:

"He is coming home with Old Pep? They stay together in Roncesvalles, and you have returned here for Ana Martínez?" She encompassed him with excitement. "Alberto López has released her, you know? There was talk that he knew of some great deceit, and used it to his advantage. I do not know the business in detail, but Ana is pure, as you know. But now, *compañero*, he is back with his wife. And respectable. The prices are lower in his shop. And Ana awaits you in your mother's *posada*. Good wine is there for you! Now that you are home there will be feasting and flamenco!" And her eyes, great shadows in her pale face, said: "Where is Nicolas?" but her voice did not ask again.

Manolo looked towards her *posada* where Diego Díaz was standing; a gaunt man and old, shrivelled in the sun; then back at the mother of Nicolas.

And took the cheroot out of his thick lips tossed it away and spat at her feet.

With his rifle slung under his poncho like a tent-pole, Manolo made his way to the shop of Alberto López.

López saw Manolo coming, and was concerned. The doorbell clanged as the gitano entered, and the shopkeeper threw wide his arms, crying, "*Madre Mía*! This is wonderful. Look who has arrived!" and called to his wife. "Come, come! Look who is back in Alanis! Our old friend Manolo!" Alberto López, sweating, mopped his throat and face, crying, "Next, perhaps, we shall have Old Pep himself, and the grandson, Nicolas. *Vaya hombre*! Are they not with you? If they were, Alanis would be complete. And most complete of all would be Ana Martínez!" His hands begged to Manolo. "Poor Ana Martínez, she has been lost while you have been away."

His goldfish eyes bulged at the room for a weapon.

Manolo reached out behind him and dropped the bolt over the door.

"Understand it, Manolo – she has been lost. Lost! A wandering soul. You went without a word, remember? True, true, there has been a little misunderstanding . . . Ah, you are here . . ." and he patted his fat wife who came with sullen eyes. "Confirm it, my love. A little misunderstanding? It is reasonable to make mistakes . . ."

Manolo tossed back his poncho and unslung his Mauser.

"Ana and me – we have been to the confessional. I myself have been on my knees before the Virgin, she who forgives the trespasses of sinners. Side by side we have knelt before the altar of Santa María – and the village looking on. Even my children! On our knees, in penitence. Think of the shame! And have been forgiven. Forgiveness is the holiest gift of God . . ." He crossed himself.

Manolo took from the bandolier around his chest the bullet that was brightly polished, opened the breech of the Mauser and inserted it; shot the bolt home.

The expression on the face of Señora López did not change.

Her husband sank to his knees before Manolo, and the sweat, which was already beading his creased face, now ran in streams to his collar, and the collar soaked and dripped on to his chest and his mouth opened and his teeth chattered, and he said: "Shoot, then, but remember your soul, Manolo Quinto! Shoot and have done with it. Cleanse me of this fornication and I will go to Eternal Glory . . . give me death to expiate my sins!" He shrieked, pulling open his shirt. "Shoot here! Shoot here . . .!"

Manolo aimed the Mauser first at Alberto's forehead, while the eyes of the shopkeeper rolled; then slowly lowered the muzzle to Alberto's mouth; then to his chest; and then to his stomach.

The crows rose in black squawks from the roof of the grain loft.

Blood spurted through Alberto's fingers as he clutched his groin.

The expression on the face of Señora López did not change. Turning, she went to the telephone.

"Wait," said Manolo, and opened the door.

"Wait?" asked she. "My husband is dying. He needs a priest. That also is according to gitano law."

"Wait ten minutes," said Manolo. "I have another visit to make."

"Ten minutes, Manolo Quinto?" said she. "Ana Martínez next?"

Manolo stepped over the shopkeeper who was rolling on the floor.

Finding Ana Martínez awaiting him in his mother's *posada*, Manolo greeted her and took her hand; not embracing her, which would have been more than she could have expected . . . and led her out into the olive fields of Alanis where the moon was big on the shoulder of the mountain.

"You know of me, Manolo?" asked Ana, and her face in that soft light was low.

"I know of many women in my travels," said Manolo. "What is another?"

"That I have been soiled by Alberto López, and have no virtue in the eyes of the village?"

"Little matter," said Manolo. "I also have much to apologise for."

"It was against my will, though," said Ana, and behind

her, on the roosting perches of a neighbour's *posada*, a cock crowed once.

They walked on and the moon was good to them and the ears of the wheat were ripe and golden in the fields, and here they lay, Ana first smoothing out her dress, which was a white stain on the stubbled gold.

"I would never have done it, but to save my father, you understand?"

The cockerel crowed again.

Manolo shrugged and wiped his bearded face with the back of his hand and listened to the distant sounds of the village, and hoof-beats.

"The Guardia is about tonight, I wonder why?" asked Ana, and her eyes were dark stains in the hollows of her cheeks.

Manolo lay above her and her throat was white under his brown hand and he kissed her lips, which were black, like lips stained with berries, and Ana said against his cheek: "I had no love for Alberto López. Believe it true?"

The cock crowed again.

And Manolo saw, in his growing anger, the barn opposite the shop of Alberto, where he had swung from the hook of the crane; like a pendulum swung, and in his brain he looked again through the window of the barn loft and saw again what he saw that day, when he had come to Alanis before, and he thought: fug this war, the nationalists and the republicans; fug Franco, Mola, Lister and Goded. Fug them all, from the revolutionary committees to la Pasionaria: fug Old Pep and Nicolas for the pain of them, fug Alberto López and fug and defile Ana Martínez.

"Manolo, Manolo . . .!" Ana was whispering, stroking his hair.

But he was not there with her in the wheat field. Instead, in his mind, he was hanging on the crane hook outside the window of the barn loft, and Ana eased her slim body now, surprised as his fingers pressed upon her throat.

She stared up at Manolo as his fingers tightened more.

In Manolo's mind the Stallion of Alanis worked industriously.

"*Manolo!*"

Ana screamed, but no sound came, for Manolo's hand was choking out her breath, and she kicked her legs, twisting her body away and his grip slackened. On all fours, gasping, they faced each other.

"Bitch!" whispered Manolo, and leaped again.

Ana shrieked, her hands up protectively: "I am with child!"

Gasping, Manolo raised his hands to his bearded face. Mouth open, he stared at her.

"I . . . I am with child, Manolo," she whispered.

And Manolo went full length beside her, and buried his face in the stubbed ground, and wept.

Thirty

RICHARD SAID, "WE must go on."

"I could stay in this place for ever," said Juana.

Nicolas looked up from the ground and saw them, not replying: there moved in him that contentment that was an apprenticeship to life. To be alive now was enough for him, and nothing to be dead tomorrow: to look upon Juana was to look upon the future.

Soon, his primitive brain told him, the *Yanqui*, much as he revered him, would be dead; his death would be as irrevocable as night follows day. And then only he, Nicolas, and the woman, Juana, would travel the mountains.

For her he would make fires and trap and cook, and there would be no other to serve or,touch her. Meanwhile, all the time the Americano was alive, he would serve him also. This was reasonable, thought Nicolas: was not the *Yanqui* also a *compañero*?

And so, when dusk fell on the third day of travel in the Pyrenees, they made camp in a hollow of the mountain track a thousand feet above the lake and five miles farther on; and from this greater height looked back into the Spanish mountains and these were bulwarks of the sky: before them the flatlands beckoned, and in the valley to the west the River Nive strangled the verdant land of waving elms with a quicksilver brilliance, and the little tributary of Lake Iradia pushed north a bright, thin finger. Out of this tributary Nicolas tickled three fish.

In the dusk Richard built a fire, shielding it with a little cairn of stones and Juana made a triangle of sticks and Nicolas gutted and cleaned the fish and skewered them with elm branches and laid them side by side over the fire so that they sizzled and steamed, and from the other side of the fire Nicolas watched Juana and thought of his mother no more, but of the woman for whom his body had stirred, and who, one day, would be his. The best fish he gave to her, presenting

224

it on a leaf and for her he fashioned a fork, so that she would not have to eat it with her fingers.

"See," said Juana, "I am privileged, Nicolas has made me a fork."

Richard, beside her on the ground, laughed and held his fish in his fingers and stripped off the flesh, holding it up and dropping it into his mouth and small white pieces clung to his beard, which was now thick upon his face; and he raised his eyes at Nicolas, saying, "What hope of a decent meal in this wilderness if Nicolas were not here, eh? He is a very great fisherman. Notice, incidentally, that I received the smallest fish," and he winked at Juana.

"One day you will teach me how to fish with my fingers?" Juana sat back on her haunches and pushed back her hair from her face.

And Nicolas replied: "My grandfather taught me this way of fishing. Since the time of ice the fish has been cold, said he. He flies to your hand like a hungry *compañero* flies to his woman's breast. And women's hands are better than men for finger-fishing, because their skin is softer, said Old Pep. Give me a dozen women and I would take them to the Santander rivers in a cart and earn myself a fortune."

"I didn't know that," commented Richard, still eating. "The gitanos can teach us a lot. Women are better at finger-fishing?"

"There are many things the *Yanqui* does not know," said Nicolas.

"You hear that *Yanqui*?" laughed Juana. "There are many things you have to learn, including how to treat a woman, presumably?"

Richard rose and slapped his legs with his sombrero, raising dust, then sat again by the fire, his hands thrust into the sleeves of his jacket. "Travelling with Nicolas is a great privilege. Not only does a man enjoy good philosophy, but he eats better than in the Mayorazgo, down the Leganitos. Have you ever eaten in the Mayorazgo, Juana?"

"Where is that?" asked Nicolas.

And Juana answered: "It is a great hotel in Madrid. Yes, many times I have eaten there, but I prefer the Plaza."

Richard replied: "Once I ate lobster thermidor at the

Plaza, and washed it down with some excellent *montilla*." Now he lay back upon the ground, his hands linked behind his head and smiled nostalgically, and stretched himself. "I'd give a lot to be there now. The beds in the Plaza are beyond description. One could sleep on such a bed and wake only for Gabriel's horn."

"You've stayed there?"

"Once, with Carla. On our honeymoon. Her father paid, of course."

"She must have had expensive tastes!"

"On the contrary, she did not. Her parents insisted, and who were we to argue?"

"What is lobster thermidor?" asked Nicolas, and Juana answered:

"It is a sea-spider; brown in the sea, but red when you boil him. You eat him hot, straight from the pot, with pepper and butter and brown bread and butter."

"Like you eat these?" Nicolas held up the backbone of his trout.

"Yes. He is trout thermidor, I suppose, but without the bread and butter."

The boy said, grinning wide at Juana. "One day I will take you to the great hotel in Madrid. We will eat the sea-spiders and drink *montilla*, eh? And if the beds are good, I will buy you one and you will lie in it all day eating sea-spiders and drinking wine until I come home from work."

"That'll cost you a bit," observed Richard, and crossed his feet and pulled down his hat to shield his face from the sun.

Nicolas replied: "The cost will be nothing to me, for I will earn it bull-fighting." Kneeling on the earth he put his hands between his knees and smiled into Juana's face. "Did I tell you that I am excellent with the bulls? Back in Alanis, before I became a man, I was the best of the boys. The men gave us capes, you know – not darts because they are not allowed – but capes. It is good practice if one wants to be a *torero*."

"You intend to be a *torero*?" asked Richard, his voice muffled in his hat.

Nicolas leaped up and took a stance. "I will be a great *torero*. Greater than Romero or Candido – as great as Manolete, perhaps, and he is the greatest of them all!"

"The money will be handy," announced Juana, turning over on the ground. "You'll find me expensive, little one. It has been said that I am the most expensive countess in Spain."

"Do not worry! I will even take you to the hotel the *Yanqui* calls the Mayorazgo, and there you will walk and men will admire you; sitting at the little tables in the afternoon, drinking coffee or the wine which you prefer."

"Bring me a bottle of San Sadurni de Noya or the beautiful *champaña* from Barcelona, and I will be content." Juana dreamed in tiredness, eyes drooping.

"You like this wine, lady?"

"I adore it. A glass or two of that and I am an idiot."

"Then I will get it from Barcelona. You ask, lady, and you will have it."

"Watch her," said Richard drily. "She's clearly a snob when it comes to the bottle. Give her vino tinto – few women can tell the difference," and he stretched his long legs, sighing lazily in the heat.

"If the lady wants San Sadurni de Noya, she shall have it," announced Nicolas. "Who is on watch?" and he rose, his jaw belligerently thrust out and loaded his Kovak sub-automatic, which he had taken from Don Pita.

"You," answered Richard, "but for an hour. Give me an hour, and I will stand us up to dawn." He turned over upon his side and nestled into the ground.

"An hour, then? After that I shall sleep with you, shall I?" Nicolas stooped to Juana on the ground and pulled up the poncho over her shoulders.

"It will be a privilege, small one," said Juana. "And I shall take the dawn watch and see the sun come up."

Juana watched the boy leave, then moved over to where Richard was lying and lay beside him and there was no sound but the singing of the cicadas and a bass croaking of male frogs from the tributary of the lake.

"You want to watch that one," said Richard into his hat. "He has a growing liking for your company. Give him a few years and he'd slit my throat for you."

"He cherishes me and plays that I am his mother."

"Don't bank on it."

227

Juana sighed and put out her arm around Richard's waist, and Nicolas, looking back, saw this. For nearly a minute he stood on a height overlooking the plateau where they had made camp; and looked down at the two figures lying together, before the hollow of the pass.

On that night, because the weather was fine, they travelled on and the mountains thumbed and steepled the sky in a silver light, bringing the plains either side of the pass through which they walked into sharp relief. But then, as midnight grew upon them, the sky suddenly darkened. Thunder clouds, ominous with red-shot fire, rolled up from the east and clattered and reverberated over the world. The clouds, until then gently lumbering before a western wind, heaved up in fury, ragged and storm-spent, thickening in the caverns of the sky and pressing down upon the Pyrenees with brooding intent. Richard, followed by Juana, glanced up, and Nicolas joined them on the narrow pass.

"It was a mistake," said Richard. "A storm is coming, and we must find shelter. It would have been wiser to stay where we were."

But Nicolas cried, shrilly: "No, no, *Yanqui*, it was better to move. The Guardia travel by day only. We will be as grass-hoppers that fly in the night."

And even as he said this, the storm broke. Lightning flashed in a startling fork across the sky, lighting the anger of the clouds, bringing all into a sudden and terrifying day, laying bare the whole vast panorama of the range. And as instantly thunder boomed and crashed in staccato detona-tions immediately above them so that Juana instinctively lowered herself to the ground and crouched there. And then came the rain, but it did not rain.

It tub-washed and bucketed from the stricken clouds, falling in great sheaves of foaming water, and they clung to each other, staring up into the unleashed fury above as flash after lightning flash illuminated their world of mountains. And even as they pressed together against the face of the pass, little rivers of water cascaded over their heads from the mountain slopes above them; now blending their roaring into an individual one as new tributaries formed, frantic for the mothering sea. Richard braced his body, turning to press his body against Juana and Nicolas, pinning them side by side against the berm of the pass while the torrents of escaping water spouted above them, splashing off the edge of the narrow road to disappear into the blackness beneath.

"Don't move, don't move!"

Ten minutes later they were still there, cornered by the sudden outrush of dominating forces, while above them the storm bellowed and gushed with growing intensity; the savage flashes among the peaks answering the obscene mutterings of thunder that grew again and again into immense volumes of sound. Then, suddenly, as quickly as it had begun, the storm ceased. The clouds lumbered away and the moon came out in plaintive beauty, as if in contrition for the savagery: the moon came out and the dull, forbidding country of the plains lived in startling beauty.

Richard said, releasing Juana and Nicolas: "God Almighty!"

And they stood, the three of them, together on the brimming pass where storm water gushed up to their ankles, sweeping up the refuse of dead leaves and clay, flying in sheets as red as blood, to the plains below. The world smiled. There was no sound but the incessant rushing of water as small brooks and streams merged and poured in white beauty over the edge of the pass, down to the plain.

Juana said, "How soon do you think we will be over the frontier?"

Richard pondered it, and Nicolas cried shrilly, "When I was here before – through Roncesvalles and Pied de Port, you understand? – it was easy. The frontier post is at Arnéguy, the gates, the doors, you see it. Here there is nothing. One could be in Spain or France."

"Of course not. Here the border is not marked."

"You were in the Pyrenees before, you say?" asked Richard, eyeing him.

"Of course!" Nicolas struck a brave attitude. "With Old Pep, my grandfather. In those days, while my father worked in Alanis, we were water-sellers."

"Of course, yes," said Juana. "Roncesvalles was Old Pep's home."

"We had a donkey and many *botijos* in bright red netting." Nicolas rose from his haunches where he was squatting on the pass, and raised his hands high, crying, "*Perra gorda, perra gorda!* Ten *centimos* we charged them for as much as a thirsty man could drink. But my mother, when she came in *fiesta* time to Roncesvalles, was the best water-seller of them all," and he struck an attitude. "*A gorda cachucho!* She was marvellous. She could sell water to a drowning man. But that was before the Guardia beat her and her beauty was lost." He stared momentarily at Juana. "Her beauty, in those days, was as yours, lady . . ."

Juana instantly shouted, to brighten his mood, "*Sardina, sardina!* My mother used to sell sardines." And she perched her broad-rimmed riding hat on the top of her head and strutted around, one hand on her hip. "*Sardina, sardina!* Like the fisher-wives shout on the Basque waterfront. You have heard them?"

"Many times!" boomed Richard. "But a countess selling sardines?"

"She was aping Dolores Ibarruri," replied Juana. "Before she threatened the life of Calvo Sotelo in the Cortes, la Pasionaria sold sardines in the Asturias."

"Something of a radical, your countess mother!" Richard lit a cigarette, blowing on it to dry the wetness.

"Your mother sold sardines?" asked Nicolas, his eyes big.

"No, no, it was only a game! But she came here many times, when I was a child. She and Old Pep would have had much in common. As I have much in common with your mother, you say?"

"Only that your hair is black and your eyes are brown, and she is the same shape of you!" Nicolas made curving actions with his hands in the air. "You know, lady? And I beg your pardon. But only in those things. Otherwise you are not my mother," and Richard glanced up at this.

"This is why the Guardia are following us," Nicolas continued, "to find Old Pep."

"If the Guardia are following us, it is because we have

killed Mola," announced Richard, sharpening his knife on a stone. "Old Pep is not the reason."

Ignoring this, Nicolas said, "In such a place as this you might find Sergeant Fernández, I am thinking. Following me, you understand?"

"Sergeant Tomás Fernández, the enemy of your grandfather?" asked Juana.

"But Sergeant Fernández is dead, remember?" interjected Richard.

Nicolas eyed him with hostility. "He is not. He is alive. My grandfather boasted of killing him, true, but one does not easily kill the Guardia sergeant. He is a cat with many lives. After the attack on the Galapagar convoy we gitanos returned to Alanis, remember? And what did we find? That Sergeant Fernández had been patrolling there. Wounded, yes, but in the saddle. There is a man! Old Pep did not believe it, but Manolo and me, we know the truth. Fernández is alive and seeks Old Pep."

"And if he has since found your grandfather's body?"

"Then he seeks me, the grandson."

Nicolas sank down on to the pass and the red mud stained his smock, and he leaned against the rock face. "Of course. For years it has been the same. Where my grandfather goes, Sergeant Fernández follows. He goes to Alanis, Fernández goes to Alanis; Old Pep travels on a donkey to Pied de Port, Fernández arrives there also on a mare."

"But Old Pep is dead. Come, be reasonable!"

"True." Nicolas watched Richard gravely. "But does the sergeant know this? He thinks that Old Pep is alive, and so he follows. And if Old Pep is dead, then he follows me, his grandson, as I say."

Richard gave Nicolas a very old-fashioned look, and a sigh.

Nicolas rose from the ground and put his hands upon his hips and lifted his face to the wind, and Juana saw in his face the hawk-like beauty of Old Pep. The boy said, his eyes half closed, "The wind is coming from the east and it brings the smell of Guardia. French gendarmes also, perhaps, for these sometimes fight together on the old smuggling tracks . . ."

"If you smell the Guardia, it is because they are seeking the

Astrada partisans . . ." said Richard. "Do not flatter yourself, youngster."

"I smell Fernández, because he seeks me, Old Pep's relative," said Nicolas. And he sniffed again at the wind. "The nose is as good as the eye in the Pyrenees."

They picked up their bundles and slung them across their shoulders and Richard carried his Winchester before him, watching the winding pass for movement; Juana came next, with the ponchos and her medical pack, Nicolas followed her, pausing at times, sweeping the vast panorama behind him with his eyes, but nothing stirred in the wildness of plains and rearing peaks save water: water that spouted from the wounds of the mountains.

Nicolas caught Juana up and walked beside her, and said: "There are times when you look like my mother, before she lost her beauty. How wonderful it is that you should be here now with me, when she has gone to the arms of Diego Díaz, the lead-labourer. So much in your face that reminds me."

"How can I compare?" said Juana.

"Perhaps, one day, you will come with me to Alanis?"

Juana pursed her lips, her face turned upward. "It is possible, Nicolas. Anything is possible."

"When all are gone and there is only you and me – together to Alanis."

Juana's smile faded. "Oh, you are a tremendous dreamer. What a child you are."

"That is where you make a great mistake, I am a man," said Nicolas. "We peasants may be thin on top, but we are not thin in the head."

"That," commented Richard over his shoulder, "is Old Pep talking. You, my son, have a very fine head of hair."

"Do not laugh at me, or I will kill you," said Nicolas.

Thirty-one

THE MOUNTAIN SLOPES were covered with riotous gentians, decorating the valleys; purple aquilegia carpeted the marsh-lands; in the long, lush grasses white narcissi waved. All was flowers and an oven of heat, and this slowed them, so that every step upward became a gasp, for the air was thinner. The savage country of the patchwork plains wavered and danced in the fierce sunlight.

But the air, fresh and clean, was filled with a scent of flowers and this scent became intoxicating and heavy with dampness even as they climbed, and Nicolas knew that soon they would come to water.

Before them, in a volcanic basis of the mountains, lonely as a desert oasis, stood a lake of astonishing blueness, a reflection of the sky. Nicolas bounded forward, shouting aloud at this discovery, and Juana shouted also, running after him with her pack rattling metallically with their cooking pots; running in a swaying, gasping race to the water, and Nicolas, in Richard's laughter, reached it first and flung himself down upon his face in the shallows and scooped up the water into his mouth and threw it about him in light-spray, so that the lakeside, with Juana splashing also, became a rainbow of a myriad colours. Then Richard arrived and knelt and drank more sedately, watching them, Juana and Nicolas, as a man watches that which is his own: and sat back on the bank and looked at the sky, and there was for him a new radiance in the day.

This woman and this boy, Richard thought – I will take them to Candas, west of Gijon in the Asturias, first, and show them my home; show them, but without telling them, the place where I made love to Carla. And so he thought of his home near Oviedo and the cafés where once he talked politics with the old Asturian fishermen, they who were beautiful in the face, and without arrogance and dependence: men who

233

could tell the brands of wine at a sniff and how to eat hot bread with the nose as well as with the mouth. And then he thought of the Basque Mascarades that came to the town to dance; the men in their Hussar-like uniforms, white-gloved and stockinged, with feathered, ceremonial caps; leaping about to the music of flutes and mandolins, the dances of the Hongreurs, which Carla had loved.

Juana and the boy were playing in the shallows, and Richard watched.

Often, in memory, he walked with Carla in the tide-swim on the shore of Pedreña, and the little waves gave way under their toes and the indentations in the sand filled with the incoming sea. Her piquant vitality was like Juana's, and filled him with delight. And they would run together on the shore, as Juana and Nicolas were running now, and Carla's hair, which was dark and beautiful, would blow alive about her head, like Juana's. Her face was golden because of the sun; brown-gold were her shoulders in the year she was seventeen.

She had come down to the shore where he, Richard, awaited her, and it was moonlight, for her train from Oviedo was late. She came down to the shore and he was waiting, because she said she would come, and seeing her, he had called to her, but she had not heard because of the surf: and had stood there, calling 'Richard, Richard!' and he heard her voice like a shearwater's cry above the thunder of the sea, and turned, seeing her. And both had run – he from one direction, she from another – and met together on the beach, and kissed, and flung off their clothes and run into the shallows, as Juana and Nicolas were running now. And there was nothing but sun, wind and sky.

Seeing Juana, Richard thought again of Carla, who was gone, but no longer did he know emptiness; and he stood up and threw off his pack, then his smock and then his shirt, and called to them, "Come on. First one in!"

Seeing Richard coming to nakedness, Nicolas came splashing out of the lake and he, too, took off his clothes so that he and Richard, naked, ran beside the lake and flung themselves down on to the hot sandy shore where the tide made wetness, and lay there gasping and shouting, and their cries echoed in the mountains.

Then Richard cried, tugging at Juana's clothes, "Take them off, take them off!" but she would not, so he pursued her while Nicolas stood, laughing and uncertain, as naked as the day, and watched. They rolled in the sand, Richard and Juana, and presently she ceased her laughing appeals and rose and took off first her jacket and then her riding shirt, and Nicolas saw her breasts, as many times he had seen the breasts of his mother during her undressing.

Because of the beauty of Juana, Nicolas remembered his mother and her marriage to Diego Díaz, the lead-labourer of Alanis, and this sickened him so that he rose to forget and went to a quiet place of rushes where the white narcissi grew. And lay down in the shallows with one hand outstretched into deeper waters where the big trout were playing, and waited; and as he waited the water of the lake lapped over his waist and buttocks and swilled hot to his chin, but his hand and arm, where it was thrust down into deep water, was in coldness. Here swam the trout, caressing his fingers for warmth; fish who had been cold for a million years.

So Nicolas waited, letting the sun of a faultless sky beat down upon his body, and in his ears was wave-lap and the sound of fish sipping, and the hiss of the wind in the faces of the waving narcissi, and in his nostrils was the scent of orchids: and heard, as the big trout touched his outstretched fingers – waving gently, so gently that they could have been brown bindweed – heard the faint sounds of Richard's laughter and Juana's cries.

And Nicolas thought: this is paradise: this is the paradise of which the priests tell, they who moan their mournful incantations. But here instead of wailing prayers, there is laughter; in place of cruelty, kindness; for misery, joy. This is that for which I have long prayed with unknown prayers; it is freedom away from the slaveries, the tortures of the Guardia.

The big trout that had nosed his wrist and forearm now slid into his outstretched fingers, and nestled there, tail gently flicking, fins paddling in the refracted light of bindweed. Nicolas waited, breath pent. Big Trout drowses with pleasure in the palm of a human hand; shifts a round eye at a lake-spider, spits at a column of marsh-gnats dancing above. Nicolas took a deep breath, twisted at the waist, turned and threw, and out came Big Trout into sunlight: up, up, a shimmering, glistening half moon of fear, wriggling, shivering to the downward plunge on to the sandy bank. Nicolas rose, knelt; down came a stone. Big Trout's iris eye was unblinking at the sun.

Nicolas was about to slide into the water again when he saw Juana.

He saw Juana not as he had seen her before, as one of the young girls washing in the river of Alanis.

There grew in him a new strength and this strength moved to his stomach and he knew a stirring in his loins. From it came a yearning, a forging in him, as iron is forged in heat and strength, and Nicolas looked upon himself and was ashamed. The mood changed and became contrition; changed again into hatred. And the hatred took him forward into the water so that he was walking towards the woman and the man who was holding her.

Then he knelt in the water and bowed his head, but the water did not cool him.

Nicolas caught two more fish, one for himself and two for the woman, it being necessary to feed and preserve that which soon would be his own. And, with the fish held against him, rose from the water and watched again.

On the other side of the lake, man and woman were standing together like statues of marble in the midday sun, and the woman's dark hair was hanging down her neck, blowing live and free in the hot wind, and the man, clasping her, pressed kisses upon her mouth.

On the other side of the valley, more than a thousand yards distant, Sergeant Tomás Fernández, recently posted to the frontier post at Arnéquy, lowered his binoculars.

"It looks like a woman," he said, and his corporal joined him on the pass, taking the binoculars and peering over the valley from the heights of the Sierra de Abodi. "I can see only three people," said he, "and they look like gitanos."

Fernández replied, reining in his big mare: "Then it will be the old crow, his grandson, and Manolo Quinto. Last time I met them it was in the Guadarrama."

"Last time you met them, Sergeant, it was nearly your last. Why not leave them and go after the others? The leader Emilio, for one. Why are gitanos so important?"

"They are important to me," replied Fernández and the livid scars of his face shone with sweat. He peered through the field glasses again. "They are making east, are they not?"

"For Larrau is my guess," said the corporal. He was hot and his mare was lame and he was cursing Sergeant Fernández. For the past three days they had been tracking the partisans: true, among them somewhere was a woman and a woman would be good sport, if they could catch her. Better be tracking the woman, he thought, than three dirty gitanos. But then he was under the command of the sergeant who hated gitanos, and presumably personal grudges had to be settled first.

"We could cut them off at the river," suggested Fernández. The three tiny figures became instantly silhouetted against the sky-line, then disappeared into the black mass of the mountain.

"At the Nive? Yes, that is possible. Unless, of course, they turn north before they reach the valley."

"Up through Pays Basque to Pied de Port, you mean?" The sergeant snapped his fingers. "Ah yes, he returns to Roncesvalles, his home – the old crow, I mean – yes indeed – he is returning to Roncesvalles and taking the others with him."

"And when we capture Old Crow?" asked the corporal.

"Capture him first, and then I will show you, my Corporal, how an old man can scream. And the grandson too, remember – there is a bonus in the grandson Nicolas."

The corporal shrugged. "Headquarters will show little interest in the skins of three gitanos, my friend. But what now?"

Sergeant Fernández wheeled his mare on the track and pulled on his escort of ten with his arm and the hooves of the horses clattered along the pass, and he shouted: "Take one man, Corporal, and go to the Nive, in case they are making east. If so, you can cut them off. I will take the others and ride north through the valley to Larrau." Reining in, he raised his binoculars once more and stared at the distant range.

Richard, Juana and Nicolas trudged upwards like drugged ghosts against the shadows of the mountains, unaware that they were being watched.

"Old Crow, the grandson and Manolo Quinto, it must be them!" muttered Fernández.

"God help you back at Headquarters if it isn't," said the corporal beneath his breath.

Thirty-two

RICHARD SAID, LOOKING at his watch, "By my calculations we are now over the border and into France. Soon, if we continue north-east, we'll come to the river."

"The river that runs from the lake?" asked Juana, and looked at the sky where the first lights of morning were banishing the dawn. To the east the sky was bright, as if beckoning them into France, and she saw beyond the plains below the last dim ridges of blueness, the mountain bastions before Alcay and the road north-east to Pau. To the north, within the horizon haze, lay unseen Biarritz and the sea; this Juana remembered from her childhood.

Nicolas's feet were cut with the stones of the pass and in the night Juana had tended them, binding them with the torn off calico hem of her riding skirt. And now he went with an awkward tiptoeing care, pausing at times to smile at her, and she put out her hand to him and he came beside her, grasping it, and once the boy raised her hand to his lips and kissed it, and Juana smiled.

By eight o'clock, their clothes steamed dry in the rising temperature, the Pyrences were ablaze with light; a whiteness that consumed the earth. With it came a heat that burned through the rents of their clothes.

"Look!" whispered Nicolas suddenly, and they stopped on the steep descent of the pass and looked down on to the winding flash of the River Nive, and standing in the shallows an ibex, a wild mountain goat, was drinking.

"You fancy fresh meat?" asked Nicolas, smiling.

Richard put out an arm and all three sank to the ground.

"Three hundred yards?"

"Four hundred, more likely."

Richard pushed up the Winchester in front of him. "Perhaps I could get him from here . . ."

"And perhaps not," said Nicolas. "You stay, and I will stalk him. True, he is small . . ." he lowered the field glasses,

239

"but he will feed us for a week. You like mountain goat, lady?"

Juana made a face.

"Do not be afraid. The way I cook him he will taste better than eating in the Mayorazgo in Madrid, eh, *Yanqui*?" and the boy's eyes shone with a strange fire, more from an unsubstantial world than one of reality.

Earlier, before dawn, Nicolas had come off watch and looked within the hollow of the pass where Richard and Juana lay, but only Richard slept. Juana, returned from washing, was sitting on her heels beside his sleeping form, and Nicolas watched, seeing her shirt where it had fallen ragged over her shoulders; and saw, too, the whiteness of her skin in the dull glow of the fire, and her hair as she combed it out in shining blackness. Thus he had seen her, and the sight of her brought again a dryness to his throat. And then, even as he watched from the pass, Juana's hands had paused in tying up her hair and she had slowly turned to stare in his direction. So Nicolas sank back into the shadows of the dawn, knowing again the loneliness of the sierra.

One day, he thought, it might be necessary to kill the *Yanqui*; this was a pity, for he liked him; and certainly, of such an action Old Pep would not have approved. But how was it possible to live the lie? One woman and two men? True, he reflected, Juana was older than him by many years, but was not that also true of his mother and Diego Díaz back in Alanis? Young men, he had heard, often sought older women for their experience of life. How would he behave, he thought, in a hotel like the Plaza of Madrid, for instance, without the guidance of a woman of the world? Did one really eat the sea-spiders with the fingers? Or drink soup from the bowl, when others, he had heard say, ladled it up to their mouths with spoons?

Such important facts a woman like this would undoubtedly know.

Nicolas looked about him at the sun-sated turrets of the Sierra de Abodi; their endless procession of pinnacled horizons hammered at the sky. Below him in the verdant valley the ibex wandered in nervous, darting walks, its startled eyes alert for unseen enemies. Nicolas gently drew back the bolt of his Kovaks rifle, and crouching, took a little track that reached a thin finger down to the plain.

And the Guardia corporal, seeing him suddenly break from the cover of the land mass, put out a restraining hand to his escort rider.

"Look," he whispered, and pointed with his whip. "Beyond the ibex . . .!"

"Where?"

"To the left, fool, to the left!"

For answer the man drew his carbine from its saddle holster.

The ibex suddenly drowsed, unmoving. Head low, it drowsed in bee-hum, a sublimation to the sun. Nearly a thousand feet above, Richard and Juana watched as Nicolas reached the boulder-strewn plain, wriggling on his stomach or darting in quick swerves from cover to cover. A stone rattled beneath his bandaged feet. The ibex raised its head in mute inquiry, then lifted its muzzle to scent the wind. Before it the river sparkled and sang and mist rose in little billows, and the bright green plateau of the oasis were spiked with bulrushes, nodding brown-bulbed to the wind. The ibex lifted its head again, hearing nothing, scenting nothing of danger save the scream of instinct. Fixedly, it stood now, forelegs splayed, staring in Nicolas's direction, for the wind had breathed on the sweat of his face and the scent shot like an arrow to the nostrils of the ibex, and it snorted, gathering itself for escape. And in the instant before it moved, Nicolas pressed the trigger of the rifle. Smoke and flame spurted; the sound of the shot clattered fitfully upwards in the heat-laden air to where Richard and Juana crouched. The ibex dropped and lay motionless. Nothing moved in the valley save a wisp of drifting smoke from the rifle. Then Nicolas rose from cover. Juana and Richard saw him running, rifle in hand, across the grass; reaching the ibex, he knelt, turning immediately to wave to them.

"He got it!" Juana delightedly waved back.

Richard cried: "Yes, but look!" and pointed to his right where two riders had emerged from the shelter of trees. "The Guardia!"

From their high vantage point on the pass, Richard and Juana watched.

"Warn him with a shot," whispered she.

"No, wait," Richard opened the bolt of the Winchester and saw the bright brass of the round in the breech, and slowly closed the breech. "Wait to see what they do."

"Come on, come on!" Nicolas now astride the ibex, waved an arm, calling them down, and his voice wailed on the heated air. They saw the flash of his knife as he set to gutting it, and his back was to the distant riders. Richard lifted his field glasses.

"Two of them, no more. One of them is a corporal."

"Fernández?"

"Nicolas was wrong – no Fernández. This is unlucky for us – we've hit a wandering patrol . . . Another day and we'd have been clear of them."

"Look!" interjected Juana, softly.

One of the riders had dismounted and had run for cover. Crouching, with his carbine trailing, he ran from the shelter of the elms and took up a position behind a boulder on the river bank. The quicksilver water wavered in heat. Richard narrowed his eyes to the incinerating glare. The man moved again, running closer to Nicolas, who, unsuspecting, was labouring with his knife on the body of the ibex; and suddenly he rose and flung off his smock and his hands, Juana saw, were red. Richard pushed the muzzle of the rifle farther up the boulder before him and pressed his cheek against the butt. The Guardia crouching behind the boulder peered at Nicolas and rose again, then dropped and squirmed on his stomach in the grass. Sweat flooded Juana's face. She whispered, "Richard, for God's sake . . ."

"Next time he rises," said he, and closed one eye, squinting down the barrel of the Winchester and the prone body of the Guardia, now two hundred yards from Nicolas, inched forward; snake-like, the man was walking on his elbows, his shoulders moving awkwardly, his knees propping out, and the vetch-grass, the hair of the river bank, waved to his progress. Unsuspecting, Nicolas worked on, pausing at times to call shrilly. Suddenly, the policeman rose, bending for a final run. Instantly, he danced like a marionette on the tip of the

Winchester's foresight. Richard squeezed the trigger. The muzzle recoiled in smoke and flame, leaping from the boulder. In the drifting smoke Juana saw the Guardia stretch suddenly to his full height, before turning slowly, to fall face down. Nicolas wheeled about, his hands sweeping for his rifle, and from the clustered elms the second Guardia, the corporal, emerged, spurring his horse. Richard fired again, missing him, and the horse and rider came on, the horse now at full gallop. Juana saw Nicolas rise, put his weapon to his shoulder and fire. But still the Guardia came on; his carbine spurted smoke as he fired from the saddle. Running for the cover of a nearby boulder, Nicolas flung himself flat: the day was suddenly raked with shrieking ricochets.

"Wait here!" Richard hand-sprung over the boulder before him and dived down the steep path to the river; Juana watched his slipping, sliding progress, his rifle held at arm's length above him. Reaching the plateau he stopped, took rough aim and fired again and again, for the corporal had leaped from the saddle and was racing for cover. Disdaining cover himself, Richard took a final aim at him. The Guardia's horse was now wandering aimlessly within the flying bullets. Juana saw smoke and dust appear on the rocks before Richard as he stood his ground and fired. Nicolas was firing also; she saw dust and splinters flying up from the crag in front of the policeman. Then, suddenly, Richard wheeled and fell, the Winchester flying out of his grasp. He lay momentarily while Juana stared in horror, then began to drag himself towards the river grass like a wounded leveret. Seeing this, the policeman rose confidently from behind his crag taking fresh aim; rolling sideways out of his cover, Nicolas fired first. The man screamed and flung up his arms, collapsing sideways, then tumbled head first over the crag. He lay there, spread-eagled, his booted legs grotesquely stuck up. Calmly, Nicolas fired again. The corporal's body shuddered to the bullet's impact. Nicolas rose and ran towards Richard from one direction, Juana came from the other. And they met beside him.

"Richard!" Juana flung herself down. Richard turned over slowly on to his back, rose on an elbow and rubbed his sleeve across his sweating face.

"Christ," he said.

The Guardia's bullet had taken him low, cutting across the lower abdomen and ricocheting off the right hip. With frantic fingers Juana bared the wound, raising the blood-soaked waistband and removing Richard's belt, which, almost severed by the path of the round, had taken much of the impact. Blood was pulsating from the flesh wound, running in red streams over her fingers as she strove to stop the bleeding.

She whispered urgently, "Can you stand? It reduces the bleeding."

With the help of Nicolas, Richard did so. From her medical bag she took a broad band of adhesive plaster and with this, kneeling beside Richard, Juana managed to close the wound. Instantly the bleeding lessened.

"It will need stitching."

Nicolas stared about him at the bodies of the two Guardia. The horse drew closer, nosing the ground in mute inquiry.

"My God, we're going to need you," said Richard.

"Can you ride, do you think?"

Richard blinked sweat from his eyes. Weakness from shock was sweeping over him in waves of increasing intensity, and the eyes of Nicolas were calm upon his. He answered, lightly, "Of course. Just help me to get on the thing."

"We go now," said Nicolas, and there was in his expression a new command. "Soon the rest of the patrol will come. Fernández will remember us for what we have done to the Guardia."

"And you're still as certain it is Sergeant Fernández following us?"

"Of course. I am a gitano. I know the ways of the Guardia. Come," and he seized the reins of the horse.

Thirty-three

BECAUSE THE WOUND in Richard's side bled again within a mile of renewing the march, Juana stitched it, using sutures plucked from the tail of the Guardia mare.

Nicolas, squatting near, watched with meticulous intent while she did this. Richard lay in the limp posture of a man without strength, his face turned away. After this, Juana and Nicolas helped him up into the saddle, and he sat there, swaying drunkenly to the animal's gait, eyes closed against the glare of the sun.

Juana was worried. He was a big man and his strength was great, but the slash of the wound betrayed its depth; while stitching it she had felt the wall of his stomach above her fingers, and though Richard made light of the wound, the intensity of the shock was in his face. There was now about his movements a lethargy; a pallor in his features that Juana had not seen before. This came, Juana knew, with the onset of desperate injury; it lay in the white, languid features of the wounded brought in from Madrid; row upon row of stretchers laid in neat lines in the hospital corridors. From these men, the seriously hurt, no sounds emerged. They lay in the parched tranquillity of their personal tragedies: a patient resignation that carried them to the advent of death.

"How is it now?" Juana asked, leading the mare.

Richard smiled, "I'm all right, I tell you."

The sun beat down on the mountains with relentless heat. The little cavalcade went with bowed faces; the mare drooped her head in paradise dreams of water.

By the afternoon of the second day of travel the sun's radiance transmitted reflections of incandescent light, a dazzling noon-tide glare: on one side the rocks emitted lambent flame, a splendour of heat; on the other, far below in the valley, the fields lay emerald and empty of movement and sound, save for occasional swooping buzzards and the pitiful bleating of sheep.

On the evening of that second day, with layer after layer of prodigious mountain peaks confronting them, they stopped in the lee of an overhanging bluff on the pass and Nicolas said, "Lady, will you speak with me?" His great brown eyes narrowed to sun-glare. "Alone."

Juana tethered the mare. Richard sat unmoving in the saddle, his eyes moving dully over the barren scene of rocks and heat, making no attempt to talk. His smock, from waist to hem, was starched with blood; dried blood was upon his hands, upon the saddle.

Nicolas said: "The *Yanqui*, he is ill, you realise?"

Juana turned away peremptorily. "Of course."

"The bullet, it has cut his stomach. His inside stomach, you understand?"

"I do not think so." She considered this again.

"It is bloody inside. I have seen such wounds before. It speaks by whiteness in his face. The stomach locks the tongue, you know? In Estremadura, during the fighting against the Moors, we killed men with such wounds." He made the motion of shooting with a pistol, squinting one eye.

"Holy Mary, don't!"

Nicolas made a face. "I tell you, it is true. Would it not be kinder? He does not talk, you see? The Americano has been wounded before, and I did see it. In the head, too, and then he was all tongue. Then he was all fists and orders, and we had to obey. Now he sits and does not speak."

"We do not shoot our comrades, Nicolas."

He smiled, his white teeth appearing in his dust-stained face. "Yes, yes, lady, nor does a gitano. Not even when the fascists came. But left them behind with the women, for care. Women are kind to the stomachs of men."

"Yes. You took them to the hospital. That is where the Americano should be, in a hospital."

"But instead, he is sitting in the saddle of a mare, lady. With his feet up in a bed such a stomach slit is wonderful. The war is over. But to sit in a saddle, to ride for miles. Would you give this pain to a dog?"

"He doesn't speak," said Juana at nothing. "If only he would speak."

"He does not speak because the blood is in his mouth."

Nicolas leaned back against the rock of the pass and tipped back his sombrero; jerked his head to where the mare was standing motionless, with Richard slumped forward, his face lowered almost to his chest. Nicolas thumped his stomach. "He bleeds in here, you will see. Soon he will be dead."

"Help me get him off the horse," said Juana.

They slept that night on the open pass within the shelter of the bluff and the moon, round and beautiful, hung over the valley. Earlier, Nicolas had gone down one of the tracks to a basin in the rocks where water glimmered, and returned with the Guardia's water-bottle filled with hot water. Then he sat on the pass and gnawed at a thigh-bone of the ibex, which he carried rolled in his poncho: Juana knelt on the pass and held the bottle to Richard's cracked lips.

"My darling," she said.

She slept beside him, wrapping her own blanket about him, and Nicolas, from a distance, sat cross-legged with Don Pita's automatic across his knees and dozed beneath his slanted sombrero, and Richard said, in sleep: "Are you there, Carla?"

The sound of his voice, so sudden in the night, awakened Juana; rising on an elbow she looked into his sleeping face.

It was the face of a man who has seen death come and lived despite it: the sunken cheeks, the grey pallor of the forehead, the stubbled beard where the sweat glistened against a skin parched dry of sweat; a parchment skin stretched tightly across cheek-bones, bringing the shadows of features into high relief. Moonlight enhanced the vision of illness.

"Carla . . ." But Richard's voice, when he spoke, was bass and strong, as if from a rent in the coffin of his soul. Juana gripped his hand.

"Yes, I am here."

He said, turning away his face, "You are coming to Pedreña again?"

Juana lowered her face. "Of course . . . I shall come."

"Down to the sands again, to Pedreña?" He moved his head from side to side. "And we will go to Santander in the spring. Did I tell you that I have a boat in Astillero?" He grunted in sleep, turning his head in wayward agitation. "Come now, I told you!"

Juana said, her voice breaking, "You . . . you did not tell me."

"A little ketch . . . five thousand *pesetas* I paid for her. We will go to Santander and out into the bay and catch sardines and squid and sell them to the tourists . . .?"

A shadow fell across the moonlit pass. Juana looked up. Nicolas was standing above them, the automatic held loosely across his forearms. He said, softly, "He dreams?"

Richard said, his voice rising, "When we are married, eh? Or even before, if your people will agree . . .?"

Juana said, staring up at Nicolas, "Leave us." And he asked, his head on one side:

"He calls you by the name of Carla?"

"Leave us, please," said Juana.

"But I thought your name was Juana, lady."

"Hush," said Juana, and with her handkerchief wiped Richard's sweating face.

"It just shows," commented Nicolas, turning away, "how easy it is to be mistaken."

Juana bowed her head. "Please go," she said.

On the morning of the fifth day of travel, with the sun making haloes of light above a distant lake, they went in silence with Nicolas leading the mare.

As if in contrition for the torturing splendour of the sun, rain fell suddenly from a single scudding cloud that raced across the sky: it fell in gentle swathes of water that revived them; trickling in cooling delight down their sun-burned bodies; lifting their faces and spirits. The mare snorted her pleasure and planted her hooves with a new vigour along the broken track. Nicolas pushed his sombrero back upon his neck, Juana raised her arms to the refreshing draughts of water. The sun blazed anew, but only with an ineffectual fire. But, by midday, the rain turned traitor and dried in the air. Steam rose from their clothes, chafing their blistered shoulders. A lustrous, glittering glare began to grow in the heavens, rekindling the damped heat of the boulders, reflecting off the face of the pass with scintillating rays of infra-red.

The day blazed with damp heat, a fusing of sun and stifling air. The mare stopped suddenly on the pass. Nicolas, exhausted, sank down on to his haunches. And Juana, twenty yards behind, started forward with a wild cry as she watched Richard slowly topple out of the saddle. He fell as she reached him, Nicholas stumbling beneath him to break the impact of the fall. Together, they laid Richard down on the pass beside the mare, who raised her head and whinnied pitifully for water.

Kneeling beside Richard's still body, they drank what was left in the water-bottle, and Nicolas said, "He is dying. You see, I told you."

Juana got to her knees, shaking her head. Her hair was down in sweated strands over her ragged shirt; her lips were cracked and colourless, her cheeks blistered.

"He is not dying," she said. "Get water."

"To get water means climbing down into the valley." Nicolas protested shrilly.

Juana shrieked: "Then do it. Climb down. I need water. When you have got it, return and help me."

"Help you?" There was a strange new arrogance in the boy's face.

"Give me your knife," commanded Juana.

Nicolas drew it from his belt. He said:

"Touch him with a knife now and he will die even quicker."

"Do as you are told. Bring water."

First, Juana bared Richard's wound, slipping down the waistband of his trousers and pulling up his bloodstained shirt. While doing this, Richard breathed with the stentorian gasps of a man already dying, but this, Juana knew, was the natural snores of the unconscious; she was grateful for his oblivion. By the time Nicolas returned with the water-bottle, she had cauterised the blade of the knife by the flame of dried sticks, ablaze with Richard's lighter.

"Help me to turn him on his side."

Nicolas obeyed.

The sight of the wound, its change since she had last seen it, astonished her.

Where before the path of the bullet was clean, a razoring cut that readily stitched and laced together, there existed now a heaped bluish mound of poison; raised at the edges by a crimson inflammation, it was now ridged with a purpling blackness.

The swelling of the wound extended over the pit of the stomach and enveloped the hip-bone; pushed into Richard's groin where the puss had spread red fingers of infection.

"*Madre Mía!*" whispered Nicolas. "And still he sits a horse?"

Juana had seen such infection before in the tossing, shuddering cages of pain in the Hospital of the Sacred Heart; even under the antiseptic conditions of a hospital, few such cases recovered, but slid into a gangrenous putrefaction; the thin red line that poisoned the limb, demanding high and instant amputation. And although the exclusion of air by plaster of Paris had proved beneficial to healing in normal cases, such methods did not help with gangrene. Richard was now whispering heatedly, twisting this way and that in growing delirium, as if in expectation of the coming surgery.

Bending above him while Nicolas shielded Richard's face from the sun with his sombrero, Juana gently swabbed the infected area clean with iodine; Richard called, his voice clear and strong: "Carla, Carla!"

"I am here," Juana replied. "You are all right, my darling, I am here."

Nicolas lifted his eyes from Richard's face.

"He is dying, I tell you. Why bother?"

Juana shook her head. "He will not die. I will not let him die. Be quiet, and hold him still."

Inserting the point of the knife, Juana cut horizontally; slowly, carefully, from hip to groin; ignoring the black fluid shot with blood and puss that instantly spouted over her hand. Richard cried aloud and momentarily fought them; with her forearms upon him, Juana pressed down with the weight of her body while Nicolas held his shoulders. Richard groaned, feebly moving his legs. The poison flushed out of him, running in brown streams over his groin and stomach, and Juana, gasping, levered her fists against his muscled body until pure, red blood began to flow from the wound. She was enduring an obliterating sickness; her throat contracted against the lust to vomit. Wiping sweat from her face with her forearms, she worked on, pressing, swabbing, until the wound was clean.

When it was clean, Richard slept, his head on one side, his breathing peaceful.

"You did him good, lady," said Nicolas, and rose.

The sun beat down in a fiery incandescence; a febrile inflammation of blood and heat.

Bending above him, Juana kissed his sleeping face.

"I am here. Carla is with you," she said.

Despite her exhaustion, Juana did not sleep; for hours she sat on her heels on the pass, with her hands folded between her knees, watching Richard's sleeping face. Once he stirred and put out his hand as if in search of her, and she held it. The mountains glowed in the June dawn; red light, tinged with cold, came flashing over the peaks, and still she knelt there, her chin lowered upon her chest in a numbing drowse; still Richard slept.

But later Juana rose and went down a track in the side of the mountain to the place of water that Nicolas had found: there, she stripped off her shirt and plunged her hands deep into the rock basin where the water flowed, and drank; then flung the water over her naked shoulders, allowing it to soak down in coldness to her skirt.

It was while drying her wet hair in the sun, throwing it about her shoulders, that Nicolas appeared on the other side of the basin.

Juana's hands, running wet in sunlight, paused, and she smiled at him, unperturbed.

While with a peasant it was necessary to act like a peasant; this she knew from childhood: there was no mock modesty in a gitano: women had breasts with which to feed their children; what necessity lay in hiding the fact? The boy's expression was proof of his innocence.

"One day you will wash like that under the pump in Alanis," said he, and put a straw in his mouth and a heel on the rock basin, and admired her, then tipped back his sombrero and grinned wide.

251

Juana moved slowly, reaching for her stained khaki shirt; throwing it up, she waved her arms into it; pulled down the hem and tucked it into her waistband.

"Ay-ee! Your waist so small, too! You are beautiful," said Nicolas.

"The Americano sleeps?" It was necessary to change the subject.

"He sleeps like a dead man, but is much alive. But he will not live long, lady. Soon the bullet will poison him again and soon you will have to cut him again." He tossed his hands about. "And so it will go on. He will die easily."

Juana said, "It is clear that you know little about Americanos."

Nicolas brightened, saying, "Your breasts are good to look upon, Old Pep said. He also said that your breasts are the finest he has seen in Estremadura, and I agree. They are large and firm, and no doubt their milk will be rich for a labourer's children. My mother, I'm sure, would be the happiest woman in all Alanis."

"Your mother?" Juana walked past him up the track and Nicolas followed, softly whistling to himself, having said nothing in particular.

"Now I begin to understand about her and Diego Díaz," he said, gasping to the climb.

"The lead-labourer she is marrying, you mean?"

The boy nodded, now walking beside Juana, helping her up occasionally with a push on the bottom. "Diego is twice her age – remember, I told you? And I did not understand. But now, I, too, feel the wind up my shirt, like my grandfather and Manolo explained to me. It is a wonderful feeling. And a difference in age? What is that? There is twenty-five years beween my mother and Diego Díaz; what is ten years between you and me?"

Juana paused on the path; she searched his face. His eyes, narrowed to the sun, smiled back into hers. Nicolas said, "All the time you wish to help the *Yanqui*, I will help also. But if you decide to let him die, I will understand." He patted the knife at his belt. "Even now, if you wish it, I would help him to die. Would it not be kinder? And then you can come back with me to Estremadura."

Juana's eyes moved slowly over his brown face.

Nicolas said: "You are not for him, for you are all Spanish; you are beautiful Spanish, and he a *Yanqui*. I, too, am Spanish. One day you will forget that I am only a gitano."

Juana slowly turned away. Nicolas added, "I would work for you and give you many children. All my life there would be no other woman in my *posada*. This I swear on the beads."

"I will bear it in mind."

He took her hand. "In my village we will eat salad, and cucumber dipped in oil; also fatted buñuelos with white sugar on top, and after *fiesta* we will lie in the field and listen to the sun go down." He peered into her face.

Juana hurried back to Richard.

All that afternoon they rested, a sleepless siesta within enormous confines of rock. The sun was pitiless, and in the shade of a boulder on the pass Juana knelt beside Richard or struggled up and down the slope to the rock basin far below, for water. This she swabbed over his face and chest, to cool him.

Lying nearby, with his back against the face of the pass, Nicolas watched, and did not speak. With Richard's Colt revolver in his belt and the big Winchester rifle lying beside him for cleaning, he sat with his little Kovaks automatic pistol across his knees, and watched.

With the coming of evening, they moved again; Juana struggling with Nicolas to get Richard back into the saddle. And Richard, slowly recovering from the poison of his wound, opened his eyes to the movement of the mare and looked about him at the blue-whiteness of the Sierra de Abodi, then squinted his eyes upwards at the position of the sun. He said: "Where are we, for God's sake?"

Nicolas came running up, joining Juana at the bridle. "You do not worry, Señor. Soon we will be with the French gendarmes; there are no Guardia here."

For answer, Richard reined in the mare and stared at the configuration of peaks that barred their way; then he looked behind him at the flatter pastures of Pays Basque. He stared upwards again, at the sunblaze, and said, "Christ, we're going west."

"East, I tell you!" Nicolas grinned good-humouredly, opening his hands. "Do you think I do not know these mountains? This is the last range before the end of the sierra – then into Pays Basque – down, down, *amigo!*"

Richard swayed in the saddle and rubbed sweat from his forehead. His eyes bright blue in his stained face, moved from Juana to Nicolas and back again. He said, bassly, "What the hell is happening, boy, you're taking us back into Spain."

Nicolas hunched his shoulders expressively and pursed his lips at Juana. "He is sick, lady. He has the sun in his head, eh?" He took from his belt the Colt revolver and spun the chamber ostentatiously, still smiling. "If you do not trust me, then why sleep up there, *compañero?* You do not trust a *gitano?*"

He nodded happily, grinning wide.

Juana whispered: "Why, Nicolas? Why?"

The boy made a childish face. "All right, you know the truth. Why do I take you back to Spain? Because I do not want to go to France." His expression changed and his eyes narrowed. "Do you really want to go to France, lady, and you Spanish?" He jerked his thumb at Richard, still in the saddle. "For him it is nothing – one place is as good as another, for he is a dirty *Yanqui*. But for us there is only Spain. How can you come to my bed in Alanis if you are in France?"

"Nicolas . . ." Juana shook her head in anguish. "It cannot be – don't you understand?"

For reply, Nicolas broke the Colt open and snapped it shut, then cried, in anger, "Let him walk to France, then, if he is a man. If I had one leg I would walk to Spain. All morning you have been bathing him with water, and tending him. Do you think I have no eyes? I told you I would take you to my mother in Alanis, and you listened. But then you went to him. You are a woman with a double mouth." He seized the mare's bridle. "Get down, *Yanqui!*"

Juana said, "If your grandfather were here he'd kill you, Nicolas."

"That is because he is an old goat gitano. And that is why he is dead." He waved the revolver at Richard. "Let him

walk. What stupidity, eh?" He laughed shrilly. "For miles he
sleeps in the saddle. Now he sees the sun and is very much
surprised! Only foolish Americanos do not know where they
are going in the middle of a war."

Juana said, her hands begging, "Go where you like,
Nicolas, but for God's sake leave us the horse!"

"Let him take it, the dirty little thief," said Richard, and
measured the distance between himself and Nicolas. The boy
shouted: "Walk, *Yanqui*! It will save me the trouble of
shooting you," and he turned to Juana. "And when he is
dead, I will come to you and take you back to Spain. If I kill
him, you will not forgive me." He drew away, pulling the
mare after him by the reins. "Walk, *compañero*! If you want to
go to France, then walk, my friend."

Standing together, they watched as Nicolas swung himself
into the saddle.

"When the *Yanqui* is dead, I will come back for you,
remember!" he cried, and he trotted the mare along the pass
that led west, to Spain.

Thirty-four

LACARRE FARM, SET in the foothills of the Sierra de Abodi, set its square windows towards Larrau and blindly winked at the moon. For the past year, according to the inhabitants of the Pays Basque, it had stood deserted; now its sagging roof glinted at the stars. In its ramshackle shippon, where Madame Ravol once laboured to keep her drunken Roberto, the corrugated iron roof of an outhouse, now a shelter for rats, clanged dismally in the wind of the sierra.

But now, in moonlight, a shadow was cast across the stone-flagged floor of the kitchen; a hand moved; footsteps echoed along the empty corridors and up the boarded stairs. Lacarre Farm, once as bare as chastity, knew again its long forgotten human warmth. A candle glowed near a raked out stove; mice, that had recently inhabited the empty larder, scattered in a sudden flight of panic.

The footsteps that shuffled on the kitchen flags approached a window.

Madame Ravol, clad in black for a lamented lover, held the candle against her chest; lifting the hem of her black, home-spun skirt, she left the kitchen. The guttering candle cast eerie reflections on the faded walls as she mounted the stairs to her bedroom.

Madame Ravol had brought a common law husband to Lacarre Farm some twenty years before, He, handsome Roberto Soler, a dashing Catalan, had seduced many and fathered none – a commendable feat of arms in the sparsely inhabited district of the Pays Basque; finding enough time in the intervals to smuggle successfully over the Pyrenees between Spain and France – jewels, wine, art; using his wife's farm as a base.

But Madame Ravol, quickly tiring of his charms, formed a liaison between herself and the French gendarmerie. Now Roberto Soler languished in a French prison for the duration of the Spanish Civil War; with luck, thought Madame, he might not survive it.

Now she had returned to her beloved France to farm her eighty-five acres alone; bearing her life of unhappy mischance – her marriage to Roberto with the fortitude of a Basque: meanwhile nurturing a hatred of anything Spanish, and Spanish males in particular. Roberto was a libertine, full of Spanish arrogance. The piety of her French upbringing in Avenses le Compte had taught Madame Ravol that those who spring from the soil should first be humble before it.

She was congratulating herself on discovering the house intact (she hadn't been back more than a day) when she paused on the stairs at the landing window and looked down on to the shippon below.

There she saw an astonishing sight in the light of the moon.

Two people were lying on the mud-stained cobbles of the yard: one, a man, was striving weakly to rise; the other, a slighter figure – and as far as one could see, a woman – was endeavouring to roll the man over; to lever him across her shoulders in order to carry him.

Madame Ravol stared in disdain. Clearly, like her lost Roberto, the man was almost terminally drunk.

Her immediate impulse was to check all bolts on the doors. To give strangers assistance never occurred to her. Smugglers were always seeking sanctuary in the Pays Basque; the ruses they employed being many and ingenious. Extinguishing the candle, she watched. And, even as she did so, the woman, who was bare-headed and dressed in a torn shirt, riding skirt and boots, sudenly knelt: unrolling a blanket she carried on her back, she covered the man on the ground. Rising, she then ran in stumbling, swaying haste to the door of the farm.

Her repeated knocking echoed in the bare hall and reverberated up the stairs to the landing. Madame Ravol shuddered, and pulled her black dress closer about her throat. Then the woman shouted, "Please open the door. Oh, please!" The rest was lost in a fitful cry. After a little while the woman began to sob in her calling and beat upon the door. Madame Ravol imagined drumming fists, the tear-stained face. Then the sobbing changed to commands of anger.

Vaguely, the farm woman wondered if the stranger had seen the light of the candle . . .

Getting no reply, Juana ran back to Richard and knelt beside him. She whispered, smoothing his hair, "We've found a house. And somebody's here, darling. We'll be all right, I tell you, we'll be all right . . ."
Richard did not answer.

Since late morning, when Nicolas had left them stranded in the foothills of the mountains, they had descended into the country of the Pays Basque proper; a lurching, stumbling journey to the lowlands; mile after mile of unrequited pain. With an arm around Juana's shoulder Richard had gone, stopping at times weakly to douse himself with water, before slipping again into the shuddering, sweating drowse of his septicaemia; an invasion that brought uncontrollable shivering, as with an ague; a raging temperature and a thirst.

The temporary abatement of the poison, after Juana had cut and drained the wound was now exchanged for the onslaught of renewed poisoning; the streptococcal red lines were creeping over his body.

Juana knew that Richard would die if she did not soon find a surgeon.

Still on the landing, holding herself in a sorcery of silence, Madame Ravol listened to the thumping of her heart; her eyes were fixed to the man lying on the cobbles.

It was the man she feared, not the woman. A man, she knew from experience, could beat a woman into helplessness. Suddenly, Richard turned over, his hands clasping his face; as he did this there came a faint tinkling of breaking glass.

Juana reached within the kitchen and pulled up the handle of the casement. The window creaked open to her touch, exposing the bare room within. Warm air touched her face; it was an exorcism of her fears. The house beckoned in savoury smells and warmth. She climbed in. Finding the hall in faint beams of the moon, she opened the door to the shippon and ran out over the cobbles, kneeling again.
"Come, darling. One last effort!"

Soaked with sweat, Richard clung to her, levering himself upright. With his arm around Juana's neck he staggered up the steps and collapsed on to the floor of the hall. Turning, Juana shut and bolted the door. The crash of this echoed in the house. Madame Ravol went slowly up the stairs, past her bedroom door, and opened a cupboard. She was cursing herself silently for not remembering the gun before. In possession of a gun she could have dominated the situation; now she was faced with these strangers in the house.

The man appeared ill; probably wounded, she reflected. Perhaps, now they were in, she reasoned, it would be better to wait for daylight before confronting them. Meanwhile, if she could somehow reach the telephone in the hall, she could contact the land agent in Larrau, he who shared with her a party line. He could then ring the frontier patrol. The Guardia, she thought bitterly, would soon put paid to refugees into France. The Gendarmerie would at least intern them. She would have to go downstairs to do it, of course . . . Despite her determination, she was afraid of the man. She could handle the woman, the woman didn't worry her. But the man . . .

Marriage to Roberto Soler had brought her to this state.

From the cupboard Madame Ravol took an ancient gun; an old fowling-piece from the First World War. It was Roberto's gun; she had kept it to maintain her peace of mind, should he return to the Pays Basque before his allotted time . . .

The touch of the big gun gave her confidence. A box of cartridges was somewhere on the shelf of the cupboard; she felt for these in the dark. Standing there, she listened to the sounds of the kitchen.

The woman, she thought, appeared to be scurrying about, knocking things over in her gasping haste. The man was groaning audibly; the sounds were eerie and the farm woman shivered. With trembling hands she broke the breech of the gun and slipped two cartridges into the double-bore, gently pressing the breech shut. The 'click' seemed to detonate in the cupboard: noises in the kitchen momentarily ceased.

Tumbling more cartridges into the pocket of her gown, the woman waited.

Then, suddenly, a voice cried again in Spanish: "Is anybody home?'' Juana ran up a few of the stairs, shouting up to the bedrooms.

Madame Ravol drew back into the cupboard. She was remembering what happened to the Widow of Alcay, who lived in a hamlet to the north-east. She had given shelter to wandering strangers and been strangled for her compassion. How could a lone woman trust anyone in the middle of a war? The person on the stairs was calling repeatedly, her voice shrill. The farm woman waited, the sweat cold on her forehead.

Spaniards. Damned Spaniards, she thought. It angered her that her house should be so invaded, and it was typical of Spaniards. Spanish Basques, no doubt; like Roberto; she hated them with a new resolve. Presently, Juana ceased to shout, but clattered back down the stairs. Madame Ravol listened to her consoling voice as she addressed the man. A tap began to run in the kitchen.

The farm woman had made up her mind. After the strangers had settled down in the kitchen, she would try to reach the telephone in the hall. If the pair tried to stop her, she would first shoot the man. Sweat broke out afresh on her thin face and she wiped it into her hair. Vaguely, she wondered if the strangers had seen the telephone wires. Surely, the man must have seen them when lying on his back; they ran right across the shippon . . .

For an hour Madame Ravol stood in the cupboard; stiff and cramped. Still gripping the gun, she had sunk to her haunches. The smells of food drifted to her nostrils. The man had ceased to groan; she heard the sound of liquid slopping into a glass. They were drinking her wine. The thought outraged her sense of property.

Juana held the wine to Richard's cracked lips. "Here, my darling, try to drink this . . ."

In the moonlight she saw his face a fiery red; his eyes slits of shadow in the puffy bulges of his cheeks. His lips were swollen, the lips of a Negro in their fullness, and white, chalk white. Richard smiled faintly. Raising his swollen hands to the cup; he tried to swallow. The red wine trickled like blood from the corners of his mouth.

"Juana . . ."

"Yes?" She knelt forward on the kitchen floor, the better to hear his words.

"You go on . . ."

"I am staying with you."

"Please. Please go on . . ."

She kissed his face; momentarily held him against her, then said, with cold practicality. "I . . . I've got to cut you again. You know that?"

He nodded, watching her.

"But I can't do it here. I thought there was somebody in the house, but there can't be. Do . . . do you think you can get upstairs? There's a bed. I saw it from the landing. If I can get you up there perhaps I can leave you and try to find a doctor . . ."

Richard nodded.

"But first, I must cut you. It can't wait, dearest – you realise that?"

The thought of cutting him again brought to Juana a heady sickness; the bile rose to her throat and she swallowed it down; this was something, she argued within herself, that had to be faced with a cold, dispassionate calmness. The presence of the wound itself, a breaching of the body's defensive wall, had induced the first infection. The furious breeding of the infection had forced her into further cutting the wound itself, which laid Richard open to a spreading of the septic emboli. Now he was experiencing painful swelling under his right arm; the increasingly laboured breathing and weakening of his voice betrayed pyaemia; islands of infection were circulating now. Meanwhile, until she could somehow get the services of a surgeon, she would have to limit, by draining again, the source of the original infection, the bullet wound. Later still, if this failed she would have to begin to cut any newly-formed abscess.

Pulling Richard up into a sitting position, Juana knelt, drew his arm across her neck and strained to rise. His boots skidding on the flagstones, Richard fought to help her, weakly gasping. In this position cramped beneath him, Juana began to drag his big body out into the hall. Richard grasped the banisters. Stair by stair, they began the heaving, exhausting climb to the room above.

From the shelter of the open cupboard door, gun in hand, the farm woman watched, her eyes shining in the faint light of the moon.

Somehow, Juana got Richard against the bed and toppled him into it. After doing this, she slid to the floor beside him; the room momentarily swam and she retched, fighting back the vomit. Richard made a strange croaking sound on the bed and she dragged herself up beside him.

He was groaning loudly when she came back to the bed with a jug of water she had got from the kitchen.

Juana said. "I will not let you die, I tell you." She held a cup to his lips.

But Richard had fainted. Within his unconsciousness, Juana worked with frantic speed.

Tearing up the top sheet of the bed to staunch the bleeding, in the light of the moon she cut him in the groin again and lay there, watching it drain into the sheet. Immediately the poison spouted. Richard awoke momentarily to the pain, staring about him like a man in dreams.

"It is over, it is finished." Juana said peremptorily, "Sleep now, my darling."

Within the raucous snoring of Richard's oblivion, Juana, lying on the bed beside him, her fingers on his wrist, did not hear the creaking of the stairs as the farm woman, Madame Ravol, went down to the telephone.

Thirty-five

TOWARDS DAWN, AFTER sleep and with the fever of his poisoning again subsiding, Richard awoke refreshed. He tried to sit up on the bed but Juana pressed him back on to the pillows.

Madame Ravol, standing on the landing, saw Richard move through the crack of the door, and pressed back the hammers of her shot-gun.

'Keep them there until the patrol arrives,' the gendarme had said. 'According to the Spanish Guardia, these are not smugglers but Spanish agents.'

'*Sacre bleu!*' Madame Ravol had whispered into the telephone.

'Hold them, Madame. We are depending on you,' said the gendarme. 'The Guardia will come as quickly as possible.'

The corrugated iron roof in the cow-house began to clatter with monotonous regularity from the shippon. Richard opened his eyes at the ceiling as Madame Ravol clicked back the hammers of the fowling-piece.

"What was that?"

"Nothing, darling, it is the wind. How are you feeling?"

"Better."

"Your temperature has dropped again." Juana leaned above him, searching his face in the blue, unreal light of the window. "The moment it's light I'm going in search of a doctor."

"In this area of Pays Basque all you'll find is Gendarmerie or the Guardia. Find either of those and we won't need a doctor. No, we must go on." He shook his head. "God, if ever I come across that accursed Nicolas . . .!" He made a fist of his hand and pressed it to his face.

"Is the pain bad?"

"It's reasonable." Richard eased his right leg, groaning almost inaudibly. "At first light . . . no doctors, Juana, we've got to get on." He rose on an elbow. The bed creaked. Madame Ravol peered at them again.

Earlier, she had looked through the landing window and down into the valley. The mountain road along which the Guardia Civil would come was a ribbon of blue in the hills. It was along this road, she reflected, that they had come for Roberto . . .

Richard said, holding his head. "Is there any more water?"

"Of course." Juana swung her legs over the bed and lifted the jug. It was empty. "I'll get some more from the kitchen."

Madam Ravol defensively stepped back against the banisters of the landing and levelled the shot-gun at the door.

The Guardia, not yet within sight of Lacarre Farm, came along the valley road in the dawn; called there by a telephone call from the Gendarmerie at the frontier. Spanish smugglers, apparently, were in Lacarre Farm, the Frenchmen had said. Possibly somebody a little more important, Sergeant Tomás Fernández, had replied. 'On the bank of the River Nive they killed two of my men. Burgos Infantería claims that they are possibly terrorists.'

Earlier still, the Guardia frontier post received a telephone call that a certain Colonel Carrasco had been abducted from the Espalón in Burgos: a little later a young agent attached to the Burgos Gestapo had arrived at the frontier post and said that his name was Ramón Barro. Republican saboteurs, said he, were trying to get through the Pyrenees into France for political asylum; that the probable route was south of the Sierra de Abodi and over the River Nive. A telephone call to the Burgos Infantería by Sergeant Fernández had confirmed Ramón Barro's credentials.

And then came the most important news of all – the assassination of General Vidal Mola. Yes, it was assassination all right, the Infantería reported, although the press, quite naturally, would try to cover it up: the sergeant considered this, his face screwed up to the sun.

"I'm only after one man and one man only," Ramón explained at the frontier.

"His name?" asked Sergeant Fernández.

"Emilio. He is known by this, but it is a code name," said Ramón.

"You're lucky," replied Fernández, "I'm after the lot – Hanson, his woman, the Monk of the Café Suizo, as they call him, and three gitanos. Also a couple of others, names unknown." He added, fingering his scarred face. "With luck, one gitano will have the face of a crow and the neck of a vulture."

"Old Pep, do they call him?"

"He goes by that name," answered Fernández.

Ramón smiled, for he had left his knife in Old Pep's back up at the air-strip, and said: "You are looking for a ghost, my friend. Don't tell me you transferred up here from the Gredos to kill a grandfather. *Madre*, what men of war!"

"Ghost or not, I will find him," said Fernández. "Meanwhile, Vidal Mola is now a ghost, they tell me. They bombed his plane, these Hanson partisans."

"Believe all you hear and you are a bigger fool than you look," said Ramón. "His pilot flew too low in the mist. Leave the rumours to women."

The sergeant replied. "For all I know it is true. The Burgos Infantería barracks . . ."

"Scandal-mongers. Bring the dogs, what the hell are we waiting for?"

In a party totalling eight, with Ramón and the sergeant leading, the horsed patrol left the temporary frontier post near Arnéquy, and the peaks of the Sierra de Abodi were ringed with ropes of light.

High on the topmost ridge of the sierra, where you took off a donkey's saddle, it was said, to get him under the clouds, Nicolas sat motionless on the Guardia horse he had stolen from Richard, and looked down into the valley of the Pays Basque. The wet roof of Lacarre Farm glistened like a dewdrop on fire.

Earlier, in darkness, while following Richard and Juana, he had seen a light glowing in the farm, and wondered if perhaps they would make for shelter there: in such a place, he reflected, the *Yanqui* could die in comparative peace, therefore the lady would not be so distressed.

Death, to Nicolas, was finality; it was the chasm at which old emotions halted, the passing of a moon. Therefore, it was necessary, he considered, to be on hand when Juana needed a man's assistance. Did not Old Pep once say that the eyes of the Virgin of Valdés de Real brimmed with tears for every Spanish widow? So it was with this lady; in sleep she had held him – yes, he Nicolas Alvarez – clasped him against her in the night's cold – as recently as before the Galapagar ambush. And he had kissed her hands in warm friendship. Women such as this were full of compassion; in his sickness she naturally treasured the *Yanqui*; yet he, in this very poisoning, gave off a most offensive smell. It was, to Nicolas's mind, only a question of waiting. Gitanos were good at waiting, he reflected; they had been doing it since the Moors. Only the marriage bed back in Alanis was worrying him. A jumble of rags in the corner of his mother's *posada*? Also, she who was by birth a countess would require something considerably better than sharing a *puchero* with the oily fingers of Diego Díaz. More, the bucket used for sitting outside would have to be very much improved; his mother, he knew, would be the first to agree.

Nicolas looked about him at the big country of pines.

At one time the land was lavish with trees, but then came man: here two pines had once been felled to make a pair of shepherd's shoes, the wooden sabots. The country had been devastated by greed. True, it was not much better back in Estremadura, thought Nicolas, but at least, in Alanis, the lady would love it as home. And he would keep her content with food and love. Was it not for this one, and for her alone, that his body had moved?

After he had seen the light glowing in Lacarre Farm, Nicolas had watched Juana enter by breaking the window; seen her return to the yard and half drag the *Yanqui* within. With luck, he now estimated, looking at the watch he had taken from Richard's wrist, the foreigner might even now be dead. Nicolas dropped his hand to Richard's big Colt. One could go down there and hasten the proceedings, of course, but the lady may not relish such interference, for women were strange. Indeed . . . and Nicolas pondered the next thought deeply . . . it might prove wise to repent a little and call at the

266

farm and offer assistance . . . even at this late stage?

With this in mind Nicolas took the Guardia horse down the foothill tracks to the flatter Pays Basque; then trotted it along the metalled road that led to Lacarre Farm. He did not notice the Guardia patrol, led by Sergeant Fernández, coming along the road from Arnéquy.

Madame Ravol, guarding the landing, heard Juana talking within the bedroom. Juana, water jug in her hand, swung open the bedroom door and came face to face with her. With wide, frightened eyes the farm woman presented the shot-gun, her knuckles straining white on the stock.

"Get back!" She retreated, colliding against the banisters.

Juana momentarily stared at the gun, shock upon her face, then instinctively dropped to avoid its discharge. Richard, sitting on the bed, rolled sideways to the floor. Shouting with pain, he scrambled on all fours towards Juana, reached out and slammed the door shut, but Madame Ravol kicked it open again. The gun exploded as Richard rose to seize it; the discharge took him full in the chest. The force of it flung him upwards and backwards, staggering him across the floor and headlong over the bed. He rolled over, limbs waving, falling in a heap between the bed and the wall, one blood-covered hand sliding down the wallpaper. Juana put her hands to her face and screamed, but made no sound; screamed again, still soundlessly. Silence. The farm woman stared at the blood-stained hand; its fingers were faintly moving, leaving a trail of blood as they slid down, down . . . Dropping the gun Madame Ravol shrieked and fled. Still on her knees, Juana heard her sabots clattering down the stairs.

"Richard!" Leaping up, Juana sprang across the room, crawling between the bed and the wall. "Richard!" Her voice was a scream that descended in pitch and force, and ending in faint, choking sobs.

Nicolas, trotting towards the farm, reined in the mare when he heard the shot; smacked her into silence on the metalled road when he heard the scream. And then he saw the black-clad figure of a woman running across the shippon. She was crying incoherently and waving her arms in fearful despair.

And even as she approached, unaware of him in her haste to escape, Nicolas spurred the mare into a gallop, leaped the farm gate and clattered into the shippon: there, he flung himself off the horse, pulled out Richard's pistol and barged through the open door into the house.

"Lady!" His voice echoed as he shouted around the hall. "Lady!"

Above the metallic rattling of the hooves of the troop and the yelping of the dogs, Sergeant Fernández heard the shot with a practised ear, and reined his mare to a halt. Hands raised for silence, the troop stood listening on the road from Arnéquy. The two wolfhounds cowered into quiet.

Ramón whispered: "What is it?"

"A shot, unless I'm mistaken . . ." Fernández looked over his shoulder: a man cried, "Yes, a shot, Sergeant."

"Where from?"

The man pointed with his riding whip. "The farm. I think I saw the flash . . ."

Fernández stared up at the sky.

The dawn was slow that morning. Rain clouds had been blundering up from the east all night: he would have liked it even darker. One thing had been certain in his mind; these people would be armed. The shot was now proof of it. If he barn-stormed the place and lost some men, questions would be asked at Divisional H.Q. Why didn't he wait for dark? Why didn't he do this, do that? Questions, always questions, from the bumbling fools who did their Guardia fighting from the mahogany desks of provincial safety.

Fernández sniffed the wind. Rain, of course, could be some sort of cover. He wondered if Lacarre Farm provided billeting shelter – farm buildings, outhouse cover of any kind? Standing up in the saddle he could see the farm clearly now, down in the valley; its roof shining in expectancy of dawn rain. Turning to Ramón, he said: "What are these people supposed to have done, then?"

Ramón smiled. "Are you not in a position to know, Sergeant? Or is it that they don't trust you with these things . . .?"

"Go to hell," said Fernández.

"For a start – an attack on the life of our beloved Caudillo at Galapagar."

"Oh yes – I was in on that," said the sergeant, fingering his face.

"Then an attack on General Mola in Segovia – a furious affair, according to reports."

"But they didn't succeed."

"They did not."

Fernández laughed bassly. "But they succeeded on the 3rd June – at Briviesca, I take it?"

Ramón said, askance, "What the hell are you talking about?"

"I am talking, little poof," said Fernández with sudden wrath, "of the death of General Mola in a plane crash. Or perhaps you never heard of that in the Burgos Infantería?" The sergeant was sickening both of Ramón's effeminate charm and his autocratic attempts to put a sergeant in his place. Fernández owed nothing at all to the élite – Gestapo or otherwise; he himself was of the Guardia, and the Guardia commanded respect.

Ramón said, nonchalantly: "God help us, man! Where do you get these fancy ideas? Mola was killed in an air crash, true – a crash in the mist. The pilot was too low, and there's nothing to prove otherwise. I told you this before."

"Nothing on paper, eh?" said Fernández. "What kind of idiots do you take us for, you people in the Infantería?" His tone changed, and he added, nodding towards the farmhouse, "What range was that, would you say?"

"About two hundred metres."

"You know these people – these terrorists? What are they like with weapons?"

"I'll tell you one thing," answered Ramón. "I shouldn't stand up in the saddle again – not unless you want what you had before, my friend. And if Hanson's in there, you won't be safe at a thousand yards."

"Who's Hanson?"

"If he's in there, you'll very soon know."

Fernández turned in the saddle, crying bassly. "Don't bunch – drop back, you lot. And watch it! I want them alive. Especially the old gitano. You hear me? I want them alive!"

With his face turned up to the now pattering rain, Ramón whistled a tune.

"Then proceed with caution, Sergeant," said he. "Preferably according to the book, if possible."

Fernández turned away his head, and spat. "You bastard!" he said.

In a sudden, quick flush of the wind, came faintly the sound of a woman sobbing.

The sergeant rubbed his sweating face, listening.

"Now, that's really something you can get your teeth into, isn't it?" said Ramón.

Even from that distance he thought it sounded like Juana . . .

Thirty-six

JUANA, HER FINGERS on Richard's pulse, raised her head as she heard Nicolas shouting from the hall. Realisation struck her with total force, and she scrambled up, gaining the middle of the room. Madame Ravol's gun was lying across the threshold of the door; she approached it, staring down at it. Nicolas continued to call; she could hear him searching the rooms below with increasing urgency.

When he reached the bottom of the stairs Juana picked up the weapon.

She had never before held a gun; the touch of it sickened her; it translated her into a world of horror, the gaping wounds and moaning of the wards. After a week in the nationalist hospital in Avila, she had taken an oath never to touch a gun. Now she stood with the muzzle of the fowling-piece wavering at the open door of the bedroom. Behind her Richard lay, legs and arms outflung. Moments ago his pulse had been fluttering in the indecision of death. Juana determined to protect him, alive or dead, from anyone.

Now Nicolas was coming up the stairs; above the scramble of his feet Juana heard his laboured breathing.

"Lady . . .!" He stood gasping in the doorway

Richard's Colt revolver was drooping in his hand. Across his back was slung Richard's Winchester rifle; his own small Kovaks pistol-automatic was on his shoulder; a travelling arsenal, thought Juana vaguely.

"Give me those . . ." She raised the fowling-piece.

"Lady, I would not harm you . . .!"

"Throw them on the floor. The revolver first!"

"You do not trust me?" Hurt was in his face.

"Throw them!"

She waited, her fingers tense on the triggers. With luck there should be another cartridge in the double-barrelled gun, but she did not know it for sure.

Nicolas threw down the revolver; unhooking its sling, he

laid his Kovaks pistol-automatic at her feet, and followed it with Richard's rifle. Then he said, looking past her, "The *Yanqui*, he is dead?"

"Nearly – thanks to you." Juana reached out with her foot and slid the weapons under the bed behind her.

Incredulity struck Nicolas's face. "But I did not shoot him!"

"You did worse. You left us and took the horse. You took his weapons. He could not defend himself."

"Lady, I have come for you, now that the *Yanqui* is dying . . ."

"Get out before I shoot you." Juana straightened the gun at his chest.

"But, Alanis . . .? I am taking you to Alanis . . .!"

"*Get out!*"

Having taken advantage of available cover, Sergeant Fernández took the last hundred yards of open country at a gallop, and led his troop clattering into the farm shippon: there he dismounted and went in a crouching, swerving run to the shelter of the farmhouse wall and flattened himself against it. His men followed his example, taking up positions in the outbuildings.

Juana and Nicolas stiffened to the sudden commotion of hooves and running feet. A dog yelped piercingly, the shrill noise echoing in the bedroom.

Nicolas said, "Guardia!"

Swinging about, he ran to the window overlooking the shippon. Juana joined him, staring down. Six Guardia horses were tethered there. The wind was rising with the new dawn; the corrugated iron roof clanged dismally. Nicolas whispered, his face close to Juana's, "Guardia – and with dogs. They are surrounding the house. Quick, we must run for it!"

Juana left his side and ran to the door, peering out.

The stairs, the hall below, glimmered emptily in faint, roseate light. She saw through the landing window the crags of the far sierra reaching up purple fingers, the razor-edged summits surmounted with crimson surplices as the dawn came slashing over the sky. Suddenly a man raced across the shippon and flung himself flat. The muzzle of a weapon momentarily shone wetly, then vanished.

When she turned, Nicolas was facing her and his Kovaks automatic was in his hands. "*Mala sombra!* Lady, will you come? Now is the only chance."

"They're all over the place, we have no chance."

"Yes, we have. The mare is on the other side of the house – not ten yards from the door. Look," and he pointed with the gun. "Down the stairs and through the hall, out of the door and on to the horse."

Juana nodded towards Richard's body. "I am not leaving him," she said.

"But he is dead, woman, and you are alive!"

"He is not dead. Soon, perhaps, he will be dead, but he is not dead yet, and I am not leaving him."

"Lady, in the name of God, please!" Seizing her arm Nicolas pulled her towards the door, but Juana fought herself free and pushed him away, crying, "You go. If you stay the Guardia will kill you because of Old Pep, but they may not kill me."

For answer, Nicolas hooked his arm around her waist and dragged her to the door; kicking it open as he reached it and spinning Juana out on to the landing. His back was to the stairs, Juana tore herself away, seeing instantly, in the moment before she regained the room, a man standing at the bottom of the stairs; he shouted: "This is the frontier police . . ." He got no further.

Nicolas wheeled to face him and triggered his gun. Light chattered from the shadows of the hall below; bullets sprayed up and down the stairs; blood spattered the landing wall. Nicolas slowly turned, and toppled into the bedroom, to fall flat at Juana's feet.

"Nicolas!" Juana knelt, then rose with the shot-gun in her hands as boots came battering up the stairs. As a Guardia's head came bobbing into her view she dived behind the door and pressed the trigger. Light flared; the pellet discharge slammed the door shut, shattering its panels. The man took it full, bawling. His shout ended in a shriek. Reaching the landing he collapsed head first against the door.

Silence.

Juana lay on an elbow behind the door. Unexpectedly, in a little wind from the stairs, it slowly creaked open. Light put a finger over the boards. Scrambling away, Juana watched it, fascinated by fear. It was as if the dead man had risen, his soul entering the room.

Faintly, then, she heard breathing. Ears strained, Juana listened. In the sepulchral, eerie nothingness, she could hear breathing. Her eyes settled on the still body of Nicolas. He was lying where he had fallen; black streams slowly searched the boarded floor of the bedroom; holding her gaze with riveting force; she wanted to be sick. Then she heard it again . . . faint breathing; she looked over her shoulder at Richard. He lay exactly as she had left him.

The breathing ceased. She heard the suppressed yelping of dogs.

Muzzled dogs? The yelping grew into a sudden crescendo of noise and she knew that the muzzles had been removed.

Soon, Juana knew, the dogs would come up the stairs.

Leaping, snarling, they would come hunting for her in the room.

A voice called from the shippon: "This is Sergeant Fernández of the frontier police. I am giving you one last chance. Come out one by one, with your hands behind your heads. I give you my word that you will not be harmed. Do you hear me? Come out one by one . . ."

Juana smiled faintly.

She had no illusions about being in the hands of the Guardia; the tales of their atrocities were real: she had seen the evidence with her own eyes up in Asturias during the Miners' Rebellion. And to the sadism of men like Major Doval could be added the names of Joaquín del Moral, the ex-republican of Burgos, Criado of Seville and Ibáñez of Córdoba. A woman in their hands would be a red letter day for the Guardia. No, she reasoned; now she had come this far, it was realism to fight and die like her comrades. Richard's body called her with relentless force; the body of Nicolas induced an overwhelming pity for his youth.

Rising, she knelt beside the dead boy, and prised his fingers free of the little Kovaks automatic. Sitting back on her heels, she examined it with interest in the growing light of the bedroom window. The cold touch of Don Pita's little weapon was in itself a final act of conclusion. There was no self-pity in it, no recrimination. Hatred was beginning to move in her; Richard was dead; a fight to the death, she thought vaguely, would bring a benediction to the things he had fought for – freedom, decency. She thought about prayer and abandoned the idea. There was little of devotional prayer in the presence of those who were planning to tear her to pieces with dogs: the blood of Richard and Nicolas was a libation she had to offer; a total, awful sacrifice of good in the face of evil.

She crept over the floor to where Richard was lying between the floor and the bed and gently kissed his face.

A strange, diffusing light was creeping into the room; raking away the shadows of the corners; a slow exorcism of spectres that moved, wraithlike, before her weary eyes. She nodded, head drooping, desperately needing sleep.

Suddenly her eyes snapped open.

A dog was coming up the stairs. Two dogs. Two dogs and a man. Above their yelps and howlings she heard the frightened voice of their handler urging them on. His boots were scrambling, their paws slithering on the stairs; other men crowding into the hall were shouting him upward; jibing in shrill falsetto, to lend him courage. The handler drove the dogs before him; and the bedroom door went back on to its hinges as man and wolfhounds burst into the bedroom; sprawling headlong as they struck the body of the dead Guardia on the landing. From the shelter of the bed Juana calmly sprayed the doorway with raking fire. Tracer bullets tore in automatic strings of exploding sparks into the bodies of dogs and man, and all three leaped upwards, gyrating like phantoms on the strings of a mad puppeteer; howling, shrieking, the man bawling oaths, and they fell; tumbled flat, all three, two dogs and a man in ricochets of lead, hopelessly entwined; paws and booted legs spasmodically jerking as death scythed them.

Silence.

Silence . . . Dust danced in the filtering light of the dawn. The dying man's fingers were drumming on the floor. Juana watched, riveted by the sight. As if playing the tempo of some long forgotten tune, the fingers tapped . . . tapped into stillness.

The Guardia groaned, then sighed, and slipped easily into death.

"Gustavo!" A voice commanded up the stairs. "Gustavo!"

Juana bent to the gun. She inadvertently touched the barrel and it scorched her fingers.

"Gustavo, are you there?" The voice called again.

A deeper voice said, "Holy Mary! Who is up there, in the name of God?"

"It is the man Hanson," said another, lighter voice. "I warned you, remember? These are professionals."

Juana narrowed her eyes. Some obscene sorcery must be playing tricks with her mind, she thought; she could have sworn that she had heard the voice of Ramón . . . an hallucination of the ears as well as of the soul. She reached out.

Richard's hand was still warm against hers, but she knew that he was lost to her; as Nicolas was lost to Alanis, and Spain was lost to savagery. Yet, despite the loss, there grew in her a need to survive. It was elemental, all-embracing; like a chord of sound, growing in strength and beauty.

And if she did not survive, she would take their enemies with her.

Why not attack, she suddenly thought? She had nothing to lose. Juana rose from behind the bed and went to the little square window that looked out over the mountains. Gently parting the lace curtains, she saw in the dawn a vast, rolling country. The sun was rising in regal splendour. It was an excellent day, she thought, in which to die.

Now, with the Kovaks pistol held before her, she stood between the dead Guardia and the open doorway and peered down through the landing window into the shippon.

There, to her amazement, two men were standing together, arguing with the confidence of men in deep debate; one was pounding a fist into his palm in emphasis of an important point of tactics. Juana took aim. The trigger moved on the pistol-automatic. A stream of tracers shattered the dawn; the landing window glass exploded before her. The two men in the shippon flung up their hands, and dropped; one lay motionless, the other writhed, flaying his legs about, shouting at his wounds.

Head down, hunched against return fire, Juana retreated into the room and dived head first behind the bed, beside Richard.

There had come to her a new courage; its intensity commanded her, obliterating all other emotion, including grief. Even the impossible odds no longer assailed her, and there was accompanying this courage a new spirit of self-preservation. It was now vitally angering to her that they sought her death.

Juana examined the magazine of the Kovaks automatic; as far as she could see the thing was nearly empty. Tossing it aside, she drew up Richard's big Winchester beside her. The Colt revolver was close to his hand, so this she did not touch. But, remembering the little Vostok pistol that had belonged to Elisa, she searched Nicolas's pockets, found it, and stuffed it into the band of her skirt. Then, lying full length, she sighted the Winchester repeater over the end of the bed and on to the open door, to where the bodies of the dogs and men lay entangled.

Minutes passed and the Guardia made no fresh move. The possibility of escape came to Juana . . . while their numbers were depleted she had to get out of the farmhouse . . .

With Richard dead there was no sense in staying to fight it out.

The thought came to her then that she might perhaps die at her own hand: one thing was certain, she thought; she didn't intend to be taken by the Guardia. To be captured meant torture. Everything the Astrada group had achieved would be laid at her door. First the interminable beatings, then the more refined apparatus of Gestapo interrogation, in which the Guardia were proving apt pupils.

Lying there among the dead she decided to make a break for it.

As if with the finality of this decision, somebody began to snore faintly in the room. With a sudden rush of Guardia activity in the shippon, it was difficult to define the position, and even as Juana held her breath to listen, the snoring ceased. And then she again heard faint breathing. It sounded as if it came from one of the men lying by the door; this coincided with a stumbling rush of footsteps in the hall and furious shouting. They were coming. Then, as suddenly, the sounds of attack again ceased. Juana lifted her cheek from the cold muzzle of the Winchester. The dawn was fuller. Sunlight was streaming through the window of the bedroom. If she intended to go, now was the time, she thought – while they were summoning courage for a final attack. Out the back way? Through the bedroom window and drop into the garden? Then a race across the fields? If one had to die then best do it fighting; not lying apathetically like this awaiting execution in the enemy's good time, and at his pleasure. Juana wiped her sweating face.

Something touched her leg. She reacted convulsively. It was a small, black kitten. It was purring softly. This, she thought, was the breathing she had heard. A kitten. Putting out a hand, she scooped it against her and lay there with the kitten against her cheek, watching the door.

The kitten licked her hand, purring louder. A board creaked on the landing. A hand grenade rolled like a little grey pineapple innocently across the bedroom floor. It rolled haphazardly, without direction. As Juana stared at it, it wagged sideways and disappeared under the far side of the bed. She managed to scramble up a moment before the explosion. The bed reared up. She was lifted bodily upon it and dropped from a height. The vacuum that followed the blast momentarily concussed her. The light-flare momentarily blinded her. But, in the ensuing flame and smoke, she saw two men appear in the doorway; dropping to their knees they raked the bedroom with automatic fire, methodically spraying from floor to ceiling. Rolling over on the slanting bed, Juana fired. The big repeater shot a yard of sparks with every touch of its trigger. One man spun, his hands clapped to his face; the other subsided, groaning, into a quiet untidy heap. Still Juana continued to press the trigger, sending round after round into the entangled bodies at the door.

From the huddle of dead there rose an arm as if in protest; slowly it rose, one finger pointing upwards, a signpost paroxysm of dying . . . then collapsed in the rigidity of death.

Silence again.

The kitten crawled in an ungainly fashion across the wrecked bed. A hole had been blown in the floor exposing the room below; Juana could smell smoke, and not just the smoke from the weapons; her nostrils were now accustomed to this. She listened to the unmistakable crackling that comes with fire. Heat moved in warm flushes, fanning her face. She began to cough. Small explosions of soundless coughing began to wrack her throat and lungs. The kitten backed away, arching its back to her agonised coughing. Panic seized Juana. Coughing would give away her position. But then, as the burning sheets and blankets caught fire, the smoke diminished. Flames spilled up. The curtains of the window flared; fire licked the ceiling. Beyond the blackening window glass the world was flooded with a sudden brilliance; the sun.

Juana's hands moved frantically on the little Vostok pistol. She released the butt-magazine, found it was fully loaded, and slammed it back into position, but failed to check it . . . Rising, she crawled across the bed and on to the floor. The carnage of the door held her momentarily, but she dragged her gaze to the window. Through it quickly, she thought; head first, if necessary – take the chance. Anything was better than to be burned alive.

Then a man's voice shouted up the stairs: "You up there! Hanson, do you hear me? I give you one last chance. I've sent for reinforcements. Meanwhile, you're trapped. But surrender, and your woman goes free – you've a woman in there, I understand . . . Surrender, and I'll spare the woman."

Standing clear of the smoking bed, Juana was measuring, through the window, the drop to the ground. It looked at least twenty feet. But nearby was tethered Nicolas's horse. If she could scramble towards it she'd at least stand a chance.

She was considering this when Sergeant Fernández came hammering up the stairs, shouting with anger.

Juana's first shot from the Vostok pistol whistled over the sergeant's head; the second shattered another pane of the landing window. The sergeant came on. Leaping over the bodies, his revolver spurted fire. The bullets missed Juana.

Leaping on to the burning mattress she levelled her weapon point-blank as the man clawed at her, but the Vostok misfired; Fernández leaped at her legs, bringing her down. Somehow, Juana eluded his grasping hands and seized the Winchester, but the sergeant was upon her, tearing it from her grasp. Kneeling above her, his fist came down and knocked her flat; the Vostok slid across the bedroom floor.

Juana was half conscious when he hauled her to her feet. Raising his fist he clubbed her down again. Juana lay face down on the smoking mattress.

"*Que va!*" said Fernández, gasping for breath.

Juana moved again, but he was the quicker. Pinned down, she saw his hand tighten on the pistol and clenched her eyes, awaiting the stunning impact of the bullet. It never came. When she opened her eyes, he was actually smiling. With one hand gripping her throat the sergeant looked slowly around the room. The fire had got a hold on the floor boards now, burning in noisy flares. His eyes, pink in his scarred face, settled on the door.

"Just you . . .?"

Juana stared up at him.

"Holy Mary," he breathed. "You bitch. You've killed all six of them!"

Now, he pulled her by the throat to an upright position, and swung a boot, catching her in the body. The blow nearly somersaulted her. Finishing up in a heap on the floor, Juana held her stomach, retching.

Sergeant Fernández, his revolver at the ready, moved around the room.

Pausing before Richard, he stooped, heaved him to a sitting position, examined him, and let him fall back again; the body of Nicolas he turned over with his foot, staring into the dead face. Hearing breathing, Fernández paused, listening, then stooped and hauled one of his men out by the leg. Still covering Juana, he felt the man's pulse; he nodded towards Richard.

"That Hanson?"

Juana could not answer; she was still fighting for breath, rocking herself to and fro against the wall. Sergeant Fernández got to his feet. He said, "A bloody countess, eh? You've made

a bloody mess here~~~~~~~ I give you credit." With watering
eyes, Juana stared back at him.

The sergeant's discipline was returning with his confidence.

Juana watched him from the corner of the room. He was a
big man, typical of the Guardia, his face most brutally
scarred. She remembered Old Pep . . .

She had seen his type in Avila seven days a week. They
were trained and fit, men born to a saddle. Possessed of the
esprit de corps of the Guardia Civil, theirs was a legendary
occupation, suppression of the peasants, for the benefit of a
ruling class. In war, their natural aptitude for brutality had
been given full rein.

The sergeant's riding whip slashed down before Juana was
aware of the intention. A sudden, terrifying pain jerked Juana
into reality.

She had expected to be shot; this had not happened: even
within the cutting pain, she was astonished at being alive.

The sergeant cried, raising the whip again, "You anarchist
bitch!" and he implemented each ejaculation with a downward slash of the whip. It tore Juana's shirt, laying red weals
on the skin beneath. It induced shrieks, not because of
immediate pain, but through the impulse of shock; she
cowered in the corner.

He beat her freely, accompanying each downward stroke
with an obscenity. Once Juana staggered up, turning her back
to the cutting pain, then swung to face him, catching the
thong in her fingers and hanging on to it, until he thrust out
his foot and bowled her back into the corner.

Fernández was enraged by his own impotence. Blood was
appearing in the rents of Juana's shirt as he shouted incoherently, calling a name.

Faintly, through a mist of agony, Juana heard the name: it
produced in her no sense; yet it was reasonable that he should
shout something that accommodated such fury.

Crouched in the corner again, trying to protect her face, she
saw through the cage of her fingers his wounded features, the
puffed eyes, the big teeth splitting his thick lips.

He was sweating badly; gasping with the effort of the

beating. He called the name again. It was a woman's name. Within Juana's deadening senses, the pain was lessening. She sank lower in the corner; the beating confined itself to a dull thudding within her sub-consciousness.

Suddenly the beating ceased. Juana peered up. The sergeant was standing wide-legged before her, his riding whip upraised, looking over his shoulder.

In the open doorway a man was idly leaning, and he repeated: "Put that away, Sergeant; it won't get us anywhere."

The Guardia obeyed. Juana opened astonished eyes.

"Ramón!" She struggled to a kneeling position, meaning to rush to him, but the look on Ramón's face rejected her. He said, evenly: "You'll never get anything out of her here, Fernández. Down at the police station there's much better apparatus." He smiled at Juana, and waved the sergeant aside; entering the room he slowly looked around it.

"My God, you have made a mess, haven't you? The last stand of the Hanson partisans."

Juana said, recovering herself. "So you were the traitor! Carrasco said it was Elisa. What has he done with her?"

"She was executed this morning. She wouldn't talk. But you will won't you? Your war's lost. The only thing left to save is your skin. Where's Pío?"

"I don't know."

Ramón approached her; his eyes momentarily danced in his small sensitive face. "You see, if we knew where Pío's gone we might clear up certain things . . . Matters that bothered me all the time I was with your partisans. Astrada was pretty thick with Pío, wasn't he? Because of your mother's radical views, republicans came and went in Pío's House. Don't tell me Pío knew nothing about that."

"He knew nothing," said Juana.

Ramón leaned against a wall, his hands in his pockets. "There's been an awful lot of action, you know, since Pío arrived on the scene. Colonel Carrasco's been abducted and it's my bet he's dead."

The sergeant, now squatting on his haunches, glared up

balefully at them both, saying, "Get her back to the station; there she'll talk in minutes."

"Yes, she'll talk, all right." Ramón came nearer to Juana and his eyes, filled with the old serenity, drifted over her. "You are going to tell us all about Emilio and Pío de Córdoba, aren't you? Do you know something?" He smiled at her. "I reckon you're the one last link we've got with the republican secret service."

There was a silence.

Beyond the window the day was bright in sun and greenness; birds sang in chorus. A little wind blew from the olive fields and it was perfumed. The dead faces in the room stared unblinkingly into the sunlight.

Ramón said: "Surely you knew what was going on in Pío's House? Nobody else did, you know. I've searched the *Somaten* and Gestapo files. Nothing, not a thing. Against Pío de Córdoba there's not a hint of suspicion . . . they've just got him down as a moneybagging fool."

"That's what he was," said Juana.

"You know what I think."

Juana didn't answer.

"I think the organisation started with your mother, but that she didn't do it alone. Pío was in on it from the start. And, after your mother's death the organisation grew. That Falangist subscriber business was as much a blind for Pío de Córdoba as it was for Carrasco. We all need a cover in espionage. Your husband's cover was his assumed idiocy, and his money."

"Yours was homosexuality."

Anger was now replacing Juana's fear; an obstinate pride was growing within her.

It appeared appalling that she should be the one to protect Pío when Richard lay dead on the other side of the room.

Would Pío even care? she wondered. Would he give a thought to this shambles in a farmhouse while he was safe in Portugal or Paris with Lucía García? The injustice of it beat about Juana now with relentless force. Yet instinct was telling her to maintain loyalty. To weaken now and expose Pío might earn her temporary freedom, but it would betray all who had suffered for republican espionage: Elisa, Consuela, who lay in a shallow grave, and her father, Señor Pelán; Old Pep and Nicolas, the sacrifice of Felipe Astrada – and all who fought for Spain.

And Richard. Most of all, Richard would be betrayed.

From her cramped position in the corner Juana could see but a small part of him; a hand and arm outstretched beside the bed's drooping blanket.

She looked at the two men before her; saw the brutal features of the sergeant interlaced with their livid wounds; she saw the delicate face of Ramón, he of the pale hands and mincing step, a sadist in another shape. From these she knew she could expect no mercy. She remembered then her mother's words: 'One day, with luck, you may be mistaken for an Asturian . . .'

Had her mother ever dreamed, Juana wondered now, of such a predicament?

Juana raised her face. Ramón had one eyebrow lifted in mild expectation of a pleasing answer. He said, softly, "I'm probably the only nationalist agent on the tail of this Emilio, the most important spy in the republican service. Get him, and we'll get the ring – people like Hans Deimler are very small fry. Who is Emilio? Is he Pío de Córdoba? He is, isn't he . . . I can see it in your face."

"If you're all that certain, why ask me?"

Ramón wandered the room. "You know what they'll do to you, don't you? If you don't talk here you will down at the station; and if we don't hear what we want there we'll send you to San Pablo for a week or two. There they will do to you what they did to Elisa – I know, you see, because she told me. They will strip you naked and strap you down on to an iron bed; they will fix electrodes on to all your most intimate places; are you listening? And they will say, as they said to her, 'Here's a bridal night for an anarchist; here is a fascist thrill for a member of the Doctrinal Vanguard,' and they'll press the light switch and you will scream and all night long it will go on, until you tell what they want to know. Who is Emilio? Just one name, Juana, and you go free – I give my word. Pío de Córdoba?"

"I tell you again. I do not know."

There was a brief silence. Then the sergeant lumbered to his feet. Reaching out, he seized Juana by the wrist and swung her out of the corner, muttering, "You're wasting time. Give her to me and I'll get her down to the station. An hour or two of the Orphean Choir . . ."

Ramón interjected, "If he takes you I can do nothing to help, you know that, Juana? Better San Pablo – God help you if he takes you."

The sergeant kicked the door wider, pulling Juana after him; within the numbing pain of his grip there came a stunning detonation, an explosive shock that blinded the sun-shot room. The sergeant's mouth dropped open and he bawled unintelligibly, his frog-like eyes bulging in his cheeks. The grip on Juana's wrist relaxed, and Ramón wheeled about, fighting to get at his pistol. Light had flashed. It flashed again as Juana dropped to her knees. Ramón's body, now above her, jerked upwards and back, flung by the impact of the heavy bullet that had struck him in the chest: the room bellowed light and sound. Landing against the wall, Ramón hung there momentarily like a crucified doll, then slowly slid down to the floor. His eyes opened wide in amazement, fixed upon Juana, then closed; he toppled forward on to his face.

On her knees, Juana stared at the dead face of Sergeant Fernández; the whip was trembling in his outstretched hand.

White smoke was rising from behind the shattered bed. Juana saw the muzzle of Richard's Colt revolver slowly slip out of sight; she heard the thump of his body as it struck the floor beside the wall.

"Richard!"

Scrambling over the sergeant she heaved at the bed, dragging it away.

Richard was lying exactly as she had left him, save that the big revolver was now in his hand. She touched the muzzle, and it was warm.

He sighed once, even as Juana watched him, and slipped into death.

Thirty-seven

KNEELING BESIDE RICHARD'S body, Juana removed from around his throat the little Pelayo medallion he wore. It was a replica of the one she had taken from the body of her mother, save for a small, black arrow that was inscribed on the reverse of the Pelayo portrait . . .

This second medallion she now wore.

From Richard's pockets she took all his small possessions; a pocket-knife, his false identification papers, what little money he possessed and a tiny photograph of a young, dark girl.

"Carla . . .?" she said, and put it back again into Richard's breast pocket.

Bending, Juana kissed his lips.

Straightening his limbs, she crossed his big hands upon his chest and stood momentarily, staring down.

It was as if he were sleeping, she thought, so peaceful did he look.

The mattress was fully alight now; flames were billowing up from the room below, shooting like a blow-torch from the hole in the floor and she began to cough again, bending low in her progress to the door. Here the body of Nicolas confronted her; stooping, she heaved it clear of the others. Kneeling, Juana checked the magazine of the little Vostok pistol; failure to do this, she reflected, had nearly cost her her life.

An unusual, an almost fanciful thought came to her then; that she would avenge the lives of these people. She rejected it, but it returned with total force. Taking the Vostok out of her belt she held it against her, staring through the smoke.

"Franco . . . *Franco* . . ." The name began to beat in Juana's head.

Clambering over the Guardia dead at the door of the bedroom, she looked through the shattered landing window, down into the shippon. She was now, it seemed, in a world of make-believe where nothing was coherent and no action made sense. Every step she now took appeared as an extension of a nightmare: in her ears was the sustained explosion of guns, the cries of wounded men.

Juana looked over her shoulder. Behind the heaped bodies of the bedroom, smoke was wreathing in strange, fantastic shapes. And out of the smoke, crawling with uncertain steps, came the little black kitten. Seeing her, it faintly mewed, close to death.

To Juana it appeared that the two of them were the only live things in the world. Going back into the burning room, she picked up the kitten and cherished it against her throat. And the last thing she saw in the shambles of the room was the face of Richard. Pale, upturned, it possessed, in death, a marvellous serenity.

Soon, thought Juana, another patrol would come from the temporary frontier post at Arnéquy. It was stupid to delay any further.

Clasping the kitten, and with the little Vostok held out before her, Juana reached the hall. Flames were spewing out of the door of the kitchen. Soon, she knew, the house would assume the proportions of a giant crematorium. Light and air struck her as she went out into the shippon. Here, clear of the fire, were tethered the Guardia horses; these she ignored. Going to the side of the house, she untethered the horse that had served them all so well; it high-stepped, wheeling, whinnying at the sight of her, dying to be gone.

The midday sun enveloped her with a blinding light; rays of vicious infra-red burned through the rents of her tattered khaki shirt. The kitten clung on tenaciously as Juana mounted the horse. Hooves clattering, it wheeled in a circle, seeking rein. Juana looked first to the east, towards France; then, straightening in the saddle, she spurred the horse and galloped it to the west. Flames were spiralling up to the eaves of the farmhouse as she went past the window of the room where Richard lay.

The sierra was calling her with unremitting force; the Spanish Pyrenees seemed to beckon with their ancient mystery. The sun was almost immediately overhead, beginning again its pitiless blaze. Even the cicadas would be silent, she thought; this would be yet another siesta without sleep.

"Goodbye," she said.

And she gave the horse its head and galloped, at full stretch, along the road that led to Spain.